THE FALLEN AENEID

COREY McCULLOUGH

THE FALLEN AENEID

2nd Paperback Edition

Copyright © 2018 by Corey McCullough

ISBN: 978-0-9966902-2-5

First edition © 2014 by C.B. McCullough

First printed in the United States of America in 2014

10 9 8 7 6 5 4 3 2

For Vanessa,
My inspiration.

Dedicating a book to you isn't enough. A whole library wouldn't be enough.

To you, I dedicate my life. Better together, always.

A Note from the Author

Dear Reader,

Thanks for checking out *The Fallen Aeneid*. As a thank you for purchasing this book, I have a couple of goodies I would like to send your way, including a map of the Oikoumene (the world of *The Fallen Odyssey* series). Admittedly, the map is rough—if it truly looked fantastic, I would have included it in the book, but it's really just something I put together for fun. Get your map and a few other freebies at **WWW.THEFALLENODYSSEY.COM/SEQUELBUNDLE.**

Thanks for reading, and ever journey on,

—Corey

EVENTS FROM THE FALLEN ODYSSEY

One year after a life-changing car accident, seventeen-year-old **JUSTIN HOLMES** was inexplicably transported from Earth to an alternate world called the **OIKOUMENE**, the home of a mystical power known as **AURYM**.

After being recruited by an old man and a fire-wielding mercenary to rescue **LEAH ANAVION**, the exiled heir to an empty throne, Justin embarked on a journey that led to the discovery of his identity as an **ETHOUL**: a powerful inter-world traveler known to some as a "fallen angel."

Pursued by the minions of a vile master, Justin encountered **DAEMYN**, the deadly antithesis of the life force of aurym. During an attack by carnivorous coblyn demons, Justin and Leah were kidnapped by servants of the dark lord **AVAGAD**, whose chief aim was to enslave Justin and gain control of his powerful aurym abilities.

While Justin's friends waged a war against a mysterious black fleet, a giant **CYTHRAUL** demon transformed Justin's left arm into a blackened, bone-armored **DEMON ARM**. All seemed lost until Justin unleashed his aurym powers for the first time through his aurstone-forged **A'THRI'IK SWORD**. He and Leah escaped from the enemy's clutches, but his powers came at a price—alerting the forces of daemyn to his precise location.

With the battle won, Justin and Leah reunited with their allies, and Justin was left with an offer from Avagad: **ONE YEAR** of service under the dark lord in exchange for mercy for Justin's friends. Given until winter to decide, Justin contemplated the proposal, and an **ANCIENT BOOK** revealed the secrets of returning home.

Justin traveled to Earth using the power of the **KEYSTONE** and discovered that mere hours had passed during the course of his weeks-long journey. But Justin knew he could not stay on Earth.

Having chosen to leave his home behind, possibly forever, the boy from Earth returns to the Oikoumene to take up his sword in the war against the demons. Yet still unbeknownst to Justin is the **TERRIBLE COST** of traveling between worlds. . . .

PART I

THROW DOWN
THE SWORD

CHAPTER 1

What had first burned with the intensity of many tongues of flame was now only a quiet, green glow spotting his eyes like the aftereffect of camera flashes. The blurry, greenish spots before his eyes, apparitions of the metaphysical, faded to black.

The tunnel was dark. The torch on the wall that had burned brightly a few moments ago was out—perhaps doused by the swirling, violent energy that had brought him here.

Alone in the darkness, Justin closed his fingers over the tiny pebble in his palm. It was warm with the expended aurym used to transport him back here. He felt or sensed the echoes of his own power hanging in the air around him. He envisioned his father's face watching him through the frosty kitchen window, the smile as he'd adjusted his glasses. A nod. And an understanding, almost accepting look on his face.

Justin lowered his head in the darkness. "I'm sorry, dad," he whispered. "I hope this isn't a huge mistake."

It had been difficult to leave, but the correct choice was clear. Home would have to wait. There was work to be done in the Oikoumene.

Justin fed a tiny sliver of spirit energy back into the gauge, turning it from an ordinary pebble into a burning emerald ember in his hand. Somewhere in this Hartlan palace, beneath these sandstone cliffs, a warm bed waited for him.

The preceding days seemed to blend together, into a single terrible night without end. Through the tortures of being held captive in the Drekwood, then doing battle against Avagad's demons, Justin had slept only intermittently and then, poorly. His weariness had come full circle; his body had been deprived of sleep for so long that it had shifted gears into survival mode. He felt no less tired, but it no longer bothered him. He didn't fight it. He accepted it. This was the new normal. He would just be tired until he died. To rest his head—on a pillow, no less—seemed almost too good to be true. Once he got under the covers, they were going to have a hard time getting him up.

Justin ran a hand through his hair, damp with melted snow from the winter of another world. He had washed and bathed prior to Hartla's victory celebration, but what he really needed was a haircut and a shave. It'd been a long time since his hair had been this long. And the boyish, patchy hairs sprouting from his chin and cheeks probably looked pretty dumb.

The glow of his gauge illuminated the hall with clean, green light as he walked. He'd had to retreat this far into the innards of the palace just to be able to hear himself think. The festivities in the main hall were no doubt still raging, commemorating a triumphant battle at Gaius by Hartla and its allies. But unlike everyone else, Justin was in no mood to party. He still wasn't convinced the events could be called a victory at all. So many had died. And those who had survived—had they really won anything? Or had they just delayed the inevitable for a darker day?

Justin looked down at his left arm. It was wrapped in black satin to hide its disfigurement, but a keen observer would have recognized how unnaturally narrow it was. Beneath the covering was a mutilated appendage made of chitinous, bony material, much like the bodies of the monstrous cythraul. He ran his hand over the satin.

Justin knew too much, now, to believe that living to see the next sunrise was any sort of victory. Living was nice, but there were worse things than dying.

His footsteps echoed down the corridor as he went. Ahead was the semicircle of light that marked the entrance to the main hall. Maybe he wouldn't go straight to bed. He could stand a drink or two. At the very least, the celebration might distract him from thoughts of coblyns, giant soldiers, cythraul, and Avagad's proposal.

One year. One of service in Avagad's army. In exchange for the safety of Justin's friends.

Justin stopped walking. He was a stone's throw from the doorway to the main hall, and his final footstep echoed for a moment after he'd stopped, reverberating down the quiet hallway.

Quiet. . . ? he thought.

Now that he stopped to pay attention, Justin realized it was not just quiet. It was completely silent.

Justin cut off the flow of his power to the gauge, and the light in his hand went dead, immersing him in shadow. He slipped the stone back into his pocket and reached over his shoulder for his sword. Ten, fifteen minutes ago, the main hall had been filled to capacity and noisy with toasting and merrymaking. He should have been able to hear something.

The cat's eye blade sang a quiet song of scraping steel as he pulled it free of the leather-wrapped, wooden sheath strapped to his back. With the heavy claymore held low, Justin crept forward. A cool breeze swept in through the corridor and tugged at his hair. He still couldn't see or hear anyone. He flexed his fingers around the sword's hilt, feeling the presence of aurym, prepared to feed it into the sword, if need be. The aurstones in the blade carried no inherent magic unto themselves but served as a conduit through which aurym could be tapped. Aurym was an ally. It was everywhere, and its physical form didn't come from him; it existed through him. He, like the sword, was a conduit through which the power could manifest. Zechariah had once told him that aurym was equivalent to a person's inner, spiritual strength, but that was not entirely true. It was more accurate to say that inner strength was a prerequisite for communing with aurym and calling upon it as one's ally. Aurym was not spirit power from within, as he had previously thought. It was divine reinforcement from without.

Justin held his breath as he pressed himself against the wall, crept to the edge of the doorway, and peeked around the corner. To his alarm, he realized the room was illuminated by a gray sky, visible through a collapsed roof. The palace had caved in. Then

Justin's eyes strayed to the floor of the main hall, and for several seconds, he forgot how to breathe. Strewn across the ground and pinned under fallen chandeliers and draped across overturned tables and lying in scattered pieces like disassembled dolls, were dead people. Hundreds of dead people.

CHAPTER 2

Their blood crusted the floor, stretching out in dark brown, asymmetrical, pin-wheeling patterns textured like rust. Dropped weapons lay alongside the bodies.

A loud clatter in front of Justin made him jump. He looked down and saw his sword wobbling on the stone floor. It had fallen out of his hands. He hadn't felt it leave his fingers.

Justin took an unsure step forward on weak legs. The sour stench of decomposition hit him, and the muscles in his throat spasmed. He covered his nose and mouth. It seemed to Justin that he had never experienced true silence before this moment.

"Leah," he said.

His voice sounded so small.

"Leah?" he called. "Leah!"

No answer.

Justin's legs carried him forward almost of their own accord. Before he knew it, he was running through the hall, checking the bodies, looking for familiar faces—seeking his friends and praying not to find them. His mind rode a deadly seesaw, bouncing between extremes, his perceptions alternating between the brink of unconsciousness and a devastatingly unsparing hyperawareness.

The bodies were everywhere. Their skin was pallid. Their bones, where visible, were the dull off-white of unfinished ceramic. Maggots writhed in every orifice. Justin knew he should be crying or even wailing at the horrors before him, but he was beyond that now, in a place that was not quite madness but surely bordered it. The still-functioning part of his mind observed that the bodies were not torn or ripped open as they would be from a coblyn attack. These people had been cut, stabbed, and hacked apart by blades.

"Leah!" he continued to cry, seemingly at random, or sometimes "Zechariah!" "Ahlund!" "Olorus!" "Hook!" "Gunnar!" Each time, his voice sounded less significant and more pathetic. His search led him to the front of the hall, to the twin thrones of Hartla, where he found the first familiar face. The severed head of Admiral Drexel Von Morix sat on one of the bloodstained seats. His hair was shorn straight across in a bob cut. His mouth hung open. His tongue looked dry.

Justin's throat spasmed again, and the muscles in his stomach and shoulders con-vulsed painfully, forcibly bending him over. He turned away.

The far end of the room was a hillside of broken stone blocks piled up to a summit where the wall and roof had once met, which was now a massive breach to the outside world. Hartla was a fortified city. If an enemy had gotten this far in—if the palace looked like this . . . .

Justin ran toward the opening in the wall. He dug his toe into a foothold at the baes of the rubble pile, pulled himself up, and started climbing. Pieces of stone teetered beneath his weight as he climbed. Rocks came loose and slid downhill behind him. He slipped and skinned his hand but ignored it and kept climbing, toward the overcast sky.

The summit was a mound of jagged debris. A fierce wind battered him as he crawled on all fours to the edge and looked out at the city. Far off, between the sandstone ridges, he saw the shimmer of the ocean. Between it and the palace, the city of Hartla was utterly destroyed.

Buildings lay in ruins. Rubble clogged the streets. Blackened, smoldering craters pocked the city. In many places, fires raged, pouring so much smoke into the air that Justin wondered if the sky was really overcast at all, or if the sun was blotted out by the smoke.

Am I . . . the only one left?

A noise from the throne room below made Justin duck instinctively behind a large chunk of stone. It was faint at first but soon grew louder.

Rhythmic footfalls. Lots of them.

Leaning against the stone, Justin peeked out and saw soldiers emerging from a corridor into the main hall. There were dozens of them. Their armor was trimmed with white cloth, and instead of helmets, bandanas covered their heads. Most held their noses against the smell of decay in the throne room.

A final figure stepped out of the corridor. He wore white-trimmed armor similar to the others, but with the addition of a flowing, purple cape hanging from his shoulders that hovered an inch above the floor behind him as he walked. On his head was a white hat with a great, fluffy feather that bobbed up and down with every step. He stopped and looked around the room, and Justin recognized his face. Gunnar Erix Nimbus.

Breathing a sigh of relief, Justin started out from behind his hiding place to call to him. Before the greeting could leave Justin's lips, Gunnar wheeled on the soldiers and shouted, "Can one of you please explain to me how we lost him? *Again*?"

Gunnar's furious tone of voice gave Justin pause. He watched for a moment, realizing Gunnar's face was contorted in a sort of rage he never would have expected from the good-natured, albeit irreverent man he'd come to know on their voyage down the Greenspring River.

"Damn it to bloody HELL!" Gunnar shouted.

Gunnar stomped across the room to the thrones. Without a moment's hesitation, Gunnar grabbed Drexel's severed head by a fistful of hair and angrily flung it across the room.

CHAPTER 3

The thud of Drexel's head hitting the wall snapped Justin back to reality. He ducked behind the piece of stone.

No, thought Justin. *No, no, no, this cannot be happening. Not Gunnar.*

Justin peeked out around the side of the boulder. Gunnar's caped shoulders heaved with rage. There was a fire in his eyes that Justin had never. . . .

Eyes, thought Justin. *Plural?*

"Could he be in the city, my lord?" one of the soldiers said.

"I tell you, he was here," Gunnar growled. "I felt him *in* the palace! He can't have gone far." He pointed at a group of soldiers. "You, come with me. The rest of you, search the city. If you find the ethoul, bring him to me. Alive. And as unharmed as you can manage."

"Yes, lord-count!"

The ethoul. Gunnar was looking for Justin. And he had felt his arrival.

A sharp tingle raced down Justin's demon arm.

If he felt me arrive, he realized, *then everyone else must have, too. Any aurym-sensitive within a hundred miles, maybe more, must now know I'm here. Maybe including Avagad and the cythraul. But Gunnar couldn't be responsible for all this! The Gunnar I know would never. . . . And where is his eyepatch?*

Then Justin remembered something—something he'd been told while onboard Gunnar's newly commandeered ship, the *Gryphon II*. There was another Erix Nimbus. A man whose imperialistic aspirations had destabilized the Mythaean Thalassocracy. A man who invaded colonies and overthrew Mythaean counts and admirals. A man who had betrayed Gunnar, his own brother, and who called himself lord-count of the Raedittean.

Of course, thought Justin. *Yordar Erix Nimbus.*

Justin watched Yordar—a near double of Gunnar—patrol the room, seemingly unfazed by the putrid horrors around him. As the lord-count changed course just to give Drexel's head a swift kick, Justin felt ashamed for mistaking this murderer for his friend.

He and his soldiers must have invaded during the night, thought Justin. *But why's he looking for me?* He reached over his shoulder to draw his sword. *Well, if he wants me, he's about to get more than he. . . .*

Justin's hands found only air. His sword wasn't there. A cold emptiness seized his stomach. Looking down, he spotted the distinctive *Y*-shaped crossguard of his sword on the ground in the throne room. The grisly scene had made him drop it in shock, and in his numb despair, it had not occurred to him to pick it back up before climbing up here.

Justin turned to look over the precipice to the city ruins outside. A mound of debris descended down to ground-level outside. There, a natural chasm separated the palace from the rest of the city, acting as a dry moat. The depths of the chasm were shadowed.

A lone bridge connected the palace with the city. He and his friends had marched across it the night before. But the bridge, like so much of the rest of the city, was destroyed. A long, wicker boardwalk spanned the gap as a makeshift replacement.

As Justin watched, Yordar's soldiers hurried across the boardwalk and into the city—a city of broken buildings, raging fires, and blackened craters. Yordar hadn't done all this. Of course he hadn't. This was the kind of destruction only cythraul, wielding the destructive power of daemyn, could deal. The craters were products of the daemyn blasts of cythraul. The hole in the collapsed cliff where Justin stood hiding was probably the result of one such attack. A daemyn blast that had, intentionally or otherwise, caused a portion of the throne room to cave in. The question was, was Yordar on the demons' side? Or he had swept in during the aftermath?

Justin squeezed his hands into fists as the purple-robed tyrant and his men searched the room. The victims in the throne room bore no wounds that would indicate a demon attack. Clearly, Yordar had done this.

Suddenly, Yordar stopped in his tracks. Then he crossed the room, bent over, and picked up Justin's sword.

Eff... thought Justin.

Yordar held up the sword and ran his hand lovingly over the forward-sloping quillons.

"He is here," Yordar said, "and he will not have gone far without this." He flicked the blade with his fingernail for emphasis. "New plan. Flank the doors. He's in here somewhere. We'll just wait him out."

Justin pressed closely against his cover, trying to lean out for a better look, searching for some way to sneak down and catch Yordar unaware—

The stone he was leaning against shifted beneath his weight. Justin stepped back in surprise as rubble spilled from beneath the stone in a small landslide. Then the huge chunk of stone wobbled, dislodged completely, and lurched forward with a crunch. Someone below shouted in alarm as the boulder broke loose from the pile and started rolling down toward the throne room.

CHAPTER 4

The boulder rolled down the embankment, gaining speed. It bounced near the bottom, slammed against the palace floor, and bounced again.

Yordar dove for cover. His soldiers tried to scatter as the boulder came down on them, and not all were fast enough. Their bodies were crushed beneath it. As Yordar landed, Justin's sword fell from his grasp. It slid across the palace floor, spinning like the hand of a clock.

"Up there!" Yordar was screaming before he even got to his feet. "The ethoul! Get him!"

Through the settling dust, soldiers rushed the debris pile with swords drawn. "Coward!" one of them shouted at Justin as they began climbing up toward him.

At ground level, Yordar hurried to retrieve the sword.

Justin acted on instinct. In his battle with the cythraul, there had come to him, entirely unbidden, the conviction that if he would only reach out his hand, his sword would be there. He was feeling it again. Something seemed to be telling him without words, *Reach out and take your sword.*

Justin obeyed. With a certainty that surpassed understanding, he extended his hand.

Yordar picked up the sword, but an invisible force wrenched it from his grasp. He cried out in surprise, and the cat's eye claymore went spinning through the air as if it were no heavier than a leaf on the wind, coming straight for Justin. The deadly weapon rocketing toward him should have been frightening, but Justin knew that its hilt was about to land precisely within his outstretched hand.

The first soldier finished the climb and drew his sword. With a sharp *whoosh*, Justin's claymore flew over the man's shoulder. Justin grabbed it from midair. The soldier hesitated. But instead of raising arms to defend himself, Justin slid his sword into the sheath on his back, turned, and jumped over the edge of the debris pile, out toward the city.

For a second, all was silence. Justin was airborne, falling, aiming for a flat platform of stone partway down the hillside made of shattered debris. But the silence was killed by a sudden, booming roar—a sound a less experienced man might have mistaken for distant thunder.

But Justin knew better. It was the call of the cythraul. One was close.

The wind whistled in Justin's ears as he fell.

Crap, he thought. *Crap, crap, crap.*

He flailed his arms in panic, realizing he'd made a terrible mistake. The semi-flat platform he'd aimed for, an overturned hunk of blasted cliff-side, was racing up at him at stunning speed. But the drop was farther than it had looked from above.

Several seconds had passed, and he was *still* falling. Even if he landed perfectly, he was coming in too fast; his ankles would snap like twigs. He braced himself for the bone-pulverizing impact.

His boots hit the rocky surface—and kept going. His weight knocked the chunk of rock loose, and instead of a blunt collision, the rock slipped free and flipped out from under him. His legs flew forward. His body slammed down. He heard an audible *crack*, and a hairline of pain sizzled up his spine. Before it could even occur to Justin that he had just broken his back, he was careening down the hillside amid an avalanche of rubble.

He bounced. The world turned end-over-end. He bounced again, and his neck jerked with whiplash.

Amid his wheeling surroundings, Justin saw the black void of the chasm. He reached out, desperately grabbing for anything to slow him down. His hands battered off rocks, but he could find no solid anchor. A hundred fists of stone pummeling his body as he tumbled out-of-control toward the abyss.

With everything he had, Justin threw out his left arm and slammed his elbow down. The impact against the rocks would have been enough to shatter human bone, but not his demon arm. Instead, the anchor of his elbow grinding against the ground turned his tumble into a controlled slide. Satin wrappings shredded like snakeskin.

Like a rudder, his elbow turned him to face the gaping maw of the canyon coming up at him. Eyes closed, teeth grinding, he braced his boots against the ground, but it wasn't enough. His feet slipped over the edge.

Justin opened his eyes. His body had stopped. His legs hung over the precipice, and from the knees down, there was nothing beneath him but empty air. He heard rubble settling around him, and, far, far below, rocks clacked and crashed at the bottom of the gorge. Behind him, a long, gouging slice marked the path where his demon arm had cut a ditch through the stone.

Wrenching his arm out of the rock, Justin scrambled onto solid ground. His palms were bloody. His heart pounded so hard that the breastplate of his Hartlan armor jumped with every beat. A stabbing pain in his lower back greeted him as he stood. Reaching for it, he found the culprit to be a sharp, jagged piece of something. It was the backplate of his armor. It had split down the middle—the crack he had heard when he'd landed—and had undoubtedly saved his life.

Before he could check for further injuries, he heard more falling rocks knocked loose by several white-armored soldiers braving the descent down the hillside. They were coming fast.

Justin took off for the broken bridge and the narrow, wicker boardwalk installed as a replacement. No time to test how stable it was. He sprinted over the lip and hit the boardwalk in stride. There were no railings of any kind, and he tried not to look down as he ran. His footfalls echoing down into the shadowed depths of the canyon.

He heard a cry of alarm as he reached the opposite side. He skidded to a halt. Turning, he realized one the soldiers descending the hill had taken a wrong step. The man somersaulted three times and slammed against the bottom, but he somehow managed not to slide into the gorge. As the man limped toward the bridge, more soldiers in white armor scrambled down behind him.

A figure emerged from the long corridor leading into the palace of Hartla—Yordar running to join them. Justin turned to run, reconsidered, then grabbed the end of the boardwalk and pulled.

"No!" shouted Yordar as he ran. "Stop him!"

The boardwalk was heavy, but it slid over the stone as Justin pulled backward. Across the chasm, the soldier who had fallen now stopped, drew his bow, and pulled an arrow from his quiver.

The opposite side of the boardwalk slipped over the edge. The end in Justin's hands was flung skyward like a trebuchet by the plummeting counterweight. The boardwalk pivoted on its fulcrum, then dropped. As it fell into the canyon, the archer nocked his arrow, pulled back, and drew aim on Justin.

CHAPTER 5

There was no cover. He was out in the open and entirely exposed. All Justin could do was duck low and try to make himself as small a target as possible.

"*Alive*, you fool!" Yordar shouted, sprinting up from behind the archer. And he snap-kicked the archer in the small of his back.

The archer stumbled forward. His arrow left his bowstring with a twang but flew harmlessly sidelong and bounced across the ground. He tried to catch himself, but it was hopeless. He didn't start screaming until he was already over the edge, tumbling down into the canyon, and then the sound seemed to continue for an ungodly length of time.

Another thunderous boom echoed over the broken city. This time, it was more than a tingle in Justin's demon arm. It felt like his marrow was being flash-boiled. He fell to his knees. His body trembled with the pain.

Definitely more than one of them, thought Justin. And *getting closer*.

Yordar started to yell something across the gap at him, but Justin wasn't sticking around to chat. Forcing himself to his feet, he took off into the city.

Hartla was deathly quiet as he ran. Everything reeked of the mixed odors of smoke and decay. He knew Yordar's other soldiers were somewhere out here looking for him. He took a random left turn, ducked down a back alley, and emerged in what looked like some sort of market district.

Justin's run slowed to a trot. Then a walk. Then he stopped. His mouth hung open.

Wooden frames of broken stalls lay everywhere. The smoking foundations of former homes oozed daemyn energy like open wounds. A fallen lighthouse lay across the street before him, broken in half where it had been blasted from its base.

Bodies were everywhere. The ones in the throne room had been mostly soldiers. These were not. And every one of them bore the distinctive feeding wounds of coblyns.

A strange smear stained the street at Justin's feet. He turned, following its trail to an object several yards away: a man. Or half of one, anyway.

Justin put a hand over his mouth and tried to avert his eyes but instead found himself looking at a corpse seated against a storefront, trying even in death to hold closed a disemboweling wound across his stomach. Justin closed his eyes, but the smell of rot overpowered him, and he gagged and retched.

I should have been here, he thought.

His legs buckled. He hit the ground on his knees. He had been so concerned about his friends, capable warriors in their own right, that it had hardly occurred to him to worry about the people who were most vulnerable: the innocent, defenseless citizens, sprawled and scattered dead before him.

Whatever happened, happened when I was on Earth. They needed me, but I was gone. If I'd been here, I could have used my power. I could have fought.

The realization was too much. Justin pounded his fist against the bricks of the street. "I could have saved them," he said.

A nearby sound prompted Justin to look up. He blinked in surprise. Standing in the street was a tiny child, a girl probably only five or six years old. She was in the shadow of the broken lighthouse. Blonde hair framed her round face, and her big, blue eyes watched him carefully.

For a moment, Justin thought he was seeing a ghost. Then the girl tilted her head, seemingly confused by his presence in the street, and said, "Justin?"

CHAPTER 6

When he didn't answer, she spoke again, in a voice like the squeak of a mouse. "Is your name Justin?"

Before Justin could answer, the pounding of booted feet erupted behind him, emanating from the alleyway he had just come from. Justin started to run for another side alley, thinking he might be able to double back and circle around to lose them, but then he realized the little girl was still standing frozen in place, staring up the street at the sound of the approaching soldiers.

Without thinking, about-faced and ran toward the little girl. She stood in front of an open window of the fallen lighthouse, and she backed away nervously at his approach. But Justin quickly scooped her up in his arms, ducked low, and stepped in through the window.

The lighthouse's interior was dizzying. The fall had shifted everything sideways, turning the wall into the floor and vice versa. He was in a small room, perhaps a living space for the lighthouse keeper. A spiral staircase hung before him at eye level. Broken pieces furniture lay everywhere, with odds and ends spilled from drawers, making it look like the home of a compulsive hoarder. Picking his way through the junk, Justin crossed the room with the little girl in his arms, making his way toward an old dining table propped on its side against the staircase.

One of the girl's tiny shoes bumped a vase lying on an overturned chair, and it fell and shattered against the floor.

Justin ducked behind the table, placed the child down on her feet beside him, and raised an index finger to tap it against his lips for silence. She watched the gesture, then nodded.

Through the sideways window, the sound of footfalls approached. Justin held his breath, but they passed by the window and seemed to fade away in the opposite direction. A few moments passed. The silence of the dead city seemed amplified to haunting extremes within this still room. In the dim glow from the window, his eyes met the little girl's. Her look said, *What now?* He shrugged at her, hoping it wasn't too obvious he was wondering the same thing.

The light from the window was abruptly eclipsed, dousing the room into shadow. Justin froze. He heard the scraping of fabric against stone—someone climbing through the window.

Feet hit the floor that had once been a wall, and a mountainous shadow extended across the room. Its owner stooped low, and Justin heard a creaking sound as he or she or it lifted up a piece of furniture. Pieces of the shattered vase jingled against the floor.

A deep, thick, raspy voice: "Well? You in here?"

It was the kind of voice Justin associated with heavy smokers and asthmatics, and it sounded shockingly loud within the confines of this quiet room. As the intruder moved toward them, Justin wondered how far he was from the table. He wondered how quickly he could rise, draw his sword, and take a swing. And he wondered how best to kill a man to prevent him from making any noise—

"Yes, I'm here!" called the little girl.

Justin's eyes went wide. He looked at the girl in horror. Before he could stop her, she popped up from her hiding place and stepped out from behind the table.

"Ah-*ha* . . ." said the raspy voice.

Justin placed one hand on his sword and stood. Silhouetted by the light of the window was a large, armored man. A brown briar-bush of a beard covered the lower half of his face, and a jagged, nasty-looking blade was strapped to his back. He was leaning over, touching the little girl's shoulder.

"I found him!" said the girl. "I found Justin!"

"Maera," said the man, "what in the spirit were you thinking, running off like. . . ?"

The armored man looked up at Justin. Recognition dawned on his face. But instead of attacking, the man promptly dropped his gaze and fell to one knee.

"My lord!" he said.

CHAPTER 7

The little girl, Maera, turned and looked at Justin. She was all smiles.

"I saw him run across the bridge, so I came to find him," she said. "I knew it was him! Would've swore it was him—with every swear word I ever heard—"

"Hush, now," the big man whispered. Then, in a bigger voice, "Sir Justin, your holiness. Never, even in the darkest hour, did I lose hope that you would return. This is truly a glorious day. My sword is at your service."

Justin cocked an eyebrow. "Sir Justin?" he said. But it was the "your holiness" that really took him aback.

The man remained piously frozen on bended knee.

"You, uh, can stand up if you want," said Justin.

The man obeyed, standing to full height and staring ahead as if ready for a military inspection. He wasn't as tall as Justin, but he was certainly heavier. He was barrel-chested, with the kind of broad, solid shoulders that implied a lifetime of strenuous daily labor. The man threw a sidelong glance at Maera and muttered, "Very good finding him, but you've still got a lot of explaining to do."

"Maera," said Justin. "Is this your daddy?"

"No," she said.

Justin kept a tight grip on his sword. "Do you know him?"

"Huh?" she said.

"Do you know who this is?" Justin said.

"Yes," said Maera, looking at Justin as if it were a strange question.

"We are part of a small group of survivors," offered the big man. "And *this* little one had us all very worried. We long ago gave up on forbidding Maera from playing out in the open, but she usually doesn't go missing for so long. And this time, I won't say a word if her grandfather wants to give her a spanking."

Maera scrunched up her nose and crossed her arms.

"So, you're not with Yordar?" said Justin.

"On my life, I'm not," the man said. "Major Lycon Belesys of the Hartla city militia, reporting for duty, sir."

Again, the use of the title "sir" struck Justin as odd. He looked at Maera. "How did you know who I was?" he asked her. As an afterthought, he smiled, trying to look friendly.

Maera shrugged and pointed at his demon arm. The black satin wrappings hung in tatters, and the bone armor of his elbow was exposed. It was unnaturally narrow, blackened like charred wood, and devoid of skin, muscle, or tendons from shoulder to wrist. Strange, leathery scar tissue marked the border between the demonic armor and his natural, human hand. Justin tore off the remaining wrappings and flexed his fingers, feeling the tug of flesh against non-flesh.

"The child means no offense," said Lycon.

"No, no, that's okay," Justin said. "You must be very smart, Maera."

Maera's smile widened, revealing a missing baby tooth.

"Our group has managed to stay hidden thus far," said Lycon, "but now, demon calls once again echo over Hartla. I fear they come to finish what they started."

"I think you're right," said Justin.

In fact, he knew Lycon was right. The discomfort in his demon arm was intensifying by the second, like insects burrowing through his veins. But, stranger still, now that Justin had relaxed enough to pay attention, he felt something else, too. It felt like a burst of energy, distant but distinct, and this one didn't feel like daemyn at all.

"We should find some better cover, sir," said Lycon.

Justin blinked, snapping out of his daze. "Oh. Yeah, okay."

As they exited the tower window, Justin saw no sign of white-armored troops, but soldiers were the least of his worries, now. Humans were one thing. Demons, on the other hand. . . .

Skirting the edge of the tower, Lycon slipped up a side street with Maera right behind him. Justin brought up the rear, and as they passed the bodies, the carnage, and the destruction, he was suddenly concerned, of all things, about what Maera's eyes were being exposed to.

She's just a child, thought Justin. *But, then again, I'm only seeing the aftermath. She probably lived through it. God knows what she's seen.*

Turning a corner, they hit a corridor choked with wreckage. Lycon started climbing, testing his weight on the debris and picking his way along sturdy pieces, but as soon as there was room, Maera hopped up and scaled it like a squirrel. She slipped through Lycon's legs and quickly passed him by.

"Careful where you're—!" Lycon said, wobbling on a loose piece of stone. He hissed through his nostrils and chuckled, "Brat."

Justin followed, trying his best not to fall or roll an ankle in the debris. He put a hand against the alley wall to steady himself. The stone surface beneath his palm was scored black with burn marks. Flames? Or the discharged energy of a daemyn blast?

Maera was waiting as Lycon and Justin dropped down on the other side. Here, the boulevard was lined with destroyed building fronts. The structures had been reduced to rubble-filled husks. The dark essence of daemyn hung over everything like a sopping wet sheet. Ducking low, Lycon and Maera jogged up the street.

"Is there any way out of the city?" Justin asked as he followed.

"When the assault began," said Lycon, "many citizens initially escaped by water, but only the first wave of ships made it out. Those that lagged behind were targeted and destroyed by the demons' black magic. There isn't an ocean-worthy vessel left around here for miles. As for the inland route, Yordar's forces have it blocked off and heavily guarded."

Lycon came to an abrupt halt in an alleyway, scanned the area, and placed Maera on her feet beside him.

"Do you remember the code?" he asked.

"Of course," she said.

She knelt down to the base of a cellar door Justin hadn't noticed. Forming her hand into a small fist, Maera landed a few quick, hard knocks against the wooden door, beating out a precise rhythm.

"As for the tunnels within the palace," said Lycon, "they were utilized for a mass evacuation into the north that I can only pray was successful. In the event that the city fell to invaders, standing protocol has always been for the tunnels to be caved in from behind, to prevent pursuit."

Justin looked up above the buildings, at the sandstone ridges surrounding them.

"Without a way out," said Justin, "these natural fortifications . . . turn the city into a cage."

"Yes, and the so-called *lord-count* has his soldiers patrolling the interior," said Lycon, "which gives us little opportunity to scavenge for supplies. Our food and water are running dangerously low."

"So, the demons attacked, and Yordar came in to finish the job," Justin said. "They must be working together."

"I don't think so, sir," said Lycon. "Yordar's forces didn't arrive until well after the demons moved on. I think it's more likely that Yordar saw Hartla's fall as an opportunity, and pounced. After our display at the Battle of Gaius, we were a threat to his power. This is how he retains his authority. By stomping us out. Ever since he arrived, the bastard's been executing survivors indiscriminately. If not for his presence, we might have escaped to the countryside weeks ago."

Justin squeezed his hands into fists, regretting that he hadn't killed Yordar when he'd had the chance. Was there not enough evil in this world already, without a power-hungry madman like that to. . . ?

Suddenly, the full meaning of Lycon's words dawned on Justin.

A thud and a creak sounded below their feet. The cellar door swung open, and a female soldier, shielding her eyes from the light, took Maera by the hand and helped her down the steps.

"Lycon," Justin said, stopping him before he could step down. "Did you say *weeks* ago?"

"Yes, sir," said Lycon.

"What do you mean?" said Justin. "How long have you been trapped here? How long has it been?"

Lycon considered, counting in his head. "I guess about five weeks, sir."

CHAPTER 8

Again, Lycon tried to step down into the cellar, but Justin grabbed him and spun him around to face him.

"What are you talking about?" Justin demanded. "What do you mean, five weeks?"

"Please, sir," Lycon said, grasping Justin by the shoulder. "We'll speak inside."

Justin wouldn't have been able to resist, even if he'd tried; judging by how effortlessly Lycon pushed him down into the cellar, he could have manhandled him, if he had to. He passed beneath an overhang and down a set of stairs. He had to stoop to keep the hilt of his sword from touching the ceiling. His first perception was that the room reeked of body odor.

Lycon shut the door behind them, slid an iron bar across it, and with that, the dank cellar was plunged into total darkness but for the open flame of one dull, lonely candle on the other end of the room. Its light reflected in dozens of tiny, moist orbs. With some alarm, Justin realized they were eyes. Twenty or thirty pairs, all looking at him. Crammed in a crawlspace.

Justin's eyes slowly adjusted. The floor was dirt. In a far corner, a bald, old man had his arms wrapped around Maera. Even by candlelight, Justin could tell that the people were unwashed and malnourished.

Lycon stood beside the female soldier who had let them in. They were the only ones with any armor or weapons. The rest were in civilian clothing, some in nothing but rags.

"Found her in the market, Feliks," Lycon said. Like Justin, he also had to stoop to keep his sword's hilt from scraping the ceiling.

"Bless you," said the old man, hardly looking up from Maera. Tears streamed from his eyes, and he rocked her back and forth, speechless with relief. "Bless you."

"Who's the new guy?" said the female soldier.

"Maera saw him running into the city from the palace," said Lycon.

"From the palace?" said the female soldier. "He was *inside*? What kind of crazy—?"

Justin was looking the other direction, but judging by the *oof* sound she made, it sounded like she'd been elbowed.

"This," said Lycon, "is Justin Holmes."

Hushed gasps filled the room. The candlelight rippled with their combined inhalation.

Maera's grandfather dropped to one knee. One by one, the others followed his example until everyone in the cellar—save Justin, Lycon, and the female soldier—knelt reverently in Justin's presence.

Lycon looked solemn. As for the female soldier, far from the veneration of the rest, she watched Justin with scrutiny and more than a little distrust.

Justin leaned closer to Lycon. "What is going on?" he whispered. "How can it have been five weeks since Gaius?"

Lycon and the female soldier exchanged a look. The look of people dealing with someone outside of his right mind.

"What happened to the city?" asked Justin.

"You mean you don't know?" said Lycon.

Justin opened his mouth to answer, but the female soldier cut him off. "Demon invasion," she said. "About a week after your vanishing act."

"Mind your tone, Private Lor," Lycon said.

"Vanishing act. . . ?" said Justin.

"There were thousands of them," she said. "Half our navy was out fighting on the other side of the Raedittean. But even at full force, we'd never have stood a chance. Fires *still* burn where the High Demons rained hell down on Hartla. Our people were either driven out or slaughtered in the streets. No help from our secret weapon, the fallen angel, who conveniently disappeared—"

"Enough, Adonica!" Lycon snapped, so loudly it made Justin jump.

The female soldier glared at Lycon. Then she placed her helmet down on the dirt floor and used it as a seat. Her blonde hair was in a braid. She tossed it over her shoulder, propped her elbows on her knees, and shifted her glare to Justin.

"Do you mean," Justin whispered, "that it's been five weeks, and these people have been stuck down here the whole time?"

Lycon sighed. "After Yordar arrived, our options were limited, sir," he said, almost apologetically. "That jackal knows no pity. At first, a few optimistic Hartlans attempted to surrender to him." Lycon only shook his head.

"That doesn't matter anymore!" someone said.

Justin turned toward the voice and was alarmed to realize everyone was still down on their knees. All but Maera's grandfather, Feliks, who was getting shakily to his feet.

"The nightmare is over," said Feliks. "Justin Holmes has returned. The ethoul has come to save us!"

CHAPTER 9

The words were like a knife to Justin's heart. Him? Save them?

Others in the cellar were standing with Feliks, murmuring in excitement. Justin looked to Lycon for help, but the major was smiling. With a sick feeling in his stomach, Justin realized that Lycon believed it, too.

Somehow, these people had heard about the fallen angel named Justin Holmes. How five weeks had passed, Justin didn't know, but now that he was back, they expected him to save them. What they didn't know, couldn't know, was that aurym was still new to him. Through nothing short of divine intervention, he had escaped Lisaac in the Drekwood, and only through miraculous circumstances had he later managed to kill the three cythraul that had come after him. Now, he could sense three *groups* of cythraul, at least five or more in each group, all converging on Hartla from multiple directions. The aurym power of his return had been like a signal flare, drawing them in.

These people thought Justin had come to save them. Instead, he had brought doom down upon them.

Amid the sensations of daemyn, Justin felt something else jump up in the distance. *That second force again.*

This one wasn't coming from any demon. It was aurym. And it was pulsing, rhythmically, intentionally, almost as if someone were trying to. . . .

"Trying to signal me," Justin thought aloud.

"Sir?" Lycon said.

Justin blinked, realizing he had been standing there, silent, for several seconds, staring in the direction of the aurym signal—somewhere out on the ocean. To the people around him, it would have looked like he was staring blankly at the cellar wall. Justin remembered a time not so long ago when he had watched Zechariah behaving in similar ways and had suspected the strange old man of being severely demented.

"Lycon," Justin said. "What happened to the others? Where is Gunnar Erix Nimbus? And Ahlund Sims and Zechariah? And Leah Anavion, Olorus Antony, and Hook Bard?"

"The princess and her soldiers marched westward to her homeland before the demons arrived," said Lycon.

"She went back to Nolia?" said Justin.

"Yes, sir."

Justin breathed a sigh of relief.

"As for the others, I don't know," said Lycon. "Perhaps they made it out. Or they could still be in the city somewhere, I suppose."

"Maera?" said Justin, scanning the cellar until he found her little blonde head in the crowd. "The place where you saw me from. Could you see the ocean from there, too?"

"Uh-huh," said Maera.

Then that's where I need to be, thought Justin.

He cleared his throat. Most of the people were back on their feet. Those who were still kneeling he motioned to stand, and they complied. He knew he probably should say something inspiring, bold, or at least encouraging—or something. But public speaking was not his strong suit. Anytime he gave a presentation in school, he looked at the back wall of the classroom, above everyone's heads, to keep from stumbling over his words.

Justin had to clear his throat a second time before he managed to get started. "I'm sorry you've been stuck down here," he said. "And I'm sorry I disappeared. It's a long story, and I'm still not sure how it happened. But please trust me, I didn't *mean* for it to happen. I'm going to try to get you all out of this city. Today. And I think I can do it, but first I need to be sure about something. For that, I need to be able to see the ocean. So, can someone please take me up to the place where Maera was?"

"I'll do it," said the female soldier—Adonica, Lycon had called her. Justin looked at her. He couldn't tell if her expressionless face spelled determination or indifference.

"Okay," said Justin. "Everyone else, when we get back, be ready to move. Got it?"

There were a few scattered nods.

"*Got it*?" Lycon repeated for him.

"Aye, aye," several voices said at once.

"Good," said Justin. As the occupants of the cellar talked among themselves, Justin leaned toward Lycon and Adonica and whispered, "How many of these people are soldiers?"

"You're looking at 'em, angel," Adonica said.

"You mean just you two?" Justin said. "Jeez."

"We've no shortage of weapons," Lycon said. "Hatchets. Pitchforks. Knives. But these are Hartla's working people. Bakers, basket-weavers—old Feliks is a brickmaker. They won't last long in a fight, sir."

"They won't have to fight," said Justin. "All they'll have to do is run. At least, I hope."

"Right," said Lycon. "Can I ask what you're looking for on the ocean, sir?"

"Only if you stop calling me sir."

Lycon smiled. "Understood, Justin."

"I'm looking for a signal," said Justin. "Something that will tell us which the direction we should be running."

"Good luck," said Lycon. "Keep him safe, Private Lor."

"Hmm," said Adonica.

After snatching up her helmet and pulling a sword belt around her waist, Adonica climbed the steps and threw open the cellar door. Overcast as the day was, Justin had to blink many times before his eyes adjusted to the light and he could follow her out into the street. The cellar door shut behind them, and he heard the iron bar fell in place with a thud.

CHAPTER 10

Adonica pulled her braid up into a spiral, then slid her helmet on. The dark steel covered her whole face except for a gap for her mouth and for two narrow, downward-sloping eye slits, which gave the appearance of a scowl. Fully armored, she cast an intimidating figure. All the more so as she whipped the bronze short sword from her belt and gave it a practiced spin.

"Are you sure you know where she was?" Justin asked.

"I got this, angel, don't you worry," she said. "Just follow me."

Justin balked at being called "angel" again—a decidedly feminine label—but Adonica took off up the street before he could protest. He had to hurry to keep up as she took a sharp right and cut up an adjoining alleyway. It didn't take long before their destination became clear. Rising from the center of town was what looked like a large stalagmite: a vertical rock column with a spiral staircase wrapped around it all the way to the top. At its head sat a lonely portico, some sort of temple fifty feet above the city rooftops.

Five weeks, thought Justin. It did explain the advanced decay of the bodies he had seen, but how? How was it possible?

Justin narrowed his eyes on the rock column, putting everything else out of his mind. All that mattered right now were the people left in this city—trapped down in that cellar. He couldn't control what had happened, but he could do everything in his power to save the ones who were left.

At least I know Leah made it out, he thought. *I hope she's okay.*

As they reached the base of the rock column, Adonica ducked low and snuck around to the front.

"Maera was up *there*?" whispered Justin. From here, he could see that the column was not entirely vertical, as he had assumed. It jutted outward slightly so that the portico hung out over the city below. "By herself?"

"Tenacious little ankle-biter, huh?" said Adonica. "This should go without saying, but anyplace where you can see a lot, a lot can see you. You sure you want to risk it?"

"I have to be sure," said Justin.

Adonica shrugged. "You're the boss."

Without another word, she started racing up the staircase, taking the steps two at a time. Justin followed.

He was seriously reconsidering his plan by the second time around the column. There were no railings or handholds. The city ruins turned before him like carousel scenery. To avoid dizziness, he tried to keep his eyes focused only on the next step.

Soon, Justin could see the river that zigzagged through the center of the city. He saw the gap between the sandstone ridges but could not yet see the ocean. Ever present was the steady, rhythmic pulsing of that unknown aurym power. If only he could get a glimpse of it, to be sure it wasn't some trick. He hadn't heard any cythraul roars for a long time, but he knew they were close. It occurred to Justin that they might be sneaking up on the city. The idea made him shudder. Despite everything he'd come to know about those creatures, he still tended to think of them as mindless monsters. It was somehow more comforting than the truth. That cythraul, in reality, were intelligent beings capable of multilingual speech, deductive reasoning, and devilish cunning.

Justin tried to ignore the daemyn energy assaulting his soul, making his arm tingle, weighing heavily on his heart. He was several steps behind Adonica, but he nearly ran into her when she suddenly stopped and ducked low on the stairs in front of him. She turned to him and pointed down.

Looking down was a dizzying experience. From here, Justin could see most of Hartla. Adonica was pointing at the palace. Justin saw the broken cliff face, the gaping hole that led to the throne room, the mound of rubble he had slid down, the chasm of the dry moat, the broken bridge—and Yordar and his troops. The lord-count stood outside the palace door, shouting orders at his soldiers. They were nailing together scavenged scrap wood, constructing a new plank to replace the boardwalk Justin had toppled.

Adonica threw Justin a look. Justin nodded. They kept moving.

On the next turn around the column, Justin finally spotted a sliver of ocean. There, on the water, perfectly visible through the sandstone ridges, was a single black ship with black sails.

"A demon ship," Adonica whispered.

As they watched, a jet of orange flame sizzled off the bow of the ship and hovered above the water. It coincided with the aurym-signal Justin had been feeling.

Ahlund.

"It was a demon ship," Justin said. "Until it was taken from them and renamed the *Gryphon II*."

"Admiral Nimbus's flagship?"

"And our ride out of here," said Justin. "I thought so, but I had to be certain. Let's go."

Justin turned to hustle back down the stairs. He had suspected back in the cellar that the aurym signal he'd been feeling belonged to Ahlund Sims, but too many lives were at stake to risk a hunch. Now, he had confirmation of what he'd hardly dared to hope. His friends were not only alive but had felt his arrival and were coming to find him.

Justin looked down again at the palace. A set of long, wooden poles had been extended over the broken bridge, spinning the gap between the city and the palace, and the beginnings of a rickety new boardwalk were being slid into position.

But Yordar Erix Nimbus wasn't looking at the boardwalk. He was looking up. Right at Justin and Adonica.

CHAPTER 11

Yordar sneered, then pointed up at Justin and Adonica, and shouted something. His soldiers all looked up. Those not working on the new bridge drew their swords.

"That was inevitable, I think," Adonica said. "Time to move."

She passed him by and took the lead down the stairs. Justin did his best to follow, amazed at how gracefully—and recklessly—she moved, taking stairs two, sometimes three at a time.

"We'll split up!" Justin shouted, panting. "I'll draw them off while you go get the others."

"You damn fool, you'll get yourself killed," Adonica called back. "*You* get the others, and *I'll* draw the soldiers away. Got it?"

"Then you're the one who'll get killed!" said Justin.

"And which of us is worth more alive? Use your head, angel."

"I wish you'd stop calling me—!"

Justin didn't finish his sentence. At that moment, daemyn's long silence was broken.

The cythraul's roar was long and low. The thunderous call was earth-shattering, but its physical sound was nothing compared to the internal effects of daemyn. The dark spiritual energy was so powerful and sudden that Justin's vision wavered. His balance faltered. He tried to stop moving, but his momentum down the stairs was too great. He took one more step, found nothing beneath his foot, and realized a moment too late that he was going over the edge.

Adonica grabbed two fistfuls of his shirt. She threw her weight backward, wrenching him back onto the stairs, and they crashed against one another, falling into the column's rock wall.

As Adonica helped him to his feet, Justin did not even have the presence of mind to thank her for saving his life. He was too busy watching the summit of the sandstone wall above the palace. At the top of the cliff, two cythraul suddenly appeared. Then two more. And then two more.

Six monsters, each ten feet tall and five feet wide at the shoulders. They were humanoid in form, with black, bone-armored exoskeletons and fleshless heads like human skulls plagued by brutal mutation—oversized, deformed, and jagged, with protruding brows and empty, glowing eye sockets. No two were identical; dimensions, musculature, and facial features varied. Justin had known them to grow human-like hair from their scalps and faces, but also animal-like horns, spikes, or antlers from their heads. Tattered bits of cloth served as primitive clothing. Giant swords, spears, and axes were clutched in bony hands.

The cythraul descended from the top of the cliff. They climbed by way of brute strength, punching their hands and feet into the sandstone for footholds and handholds. The effect was like insects climbing down a wall. Shards of rock broke free and rained down on Yordar and his soldiers. A piece of sandstone the size of a twin bed landed on one of the men, flattening him. Another piece hit the newly built bridge, snapping it cleanly through the middle and dropping its broken pieces into the gorge.

The lord-count and the rest of his soldiers turned to flee into the palace. Judging by their reactions and the cythraul's lack of concern for them, Justin's theory of Yordar and the demons working together seemed debunked.

Turning to Adonica, Justin could see her eyes through the slits in her helmet. There was no fear there. Only fire and galvanized anger.

"Come on!" Justin shouted.

The stairs beneath Justin's became a blur as he raced for the streets below. On his next trip around, he spotted one of the cythraul on the wall, a stout monster with long horns jutting from its temples like a steer, plummeting toward the ground. Justin thought at first that it had lost its grip and was falling, but a steady gouge was being torn through the cliff in the monster's wake. Justin realized that it had a giant dagger wedged into the sandstone, and it was carefully turning the weapon to direct its sliding descent down the wall—reminiscent of Justin's own descent down the palace debris pile earlier.

A deafening explosion from the opposite end of town was followed by many more booming roars. They were closing in from every side.

Justin and Adonica hit the street at a sprint. Splitting up was pointless, now, and they both knew it. As they cut through the alleyways, Justin could no longer feel the aurym-pulses of Ahlund's signals. Daemyn was everywhere, overriding his senses.

"Almost to the cellar," Adonica said as they ran. "Just a couple more blocks!"

Justin couldn't reply. His brain was foggy, and his demon arm was alight with a piercing, agonizing fire. There had even been times when the mere presence of a single cythraul nearby had been enough to make Justin lose consciousness. Other times, daemyn sucked him into a realm where Avagad spoke to him in person. Neither was permissible. Not now. Not when so many people needed him.

They turned a corner, and Justin was relieved to see that Lycon hadn't waited for them. He had acted on his better judgment, and the Hartlan refugees were already filing out of the cellar into the street, with Lycon giving assistance to any who needed it.

"Private Lor, lead the way to the harbor!" Lycon shouted.

"Aye, aye!" said Adonica, saluting with her sword. "Everyone, follow me!"

Adonica led them off down the street while Lycon helped the last of the refugees out of the cellar. It was frail old Feliks and his little granddaughter Maera. Justin stepped forward to help—

And the building facade exploded.

In an instant, the entire city block became a hailstorm of stone, brick, and mortar. Justin felt his skin break open from the rubble pelting his face and hands. Lycon's body flew backward, hit the ground hard, and flopped across the street. Feliks and Maera were briefly visible beneath the avalanche. Then the rooftop caved in, and the wall collapsed on top of them.

"No!" Justin screamed.

The silhouette of a monster materialized behind the dust. It came forward, wading through the broken building as if the hundred-year-old stone foundations were no stiffer than tall grass. Its bone armor plates shifted against one another like an insect's exoskeleton. The mouth of its fleshless skull was open wide in a demonic roar, venting poisonous, yellow fumes between its bladed jaws. At first, Justin thought two tusk-like horns grew from the monster's face, but, as it came closer, he realized the tusks belonged to the yellowed skull of an elephant, worn atop the cythraul's head like a helmet.

But as the cythraul walked closer, Justin realized it wasn't walking at all. It was riding.

The cythraul sat atop a giant mount: a bone-armored horse seven feet tall at the shoulders. Its face was jagged, black, and skinless, with teeth and tendons exposed. Hooves stamped craters into the street—*eight* hooves, in fact. Four legs in the front, and four legs in the back, more arachnid than mammal.

The cythraul looked down at Justin. Clasped in its right hand was a flail: a long, metal rod trailing a chain with links as thick as a man's hand. At the end of the chain hung a spiked mace-head the size of a La-Z-Boy. It raised its opposite hand, pointed a giant, skeletal finger at him, and roared, "THE ANGEL. RETURNS. . . . JUSTIN! HOLMES!"

The monstrous horse reared and kicked its front four legs, screaming a ghostly whinny. Justin's eyes narrowed in a scowl.

The cythraul raised its weapon. Justin drew his sword.

PART II

CARESS

OF

STEEL

CHAPTER 12

The demon horse's legs came down. The cythraul cranked the flail over its head like a lasso. The chain went taut. The recliner-sized mace sailed through the air, orbited the cythraul like a planetoid, and came whistling toward Justin.

Justin leaped forward instead of back, channeling a small flow of aurym through his sword. The a'thri'ik shards in the blade bloomed emerald. The flail's spiked mace-head went wide around him, and Justin hacked at its tether. A normal sword would have shattered or swatted aside, but with a flash of green and a sizzle, the aurym-powered cat's eye claymore cut through the chain. The giant mace-head flew loose, careened across the street, bounced, and crashed through a building with the efficiency of an industrial wrecking ball.

The loose end of the chain caught Justin's in the side, throwing him to the ground. He shouted in pain and rolled to his feet as the cythraul, undeterred, shifted strategies. It brought the loose chain back around at him like a bullwhip. It slammed into the street a few yards from Justin, splitting brick.

The cythraul reeled the chain back with a practiced flick of the wrist. With no small degree of alarm, Justin suddenly realized that a bullwhip made of a chain was no less deadly than a macehead. On the contrary. The cythraul's weapon was no longer weighed down by the mass of the wrecking ball at the end, and its attacks were now twice as fast. If anything, Justin had done it a favor.

Empty eye sockets stared at Justin beneath the elephant skull helmet. The cythraul appeared to be enjoying itself as it hauled back for another swing of its massive, chain-link whip.

Justin willed the full force of his aurym into the sword. The blade glowed a blinding green. He visualized his power manifesting into a wave of deadly energy, tearing the monster apart.

But suddenly, he realized he couldn't use it—not here.

In his moment of hesitation, the cythraul attacked. Chain came at him again in a horizontal slice. He ducked it but felt the rush of air as it whizzed over him—dangerously close to taking his head off like a dandelion under a string trimmer.

Okay, that was way too close, thought Justin, backing away with his glowing sword raised.

But he couldn't use his aurym. Just the day before—by his reckoning, anyway—he had witnessed his power burn through the earth. He'd seen it decimate the solid stone structure where he'd fought Lisaac, and Lisaac's body had been burned to dust. He'd seen his aurym shred through cythraul like paper. He had also seen the side effects. He remembered Leah clutching a wound at her hip, blood dribbling through her fingers, burned nearly to the bone by the peripheral energy of his power.

Lycon lay in the street nearby, unconscious or dead. The mound of stone and rubble that had fallen on Feliks and Maera was only a dozen yards away. They might still be alive under there. If he used his power to kill the cythraul, what if it hit them, too? And what about the rest of the city? He had only called on aurym a couple of times before and wasn't certain about his ability to control it. A wide, open area was one thing. But what if his aurym hurt or killed an innocent bystander?

Justin could feel the daemyn energies of other cythraul coming this way. He heard the stomping of their feet. Buildings being pushed over. Whatever he was going to do, he had to do it fast.

He jumped back to avoid another swing of the chain. The place where he'd been standing erupted in a shower of broken bricks and rubble, throwing dust and dirt into his eyes. The demon horse came forward, snapping a mouth full of flat molars. The animal stank of sulfur. The cythraul raised its free hand and pointed its palm at him. A ball of swirling, black energy appeared in its hand. Purple lines of electrical energy danced through the center. A daemyn blast, like the ones that had reduced whole neighborhoods of Hartla to craters, aimed right at him.

Maybe I don't need an open space, thought Justin. *I just need the right angle!*

Justin sprinted at the cythraul. The monster tried to take a swing at him, but Justin dodged and circled to the side. A horse hoof kicked at him. He ducked it and ran beneath the demon horse's legs. He lost his footing in the effort, tripped with a cry, and landed on his back—looking directly up at the horse's underbelly.

Bingo.

Justin swung his sword. Aurym surged through the blade as spirit became substance.

Shining beams of light flashed and spiraled. An eruption of molten, emerald energy shot from his sword and coursed upward, into, and through the demon horse's stomach.

CHAPTER 13

Eight legs fell kicking spasmodically—four backward and four forward—as the horse split in half. One of the cythraul's legs fell, too, ripped out of its hip. Closing the tap of his power, Justin lowered his sword. The rest of the cythraul's body rode a geyser of aurym like a rocket, rising higher and higher above the city. Finally, at its zenith hundreds of feet over Hartla, the energy exploded. A fireworks show of green aurym energy bloomed across the sky, swallowing up what remained of the cythraul.

Horse pieces and slimy, black viscera were still raining down on Justin as he jumped to his feet. He sheathed his sword, sprinted to the fallen building, and plunged his hands into the rubble.

"Maera!" he shouted as he dug. "Feliks! Can you hear me? Hold on!"

Cythraul roars were everywhere, now, getting closer every second. But he didn't care. He used his bare hands to swipe through the looser rubble. Larger stones he wrenched and rolled off the pile. The bigger pieces of building and rooftop pushed his muscles to the limit. But finally, beneath some shingles, he uncovered a chunk of solid stone—a section of wall bigger than him. He found an edge and wedged his hands under it. He braced himself, bent at the knees, and pulled with all his might.

It didn't move.

"Ah, come on," he whispered to himself, trying to talk down the panic. "You can do this. Come on."

He repositioned his hands. He dug in, got down, and tried to shoot up. He shouted with the effort. The edge cut his hands. The stone wobbled, but no more.

It was too heavy. He couldn't lift it.

Justin's throat seized up. No. This was not happening. No. No. . . .

He hauled back and swung his demon arm into the block like a hammer. He felt the tremor of its impact. The unfeeling elbow was impervious to pain. He struck again and again, praying with each strike that the stone would shatter or crack or at least give a little.

Nothing.

"Come on," he hissed, eyes suddenly wet. "Come on, Justin! Harder!"

His arm rose and fell like a hatchet to timber. Puffs of dust rose with every hit, but the stone was unyielding. Whether trapped or dead, he couldn't get to them.

"They're in there!" Justin sputtered, tears flying from his lips. He braced himself for another lift. "They are *trapped* in there! Be strong enough, Justin. *Be strong enough!*"

A second pair of hands suddenly grabbed the section of wall beside his. Justin looked up sharply. Lycon stood beside him. Blood ran down his face from a head wound, matting half his beard.

"All right, together on three," Lycon said, squatting down beside him. "Just like lifting a beer barrel. One, two, *heave!*"

Justin and Lycon lifted as one. Justin screamed like a powerlifter. Tendons stood up in Lycon's neck, and veins bulged in his hairy forearms. And the wall lifted.

Stones spilled off the top. When the wall reached their midsections, Lycon, at great risk to himself, stepped forward and wedged his whole body under. He seemed to savor the experience as he pushed upward beneath it like a jack lifting a car. With a final heave, the wall fell back.

A limp hand was visible through an opening beneath. Lycon pushed away more stones. Justin grabbed the hand and pulled. He half lifted, half dragged Feliks out of the pit. The old man wasn't moving, but tight under his arm, crying, was Maera.

"Alive!" Lycon shouted, helping Justin pull the girl free. "I don't believe it! He must have pulled her back down through the cellar door as the wall fell. Shielded her with his body!"

Justin's hands shook as he checked Maera for injuries. Not just alive. Unharmed. Tear-tracks of clean skin striped her dirty face.

"Are you all right, Maera?" Justin said. "Does anything hurt?"

"Grandpa," she sniffed, looking down at Feliks.

"It's okay, sweetie," said Lycon. "I'm sure he'll be. . . ." He seemed unable to finish the sentence.

Earth-shaking footsteps caused Justin to look up. A larger-than-life shadow passed through the adjoining alleyway but kept moving. A lucky break.

"We've got to move," Justin whispered. "If we don't make it to the harbor now, we never will."

"We'll make it," said Lycon.

Gently, Lycon picked Maera up and handed her to Justin. Then he slung Feliks's body over one shoulder. Justin took one last look at the recliner-sized mace-head stuck in a nearby building, and they ran.

Maera clutched Justin tightly as he ran. Her tears soaked the collar of his shirt. He could see the gap between the sandstone ridges as they emerged from an alley and raced down the main thoroughfare toward the harbor.

At the end of the thoroughfare, Lycon skidded to a halt. Dead bodies were everywhere—fresh dead bodies. Their white-trimmed armor identified them as Yordar's soldiers. They had been ripped open and torn apart, disemboweled and feasted upon in the characteristic method of—

Claws skittering against stone. Ape-like shrieks and howls above the rooftops.

"Go, go, go!" shouted Justin, and they resumed running.

Justin looked over his shoulder as, all at once, a solid stream of hairless, leathery, child-sized bodies spilled out into the street. From multiple adjoining alleyways, the streams converged, forming a roiling sea of black bodies: a loping, galloping, crawling herd, as thick and viscous as if the streets had been flooded with tar.

Coblyns.

Lycon hurdled over a corpse and swung wide around a fallen monument. Justin did his best to keep up. Behind them, the coblyns bayed like hounds on the scent.

"Almost there!" shouted Lycon.

Justin could see it. The harbor. The ocean. And the *Gryphon II*. Adonica was half-way up the ship's gangplank, still helping Hartlan refugees aboard.

A cythraul emerged from amid the ruins, sitting straight-backed astride yet another demon horse. A hornless, hairless head sat atop spiked shoulders. A giant, rusty trident was in its hand.

The cythraul seemed wholly unconcerned with the escapees at the harbor. Instead, it spurred its horse forward and quickly placed itself in front of the *Gryphon II*, facing Justin and Lycon, cutting them off from the ship. Had its fleshless face been capable of emotion, it might have smiled. It had been waiting for him. They were trapped between it and the coblyn herd rushing up the street behind them.

The cythraul raised its trident—

A jet of flame erupted behind the cythraul. The demon horse whinnied and bucked strangely, nearly throwing the cythraul off. A long, black object fell and rolled across the pier: one of the demon-horse's back legs.

CHAPTER 14

The demon horse tried frantically to find its footing but could compensate for its missing rear leg. But the weight of its giant rider was too much. There was an audible snap as one of its other back legs broke under the pressure, and its whole body toppled sideways. The cythraul attempted to dismount, but it was too late. Horse and rider both tumbled sidelong and fell into the bay. They sank beneath the water's surface, leaving only a horse's severed leg on the dock and a tall warrior standing over it, flames dancing across his longsword.

"Ahlund!" shouted Justin.

Ahlund strode toward them. Black demon blood was splattered across the thick stubble on his jaw. He said nothing, only gestured toward the ship and began covering their escape by pouring gallons of liquid fire onto the charging coblyns.

As he passed beneath the sails of the *Gryphon II*, Justin heard a series of buildings falling in the city behind them. He raced up the gangplank. On deck, Adonica and several other soldiers fired arrows at the coblyns. Lycon was right behind Justin.

Ahlund took the plank in two long-legged strides. He moved calmly, seemingly unconcerned that coblyns were climbing up the plank behind him. As soon as he reached the deck, Ahlund turned and hacked his sword in a fiery circle. The plank went down in two flaming pieces. Black bodies fell with it, snarling as they plunged into the water.

"All's aboard!" someone shouted. "Row, row, row!"

The *Gryphon II* began moving. Oars rose and fell, slamming against the water. Coblyns at the harbor leaped into the water to swim after.

At the pier, a massive black hand reached out of the water—the cythraul Ahlund had dunked. It grabbed hold of the dock platform, trying to pull itself up, but the boards snapped and shattered, and the pier was pulled down by its weight.

The city of Hartla had become a literal hell. Smoke poured into the air. An ocean of black bodies clogged the streets beneath a ceiling of smoke. A group of cythraul several streets back was punching through buildings, trying to reach the harbor, but the *Gryphon II* was leaving it all behind.

A cythraul charged through a storefront as easily as walking through a curtain. It trampled coblyns as it sprinted. By the steer-like longhorns sticking out of its temples, Justin recognized it as the cythraul he had seen sliding down the cliff wall. It reached the pier in a few strides and didn't hesitate for a moment. It raised its hand. A black ball of daemyn appeared, and it fired.

"Hit the deck!" someone screamed.

"Get down!" Ahlund shouted.

The cythraul's aim was true. The blast of daemyn flew at the *Gryphon II* like a loosed projectile. It was low—so low that it would hit the hull almost at water level, and Justin knew from experience that the impact would shred the ship like tissue.

Justin had no time to think about what he was doing. He put Maera down. He dashed past Lycon, Ahlund, Adonica, and a few dozen others to the rear of the ship. Grabbing the closest mooring line, Justin kicked off the deck and jumped overboard.

He plummeted toward the churning waters. When the line reached its end, it went taut, wrenching his shoulders. The rope sliced his palm, and he swung like a pendulum.

Justin's body slammed against the ship's hull. The daemyn blast bore down on him—a ball of darkness as colossal as a solar eclipse.

He pushed off from the side of the ship and reached for it with his left arm.

Justin felt the impact. His world turned black. The roaring of colliding energies assaulted his ears, and for a terrifying moment, he thought it hadn't worked. He had done it before, but maybe conditions had been different; maybe it didn't always work the same way.

But then he noticed a barely perceptible movement to the darkness—a rotation, with his demon-arm as the central point. His body seemed suspended in mid-air as if caught in zero gravity. He felt the rope flailing wildly against his grip, pulling, sliding through his hand, slicing deeper into his palm.

Like a galaxy turning on its axis, the daemyn rotated. With every second, the rotation speed increased. It spun inward, warping and collapsing. Daylight became visible at the edges, and the light grew as the daemyn was drawn steadily into Justin's arm.

The darkness folded inward, and just like that, it was gone.

Justin was barely aware of what was happening as his body swung back and thudded against the hull. He had slid so far down the rope that his feet were dragging in the water, leaving twin wakes. He felt something touch his shoulder. A second rope tossed down to him. He grabbed it numbly and wrapped it around his arm. His ears rang as they pulled him up.

Justin felt his body hoisted over the railing and lowered onto the deck by many hands, but he was too drained to help. He made no attempt to stand or sit. He just lay on his back. People tried to speak to him, but he couldn't hear them. He tilted his head to look through the rungs of the ship's railings. The *Gryphon II* had passed through the mountain-like peaks of the sandstone ridges. They were in open waters. He closed his eyes and let his head fall back against the deck.

A boot nudged his shoulder. He looked up. Ahlund Sims and Gunnar Erix Nimbus stood looking down at him. Ahlund was impassive as ever. Gunnar was smiling wide enough to reveal his gold tooth. Justin could hardly hear his own voice as he said, "Well. I'm back."

CHAPTER 15

The cold wind of a late autumn morning cut across the Orlia Flats. The sky was clear, but any heat from the sun was swept away by the dry wind.

The Flats were young by worldly standards. Though none could say the exact year they had formed, historic maps survived from a time when this entire region had been ocean. Now, it was a wasteland. Fields of black, volcanic basalt stretched on for miles without variation, save the occasional ripple or fissure. The jagged, peninsular expanse jutted out from the northwestern corner of Athacea like a great snaggletooth, creating a narrow channel between it and the smaller neighboring continent of Endenholm.

Leah Anavion found herself wishing she could see that channel, now. Not for the ocean view; she'd had quite enough of that. She wanted to see the place where the Orlia Flats ended. She'd been told there was a sheer wall of columnar formations, like massive stone reeds that dropped straight down into the ocean. Their tops, she'd heard, were polygonal—three, six, and even eight-sided shapes as equilateral as if taken out of a mathematician's sketchbook.

Unfortunately, she did not have the luxury of being distracted by nature's marvels right now, because something out here was very, very wrong.

Leah sat on steedback in the middle of an army. Her army. Two thousand infantrymen, one thousand cavalrymen, two hundred spearmen, and five hundred archers, supported by some fifty healers and a bevy of smiths, fletchers, cooks, and armorers. They came from all across the southern Raedittean, from the Mythaean colonies of Hartla, Syleau, Winhold, Arillion, and Lyphix and from the coastal nations of Skyre and Castydocia. They were fighting men—and quite a few fighting women, too—from varying homelands, creeds, and races. But above all, they were soldiers.

Beside Leah and also on steedback, Olorus Antony made an impatient, grumbling noise in his throat. His auburn hair shone even redder than usual in the morning sun. His beard had been allowed to grow unchecked for some time, and even the formal attire of a Hartlan commander, dark leather armor with fine, orange trim and iron gauntlets, couldn't keep him from looking more like a mountain man than a lieutenant. Strapped to his back were his spear and his kite shield. Leah wore the ceremonial garb of Hartlan nobility: plated armor trimmed with satin and hanging with decorative furs. Instead of the headdresses customary of Mythaean nobles—like the Von Morixes' heavy, horned helms and Gunnar's boisterous feathered hat—she had opted for a simple hooded cloak of blue and silver, the colors of Nolia. A steel saber was sheathed at her belt. It was not yet clear whether it would see use this day.

The coalition had begun as an unofficial partnership formed when allies of Hartla helped drive off an enemy fleet during the Battle of Gaius. But as more and more demons threatened western lands, tensions in the Raedittean Archipelago grew, and the alliance developed into a formal political confederation. The Von Morixes of Hartla initially referred to it as the "New Mythaean Alliance," but the consensus now seemed to be that they were the "Athacean League," and she, the young princess of Nolia, was considered a founding member.

Her army stood at a halt. The silence was broken only by the whistling wind. Temperatures had dropped precipitously throughout the past week, and the air on the Flats was so dry that it carried not even a hint of smell. Leah tugged the hood tighter against her neck, but the wind still managed to get in, scratching like cold sandpaper over her lips and nose. She resisted the urge to rub her hands over her arms for warmth. She could not afford to look weak in front of her soldiers. Not when it had been her choice to brave the Flats in the first place.

And certainly not while there was another, unexpected army lined up in defensive positions ahead of them, as if ready for battle.

As if they were waiting here for us, she thought.

The original plan had been for Leah and her forces to march across upper Athacea to her home country of Nolia. There, peacefully or otherwise, she would take back the throne from the usurper, Prime Minister Illander Asher. Months ago, Asher had orchestrated the assassination of the royal family—except for Leah, whom he left to accuse of the crime.

Reclaiming her place on the throne would not only mean Leah's redemption; her family would be avenged, and the true mastermind would be held accountable. The League as a whole also stood to gain from the arrangement. Nolia was one of the largest countries on Athacea. If she took back the throne, Nolia would become a contributing member of the League, significantly increasing its military strength. So, with Olorus Antony and Hook Bard at her side, Leah had set out from Hartla with an army four thousand strong.

Leah let out a long breath. They were now, finally, only a day's march from Cervice, Nolia's capital city. If Asher resisted diplomacy, it could mean a military engagement against the very people Leah meant to free. Now, an unknown army stood before them. Had Asher learned of the League's plans and sent these soldiers here to stop her? And would she be forced, today, to bloody her saber against her own countrymen?

If this all went awry, the blame lay on her. She was the one who'd decided to approach via the Flats. According to an existing treaty between Nolia and Endenholm, neither country was permitted to have a military presence on these lands. Historically, the two nations were perennial adversaries, but this demilitarized zone had kept relations cordial for over a century. The treaty's stipulations only applied to the two countries in question, which meant, in theory, that the League's army could march all the way up the Borderwoods of Nolia without breaking any laws. It also meant—if both countries were adhering to their treaty—that the Flats should be empty.

Instead, there is an army waiting for me, she thought. *Why did I ever think I could do this alone? Justin . . . where are you?*

"Here he comes," Olorus announced from beside her.

Leah looked up and spotted a lone rider silhouetted against the horizon. The steed's hooves clopped loudly against the basalt. The front line of soldiers parted to make way. The strip of cloth tied over the rider's forehead held back his long, dark hair, even longer than Leah's now, and covered the scarred brand of his past life. His calculating eyes darted furtively around the crowd—alliance or not, Sergeant Hook Bard was still un-comfortable around so many people.

Leah demanded no report. She waited until the silent soldier was ready. He let go of the reins and raised his hands.

"There are more of them than we thought," he signed.

Leah scanned the soldiers around her. None in this group, to her knowledge, could read Hook's signs except for Olorus and herself. She tried to keep a blank expression as she raised her hands and signed back, *"An enemy army?"* She felt clumsy doing it. She understood the signs well enough but was not very good at making them.

"An army, yes," replied Hook. *"An enemy, perhaps not. When I got near, they seemed to be sending a rider out to meet me."*

"Do they want to negotiate?" Olorus asked—the first verbal words of the conversa-tion.

Hook shrugged. *"I did not stay to find out. Diplomacy works best when both parties are able to speak."*

"Even if you could speak I wouldn't send *you*," Olorus said. "I've seen too many times what your idea of diplomacy looks like."

Hook smiled.

"Could you tell who they were?" asked Leah.

"Our neighbors from across the channel," signed Hook. *"Endenholm."*

"Then they've violated the treaty," said Olorus.

"Maybe they think that is why we are here," signed Leah. *"To drive them off the Flats."*

Hook shrugged again.

There was only one way to find out. "Okay, boys," she said. "Let's go say hello."

CHAPTER 16

It was growing colder by the minute as Leah, Olorus, and Hook slowed their steeds to a trot on the volcanic field between the two armies. Leah's steed raised its long trunk, sniffed at the air, and stomped one hoof anxiously.

Endenholm had sent only one representative. He stood beside his steed, waiting for them. He was a young man, probably about her age, not very tall, with close-cut, red-dish hair typical of the Enden people. Red sideburns connected at a thin chinstrap of a beard. His upper lip was clean-shaven. His eyes were defiant. But nervous.

Good, Leah thought.

She brought her steed to a halt a dozen paces from him and dismounted.

"So you *are* Nolian," the man said.

Leah said nothing. Olorus and Hook took up positions alongside her. The man's neck shifted with a hard gulp.

"I am Marcus Worth," he said. "I am captain of these men. We only wish to pass through."

"What is your destination?" asked Leah.

He hesitated. "Ronice."

Leah felt her nostrils flare. "You are marching a foreign army to a Nolian city, and you expect me to let you pass? No. I will not let you pass."

Marcus Worth's face tightened.

Leah cocked an eyebrow.

"It may be a Nolian city," he blurted, "but many traders and craftsmen from Endenholm do business in its markets! Some of us have family there."

Leah squinted. His tone confused her. "Did your king authorize this invasion?" she asked.

"What manner of insult is this?" Marcus Worth growled, suddenly livid.

"Watch your tongue," Olorus growled right back. "Another outburst like that—"

"The king of Endenholm is dead," Worth cut in.

"Dead?" Leah breathed.

"Of course! Everyone is dead!" he shouted. He opened his mouth to say more, but instead, he took a deep breath and let it out slowly.

"Spit it out, soldier," said Olorus.

"As if you don't know," grumbled Worth. "For weeks, we begged Nolia to send aid! Food. Supplies. Strength of arms. Anything! And we got nothing. Now, you dare to pretend our pleas fell on deaf ears?"

Hook started forward, clearly unhappy with the soldier's choice of words, but Leah grabbed his arm to keep him in place.

"Captain Worth," Leah said. "I have not been in this part of the world for some time. All this is news to me. But you still haven't told us why armed foreign soldiers marching on a Nolian city."

"My Lady," Worth said with forced composure. "Endenholm has been overrun. Its cities are burning. The soldiers you see before you are quite possibly *all* that escaped. Our country is no more."

"Overrun?" Olorus said. "By what?"

A haunted look crept into Worth's eyes. "You would not believe me if I told you."

Leah set her jaw. "Try me."

CHAPTER 17

There were nightmares—nightmares where people he knew were snatched away before his eyes and eaten by shadows. There was a light in Justin's hands, but for each step he took forward to drive back the darkness, more shadows pressed in from every side. It was either save the people he loved, or let the light die. It was a turn-based system. And for every step he took, the opponents hidden in the darkness took two, burning, destroying, and hurting as they went. He saw predators without form or substance break through a frosty kitchen window and abduct his father out of his wheelchair to the tune of a screeching guitar—the solo during the interlude of a twelve-minute-long track from one of Benjamin's 1970s progressive rock records that was spinning in the background. The scene faded to black, and his mother emerged from the darkness, trying to crawl out of a wreck of twisted metal. She called his name just as sinewy, childlike hands grabbed her by the ankles and dragged her back in. Ahlund and Gunnar were beheaded by black blades. Zechariah's hand was ripped off, then his arms, then his legs. Olorus and Hook burned in dark fire. The screeching guitar wailed as a bone-armored hand closed around Leah's throat.

Justin's eyes shot open. He grabbed his sword from where it lay on the bed beside him and sat there, panting.

Bed, he thought. *I'm in a bed.*

A bed where? Not his bedroom, of course. Was it an old man's shack on the Gravelands? A hut in a mountain village? Some devious illusion within an unending nightmare?

Wherever it was, the room was small and dark. There was a swaying in Justin's stomach that he mistook for nausea until he realized that the world around him actually was moving. The room creaked with motion. Tiny cracks of light could be seen between the boards of the ceiling. He heard the clomping of footsteps and the sounds of people hollering at one another.

Slowly, it came back to him. Escaping the city with Maera in his arms. Boarding the *Gryphon II*. The cythraul's attack. Jumping overboard. Ahlund and Gunnar.

Maybe he had passed out from exhaustion after that. Whatever had happened, he didn't remember the walk to this room. Some subconscious part of him must have remembered lying down to rest because his hand had known exactly where to reach for his sword.

Justin tried to remember the last time he had gotten a full night's sleep. Before the celebrations at Hartla, and before being picked up from the northern coast of Athacea, he had dozed for a few minutes while Leah healed him after his battle with the cythraul. Prior to that, he'd been the prisoner of Avagad's giant henchman, Lisaac, and the only sleep during that hellish week had been naps on bare earth, punctuated by beatings, healings, and more beatings.

Justin chuckled to realize that the last time he'd slept in a bed was onboard the original *Gryphon*. And if five weeks really had passed during his five or so minutes on Earth, then by Oikoumene time, he hadn't slept in over a month. The thought reminded him of something he'd read in a book given to him by Avagad. *The Book of Unfinished Dreams*.

My arrival in this place was certainly none of my own doing. But I am grateful that I was able to decipher the mystery of the Keys of the Ancients. Without the Keys, I never would have been able to return home. Nor would I have been able to come back to Antichthon again. But, of course, by now, I have come to understand that traveling between the worlds comes at a terrible price.

"A terrible price," Justin whispered.

In the book, the writer claimed to be a traveler from Earth. Thanks to the writer's clues, Justin had discovered how to return home using his gauge—also known as a keystone. Now, the book's warning about traveling between worlds seemed to have been confirmed. Minutes on Earth passed as weeks in this world, a place the writer had called "Antichthon." Could this time disparity have been the "price" referred to by the mystery writer?

Justin couldn't deny that his journey home had come at a terrible price. As harmless as those five minutes had seemed, innocent people had suffered and died because of his decision. If he hadn't left, many of them might still be alive. That knowledge gutted him.

And what if I'd stayed longer? thought Justin. *What if I'd gone inside, visited with dad and explained everything? How much time would have passed then? Or what if I'd decided to sleep in my own bed one last time?*

Justin shuddered, wondering what sort of passage of time he'd have been greeted with, then. Years? Decades? What would Avagad and his demons have done in that time? And would any of his friends have survived it?

Leah . . . thought Justin.

According to Lycon, she had departed Hartla before the attack. All Justin could do was pray she was all right—and hope she didn't hold his disappearance against him.

Justin stood from the bed. He had seen Ahlund and Gunnar on deck, and Zechariah was bound to be somewhere around here, too. Maybe they knew something about her.

At the foot of the bed, Justin found a set of clothes and boots. On the floor was a bucket of fresh water with a rag floating in it. He undressed, and each sweaty, dirt-encrusted, bloodstained layer he peeled off felt wonderful.

He dunked the rag into the bucket and wiped it over his face. Nothing had ever felt cleaner than that cool, fresh water. Funny, to think of his former life in a world where getting properly clean required nothing less than scalding hot water, brand-name shampoo, and scented antibacterial soap. He dressed but couldn't really tell what the new clothes were like in the dark of the cabin. He felt like some sort of desert trader.

Draped over the bedpost was a long strip of black cloth. No mystery what that was for.

Justin examined his bony, black arm. For some reason, Leah had been unable to heal the wound. The arm was still functional and surprisingly strong, but it looked more like a burnt tree branch than a human appendage. He tucked the end of the cloth under his armpit and wrapped the demon arm as if he were dressing a wound. Hiding the mutilation helped, but it was still shockingly narrow. He hoped Leah or some other healer would learn how to heal the cythraul's touch in the future.

He fitting his sheathed claymore to his back and left his room. He had to shield his eyes as he climbed the stairs and stepped out on deck.

Even after his eyes adjusted, there was too much to take in. The deck was crowded with sailors, soldiers, and civilians. For as far as the eye could see, the world was blue sky over blue ocean.

He took only a few steps before realizing the voices around him had faded to hushed silence. He stopped and looked around. Everyone was staring at him.

Justin started to look himself over, wondering if he'd put on women's clothing or something. Then one of the civilians, a face he recognized from the cellar in Hartla, dropped down to one knee. Others followed the man's example.

"No, don't do that," said Justin.

But nobody was listening. A ripple effect spread. Soon, almost everyone on deck was bowing.

Guilt welled up inside Justin. These people were the lucky ones. Many others were dead, all because of Justin's actions. These people should have hated him for what he'd done. Instead, they were on their knees, looking up as if waiting for him to do something.

What do they expect me to say? thought Justin. *I have nothing to give. I can't even tell them they're safe now because they're not. Nowhere is safe anymore.*

Justin's eyes found a little face in the crowd, framed by blonde hair. Maera was on one knee. Beside her, Feliks leaned heavily on a cane. Alive.

You do have something to give, a voice in Justin's mind seemed to say—a source outside himself. *Hope.*

Justin squared his shoulders in a show of resolve he did not feel. He reached over his shoulder and grabbed the hilt of his sword. As he drew it from its sheath, he willed his aurym into the a'thri'ik stones in the blade. It glowed like a green beacon as he raised it high into the air.

The people stood. Soldiers raised weapons to mimic his stance. Sailors raised whatever happened to be in their hands and cheered. Men, women, and children threw their fists into the air, whooping out war cries and hurrahs.

Sensing a familiar presence, Justin turned. Ahlund stood beside him. He did not know if the mercenary had been there all along or if he'd walked up in the middle of the commotion. The man had a way of appearing out of thin air. His stone-etched face was unreadable.

"Come with me," he said.

CHAPTER 18

Ahlund led Justin below deck. Partway down the hallway, Justin stopped.

"You're angry with me," he said.

Ahlund came to a halt but did not turn around. He said nothing.

"Back at Lonn, I promised you I wouldn't run away anymore," Justin said. "Ahlund, I kept that promise. I did not run away. This was an accident."

"It was against your will that you left, then?" Ahlund said, still not turning around.

Justin opened his mouth, but the answer caught in his throat. "Well, no. I did mean to leave, but I didn't mean to be gone as long as I was, or to—"

Ahlund resumed walking. "Then that's not an accident. What you're describing is a mistake. A costly one."

Justin raised his hand, but Ahlund rounded the corner. Justin dropped the hand to his side and hung his head.

"This again," he heard Ahlund say from around the corner. It took Justin a moment to realize he wasn't talking to him. "For the last time. No."

"You still treat him like he's a small fish!" Gunnar's voice exclaimed. "For all your talk of devotion to the war, you've never understood that *he* is the linchpin. It would make all the difference if we—!"

"The linchpin of the wrong mechanism," said Ahlund.

Justin followed the voices. Partway down the hall, he found them in a small room.

There were two chairs, and Gunnar was using both—sitting in one, his feet propped on another. A long-stemmed pipe was between his teeth, and he smoked it vigorously, puffing out thick, white clouds that floated in spirals.

Ahlund leaned against the wall with his arms folded, still as a statue. Scattered across the surface of a nearby table were a dozen or more maps, overlapping one another, spotted with pushpins and lined with scribbled notes in a language Justin could not read.

"For all we know, he's already dead," Gunnar said. "His guards were wiped out, and the demons will move on soon. If he is dead, all we need is proof. If he's alive, he's trapped and helpless. We'll never get another shot like this."

"It isn't worth the risk," said Ahlund. "Do not forget who the real enemy is."

"We won't stand a chance against *anyone* if we can't undo the corruption Yordar has spread across the Raedittean." Gunnar removed the pipe from his teeth and jabbed its stem in Ahlund's direction. "You want to talk about risk? The risk is neglecting to tie up a loose end. Defeating that man isn't enough—I should know. As long as he's

alive, he's dangerous. If he makes it out of Hartla and has time to restore his strength—
!"

"That is not where our resources are best spent," Ahlund said.

Gunnar slammed his fist on the table. "He's a war criminal! And you want to let him go! Saving innocent lives isn't worth our resources? You want to leave the Mythaean people at the mercy of a tyrant?"

"I would put the Mythaean people in chains, myself!" Ahlund growled, his voice brimming with uncharacteristic rage. "Better that they *live* under a tyrant than be eaten alive and stamped out of existence by Avagad's armies."

"You know about Avagad?" said Justin.

Gunnar looked at Justin but said nothing. He turned his pipe over to empty the contents onto the floor, then stomped out some red embers. Far from the jovial scoundrel Justin remembered, he seemed weary and frustrated. Ahlund, on the other hand, would not even look at Justin.

Justin cleared his throat. "Is it true?" he asked. "About the time?"

"What about it?" Gunnar asked, tossing his pipe across the table.

"Has it really been five weeks since Gaius?"

"Feels more like a lifetime," said Gunnar.

Despite his six-foot-four frame, Justin felt small before these men. Neither was happy to see him. They seemed more annoyed at having their argument interrupted. Only yesterday, he had been celebrating a great victory alongside them—yesterday for *him*, anyway. Now, things were different.

"I didn't abandon you," Justin said, hardly louder than a whisper. "I swear, I didn't mean to be gone all this time. It was an accident."

Ahlund still wouldn't make eye contact. Gunnar hardly seemed to be listening.

"I'll never..." said Justin. "I'll never be able to explain everything that happened after we got separated in the Drekwood, but during that time, I learned about a way for me to go home. I tried it, and it worked. But I was only there for *a few minutes*, I swear! When I came back, five weeks had somehow passed here. Gaius, the celebrating at Hartla, all that stuff happened *yesterday*, to me."

Gunnar wore a look that said he wanted to believe him, but it was clear he didn't. Ahlund didn't react at all.

"Don't ask me to prove it, because I can't," Justin said, "but I'm telling you the truth. Where's Zechariah? Maybe he can vouch for me. Maybe he's heard of something like this before."

"He's gone," said Ahlund.

Justin felt the blood drain from his face. "Gone?"

"No, no, not dead," sighed Gunnar. "Not as far as we know, anyway. Just gone." Neither he nor Ahlund seemed eager to elaborate.

"Look, I get it," said Justin. "You have every right to hate me, but don't think for a second I don't hate myself more. All those people in Hartla, dead in the streets. It's my fault. I could have helped."

Gunnar ran a hand through his curly, black locks. "Blast it all," he said. "I wish Zechariah were here, too. The old man had a way of sorting these things out."

"Where is he?" asked Justin.

"South," said Ahlund.

"Apparently, he has political ties with the empire of Raeqlund," said Gunnar. "He anticipated that even if we managed to get all the forces of the Raedittean and Athacea on our side, it still wouldn't be enough. He hoped to secure a military alliance with them. So he left the two of *us* in charge of fighting the war here."

Justin did not miss the icy glare Gunnar shot Ahlund for emphasis. It seemed the argument Justin had walked in on was only the latest incident in an ongoing conflict between them.

"Lycon told me that Leah's trying to get her country to help, too," said Justin. "But I don't understand. What war?"

Gunnar laughed aloud. "Damn, kid. Either you're scary-committed to your story, or you really have been gone a while."

CHAPTER 19

"At the Battle of Gaius," said Gunnar. "Hartla called on its allies to help fight a demon fleet. Syleau, Winhold, and Arillion responded—a remarkable thing. We Mythaeans are not normally known for being good neighbors. Remember the victory celebration? Well, it didn't last. Olorus, Hook, Leah, and I were battling a demon fleet in the eastern Raedittean not four days later. All while Zechariah searched for you."

"And I was with the Von Morixes," said Ahlund, "leading forces on the ground against an inland push by a combined army of coblyns and barbarians."

"Coblyns and barbarians?" breathed Justin.

"Oh, yeah," Gunnar said. "Gaius was like kicking a hornet's nest. The demons retaliated in force—more of them than we would have guessed even existed. News spread. Outlying territories came under attack. Lyphix, another Mythaean city-state, joined the cause, followed by the Athacean kingdom of Skyre. When the demons launched an invasion of Castydocia—that's a coastal nation in northern Athacea—we beat back the gut-sucking little devils as a gesture of goodwill. So Castydocia joined us. More cities and countries followed. Even some islander tribes from across the Raedittean joined up. Soon, we weren't just a Mythaean alliance anymore. People started calling us the Athacean League, and the name stuck. As the founders, the unofficial leaders of the outfit are the Von Morixes, Zechariah, Ahlund, Leah, and yours truly. Not everyone liked the League. My brother least of all."

"Doesn't seem like he likes much of anything," said Justin. "I don't know if he wanted to kill me or what, but he was pretty eager to—"

"You saw Yordar?" Gunnar cut in. "At Hartla? Is he alive?"

"He and his soldiers were coming after me when the cythraul showed up," said Justin. "The last I saw, he was running into the palace and the tunnel caved in."

Gunnar shook his head. "And ten to one odds he made it inside."

"Gunnar's brother was an unforeseen complication," said Ahlund.

"He saw the League as a threat to his autocracy," Gunnar said. "He declared war against us, causing a rift in the Thalassocracy. He already had a small confederacy of city-states, and more chose to join him rather than face his wrath. Others joined the League, hoping to stop him. The Raedittean Sea is now the main battlefield of a three-sided war between the League, Yordar's confederacy, and Avagad's demons. We were holding our own for a while."

"Until Hartla fell," said Ahlund.

Gunnar sighed. "Zechariah departed for the south. Then Leah marched west. The Von Morixes started getting ambitious in the fight against Yordar, and Ahlund and I were coordinating strikes against the demons. In hindsight, we were spread too thin. There weren't enough of us to defend Hartla when the demons attacked in earnest. Hardly a force in the world could have stood against so many cythraul and coblyns. We had to evacuate. A lot of good people didn't make it out."

"No one went back?" said Justin. "To rescue the survivors?"

"Hell, we tried, but Yordar beat us to it," said Gunnar. "Even with half the city destroyed, Hartla's defenses are still a work of military genius. With only a few hundred men, Yordar managed to repel our attempts. We've been preparing for another strike, hoping to rescue some of our people who are still unaccounted for. Like Drexel. He stayed behind to oversee the controlled cave-in of the tunnels. We haven't heard from him since."

"I found him in the palace," said Justin, wincing. "Some of him."

Gunnar made a noise like he'd been punched in the stomach.

"Are you sure?" Ahlund asked.

Justin nodded.

Gunnar hung his head. "This will destroy Wulder."

"We should count ourselves fortunate," Ahlund said. "Athacea and the Raedittean have seen little of what Avagad has to offer. We're fighting one war. He is fighting multiple wars across the Oikoumene. And winning. He sacks our cities and defeats our armies all while toppling more powerful empires half a world away. Refugees flood Darsida from the far east, driven from their homelands. The Ecbatan Empire is being chipped away by demon forces, province by province. If the nations of the Oikoumene could collaborate, we might prove formidable. But much like our mistake at Hartla, mankind is spread too thin, too preoccupied with petty personal feuds against one another to unite against the real enemy."

"I appreciate the semi-veiled cut," said Gunnar. "Oddly refreshing to hear you revert to passive aggressiveness. And as long as Yordar breathes, the Raedittean suffers for it. Personal, this may be. But petty? Not hardly."

"How did you find out about him?" said Justin. "Avagad, I mean."

"It was Zechariah who first told me the name," said Gunnar. "Leah said she'd heard it, too, from the men who kidnapped you. Nobody knows who he is, but it's said he rules the demons. You probably know more than we do."

Justin shrugged. "Not too much. He doesn't seem very old. He always wears a crown and white armor. He said he was a king, but I don't know if that's true. He'll say anything to—"

"Wait, wait, wait," Gunnar said, waving his hands to stop Justin. "Are you trying to tell me you *met* Avagad? The overlord of the demons. The enemy of all mankind—you had a chat with him?"

"Remember in the Drekwood, when I got sick?" said Justin. "That was the first time I spoke to him. Somehow he was able to get into my mind. It happened a few more times after that. He tried to trick me into joining him. When that me didn't work, he threatened me. And tortured me."

"Tortured you?" said Gunnar, his face a mixture of surprise and anger.

"He changed your arm?" said Ahlund.

Justin flexed his left hand and nodded, remembering the burning pain when the cythraul had picked him up—the touch that had transformed his human flesh into demonic bone armor.

And he remembered the promise of what Avagad would do if he did not cooperate: turn him fully. Make him his servant.

"I'm sorry, Justin," said Gunnar. "You go through all that, then come back to this. . . . Not right of us to attack you." He paused, stroking his braided mustache. "Yordar's death would change everything. It could end the war between the Mythaeans. All we have to do is prove he's really gone."

"We barely escaped Hartla the first time," Ahlund said. "By grace alone, we made it out a second time. To go back for a third would be tempting fate."

"With Justin, we finally stand a chance against those things!" Gunnar said, squeezing his hand into a fist. "If we were to launch a calculated assault. . . ."

But Justin was hardly listening. He was suddenly thinking back to something Avagad had said. He had offered to spare Justin's friends—and to give him the *Book of Unfinished Dreams*. As payment, Justin would serve as a commander in his demon armies for one year.

"I'm not a soldier," said Justin.

"Of course you aren't," Avagad said. "And I would never ask you to be. Your friends are the ones who want war. All I want is peace. The people of the Oikoumene should be united, not torn apart. Together, we can achieve this. I don't expect you to devote your life to my cause. Just a single year. Your role will only be symbolic, and after that, you will be free to leave and do as you see fit—I give you my word. Why, with the secrets of this book, you might even find a way home."

"Justin can mean the difference in this war," Ahlund was saying in the present. "But you are prepared to risk him to settle a family squabble."

"We have to act now," said Gunnar. "This could be the turning point in the war for the Raedittean!"

"When I met you," said Ahlund, "you were on the run from your past. We had to drag you practically kicking and screaming back to the Thalassocracy. Now, you are no better than the rest of your Mythaean kin. Gnawing at one another like bilge rats aboard a sinking ship. So hell-bent on destroying one another you cannot see that you're all doomed."

"Then where would you take Justin?" demanded Gunnar. "Out to the front lines to mow down enemy foot soldiers?"

"I hardly expect you to fight a war," Avagad had said.

"He needs to be trained," said Ahlund. "His power must be refined. Only then can it be utilized for its true worth."

"As long as we're digging up personal history," said Gunnar, "the Ahlund I met in Lonn was a *fighter* first. You have softened."

"The man you met was a cutthroat," said Ahlund. "You should thank your pagan sea gods that I changed when I did."

"Fear drives your decision-making," Gunnar replied. "Justin has returned. Nothing can stop us now."

"Your friends, however," Avagad's voice rang in Justin's head. "That is exactly what *they* will expect from you."

Justin didn't say a word to either of them as he left the room and walked down the hallway.

The arguing stopped. Footsteps hustling after him.

"Justin!" Gunnar called. "Hey, where are you going?"

"Don't know," said Justin without looking back. "Why don't you two let me know when you figure it out?"

CHAPTER 20

The two armies kept their distance from one another—four thousand men and women of the League, and two thousand Enden soldiers. At the center, Leah Anavion, Olorus Antony, Hook Bard, and Marcus Worth convened around a fire.

Olorus tossed another armful of kindling into the flames. "I don't understand it," he said, sitting back down. "The League fights demon fleets and armies in the Raedittean. And we receive reports of even worse devastation in the east. Now, you say they're coming out of the west, as well! Is the Oikoumene surrounded?"

"I tell you only what I have seen with my own eyes," said Worth.

Leah shifted uncomfortably. Worth's account was all too familiar. He told of armies of coblyns behaving as soldiers, and though Worth and his men had never heard the word "cythraul" before, they described monstrous demon giants leading the invasion of Endenholm.

Endenholm was a small landmass, an island nation separated from Athacea by the narrow channel between it and the Orlia Flats. Its people were fishermen and traders, and they did not have a very strong military force, which had proven fatal.

According to Worth, Endenholm's first warning was from Lundholm, a small country on the edge of the desert in Otunmer. Since time immemorial, southern Otunmer had been a land of barbarians, but something had begun driving tribes of Eeth out of their desert homelands and into Lundholm territories, causing friction. Soon, Lundholm was in the grips of full-scale war—not against barbarians, but against a dark force pushing across the desert. What followed was an abrupt halt in communications. An influx of refugees to Endenholm brought the news. "Monsters" had destroyed Lundholm.

Soon, demon fleets were assaulting Enden shores. Cythraul and coblyns unloaded and overran their cities, burning and feeding as they went. According to Worth, Endenholm had mounted an admirable defense. At first. They had asked Nolia for assistance. Nolia, to Leah's outrage, had flatly refused.

Weeks later, the demons took the capital city and soon all of Endenholm was burning. Only wandering groups of survivors like Marcus Worth and his two thousand soldiers had escaped.

Leah ran a hand through her dark hair, scratching her head. If she followed the timeline correctly, the demon invasions of Lundholm and Endenholm would have occurred around the time she was a guest in the Cru village in the mountains. Long before she or her friends had seen coblyns behaving as soldiers, or had understood the true threat to the Oikoumene.

Worth and his soldiers had fled Endenholm across the channel to Nolia hoping to find safe haven in the capital or one of the outlying cities. He claimed they had marched, unchallenged, through Nolian lands for days, encountering only abandoned outposts bearing signs of battle.

I have been naïve, thought Leah. *I assumed the danger was out there in the wilds. That back home, things were normal. As yet untouched by the demon invasion. But it may be worse here than it is in the Raedittean.*

What am I coming home to?

"So," said Worth from across the fire. "People in the west flee east, and people in the east flee west. I imagine it's getting crowded in the middle. At times like this, I wonder what my father would have done."

"You are not the only one, Captain," Leah said. "I know one thing. My father would not have sat idly by while your country burned. And neither would I. The prime minister of Nolia will pay for what he has done. You have my word."

Worth cleared his throat. "Lady Leah, I can't attest to the current state of your country, but it was wrong of me to insult you. Clearly, my anger was misplaced. All I knew was that Nolia had betrayed us in our time of need."

"Do not blame Nolia for that," Olorus said. "As the princess has said, this is the work of an individual. Asher betrayed *his own* country, in addition to betraying yours."

There was a pause, and Leah looked up just in time to catch the end of Hook signing something.

"*. . . And force-feed it to him.*"

"That, I would pay to see," said Olorus.

"The trader caravan I mentioned told us that Ronice is surrounded," said Worth. "Under siege by barbarians. They said its walls were still standing, but its people are trapped. The Nolian government has sent no support."

"And that is why you march to Ronice," said Leah. "To defend those who cannot defend themselves. Even as conniving as our prime minister has become, I cannot believe even he would abandon one of our own cities."

"I only repeat what I was told," Worth said. "Nothing would please me more than to be mistaken."

Leah chewed her lip. "We go to Ronice, then," she said. "Together."

"If we leave soon," Olorus said, "we can pass through the Borderwoods under cover of dark and arrive by morning."

"You would use your foreign army to assist us?" said Worth.

Leah did not miss the slight inflection he put on the word "foreign." It was not outwardly aggressive, but certainly significant. People in these parts tended to have darker skin tones, like Leah, and hair that was either black like Leah's or, like Worth and Olorus, red or auburn. To see thousands of brown-haired, white soldiers from upper Athacea, and tanned, blonde-bearded Mythaeans, would have unsettled many people from this corner of the world.

"The League doesn't abandon people in need," said Leah.

Not when I'm in charge, at least.

"We ought to inform the Jays regiment of our intentions," said Olorus.

"Right," said Leah.

The Jays Olorus referred to were the Nolian Borderwoods Guard, better known by their nickname, the Hell Jays. It was Olorus's old unit. Experts in stealth and wilderness survival, often spending weeks living in open country hunting coblyns and any other rogue dangers that posed a threat to Nolian life. Leah had intended to bypass their fort in the Borderwoods, but Olorus was right. The circumstances had changed.

"Don't you think local regiments will be taking orders from your prime minister?" said Worth. "They might not react favorably to your presence."

"We'll send a delegation to explain ourselves," said Leah. "I cannot imagine, when they learn of Ronice, that they would bar our passage."

"Many of the men posted there are friends of mine," said Olorus. "They will see the honor in our mission."

"I think you are right," Leah said.

I hope.

CHAPTER 21

The shifting of shadows behind the light of their torches made the forest look as if it were moving. Even in the Borderwoods, there was a cold bite in the air. A blanket of dry leaves matted the ground and rustled underfoot with every step. The bristles of hemlocks were the only greenery.

Human bodies littered the ground. Their torn, bloodied uniforms bore the Nolian coat of arms.

The combined forces of the League and Endenholm waited half a mile back while Leah, Olorus, Hook, and Worth surveyed the carnage that had once been the Hell Jays' outpost. Leah kept her hood pulled over her nose and mouth as she walked. It was not cold enough for the corpses to have frozen, and their decay was well advanced, producing an unbearable smell. How long these men had been allowed to lie here unburied, she could only guess. The condition of the bodies—ripped open, torn apart, and scattered—might have led one to conclude that carrion-feeders had been scavenging here. Leah knew better. She knew a coblyn attack when she saw one.

Hook placed a hand on her shoulder. It was meant to comfort her, but it only made her jump. Turning her torch to one side, Leah saw a man's lower half on the ground. The putrefied flesh was gray and swollen. The upper half was nowhere to be found.

A rustling of leaves announced Olorus's return.

"It's worse, at the fort," he said. Anyone less acquainted with him might not have noticed the strain in his voice. "The storerooms are still fully stocked. If there were any survivors, they never returned for the supplies. Or their fallen. There are . . . claw marks on the fortifications."

"Madness," Leah heard Worth whisper.

"They came from both sides," Hook signed. *"Two hordes. One from the heart of the woods, the other from over the Flats. A cohesive, organized attack. An assault."*

"Like Endenholm," Worth said. "Monsters waging war like men."

Without warning, Olorus slammed the toe of his boot into a tree trunk, kicking loose a hunk of bark. "Curse them!" he growled. "This outpost was never meant to defend against an army! The loss of life is bad enough, but the idea that good, honorable men—my friends, who gave their lives for their country—would be left to rot here, like. . . !" He trailed off, turned, and kicked the trunk again.

"Asher deserves death for this," signed Hook.

"I will be happy to give it to him!" Olorus shouted. "In all the time these men lay rotting, how could he have sent no one to collect their remains? Or to reinforce this place against further attack?"

"You are asking the wrong questions, Olorus," Leah said.

Olorus, Hook, and Worth swiveled to fix their gazes on her, all surprised by her bluntness. Even she was not sure where it had come from. It sounded more like something her father would have said.

She turned back and forced herself to look at the lower torso on the ground, memorizing its details. She didn't want to look at it; she had to. So she would never forget. She tried to moisten her lips, but her mouth was dry and smacked stickily as she spoke.

"What we should be asking is," she said, "if this is what has happened to our outpost, and if Ronice has been forsaken, then what has happened to the rest of our towns and cities? You ask how Asher could have sent no reinforcements. I ask, are there any reinforcements left to send? Or anyone left to send them?"

For several long moments, no one spoke. Hook may have signed something, but Leah didn't see it. She was still staring, noting how yellow the bones were. Even during her years as a healer, she rarely saw exposed bone. She'd always been led to believe they were whiter.

"Gather the army," she said. "We march for Ronice. Now. This is no diplomatic venture anymore. It is a rescue mission."

CHAPTER 22

Justin sat on the bed in his cabin, sharpening his sword the way Zechariah had taught him, using clean, gentle strokes with the stone, careful to keep the angle consistent.

The door opened, and there stood Ahlund Sims. "I should not have doubted you," he said.

Justin finished one last scrape of his sword and laid it down. "I shouldn't have left," he said.

Ahlund had to duck to get through the doorway. "I knew you were going to be in Hartla," he said, shutting the door behind him. "The first time you arrived, on the Gravelands, I woke the night before, and a voice told me to go out onto the plains to find you."

"Zechariah told me about that," said Justin. "I didn't know it was a voice, though."

"Not an audible voice," said Ahlund, "but a message, nonetheless. A similar event happened yesterday. We were at Castydocia, reconvening after a strike in the north. A voice told me I would find you at Hartla. I sought out Gunnar, we gathered some soldiers, and we set sail." Ahlund paused a moment before continuing. "Zechariah once went to great lengths to convince me that aurym was at work in all this. That some end was in store that was greater than we could foresee."

"He told me stuff like that, too," said Justin. "I usually didn't believe him."

"Nor did I," said Ahlund. "But over the course of our journey, he made me see the light. I am not the same man you met on the Gravelands. That man was broken. Faithless. A cutthroat."

"But you were already listening to aurym on the Gravelands," said Justin. "You found me. And you went after those men to save Leah—saving my life in the process. Then you sacrificed yourself so the rest of us could escape."

Ahlund looked at Justin. Then looked away.

"Those things are true," he said. "But they are not the whole truth. Listening to aurym that night was the only good and true thing I had done in a very long time. My sword was for sale to the highest bidder. I was in Deen because I had been hired to protect Nolia's princess and keep her in hiding on the Gravelands. That, I did. She believed me to be her stalwart protector, and I let her believe that."

Ahlund put his back against the door and slowly crossed his arms.

"What Leah did not know," said Ahlund, "was that her enemy, Prime Minister Asher, offered me much more. The job was to keep up a ruse of protecting her. Until he called on me. Then I was to deliver the princess to him. She would be the scapegoat for Nolia's regicide, which had been committed by other mercenaries, like me, greased by Asher's fortune."

". . . What?" said Justin.

"I played a different role than the mercenaries who killed the king and queen that night, but I am no less to blame. I accepted the first half of Asher's payment and took Leah to the Gravelands. I fully intended to betray her as planned."

"No," said Justin. "No, when those men kidnapped her, you went after them for—"

"For reneging on our deal. Those soldiers may not have known it, but they had been sent to strong-arm me so Asher could retain the second half of my payment and get the princess back to Cervice quietly and on his own terms. He was probably worried I would try to leverage our deal for a better one. Smart man. I killed the soldiers he sent because they were robbing me of my wages. As I said, Justin, the man I was, was a cutthroat."

Justin felt a look of revulsion warping his face and made no attempt to hide it.

"Zechariah saw through my deceptions," Ahlund continued. "You probably did not realize how precarious our alliance was, in the beginning. I did not believe you were an ethoul, but I could not deny that certain events were beyond explanation. When those cythraul appeared on the Gravelands, I realized things were happening that were more important than wages. My sacrifice that day was real. I was truly ready to offer my life. But aurym was not ready for it to be taken. I survived. And though I did not deserve it, perhaps deserved it less than any man ever has, I was given a second chance.

"Justin, I tell you this because you must understand. . . . The old man was right. Something is at work. You feel that you are to blame for the things that happened. What you neglect to realize is that in the light of eternity, a day is like a thousand years, and a thousand years is like a day. We are dust. But we are being orchestrated for a greater good. Even a traitorous mercenary, a black-hearted murderer, guilty of so many wrongdoings. . . . Even a man like that can be redeemed and become a tool for the light."

Justin could still feel the disgusted expression lingering on his face. News of such a casual betrayal took him back to a time when this mercenary had struck dread in his heart. He had been right to fear him all along. But now, he sounded more like a priest than a warrior.

A few moments passed. Neither man seemed to know what to say.

"When Zechariah departed for the south," Ahlund said, finally breaking the silence, "he left something for you, should you return during his absence." He reached into his jacket and withdrew an envelope. "I think it is time I read it to you."

He hesitated.

"Justin," said Ahlund, "before I read this, I want you to know, the man I was is dead. I was a slave to gold and power and treachery. No longer. I am a servant of aurym, and aurym has chosen me to guide you. I do not deserve amnesty for my actions, and regardless of whether you ever trust me again, I will do everything in my power to protect you with my life. I will not deceive you again, for any reason."

"Okay," said Justin.

Ahlund opened the envelope.

CHAPTER 23

Justin had never paid much attention to the sun here in the Oikoumene. Out of all the strange differences between this planet and Earth, he had barely contemplated one of its most prominent entities. But then again, he'd never paid attention to the sun on Earth, either. It was just there. And hard to look at.

He leaned on a railing of the *Gryphon II* as the golden disc climbed over the horizon. The clouds cast pink and red pixie-dust hues over the sea. He saw no noticeable differences between it and Earth's sun, but he wasn't the most observant person to begin with. Maybe this one was a little bigger and a little whiter. Or maybe he was just imagining things.

Justin looked over his shoulder. Gunnar stood at the helm of the ship, surrounded by sailors and soldiers. Lycon Belesys and Adonica Lor were with him, along with scarfaced Borris and chubby Pool. Justin had just learned that their third companion, Samuel, was dead. The little, white-haired sailor from Lonn had been killed by a wayward arrow in a naval battle someplace Justin had never heard of before, far, far from home.

Samuel was the second of the sailors from Lonn to die. The first, Vick, had been slain by a cythraul in the Drekwood when he bravely put himself in harm's way by taking the unmanned helm of the original *Gryphon*. Neither Vick nor Samuel had been obligated to give his life for this fight—a fight they barely understood. They weren't soldiers. They were just fishermen. But they had died heroes.

"'Justin,'" Ahlund had read from Zechariah's letter. "'If you are hearing these words, it means you have returned to us. I sincerely pray, if this letter finds you at all, that it finds you in a state of relatively sound physical and mental well-being.

"'I once told you that the choice to refuse responsibility, even the gift of life itself, was one of free will. I also told you that individuals are not given such responsibilities if they are going to refuse them. That is the defining quality of destiny. I still believe that statement, and I also believe that you will return to the fight when we need you most, whenever that may be.

"'The Oikoumene today hardly resembles the peaceful, bountiful world of my youth. And yet, I fear that the war and bloodshed we have seen in this little corner of the world is nothing compared to the turmoil in the east, on the front lines of Avagad's assault. Like the Demon Invasions during the times of the Ancients, it seems daemyn's minions aim to enslave humanity to feed upon us like cattle. How Avagad stands to profit from such an arrangement, I do not know, but if we do not stop them, humanity will be conquered and brought under a second Age of Captivity.'"

At the wheel of the ship, Gunnar concluded his briefing by reciting, "Through wind and tide and squall and foe!"

"We shall ever journey on!" the voices around him replied in unison.

Justin turned toward the group, catching the eye of Lycon Belesys. Justin waved him over, and the major hustled smartly to him.

"Justin," said Lycon with a salute.

Justin smiled a little. He had managed to break Lycon of calling him "sir." Now, he used "Justin" wherever he would have used "sir" before, and somehow made even a first-name basis formal and stuffy.

"I haven't seen Maera or Feliks for a while," Justin said. "Are they doing all right?"

"Private Lor has been keeping an eye on them," Lycon replied. "Maera is fine and is causing as much trouble as ever. Admiral Erix Nimbus had to fetch her from the top of the main mast last night! As for old Feliks, he broke a leg during the building's collapse but was otherwise none the worse for wear. Last I saw, he was talking up a storm to anyone who would listen, telling them what happened and praising your name."

Justin felt an involuntary twitch in his cheek at the word "praising."

"'But there is some good news,'" Zechariah's letter had continued. "'Sometimes, we hear of resistance to Avagad's invasion. Men and women, soldiers and civilians across the Oikoumene, banding together. Even after their nations have fallen, they rise up in rebellion, launching hit-and-run strikes against the enemy. They fight not for military or political motivations; theirs is a battle of faith.'"

"How's your hand?" asked Lycon.

Justin looked down, only now remembering how badly the rope had cut it during his jump overboard. Someone had healed it while he'd rested, and it now bore only the white line of a scar. Had he not known better, he might have said the injury was years old.

"Feels fine," said Justin.

"Glad to hear it," said Lycon, nodding with satisfaction.

"Wait—you did it?" said Justin. "I didn't know you were a healer."

"Not a very good one," said Lycon, "but I've got a little of the gift. Enough to stop a bleed-out in battle or close the occasional cut."

Justin's gaze wandered to the jagged weapon strapped to Lycon's back. He had noticed its strange size and shape before, but only now, in a state of relative calm, did he recognize it for what it was. His jaw dropped.

"That's a cythraul blade," said Justin.

Lycon reached over his shoulder, pulled the weapon free, and presented it to Justin. It was a long, jagged scimitar forged of strange, black metal. The blade was nicked and scraped with the weathering of old battles. Justin took it and nearly dropped it, it was so heavy. His arms jerked downward, making the big Hartlan laugh. It was a wonder Lycon could even walk with something so heavy strapped to his back.

"Is it just for looks, or can you actually swing this thing?" Justin asked, handing it back.

"It took some hard training, I'll admit," Lycon said, as he slid the blade back home in its scabbard. "The cythraul wielded it with one hand, if you can believe it. Says a thing or two about their strength. Whether demons are to be considered alive or some form of living dead, I do not know, but if you ask me, no life form should ever have so much power."

Justin looked down at his demon arm as the words of Zechariah's letter came back to him with chilling force: "'Your name is known, Justin. Stories of the fallen angel with the demon arm, who single-handedly defied the demons and saved Athacea, have spread like wildfire across the Oikoumene, giving hope, and inspiring people to rise up and act. It has spurred a movement in your name.'"

"Justin?"

He looked up to find Lycon watching him, looking uncomfortable. Justin started to apologize for spacing out, but Lycon beat him to it.

"If you'll excuse me, Justin," he said, "I'd like to tell some of the other men the news."

"The news?" said Justin.

"Our change of destination," he said. "To Esthean. Good day, Justin."

By the time Justin thought to respond with a "good day" of his own, the major was too far away to hear it.

Justin hadn't recognized most of the place-names thrown at him since his return to the Oikoumene, but Esthean was one he did remember. It was the hidden city of the Ru'Onorath, an order of aurym warriors that Ahlund had once belonged to. Esthean had been, briefly, their destination during his previous journey. Before that journey went wildly off-course.

I guess that means Ahlund won the argument, thought Justin. *He's taking me to the Guardians of the Oikoumene. To train me as a warrior. As a weapon.*

The final words of Zechariah's letter echoed through his mind.

"'These freedom fighters call themselves the Holy Army—devotees of Justin Holmes, the fallen angel.'"

CHAPTER 24

Ronice was an island amid a sea of black.

"Barbarians," Marcus Worth said beside Leah. "I think not."

Perhaps the trade caravan Worth and his men had met up with had mistaken this army of coblyns for barbarian men. Or maybe there had been barbarians here, but the coblyns had driven them off.

The walls still stood, but Ronice's main water source was a tributary of the Cervice River almost a quarter-mile from those walls. There were bound to be some wells within the city proper but surely not enough to support the entire population. If this had been going on for longer than a few days, water reserves would be dangerously low.

Leah, Olorus, Hook, and Worth sat on steedback at the summit of a hilltop, looking down at the city. Scattered across the countryside before them were bodies of humans and coblyns alike. The League and Enden armies, a combined force of six thousand, were spread out behind them. Leah estimated two to three thousand coblyns sieging the city. To someone less acquainted with demons, it would have seemed an easy victory was at hand. Again, Leah knew better.

With one hand holding a spyglass, Hook worked his opposite hand in the air, signing, *"No cythraul in sight."*

"What's he saying?" asked Worth.

"They've got to be close," Olorus said, ignoring Worth. "Coblyns only behave as a unit when there are cythraul around to keep them in line. Otherwise, they're animals."

"If there are cythraul," signed Hook, *"why have they not destroyed the walls?"*

"We'll have to risk it," said Leah.

"Risk cythraul, my lady?" Olorus said. To his credit, he tried to say it politely. "There is no quicker way to decimate our numbers than to risk the High Demons' daemyn blasts."

"Daemyn?" Worth said. "What is that?"

Olorus shook his head. "You have a lot to learn, soldier."

"It is possible these coblyns are following the orders of a cythraul master from a distance," Hook signed. *"Still, we should advance with caution. Set up closer and have our archers hit them with a few volleys. Their response will give us a better idea of how to proceed."*

"A shame that our young friend isn't with us," Olorus said. "Based on the stories I've heard, Justin would make short work of these odds and still win the day even if cythraul *did* appear!"

A lump formed in Leah's throat. She had been trying not to think about Justin. The last time she'd seen him had been during the celebration at Hartla after Gaius. When she couldn't find him later, she had assumed he was spending some much-needed time to himself. But if Justin's disappearance was a self-imposed exile, he had yet to return from it. It had not been until the morning after, when *no one* could find Justin, that the reality set in. An initial search party recovered only the toga he had been wearing during the ceremonies. There was no sign of a struggle, and no known enemies were ever found within the city. No one knew what had happened to Justin. He had simply vanished.

Rumors begin to spread of an ethoul—a powerful fallen angel—who had come down to slay many demons before ascending again when his work was done. He would descend again, like the angels of legend, when their peril required divine intervention. Others claimed he was still out there somewhere, and stories sometimes reached Leah that Justin had been seen hundreds of miles away or even half a world away performing some miracle or wiping out a demon horde. The "Holy Army" had formed out of support for him. It was a group devoted to the divinity of Justin Holmes and championing his cause against the demons.

It was strange to hear people speak of Justin in such a manner. Leah had seen his extraordinary aurym power firsthand, but he was still just a person. It worried her to think he was in trouble somewhere or, worse, that something had happened to him while she had been celebrating with the rest. He had protected her out there in the wilderness. It pained her to think she hadn't been there to return the favor when he'd needed it.

Leah cleared her throat, forcing herself back to the present. What had happened to the Nolian government? Why would they ignore Endenholm's pleas and abandon Ronice, a Nolian city, in its time of need? What would she find at the capital city?

And is there a capital city left? she wondered.

Flaming arrows were being fired down from the Ronice city walls into the conlyns. But the demons were undeterred. They threw themselves mindlessly at the gates, tearing at stone and wood with tooth and claw. Eventually, they would get through. The only question was whether starvation and disease would have killed everyone inside before that happened.

"To hell with the risk," said Leah. "We're going down there. No archers. A full charge. We hold nothing back."

"Are you certain, my lady?" asked Olorus.

"Certain as death," she said.

"Shall we split into columns, then?" asked Worth. "Drive them back to either side of the city and come down from multiple angles?"

Leah shook her head. "Coblyns do not retreat, Captain Worth. Driving them back is not our objective. We charge to exterminate them to the last, nothing less." She turned to Olorus. "Bring the cavalry forward, please. I will lead the charge."

Hook lowered the spyglass and shot Leah a look. Worth gaped at her but said nothing. Olorus only smiled as he cried, "Cavalry! Forward!"

Leah heard the clomping of hooves as the lines repositioned. The hood of her cloak was drawn up to guard against the wintry breeze, but now she threw it back. She closed her fingers around her saber and raised it high into the air. She did not wait to see if they were ready. She kicked her steed into a gallop and went thundering down the hillside. Hatred filled her heart. Hatred for Asher. Hatred for the demons. Hatred for Avagad and anyone who followed him. She would take them all on by herself if she had to.

She shouted a war cry as she neared the coblyns, and her voice was echoed several thousand times over by the cavalry and infantry following close behind her. She did not slow as she reached the black mass of coblyn bodies. She plunged into the fray with blade swinging.

PART III

SHIP BE STURDY,

NO MERCY THE SEA

CHAPTER 25

Razor-sharp claws landed glancing blows against Leah's legs, but she didn't care. The walls of Ronice were close. She stabbed her saber through a coblyn's head, then hacked off a pair of limbs on her other side. She turned to find a bat-like face bearing down on her, fangs bared, but it was ripped out of the air by the well-placed strike of a spear. It squealed in protest, and Olorus laughed as he threw it to the ground and trampled it beneath the hooves of his steed.

The soldiers of the League pushed forward, hacking and slashing as if clearing their way through thick brush. The animalistic fury of these beasts did not faze her soldiers; the war in the Raedittean had made them veterans of demon combat. Olorus and Hook were by her side, stabbing with their spears and blocking with their shields. Marcus Worth was not far behind, leading soldiers from Endenholm arranged in tight, turtle-shell formations, their circular shields raised in phalanx position.

"To the walls!" Leah cried. "Cut them down! No mercy!"

A coblyn leaped at her like a jungle cat. Raising her left arm, she felt the creature's teeth smash into the plate of her gauntlet before she brought her sword down, splitting its body in two and spilling black blood across her front.

Through the fray, she could see the river tributary, the overlook from which they'd ridden down, and the farmlands surrounding the city. There was still no sign of any cythraul.

Yet, she thought.

It had been proven, first on the beaches of Gaius and later in battles across the Raedittean, that cythraul were not invincible against human weaponry. They could be killed. With strategic advances, they could be swarmed, overwhelmed, and brought down. But it always came at the cost of many lives. A cythraul might kill fifty soldiers with a single blast of daemyn energy. A swing of a fist could reduce a man to a slimy pile of broken bones. To order a charge against a cythraul meant knowingly sending people to their deaths. They were to be engaged with extreme prejudice.

Olorus, Hook, and the rest of the League chopped and hacked with smiles on their bloodstained faces. Demon bodies and body parts fell in their wake as they pressed in. Already, they were almost to the walls. It was a laugher. If coblyns could have understood the concept of retreat, the battle would have been won, but they would have to be slain to the last.

Atop the fortifications, most of the archers had stopped firing and were shouting cheers of triumph. A thrill of hope fluttered in Leah's heart at her first clear view of the colors they wore. Blue and silver. The colors of Nolia. She was home.

As the last of the coblyns went down, the cheering of the archers on the walls was joined by the six thousand soldiers around her. But Leah did not smile. She did not raise her voice in triumph. She quietly sheathed her saber and rode toward the front gates. The gates opened, and Olorus and Hook took up positions behind her.

As she entered, people began to recognize her. Soon, she could hear her name being whispered all around her. People called out things like, "It's the princess!" And, "She is alive!" "Leah! Leah!"

Soon, it became chanting. Then cheering.

"Leah! Leah!"

She tried to keep a stern face as she directed her steed down the cobblestone road. "Olorus, Hook," she said, shouting to be heard over the crowd. "Tell our men to gather water and bring it into the city, immediately. Distribute rations from our own supplies."

"Our supplies are running low, my lady," said Olorus.

She shrugged. "Time to put new notches in our belts."

Olorus smirked. "Yes, my lady." Before he acted on her orders, he stood up in his saddle, raised his spear high, and roared, "All hail Princess Anavion of Nolia!"

The crowd chanted, "Hail! Hail! Hail!"

CHAPTER 26

Gunnar watched the approach of the contrasting colors ahead: white sand, turquoise water, and brilliant green jungle foliage.

And above the jungle, murky, gray smoke.

Seated around Gunnar in the dinghy were Ahlund, Justin, Lycon, Adonica, Borris, and Pool, who worked the oars with long, steady strokes to propel the tiny boat toward the beach. The seawater was so clear Gunnar could see a full twenty feet straight down, to the very bottom of the shallows.

The island was small, probably less than two miles from end to end. Gunnar's maps didn't have a name for it. Tribes of islanders called places like this home. The *Gryphon II* would have passed it by, but the amount of smoke pouring into the sky from its center—more smoke than any number of cooking fires would have produced—had made Gunnar suspicious. He could smell the smoke from here. Esthean was still a day away, but it merited an investigation.

Ahlund hadn't liked the idea very much, but that was normal; he didn't like much of anything. His opinion didn't matter, anyway. These were Mythaean waters, and any activity within Thalassocracy territory was Gunnar's business. The smoke might be an indication of some sort of trouble, and he was obligated to check it out.

At least, that's what he had told everyone.

In truth, Gunnar didn't know what his duties or obligations to the Mythaean Thalassocracy were. Yordar's imperialism, coupled with the formation of the League, had been a catalyst for major change, splitting the Thalassocracy down the middle. It had led to more aggressive politics across the Raedittean, creating factions and new alliances. Individual city-states weren't being left to govern themselves anymore.

Gunnar could read the writing on the wall. Old Mythaean traditions were on their way out, and it seemed unlikely that such an unstable system would ever be resurrected. In fact, the formation of the League may have unintentionally ushered in the fall of the Thalassocracy. As a direct descendant of the High King who had first united the Raedittean, Gunnar wondered if he should feel ashamed for his part in dismantling his ancestors' ocean empire. But the hell with it.

All things considered, whether or not it was his responsibility to investigate a suspicious-looking island, who could say? But it was a welcome distraction and gave him a little more time to talk things over with Ahlund and Justin, to figure out where they really stood.

Plus, thought Gunnar, *any chance to annoy Ahlund a little is worth it.*

Ahead, a school of aquatic animals cut through the water. At first, Gunnar thought they were porpoises hunting the shallows, but the shadowed bulks of their bodies were too big. One rose up, and a tall, bony sail cut the surf like a blade.

"Dimetrodiles," said Adonica.

"Lot of them," said Lycon.

"I seen me a 'dile, once," Borris said, speaking in his characteristic lisp, caused by a badly healed scar on the side of his mouth. "A big mother, it was! Sunnin' itself on the banks of the Greenspring. Musta swum from the sea all the way upriver to Lonn."

"Says the same feller," said Pool, sucking in a labored breath as he worked the oars, "who nearly browned his britches on account of he thought a dead sucker-fish were a sea serpent's eye stalk."

"*One* time!" said Borris. "You're like a dog with a bone—let it go, mate."

"Weren't no sea serpents in Lonn," said Pool. "Weren't no 'diles, neither."

"No 'diles, my foot!" Borris said. "That's what happened to the old schoolmaster. Got his arse bitten off taking a skinny-dip. Ask anybody."

"Are they dangerous?" Justin asked.

"All those big bastards care about is food," Adonica said. "They don't tangle with anything that can bite back. As long as you're not in front of them in the water, they won't even know you're there."

"Sure," said Ahlund. His voice was expressionless, but Gunnar detected many unsaid words behind that comment.

CHAPTER 27

"Shoo! Get!" Lycon hollered, waving his hands and kicking at the sand.

It was almost funny watching the bloated, hulking bodies of six dimetrodiles fleeing a single man. The green, scaly predators were five feet long, with short, wide faces and yellow teeth overlapping their jaws. Vertical spines jutted out of their backs connected by a membrane of skin, creating a parabolic crest. They *looked* fierce, and in the water, they might have made mincemeat of Lycon. But on land, they were just lumbering sacks of fat whose speed would barely rival a tortoise.

Their tails dragged lines through the sand as they plodded down the beach toward the water. Lycon even gave one's tail a little stomp as it went. It opened its mouth to hiss at him but kept moving.

Only one thing could have lured those things out of their comfort zone, thought Gunnar.

An easy meal.

Gunnar, Ahlund, Justin, Lycon, and Adonica had waded to shore, leaving Pool and Borris in the dinghy out in the shallows. Behind them, in deeper waters almost half a mile away, was the black silhouette of the *Gryphon II*. As the 'diles retreated into the surf, Lycon kneeled to examine the ground and brush off a pile of the meat they had been eating. Adonica leaned over to get a look, but she quickly turned away, making a noise in her throat and putting her hands on her knees as if about to be sick. Justin looked, too, and mumbled something under his breath.

Ahlund reached down and picked it up. He held a badly chewed human arm by the wrist.

"Spirit's sake," Adonica said, breathing deeply to stave off queasiness. "I didn't think they were man-eaters."

"They're not," said Ahlund. "But they are scavengers."

He turned the arm over to get a better look. The skin was dry and studded with teeth marks. The muscles were stiff. The loose skin hanging from the torn shoulder was etched with a set of black, interconnected circles running down toward the wrist like the links of a chain.

"Tattoos?" said Lycon.

"Tribal peoples," Gunnar said. His one-eyed gaze wandered to the column of smoke rising above the trees, dark and thick. "They were attacked. Somebody killed this man . . . inventively."

Ahlund tossed the arm over his shoulder. It landed on the sand and rolled a few times down the beach.

"What do you mean, inventively?" asked Adonica.

"Take a closer look at that arm, soldier, if you can," said Ahlund. "No blood at the bite marks. It means he or she was long dead by the time the animals got here. But there was massive bleeding at the point of separation at the shoulder."

"You mean. . . ." said Justin, and though his words were even, his face betrayed his feelings: disgust and horror. "You mean somebody got their arm cut off and tossed to the scavengers?"

"I don't know about that," said Gunnar. "Doesn't look like a cut, to me. Notice the raggedness. The trailing material. The torn skin."

Adonica's neck lurched, and she turned away again.

"The arm was . . . *pulled* off?" said Lycon.

"And they were alive when it happened," said Ahlund.

The words sent a chill down Gunnar's spine. He drew his cutlass and started up the beach toward the jungle. "Come on," he said. "Let's check it out."

CHAPTER 28

As Gunnar marched toward the tree line, Ahlund, Justin, Lycon, and Adonica drew their weapons and followed. Visibility dropped as they entered the forest. The sunlight through the canopy created stark, solid-looking beams in the smoke. The hot, humid air was like walking through a damp curtain.

Gunnar had to squint his eye against the sting of the smoke. Before long, he found himself coughing. He was starting to wonder if he'd strayed off course when he finally spotted something through the smoke: a palm-thatched rooftop.

A noise in the forest drew him to a halt, but its quick, rhythmic crashing implied an animal fleeing at their approach. More scavengers, maybe.

Hopefully.

As they approached the structure, more buildings materialized through the smoke.

"By the spirit," Lycon whispered.

"My God," said Justin.

The only huts still standing were those in the immediate vicinity. The rest of the village had been burned to the ground. Scattered everywhere, as if picked up and dropped by a great wind, were manmade goods. Worked wood. Woven baskets. Bowls made of coconut rinds. Toys made of seashells. At Gunnar's feet lay an overturned basket with half a dozen spilled guava fruit, still fresh. Smoke poured from the husks of buildings.

Corpses lay everywhere. Some were intact. Others were not.

Gunnar spotted a group of muscular men dead on the ground nearby. Bows and obsidian-pointed arrows lay around them. There were strange, ragged holes in their chests—where their hearts should have been.

"Did you hear that?" Adonica said.

She stood beside Justin, her head tilted to one side. Before anyone could ask for an explanation, she turned and took off running.

"Private Lor!" Lycon shouted.

Justin jogged after her, followed by Lycon and Gunnar. He saw Adonica hop over a fallen tree and disappear into the foliage along the outskirts of the village.

Gunnar almost tripped over a body as he ran and realized, to his surprise, that it was a man without any arms. Then he saw another. And another. All of them had had their arms ripped out of their shoulder sockets.

Adonica, Justin, and Lycon stopped near a patch of wreckage. Finally, Gunnar heard it, too. A voice. He did not recognize the language, but the meaning was clear enough. A cry for help.

They ran toward the sound. In front of a flaming hut, they found the source.

An elderly man lay among several other bodies. When he spotted them, he shouted louder. Adonica made it there first, but Lycon was a close second, sliding to the ground on his knees to examine the man. Gunnar and Justin stood watching.

The man was ancient-looking, with feathers in his hair and a yellow, spotted feline hide tied across his shoulders. His tattooed chest was slick with blood. Like many of the other victims, a ragged hole had been punched through his body, but it had missed his heart. The wound, close to the collarbone, was like a deep, blunt indentation. Gunnar had never seen anything like it. He was at a loss for what sort of weapon could cause such an injury.

"We're here to help," Lycon said, holding his hand over the wound and willing his healer's aurym into effect.

"Looks like the tribe's shaman," said Gunnar.

The shaman's eyes took turns on each of them. He drew quick, shallow breaths as Lycon healed him. His eyes looked dull.

"The whole village," Adonica said, looking around. "Demon attack?"

"Don't know," said Gunnar. "Justin, what do you think?"

Justin blinked in surprise. "Uh, it. . . . It could have been cythraul, I guess, but there must not have been any coblyns with them, because the bodies are, well, you know."

"I'm losing him," Lycon said.

Gunnar heard a noise behind him. Turning, he found Ahlund Sims looking down at the injured man. He looked at Gunnar and shook his head.

The tendons in the old shaman's neck stood up. His jaw clenched violently. He raised his hand, grasped Lycon's fingers, and pushed the healing hand away.

Lycon hung his head. "I'm sorry," he said.

Ahlund drew his knife. He stepped forward and leaned down over the man.

"Wait!" Justin said, grabbing Ahlund's shoulder. "He's trying to say something."

"H—h. . . ." the shaman stammered. "H—hyd! Hyd. . . !"

"Hyd," Lycon repeated, trying to comfort him.

"In—inn—o. . . ." said the man.

With his final breath, so loud that it made Gunnar jump, the old man cried, "*Inn—o—cen!*"

CHAPTER 29

Gunnar emerged on deck wearing his cutlass and not much else.

Night had fallen, and there was still not a cloud in the sky. He was barefooted and bare-chested, wearing only a pair of trousers and his sheath. Bumped, pinkish scars lined his chest, leaving tracks of bare skin where the hair no longer grew. Day-old stubble coated his face, and the twin braids of his mustache hung low. The locks of his long, black hair rested on his back.

Only a few of the *Gryphon II*'s sailors were on deck. He paid no mind to their stares as he crossed the deck barely clothed. On any other night, he might have made some sort of sarcastic comment. But tonight, he didn't feel like joking around. He didn't feel like saying much of anything. So he just raised the bottle to his lips for a swig. It burned on the way down.

Times like these, I do miss the Brig, he thought.

The Lonn people may have smelled like fish, but, nice thing about owning a bar, you never lacked a drinking buddy.

A lone figure stood at the ship's stern. A tall man—not as tall as Ahlund, but tall by most standards—leaned against the railing, looking out over the sea. Black fabric wrapped his left arm.

Just for fun, Gunnar took a running start and hopped over a set of barrels before ambling to the stern. Justin turned to look at him. A funny expression crossed the boy's face when he realized the admiral was barely dressed, and it made Gunnar laugh. He was a good kid, but he was cursed with the misfortune of an overly expressive face. Never any mystery what was going on in that head.

"Couldn't sleep," said Justin.

"Likewise," said Gunnar. "I always have this problem. Never fails. When there's a good bed to be had, that's when I can't sleep. You think Private Lor would sing me a lullaby?"

Gunnar offered Justin the last of the bottle, but he shook his head.

"Want to see how I drink for free in any tavern in Athacea?" asked Gunnar.

"Sure," said Justin.

"I'll bet some guy I can fit a full-grown flower into an empty bottom without losing a single petal."

Gunnar drained the final mouthful and sat the empty bottle on the railing beside him. He reached into his pants pocket and dropped a seed into the bottle. He traced his finger in mid-air, willing some aurym into the tiny vessel. Its exterior shell cracked open. Brown roots spread across the bottom, and a stem grew upward. A bud formed and spiraled open, blossoming into a single, yellow flower with spiked, red-speckled petals, perfectly contained within the bottle.

"Not bad," said Justin.

"In the real trick, I cover the bottle with a handkerchief and slip the seed in while I show them a different flower. If people know the secret of your magic trick is actual magic, they're never impressed. Which is ironic when you think about it."

"I could see that," said Justin. "Are we getting close to Esthean?"

Gunnar sighed. "All work and no play—you're getting to be as bad as Ahlund. Yeah, we're close. We should be able to see the shores of Darsida by morning."

"The shores of what?"

Keep forgetting he's not from here, thought Gunnar, scratching his chin.

"Well," said Gunnar, "the Oikoumene is mostly water. The place where you've spent most of your time is Athacea, a small landmass with the Shifting Mountains, the Gravelands, Hartla, and all that. West of Athacea is Endenholm, and to the southwest is Otunmer, a big continent. Mostly cold, dry deserts that turn to snow and ice as you head south. On every map I've ever seen, Otunmer just kind of trails off. Not sure anybody really knows how big it is. You still with me?"

"I guess," said Justin.

"Right now, we're in the Raedittean Archipelago, the place my people call home and heading toward Darsida. Darsida is the centermost continent of the Oikoumene, four or five times the size of Athacea. But we're not landing on Darsida. We're riding the Strongwinds north, to the tropical regions along the equator."

"North to the *tropical* regions?" Justin said.

"You don't know what tropical means?" asked Gunnar.

"No, I do. But if it's to the *north* of us. . . . Never mind. I guess that means we're in the southern hemisphere, and the equator is to the north. That explains why it's been getting so much warmer. The jungle today was sweltering."

Both men were silent a moment. At the mention of the jungle, Gunnar's mind went to disembodied arms, the smells of smoke and blood, and the dying words of an old man.

Hyd. Inn—o—cen.

"Where is Esthean, then?" Justin said.

"No one knows except those who've been."

Justin cocked an eyebrow. "Mysterious."

"It's a large, tropical island," said Gunnar. "That really is all I know. Ahlund would only tell me to stick to the Strongwinds till we see the shores of Darsida, then veer west."

Gunnar shrugged. He hoped it wasn't evident how annoyed he was at being ordered around on his own ship.

"Isn't there another continent?" said Justin. "You mentioned it the other day."

"Erum," said Gunnar. "Way out in the far east."

"And that's where Avagad is?"

"So they say. You all right, kid?"

"Not really," said Justin. "I don't like. . . . It bothers me that the demons aren't just fighting us anymore. They're fighting regular people—people like those islanders who have nothing to do with the war." The boy squeezed his hands around the railing, and Gunnar heard his knuckles crack. "I am not okay with that."

"Ahlund seems to think his pals at Esthean will have some answers," said Gunnar. "Hopefully, when you find them, they'll have some advice."

Justin nodded, but then his head snapped toward Gunnar. "You mean we, don't you? When *we* find them."

Gunnar hesitated.

"You're not coming with us?" said Justin.

"Nice as a break sounds, this is no time to take a holiday," said Gunnar. "I've got a shipload of refugees here. This detour to Esthean was a concession to begin with. Now, it's my responsibility to get these people to safety. And I couldn't in good conscience hand that duty off on someone else, as much as I might want to. What if something happened on the way? No, I wouldn't feel right not seeing it through personally."

"Will you go back to Hartla first? To look for your brother?"

Gunnar had started to yawn, but he clamped his mouth shut in surprise at Justin's words.

"The idea had crossed my mind," said Gunnar. "You've got me pegged."

Justin said nothing. There was no judgment on his face. Only interest.

"Look," Gunnar said, leaning close so no one else would hear. "Hartla's on the way to Castydociana anyway. If there's any sign of trouble, we'll steer clear. But if it looks safe, I can duck in real quick and see what I find. Thanks to you, I know where to look. If Yordar survived Hartla, he'll be more dangerous than ever. He'll feel belittled, and he'll put every ounce of his energy into rectifying that. He will come after us and our allies with everything he's got. He is obsessed, Justin. I have to stop him."

"Are you trying to convince me," asked Justin, "or yourself?"

Gunnar leveled his gaze at him.

"Sorry," said Justin. "Maybe that wasn't fair."

Gunnar sighed. "You better get some sleep, kid. You're gonna need it."

"Do you know what those words meant?" asked Justin. "The ones the old man in the village said before he died?"

"Must've been something in his language."

"Uh-huh," said Justin. "Okay. Good night."

"See you tomorrow," said Gunnar.

Gunnar watched the moons over the ocean as Justin left. He reached for the bottle for a drink, remembered the only thing left in it was a flower, and flicked it with his fingertip. It tumbled overboard and hit the water with a plunk.

CHAPTER 30

"You must understand," said the mayor. "At first, his words seemed wise. In such uncertain times, emergency procedures seemed to be in our best interest."

"So *you* approved this?" Olorus demanded. "On your own? The city council had no say in the matter?"

"Asher's first order was to disband the city councils!" the mayor said pleadingly. "He said it was to cut down on bureaucracy and stabilize local power during this time of crisis. We had heard of a black terror sweeping through Lundholm and Endenholm, but we did not think Asher would ever allow it to cross into Nolian lands! More than anything, these measures were meant to keep the people calm and assured. If I'd ever dreamed it would come to this, I'd have been the first to stand against it."

Leah leaned back in her seat, trying to hide her disdain. She didn't want the mayor of Ronice to think she was angry with him. He had done nothing wrong, personally— except to obey the orders of the clearly inept tyrant who had usurped the throne.

The room in which they sat was a large dining hall. Its walls were finely decorated. A roaring fire burned in the hearth, and, for the first time in several weeks, Leah wasn't cold. At least that was something to be cheerful about.

Hook Bard and Marcus Worth were with the soldiers in the League's camp outside the city walls. She had assumed this meeting with the mayor would be strictly professional. Instead, she and Olorus sat at his personal dining table, each with a great, fat leg of duck and a chalice of wine on the table before them.

The mayor, a sweaty, thin-haired man seated at the head of the table, had spent several minutes filling her in on the events of the past month. It had been while Leah was in the wilderness with Justin, Zechariah, Olorus, and Hook that the first reports of demon activity started coming in from Lundholm and Endenholm. But Prime Minister Asher had thought it more prudent to ensure Nolia's safety than to send aid to its allies.

As the reports increased, Asher had even gone so far as to partially evacuate cities and towns west of the capital. Caravans of people were moved east, where, Asher assured them, they would be safe. The western settlements had been left under standing guard, which reduced entire cities to mostly empty military fortresses. Citizens who opted to stay in their homes did so at their own risk.

That was how Ronice had come under siege. Half its people—including, to his credit, the mayor—had decided to stay rather than evacuate. When the coblyns attacked and surrounded the city, it was all the city's remnant could do to keep them from breaking down the gates. The people were alone and abandoned, with no open lines of communication with the outside world, and it had been that way for weeks.

"Did Asher not consider the consequences?" said Leah. "Did no one stand up and tell him that 'partial evacuations' would imperil our people? That this would displace families from their homes, disrupting normalcy in already uncertain times? That local economies would collapse under such duress?"

The mayor wiped his face with a handkerchief. "My lady, it all happened so quickly. At the time, no one knew what we were truly up against."

Leah's hand tightened on her fork. The pewter bent beneath her thumb.

"Asher! The fool. How out of touch can you get?" Olorus finished the comment by sucking a heavy swallow from his chalice.

"Creative solutions formed from the safety of armchairs in warm parlors rarely translate," said Leah. "If the rest of Nolia consented to his evacuation plans, it shows how strong his influence is—and how corrupt our government has become."

"I assure you," said the mayor, "no such corruption exists, here. Ronice is loyal to the true leader of Nolia, my lady. The people are joyous at your return. Our town guard has pledged its allegiance to you, and the city is at your command. I always knew you were not the criminal he said you were. Say the word, and I will do whatever you ask of me. I will step down. I will take my place on the front lines of battle! Just say the word, my lady!"

Leah was partially ignoring the mayor by now. She'd never had much patience for the dramatic displays and longwinded exaggerations so typical of politicians.

Honesty required few words. She once remembered her father telling her that if you kept your "yes" meaning "yes" and your "no" meaning "no," then "yes" or "no" was all you'd ever need to say. Or something like that—he had worded it more eloquently. She frequently found herself wishing she had paid better attention to him . . . while she still had the chance.

"It brings me no joy to do this," said Leah, "but Asher has caused so much damage that I can see no other way." She paused. "At this point, Asher's plan may be the only thing that can save us *from* Asher's plan."

"I do not understand," said the mayor.

"Take them all to Cervice?" said Olorus.

Leah nodded. "We are four thousand strong. Six thousand if Worth and his people come with us—I haven't invited them yet. Those sorts of numbers would be more than enough to protect these people on the journey to the capital."

"You mean to fully evacuate Ronice?" said the mayor.

"My people can't stay here," said Leah, "and to leave you unprotected would only result in further disaster. But perhaps at the capital, the people of Ronice will find sufficient protection. When the original evacuation took place, you decided to stay in your city. I would have done the same thing. But now, things are different. The devils that tried to beat down your doors were but a taste of what may come. I will not force anything on you or your citizens. Ronice will decide Ronice's fate."

"We'll have a vote," said the mayor. "The remaining members of the town council won't be hard to track down—"

"Not the town council," Leah said. "The town guard and the soldiers who risked their lives and volunteered to protect your people—*they* have proven their loyalty to your city in word and deed. We'll put it to a vote among them."

"Do you think," said the mayor, "and pardon any disrespect. But do you think that Cervice will *accept* your return, my lady?"

"If, by Cervice, you mean Asher and the current governing body that rules the capital," said Leah, "they will have no choice in the matter."

C H A P T E R 3 1

The mayor offered quarters in his estate for Leah and her advisors, but she opted instead for a modest, second-floor room at the local inn. Looking down from her window, she watched soldiers of the Athacean League help citizens of Ronice load carts and wagons with as much as they could carry. The city that had almost become these people's tomb was being left behind.

Leah turned away from the window. Its corners were frosted with the chill of the coming night. This autumn had proven colder than usual, and if things continued this way, winter would be difficult, especially for people displaced by the instability of wartime. She just hoped enough beds could be found at Cervice for everyone.

The whole situation had the potential to become a real mess, but, in this case, one mess was needed to clean up a bigger one. Before departing from her meal with the mayor, she had learned that Asher had implemented a steep "personal security tax" to offset the expenses of the evacuation efforts. Farm animals had been seized. Granaries and storehouses had been emptied. As a result, Ronice was even lower on food and supplies than Leah would have guessed. Under Asher's laws, anyone brave enough to stay behind, like these people, were punished with looted storehouses and empty coffers. It made Leah sick.

Two quick knocks on the door shook her from her thoughts.

"Yes?" she said.

Hook ducked in. *"Marcus Worth,"* he signed.

Leah nodded.

Hook stepped aside to admit Worth. The young man scratched at the chinstrap of his narrow, red beard as he entered. There was no sword at his belt, and she wondered whether he had left it behind of his own volition or if Hook had confiscated it.

"Is there something I can help you with, Captain?" she asked.

"No, my lady," he said, chuckling a little. "You have helped us more than enough! Several of my soldiers have located loved ones who chose to remain here in the city— travelers and merchants who happened to be in Ronice when the tragedy struck. One of my men was even reunited with his wife."

"Nice to hear a love story with a happy ending," she said. "Our partnership was mutually beneficial, then."

"To say the least," said Worth. "And now, word has reached me that you have offered us sanctuary in Cervice, as well."

"We leave first thing in the morning," said Leah. "It will be a two-day march to the capital city. Any or all of you are welcome to accompany us, but let me be clear: I cannot promise much what will happen when we get there. If the rumors are true, and evacuations like this one have taken place all across western Nolia, Cervice may be painfully overcrowded. Your people may have to make camp outside the walls, simply out of necessity, but you will be afforded equal protection of arms and all the amenities we can spare, no less than our own citizens."

"Thank you," said Worth. He crossed the room to the window, hands folded behind his back. "These people," he said, gesturing out the window. "For the first time in a very long time, they are hopeful. I can see it in their eyes. It is rumored that the vote for your plan of action passed unanimously."

"I can't really vouch for that," said Leah. "I only know it passed."

Worth wetted his lips awkwardly. "I thought, at first, that you had come to Ronice simply to gain the trust of my people," he said. "I thought you had ulterior motives of adding our swords to your cause. But to see you lead the charge yourself. To see the kindness with which you treat these people, at the expense of your own mission—to see you in battle, a girl of so few summers, and so fair. . . ."

His eyes darted away from Leah's to look at the floor, as if suddenly realizing what he was saying. It almost made her smile. It reminded her of something Justin would do.

"My lady," he said. "We few remnants of Endenholm will join you, if you will have us."

Leah nodded. "It will be an honor."

CHAPTER 32

In the morning sun, the dark ocean depths ahead gave way to a band of bright aquamarine in the shallows. In the distance, a white-sand beach gave way to a line of mantis green: a jungle with trees so thick that they looked at this range to form a solid barricade. Rising up above the jungle were verdant domes of lushly wooded mountains.

It looked, to Justin's Earthly eyes, like a picture-postcard from a tropical vacation paradise. But somewhere deep in that jungle was Esthean, the forbidden city, home to aurym warriors known as the Ru'Onorath—or, simply, "the Guardians." Soon, Justin and Ahlund would depart from the *Gryphon II* for the shoreline to travel on foot to their city.

Justin wiped the sweat from his brow. The ocean breeze did little to ease the relentless heat in these tropical latitudes. During their discovery of the island village yesterday, he had been amazed by the heat, but that was nothing compared to today. The temperature must have broken ninety degrees—and it was still early morning. Having grown up in the northeastern corner of the United States, he had felt at least somewhat familiar with the temperate and sometimes chilly climate of Athacea. This place, however, was unlike anything he had ever experienced before.

Heck, I've never even been to Florida, he thought.

To him, north meant cold, and south meant warm. It was just the way his world worked. Upon learning that they would be sailing north—and at the outset of winter, no less—he had expected snow and freezing temperatures. Instead, they were enduring relentless heat. It was clear that he was in the southern hemisphere of this planet, and by moving north, they were nearing the equator.

All of Justin's worldly possessions were on him. The loose-fitting clothes he'd been wearing for the past few days felt good in the ocean breeze, and while they would offer no protection from a club or a sword, he thought that wearing armor in this weather would have resulted in heat stroke, anyway. His cat's eye sword was strapped to his back. Additionally, Gunnar had given him a pack filled with supplies like rations of cured meat, a hunting knife, a hatchet, bandages, and a metal canteen filled with water that hung from the pack's outer lashings. His gauge-stone was in there, too. It was the only physical object, other than his sword, to which he felt any connection.

Ahlund leaned against the ship's railing nearby, silent, still, his face shrouded by his hood, watching the beach ahead. Justin had thought that he trusted Ahlund Sims. Would have trusted him with his life. But with everything that had come to light, he wasn't so sure anymore.

The *Gryphon II* was still at least a mile away from its island destination, and although Justin did not know what lay ahead for him, the prospect of dry land was an attractive one. Thankfully, he hadn't experienced any seasickness during this voyage, but the limited space made him feel trapped. Perhaps worst of all was the drinking water. It was stored in barrels below deck, and the longer it stewed in those containers, the fouler it tasted. It hadn't been good to begin with, and with each passing day, it got worse. Every time he took a drink, he swished the water in his mouth, hoping his teeth might somehow filter out some of the staleness. Usually, all it did was stain his mouth with the flavor. The canteen at his side was filled with it. He hoped they would find some fresh, clean water quickly. He was tired of scraping the aftertaste of this stuff off his tongue.

The destroyed village they'd encountered the day before weighed heavily on him. The nature of the bodies seemed to suggest that coblyns had not been involved. The wounds could possibly have been caused by cythraul, but there were no other hallmarks of a cythraul attack—no craters blasted in the ground or lingering presence of daemyn energies. He didn't know what to make of it.

A cold tingle ran down his demon-arm. It climbed through the human flesh of his fingers, slithered there for a second, making his fingertips go numb. He looked down at his hand and squeezed it into a fist to make the numbness go away. It had never done that before.

"Justin!"

The sound of his name jolted him from his daze. He turned to find Adonica Lor approaching with little Maera and her grandfather, Feliks. Justin had hardly seen Maera since they had boarded the ship. The few times he had, she'd been jumping or skipping or sprinting past him. He had seen even less of her grandfather. Feliks leaned heavily on Adonica's arm as they stepped forward.

"Before you leave," said Adonica. "Feliks and Maera wondered if they might have a word."

Justin smiled, kneeling down to Maera's level. "How are you feeling? Okay?"

Maera, suddenly turning shy, clung to her grandfather's leg and offered only a slow, dazed-looking nod.

"Master Holmes," Feliks said, in a voice that sounded even frailer than he looked. "We have not been properly introduced, but my name is Feliks Evin."

"Justin Holmes," said Justin, standing back up to normal height.

"I know *your* name quite all right!" Feliks said, laughing.

"Oh," said Justin. "Well, it's nice to meet you. Glad to see you're on the mend."

"Master Holmes, I have lived in Hartla all my life," said Feliks. "I've worked a kiln ever since my granddaddy first taught me how to fire clay, and if my granddaughter ever learns to keep still for two moments at a time, I hope to someday teach her the trade as well." He paused to clear a rattle from his throat. "In all my years, I have never been this far from home, but I am hopeful that someday, we will be able to return to Hartla again."

"I hope so, too," Justin said. "I'm sorry about the city, and for—"

"So am I, young man, so am I," Feliks said. "It is too bad, but it is no fault of yours. These are the things that happen when men who have power desire more of it. The ones to blame are that Yordar and that man they call Avagad who commands the demon creatures. Men like that carry out their schemes, and little ones like us are made to suffer. It is a relief to know that, in the midst of it all, there are also men like you who fight for us." He raised a gnarled hand in Justin's direction. "I wanted to thank you for saving both our lives."

Justin took the hand gently. The grip that he received back was surprisingly strong, and Feliks pumped his hand up and down several times.

"You have made it possible for this old man to pass on his humble trade." Feliks kept hold of Justin's hand and kneeled, urging him down toward little Maera. "To the next generation."

Justin took Feliks's hint and crouched so that he was again eye-level with Maera. She had her head down as if examining her shoes. Justin smiled and offered her a handshake. Instead, she wrapped her arms around him, squeezed tightly, then let go quickly and ran away. Justin laughed.

"Thank you!" she called back as she ran.

"She won't forget this," Feliks said. "And neither will I. The Evin family will always be indebted to you, Justin Holmes." He leaned forward and lowered his voice as if the last part were a secret. "And I assure you, anyone willing to listen will hear of it!"

With that, Feliks began shuffling off, still leaning on Adonica's arm.

"So long, angel," Adonica said over her shoulder. "Next time you show up and save all our lives, try not to take so long, will ya?"

"Guess I'll see you then," Justin said. She cracked a smile at him.

As they walked off, Justin heard the clanking of giant chain links being unreeled to drop the anchor. Justin looked out toward the shoreline, still a long way away.

"The dinghy will take us ashore from here," Ahlund said.

Justin turned to find him standing behind him.

"It's time," said Ahlund.

"Have you seen Gunnar?" asked Justin.

"I'll find him, lad!" Pool shouted and hustled off through the crowd. Only now did Justin notice how many people had turned out to see him off.

Pool returned with Gunnar, Borris, Lycon, and a congregation of the Hartlan refugees. Ahlund wordlessly crossed the deck and climbed into the waiting dinghy hanging over the side of the ship by block and tackle.

"It was a pleasure, Justin," said Lycon, again enunciating his first name with more formality than "sir" had ever carried.

"Likewise," Justin said. "Maybe we'll meet again somewhere down the road."

Lycon patted the strap of the cythraul blade slung to his back. "And then, I'll show you what this thing can really do."

Justin turned to the sailors from the original *Gryphon*, nodding to each of them in turn. "Borris. Pool. See you later."

"Give 'em hell, boy!" Pool said, snapping his heels together and offering a sloppy salute.

"Don't do nothin' I wouldn't," said Borris with a wink.

Justin turned to Gunnar. The admiral smiled.

"Through wind and tide and squall and foe," said Justin.

"Yeah, yeah, yeah . . ." Gunnar said, smacking him hard across the back.

The crowd watched Justin climb into the dinghy with Ahlund. The oarsman worked the pulley, lowering the boat down over the side of the ship. After they hit the water, Justin did not look back. Whether he would see any of those people ever again, he did not know. He preferred to remember his final goodbyes as they were.

Beside him, Ahlund sat silently, face still hidden by the hood of his cloak. Justin kept his eyes trained on the unknown shores ahead.

CHAPTER 33

They were still a ways from the beach when Justin felt the boat shift beneath him. Ahlund stood and hopped over the side into the waist-deep water. He said not a word to Justin or the oarsman, nor looked back as he waded through the water toward shore.

The beach was pristine. The weather was warm, breezy, and comfortable. The waters were calm, without a single wave. Palm trees swayed. Fallen coconuts lay half-buried in the white sand. It looked like paradise.

So why does it feel so . . . wrong?

Justin checked the water for any dark shapes or dile fins, then stepped off. The sea was warm as bathwater. The sand felt like a bed beneath his boots. He waved goodbye to the oarsman and started up toward shore, wondering why such an idyllic place would awake in him such unexplainable dread.

He pulled himself out of the surf onto white sand that was as flat and unmarked as pavement. The palm trees along the beach were, to his surprise, as tall as mountain pines, but they were dwarfed by the trees behind them: an enormous species of tree he didn't recognize, with large green leaves and a pale trunk. The wooded mountains were blanketed in thick, white mist rolling on for unknowable distances. A strange chorus of animal voices, the likes of which he had never heard before, resounded through the jungle.

Turning, Justin looked back across the crystal waters. The dinghy was sailing back to the *Gryphon II.*

"I feel troubled thoughts within you," said Ahlund.

Justin turned to face him, blinking in surprise.

"I cannot read thoughts," Ahlund clarified, "but just as aurym can create ripples of power, the aura of the soul can sometimes be sensed as well."

"I just. . . ." said Justin. "I don't know. I just have a very bad feeling about this place."

"Your senses are still raw and unrefined."

"Huh?"

"You have proven that you can hear aurym speaking to you. The difficulty at this stage is learning to differentiate it from the other voices clamoring to be heard. To learn which feelings are aurym, and which are merely the byproducts of emotion. That distinction can mean the difference between life and death. Emotions are only unrefined instincts—the driving force behind basic human needs. Fear. Hunger. Lust. Elementary building-blocks of self-preservation no better than an animal." He pointed at Justin. "But *you* must be above such base feelings. Few are blessed with the gift to hear aurym. Fewer still learn to heed its voice and to understand that it is an ally, not a tool."

"How can I tell the difference?" asked Justin. "Between aurym and ordinary feelings?"

"Emotions are based exclusively in self-preservation," said Ahlund. "But following aurym means denying the self as the basis for existence. The more committed you are to aurym, and the less committed you are to preserving the self, the more aurym will preserve you. It is a great paradox."

"So, if I'm feeling something about this place," said Justin, "it might just be that I'm freaked out. Or it could be aurym trying to warn me. Is this jungle like the Drekwood?"

"No," Ahlund said. "The Drekwood was spawned of daemyn. It is an unnatural and evil place. This place is natural and without blemish, but it is well shut off from the rest of the world. Wickedness that should not be allowed to exist can thrive in places like this, unchecked."

"I thought this was where the good guys were."

"There are other, more direct routes to Esthean, but well-traveled roads may be watched. It is preferable that we move through the cover of the jungle."

Justin turned to glance over his shoulder. The dinghy had been hoisted up. The *Gryphon II* had pulled up its anchor. Its black sails were unfurled, and it was drifting into open waters.

"Let's move," said Ahlund.

He started up the beach, toward the jungle. Justin followed.

CHAPTER 34

Growing up, Justin had sometimes heard people talking about the weather say, "It's not the heat; it's the humidity." It had always struck him as a rather stupid and pointless assertion, but now, he was starting to understand the truth of that statement.

The jungle's sticky, spongy floor felt alien beneath Justin's feet. Sweat plastered his body like a second skin. Barely a glimpse of sunlight made it through the thick canopy, and for hours, he had been walking in the shade. In his experience, shade was supposed to be cool, but here, it was worse in the shade than anywhere else. Never in his life had he experienced such unrelenting, sunless heat. The jungle radiated moisture, and the thick confines of the vegetation held it in like a hot sponge. Water vapor hung in the air and wafted like smoke with their passing. Justin's hair and clothes were as damp as if he'd stepped through a waterfall, all from the humidity.

Justin was rather tall. Usually, the geometric constructs of man made him feel awkwardly big, but here, in this land of giants, he and Ahlund were petite. Some of the tree trunks were twelve feet wide, and the tops rose to misty heights unseen. The undergrowth grew higher than their heads. Giant, prehistoric ferns grew bigger than houses. Songs from thousands of birds belonging to hundreds of species echoed around them, creating a continuous, screeching, whistling, whooping soundtrack.

Despite the birds' prevalence, Justin almost never saw them. He couldn't see anything but bark, vines, and leaves—and bugs. Caterpillars dangled from strands of silk. Armies of ants scaled the trees. And bees the size of sparrows whizzed from giant flower to giant flower. There were brightly colored butterflies, and dragonflies with wingspans a foot long. But most of all, there were mosquitoes. Justin found himself wishing for more clothes, despite the heat, just to stave off their incessant biting.

Justin remembered learning in school that jungles were highly competitive ecosystems, and the ongoing competition for survival meant that organisms developed fierce defense mechanisms. Seemingly harmless plants and animals could be toxic or poisonous. He tried to remain hyper-vigilant about not touching anything.

Ahlund led the way, hacking through the underbrush with a long knife, but it was still a matter of simple, brute strength to push through much of the vegetation. More than once, Justin was sure a snake had dropped onto his shoulders, only to find, after making a fool of himself, that it was a vine or a piece of a branch.

Justin ducked beneath the frond of a giant fern and wiped a handful of sweat from the back of his neck. "How can it be this hot?" he said, panting. "We're not *that* far from Hartla, are we? It wasn't hot there."

Ahlund came to a halt at the base of a log almost twice as wide as he was tall. Justin was relieved to notice that his hair and clothes were almost as soaked as his. Maybe he was human after all.

"The cold south winds give Athacea uncommonly harsh winters," said Ahlund. He knelt down to examine a patch of scaly, coral-like fungus clinging to the rotting base of the log. He ran a finger over it and smelled the residue, then broke off a portion, put it in his mouth, and chewed. He snapped off another piece and tossed it to Justin. "Chew," Ahlund said. "Don't swallow."

After a few moments working up his courage, Justin popped the fungus into his mouth and started chewing. It squished between his molars, pumping out a watery juice with the sweetness of honey. Other than the pieces of bark between his teeth, it tasted marvelous.

"So, is it winter, now?" asked Justin.

"In the tropics, there is no winter," Ahlund said. He started moving again, and Justin hurried to keep up. "There are only two seasons. Wet, and dry. Be thankful it is the dry season."

"But, on Athacea, I mean," said Justin, "is it winter there?"

"Yes," Ahlund said. He spat the fungus out.

That's it, then, thought Justin. *Avagad gave me until winter to decide, and now, time is up. So, what happens now?*

The sweet juice of his fungus treat was gone, and the spongy remnants tasted like mud. He spat the spent body out onto the ground and kept walking. Somewhere deep within the chitinous, bone-armor plating of Justin's demon-arm, electrical pinpricks seemed to crawl toward his hand. For the second time today, his fingers went numb. He massaged them with his opposite hand.

Weird, he thought.

PART IV

TAKE

A

PEBBLE

CHAPTER 35

During the day, the thickness of the trees made the jungle a realm of perpetual twilight. And when night fell, it fell hard, and it fell fast. The only light was a tiny fire casting strange and unearthly shadows across the greenery.

With a quick, overhand swing of his hatchet, Justin split the little tree he'd cut straight down the middle. The inner fibers were green and oozed with moisture. He tossed it to Ahlund, who placed it in a pile beside the fire, holding his white-hot sword over it to dry it.

Justin grabbed another piece and readied it to be split. Between swings, he wiped the bugs off him. They were even worse at night. The very ground moved with them. Every surface was covered with them, including his body. His skin was bumped with bites. He had tried to fight them off at first, but, after a while, he just did his best to ignore them.

He tossed more kindling to Ahlund. His arms burned from splitting the wood. His legs burned from walking all day. He felt drenched to the bone but knew he was probably dehydrated. Throughout an entire day of walking, they had stopped to rest only twice, and then, for less than ten minutes. They had eaten nothing save the juice of fungus. The ordeal had Justin so burned-out that he was almost as quiet as Ahlund.

"That should last us the night," Ahlund said. They were the first words between them in hours. Even their work on the fire had not been communicated. Ahlund had simply stopped walking and started working, so Justin had started chopping.

Justin carried the last of the kindling to the fire and dropped it into the flames. He stood there for a moment, holding his arms over it. The heat was unbearable, but the fire discouraged the bugs and dried the sweat from his skin.

"Get the canvases and ropes out of your bag," Ahlund said. "Make yourself a hammock."

"A hammock?" said Justin.

"The ground is dangerous," is all Ahlund said.

What Justin had really meant was that he didn't know *how* to make a hammock, but he was too tired to argue the point. He grabbed his pack off the ground—

Justin shouted and jumped back, nearly falling into the fire. Resting unmoving beneath the place where his pack had been was a fat, coiled pile of scaled muscle. The firelight reflected off its red skin. Uncoiled, it might have been as long as four feet from tail to head. Part of Justin expected the snake to come after him. Instead, it just sat there, watching him with orange eyes from an arrow-shaped head, motionless—not even so much as a characteristic flick of the tongue.

Ahlund reached down and grabbed the snake by the tail. It uncoiled as he pulled it off the ground, and he turned and tossed it. Its airborne body flopped like a rubber hose, then crashed down somewhere in the bushes.

"The ground is dangerous," Ahlund repeated. "Make a hammock."

Justin placed a hand over his pounding heart and breathed a sigh of relief. "Okay," he said. "What about dinner?"

"Not tonight," said Ahlund.

"Not tonight? We haven't eaten all day."

"We are fasting."

Justin blinked. "Since when?"

"Fasting demands less from the body than it does from the mind," Ahlund said. "The longer you can fast without knowing it, the easier it is."

Justin felt his stomach growl. His hunger, only a persistent nagging before, seemed to morph into agony.

"I don't remember signing up for that," said Justin.

"Do you remember what I told you about feelings and emotions?" Ahlund said. "Denying the drive for self-preservation requires more than just a conscious effort. To realize the spirit-self, it requires inner transformation. You must rise above the primitive animal-self, in both mind and deed."

"So, I'm supposed to starve myself?" Justin said. "You know, I've heard of stuff like this before. If you deprive your body of its basic needs, it starts hallucinating mystical experiences, and—"

"That is not the Ru'Onorath way," Ahlund said. "A clear mind is essential. Such delirium would not be tolerated. Fasting is a healthy catalyst to prepare for the physical and mental demands of spirit-warrior training."

"Whatever you say," said Justin.

Ahlund's eyes narrowed angrily on Justin.

"What?" said Justin.

"Make. A. Hammock."

Justin sighed.

As he reached for his pack, a noise in the jungle brought him to full alert. It began as a rustling, then grew nearer and louder until suddenly, the leaves all around him were crashing with movement.

Pouring rain hit him, washing over his already saturated hair and clothes. The sound of it smacking the leaves around him sounded like applause. The fire went out in an instant.

Justin looked at Ahlund. "Dry season, huh?"

CHAPTER 36

Sunrise was still an hour away, and only the bigger of the two moons was visible through the clouds. Its glow illuminated the peaks ahead: the sandstone ridges of Hartla.

Right on schedule, thought Gunnar.

For the second night in a row, Gunnar had been unable to sleep. This time, he'd volunteered to man the wheel through the night. It felt good to do his own steering sometimes. It put him in touch with the ocean, the wind, and the currents. Beneath his patch, the place where his missing eye should have been was burning. It did that, sometimes. It had never quite healed properly, but that might have had something to do with his modifications.

"I don't know if your friends would be happy about this."

Gunnar looked over his shoulder. He had not heard Adonica Lor's approach. "Then I've got the advantage over you," Gunnar said. "I *know* they wouldn't be happy about it. And you aren't either, are you?"

"That is a really stupid question."

Gunnar cocked an eyebrow. "There someplace else you'd rather be?"

"I spent the better part of a month in Hartla, in a basement," said Adonica. "Forgive me if I'm not eager to pop back in for a visit." She stepped in front of the wheel, forcing him to look at her. "You *told* us we were going to Castydociana to join up with Wulder and the League fleet. And to deliver these refugees to safety."

"That's where we're going," said Gunnar. "After a slight detour. Tell me, Private Lor, why did you become a soldier, anyway?"

"Would you ask that same question of Lycon?" asked Adonica.

"No."

"Because he's a man."

"No, because his answer would probably bore the pants off me. Have you ever actually talked to that guy? Dull."

"You're only asking me because I'm a woman."

Gunnar sighed. "Private Lor, I met you only a few days ago. I only know two things about you. I know you're a soldier, and I know you're a woman. I'd ask you how you became a woman, but I think I have a pretty good grasp of it, biologically speaking—"

"Many people hold you in very high regard," Adonica cut in.

"Thank you," said Gunnar.

"Not a compliment," said Adonica. "Just as many people think you are a pompous ass who gets by more on luck than competence."

"What else do they say?"

"That you talk too much."

"You prefer the strong, silent type, I take it," Gunnar said. "I've got a friend who'd be perfect for you. Do you have anything against blind dates? What about mute dates?"

"These people won't say it," Adonica said, "and neither will Lycon because he respects you too much. So, I will. It's not fair to take these people back to—"

"Yordar was at Hartla," Gunnar interrupted her. "He is the heart of our opposition in the Raedittean. I know it's not fun, but we have a duty to the League—"

"You're not doing this for the League," Adonica said, interrupting him right back.

Gunnar felt his cheek twitch.

"Go ahead and lie to Lycon and everyone else," said Adonica. "Tell then about how finding Yordar will shorten the war. But don't try to feed me that same line of rubbish. I know obsession when I see it."

"He's my brother," said Gunnar.

"I know," she said. "That's what makes me wonder. Are you trying to kill him? Or are you trying to save him?"

For once, Gunnar had no words.

"Either way," said Adonic, "it's not my place to say this, but the man's worth it. He made his own desires more important than the lives of innocent people. Be careful not to make the same mistake. War is no place for personal vendettas."

"You're right about one thing, private," said Gunnar, without looking at her. "It isn't your place to say that. Dismissed."

Adonica shook her head.

She started to walk away but turned back. "To answer your question, admiral," she said. "I became a soldier because I wanted to defend those who cannot defend themselves. I will do so until my dying breath, and when I go, spirit willing, I'll take some of the sons of whores who hurt innocent people down with me."

Adonica left. Gunnar did not watch her go. His eye was fixed only on Hartla.

CHAPTER 37

Ahlund led the way, hacking at foliage with his long knife. Whether he navigated from memory or something else, Justin did not know. He had said it would be a two-day trip to Esthean, but the rain was slowing everything down. Justin's clothes were saturated. His hands were wrinkled, and blisters were rubbing raw on the tops and sides of his soaking feet. The rain pounded relentlessly.

It had poured all night and showed no signs of stopping. It made sleep nearly impossible. Covering up with one of the spare canvases had helped but had also invited in all manner of crawling and slithering things just as eager as him to stay dry.

Throughout the morning, Justin's demon arm had pulsed with numbing pinpricks from the inside-out. The sensation was now a constant, numbing tingle. His left hand felt as though it had fallen asleep. Flexing and massaging the fingers helped a little, but, try as he might, he couldn't seem to get the feeling back into them fully.

They didn't stop traveling until midday, and even then, sitting down was unwise, thanks to the snakes and whatever else awaited them on the ground. And still no food.

Standing under the frond of a giant fern and drinking from his canteen, Justin tried not to think about how hungry he was.

"I've been meaning to ask you something," said Justin. "My sword. It is a, you know, *Ru-ON-or-rath* sword?"

"Why?" asked Ahlund.

"Well, it has aurstones in the blade," said Justin. "The only other sword I've seen like that is yours. I found this one on a dead guy in the caves under the Shifting Mountains. Do you think he was a Guardian, like you?"

Ahlund tilted his canteen, drained it to the last drop, and held it out between the fronds to let rainwater spill into the nozzle. Justin emulated the technique. Maybe filling up his stomach with water would distract him from the hunger.

"The same thought occurred to me," said Ahlund. "But I do not remember any Guardian who wielded a blade like that."

"The body was a skeleton, so he was probably from way before your time. Or, wait. . . . Don't tell me you're thousands of years old, too."

"No," said Ahlund.

"Good."

"Forging aurstones into blades is a Ru'Onorath tradition, but we are not the only, nor the first, to do it. The art was practiced as far back as the time of the Ancients. You also found an a'thri'ik cavern beneath the mountains. Perhaps the person who owned the sword had traveled there to retrieve more stones. Or maybe he was just a treasure-seeker who found the sword there. We will probably never know, for sure."

"For all the talk of aurstones, I barely ever see them," said Justin. "Gunnar, Zechariah, and Leah all have aurym abilities. So did Lycon. But I never actually saw any of their stones."

"Leah's was in a ring she wore on her finger," said Ahlund. "But most aurym-wielders choose to keep their aurstones hidden."

"Because they're valuable?" said Justin.

"To their users, yes. There are many different kinds of aurstones. Gauge stones, y'thri'ra, are easy enough to find. And healers' stones, y'thri'y, are quite common. Others, however, are rare and not easily replaced if lost or stolen. Consider Zechariah. Without his stone, he would lose his strength and agility. Not all at once, but slowly. And painfully. Age would catch up to him, bringing on senility and disease. Losing his stone, or having it stolen, would be the death of him. Something he has worked hard to avoid."

"So, where does he keep it hidden?" said Justin.

"I do not know," said Ahlund. "I've never seen it. As for Gunnar, whatever type of aurstone he uses must be rare indeed. I have never seen an aurym ability like his before. I've never seen his aurstone, either, though I do have a guess at where he keeps it."

Justin arched an eyebrow in a silent question.

Ahlund raised one finger and tapped just below his right eye.

Justin smirked at the idea of an aurstone underneath Gunnar's patch, lodged into the socket of his missing eye. "It would be like him," said Justin, "to hide it in plain sight like that."

"Hiding aurstones," said Ahlund. "Another example of the desire for self-preservation. The Ru'Onorath forge our stones into our blades for all to see, to stamp out that instinct. It binds us to our weapons. And it means that without them, we are able to be bested naturally."

"Sounds kind of risky," said Justin.

"The greater risk is for someone to be so powerful that he is unable to be defeated, ever," said Ahlund. "The Ru'Onorath way ensures that even a person wielding seemingly insurmountable power can have it taken from him if his enemy is cunning enough. A man like Gunnar, for all his good qualities, will never know aurym as anything more than a tool to be used. A means to an end. Magic. Power. But you and I know the truth. Aurym is our ally. And an ally is more powerful than a weapon."

"Is that a Guardian proverb?" said Justin.

"Paraphrased," said Ahlund. "You will learn for yourself when you meet Cyaxares."

"See-axe-a-*what*?" said Justin.

"Leader of the Ru'Onorath."

The sound of something hitting the ground beside Justin distracted him from the conversation. He turned and saw his canteen on the ground, all the water he'd just collected spilling out into the leaves.

He looked up at his left hand, at the end of his demon arm. His grip was open, but he hadn't meant to open it. He tried to close it again, and numbness tingled in his palm. The fingers would hardly move.

"Let's go," said Ahlund, unconcerned with Justin's apparent clumsiness. "We will not reach Esthean today, but there is a landmark I have in mind. We should be able to make it there by dusk."

Justin picked up his canteen with his good hand. They were on the move again.

CHAPTER 38

A giant chunk of cliff-side had fallen across the dry moat that separated the palace of Hartla from the rest of the city. One at a time, Gunnar, Lycon, and Adonica climbed atop it and hurried across.

As soon as Gunnar's feet hit the other side, he raced toward the outer wall, ducking low to stay in the shadows. He strained his ears, but all he heard was the far-off cawing of seabirds.

Lycon and Adonica took up positions beside him. For the sake of remaining undetected, only the three of them had entered the city. But it was becoming increasingly apparent that there was nothing to hide from. Only corpses in the streets and the crows and vultures tending to them.

Adonica nudged Gunnar and pointed. Scattered around the caved-in palace entrance were several dead soldiers in white-trimmed armor. Some had been caught in the cave-in. Others lay at the edge of a large, charred crater left by a cythraul's daemyn attack.

"Yordar's men," Adonica whispered.

Gunnar scanned the rubble. "Think we can find a way through?"

"We may not have to, sir," said Lycon. "Follow me."

The big Hartlan backed out of the shadows and snuck along the edge of the chasm. Gunnar and Adonica followed him around the side of the palace entrance.

Lycon stopped and kneeled before an iron-barred storm drain. It appeared to be mortared into the ground, but when Lycon grabbed the bars and pulled, the entire drain swung outward on a set of well-disguised hinges. Gunnar craned his neck to peek inside. The rungs of a ladder were bolted into the rock. The ladder led straight down, disappearing into the shadows.

"A secret entrance?" said Gunnar.

"No, a secret exit," said Lycon. "Normally, it is locked from the inside."

"Lucky for us, then," said Gunnar.

Lycon and Adonica exchanged a strange look. Neither said anything, but the comment seemed to have rubbed them the wrong way.

Lycon adjusted the sheath on his back and started down. He didn't descend far before his feet touched solid ground.

"The torch is missing," he called back.

"No other light source?" asked Gunnar.

"I have some flint," said Lycon, "but nothing to light."

"We'll have to make do," said Gunnar. "After you, Private Lor."

Instead of taking his cue, Adonica glared at him. It was no secret she wasn't happy to be here, but she and Lycon were the only soldiers who had spent time in Hartla *after* its fall. They were the best guides, and to bring additional people would have been too risky.

Gunnar glared back at her, but she didn't budge. "Fine," he said, and he pushed past her and descended the ladder himself.

The tunnel was narrow, with a ceiling so low Gunnar felt the feather of his hat scraping the ceiling. He blinked his single eye, trying to force it to adjust to the darkness, and heard Adonica reach bottom behind him.

A sharp *snap* resounded ahead as Lycon struck his flint, producing a spark that illuminated their surroundings momentarily before plunging them back into complete blackness. Running his hand along the wall, Gunnar kept moving.

Snap.

In the light, Gunnar saw a closed door to his left, but Lycon walked past it.

Snap.

The spark of the flint illuminated Lycon standing ahead—and something on the ground in front of them.

CHAPTER 39

"Watch. . . ." Lycon whispered, faltering. "Watch your step, here."

Snap.

In the light of the next spark, Gunnar saw that Lycon was a few steps up a spiral staircase ahead. At the base of the steps, a body lay on the floor.

By the time the next spark came, Lycon was partially around the corner of the stairs, which made it difficult to discern any features of the person on the ground. He was a thin little man dressed in the house colors of Hartla—a servant or a cook, based on his attire—lying with his head lolled to the side as if he'd fallen asleep. His hand seemed to be reaching up the stairs, not down them.

Gunnar now realized why his "lucky" comment had been so poorly received. The source of their luck, it seemed, was a man who had *not* been so lucky. But this man hadn't been fleeing the palace when he died. He'd been going back in.

Trying to save the people inside, thought Gunnar.

He took a deep breath and stepped over the dead man. He couldn't see anything in the darkness, but he was certain Adonica's glare was boring into the back of his skull.

At the top of the stairs, Gunnar heard the squeak of hinges. A spark of the flint illuminated Lycon opening a door. Shelves lined the walls—

An earsplitting *crack* erupted from ahead, causing Gunnar to jump and grab for his sword, but no noise followed except a strange swishing and wobbling.

"Lycon?" whispered Adonica.

"Sorry," he said. "Knocked over a broom. We're in the pantry of the palace kitchen."

"A broom?" hissed Adonica. "You damned near gave me a heart attack—"

"Keep your voice down, private," said Lycon. "We're not far from the main hall."

After a few more sparks and a few more steps, Gunnar began to see the outline of Lycon's shoulders ahead of him without the aid of the flint. The major crept at a turtle's pace, ducked low and examining his surroundings methodically. Gunnar felt his hands shaking. It was all he could do just to remember to breathe, and their slow progression only made it worse.

A sour stench assaulted his nose. Decay.

Gunnar could stand it no more. He hurried past Lycon, toward the source of the light: an arched doorway ahead.

"Careful, admiral!" Lycon whispered.

Gunnar paid him no mind. He kept moving, passing through the doorway and into the main hall. Several buzzards saw him and abandoned their meals to take flight.

Climbing high on the wing, the birds sailed out through the crumpled ceiling, into the sky. Hundreds of bodies lay scattered across the floor. Most were Hartlan soldiers and were several weeks old, bearing the marks of killings by the sword. A giant boulder rested against the wall not far from Gunnar's position. Fresher bodies, more of Yordar's soldiers, lay around and beneath it.

"Search the bodies," Gunnar said, looking over his shoulder. "If he isn't here. . . ."

He trailed off at the expressions on Lycon and Adonica's faces. Neither was paying any attention to him. They were looking around the palace hall. At the destruction. At the corpses on the floor. Lycon looked horrified. Adonica looked defeated.

Gunnar hustled toward the collapsed tunnel. Several fresh, white-armored bodies had been half-crushed in the cave-in. It looked like they'd been trying to get into the palace, when. . . .

Gunnar pulled up short. His blood ran cold.

It was never easy to look at a dead person. People who died natural, nonviolent deaths usually weren't too bad; they sometimes even looked dignified or peaceful, as if in the middle of a pleasant dream, forever. But people killed in the midst of physical struggle did not always leave peaceful-looking bodies. Battle sometimes left its casualties in unseemly or demeaning positions.

It was hard to look at a dead man. Harder still, when the dead man was your own brother, partially crushed by a cave-in. With both arms ripped off.

"Yordar," Gunnar whispered.

His skin was pale. The eyes were open as wide as they could go. His legs were crushed. His shoulder sockets were empty. Where the arms should have been were instead only rust-colored stains splayed out across the stone like a grisly snow angel.

Beside Yordar lay his arms, crossed perfectly atop one another with palms face down. It was not the sort of position that could have occurred naturally. Someone—or something—had placed them that way.

A few feet away was a human head. It was Drexel Von Morix. It sat perfectly upright, facing Yordar. As if it had also been placed there intentionally.

Gunnar had known what he might find here. But now that it was in front of him, he realized he hadn't prepared himself for it. For some reason, Yordar being dead had felt like the least probable of all possible outcomes. After everything the man had done—a lifetime of brutal conquest, all the atrocities he'd gotten away with—it had started to feel, to Gunnar, like his older brother was invincible.

Even now, part of Gunnar thought it was some trick. It wasn't really him. Maybe it was a double made to look like him. Or maybe he wasn't really dead, but I just waiting for Gunnar to turn his back so he could stand up and fight another battle.

The idea was crazy, of course. Yordar wasn't going to stand up. He never would again.

"He seems to be the only one, admiral," Gunnar heard Lycon say. He turned and realized for the first time that Major Belesys was standing right beside him.

"The only one, what?" said Gunnar.

"The arms," Lycon said.

Looking around, Gunnar saw that he was right. There were many bodies, but none of the others had received this treatment.

"Just like the islanders," said Gunnar.

And judging by the blood, Yordar had been very much alive when it had happened. The last things he would have seen were his own arms, tenderly crossed on the ground, and Drexel's head staring at him.

Several yards away, Adonica kneeled over a body. She had her back to them. She stroked the man's cheek with a quivering hand. Someone she knew.

"Whoever did it," said Lycon, "they didn't take any, uh, spoils, sir. The rings on Yordar's fingers. And his medals. He wears a small kingdom's worth of goods. I wouldn't think any man would leave all that behind."

Demons, then, thought Gunnar.

"Justin warned us Admiral Drexel was dead," said Lycon. "Still, I guess I didn't want to belive it. Wulder and the entire League will be grieved to learn of his fate, but they will celebrate the defeat of the false lord-count. You were right, admiral. It will be a great blow to Yordar's confederacy."

"Yeah," said Gunnar.

Adonica stood from examining the body and approached them, but she wouldn't look at Gunnar or Lycon.

"If that was a friend of yours, Private Lor," said Gunnar, "I'm very sorry for your loss."

"All of them," she said.

"What?" said Gunnar.

"All of them," she said, "were friends. I knew all of them."

Gunnar gaped at her. "You knew all of—?"

"This is my unit," she said. "I was separated from them in the chaos, just before the bridge went down. This is no surprise. I knew they were here. And I knew it wouldn't be pretty. Sir."

"I . . . didn't know," said Gunnar.

A silence followed in which Gunnar seemed unable to stop looking at Yordar's arms. Adonica was the one who finally spoke.

"We can't bury them all," she said. "But let's at least cover Admiral Drexel and Yordar."

"I'll gather some stones," said Lycon.

Lycon and Adonica turned to do just that, but before Adonica could take a step, Gunnar gently took her by the upper arm. She looked down at his hand, and he quickly let go.

"I'm sorry," Gunnar whispered. "Why didn't you say anything?"

"Would it have mattered?" Adonica said.

There was no venom in her voice. Not this time. But the words still hit Gunnar like a cythraul's fist.

Without waiting for a reply, Adonica turned and joined Lycon gathering stones.

A few minutes later, Drexel's burial was complete, and Yordar was nearly covered in a mound of carefully placed stones. A small space had been left open for his face. It was, traditionally, the last spot to be covered during a "burial at field"—the Mythaean custom for those who lost their lives on foreign shores.

Gunnar held the last stone in his hands. Adonica watched quietly, and Lycon stood with head bowed, holding Drexel's horned helm, which he'd found discarded in a corner of the hall.

Gunnar did not care enough for Yordar to weep, but he cared too much not to grieve. He'd tried to kill Gunnar—had sent Gunnar's life into a downward spiral he would never recover from. The man had been a tyrant, a murderer, and a traitor. No one could doubt that the world was a better place without him. But he had still been his brother.

Gunnar placed the last stone over his brother's head. "May you find peace, Yordar," he said.

Though you do not deserve it, he thought, and he felt bad for thinking it.

Gunnar slipped a single jeweled ring onto his finger. It was the only thing he had removed from his brother's body. The rest of the medals, jewelry, and fine adornments were buried with him. By right and inheritance, they all belonged to Gunnar and certainly would have made for pretty plunder, but worldly goods were all Yordar had gained from his existence. He left no offspring that Gunnar knew of. The gold and jewels were all Yordar's life had amounted to, and it seemed wrong to take from a man's only true accomplishment away from him.

Lycon cleared his throat. "We should get going, sir," he said, "if we're to reach Castydociana by tomorrow."

"Thank you both for coming here," said Gunnar. "I hope someday we can return to give the rest of these people the burials they deserve. I think . . . I think maybe you were right, Adonica. War is no place for personal vendettas."

As Gunnar turned away from his brother's grave, the words of a dying tribal shaman echoed through his mind.

Hyd. Inn—o—cen.

CHAPTER 40

"Stay down," whispered Ahlund. "Follow me. And keep quiet."

Justin did not need to be told twice.

They crept along the top of a rocky embankment—one of the only geomorphic elements they had encountered since entering the jungle. Trees jutted out from between the rocks and stretched long, slender trunks upward. Through the veil of their branches, it was impossible to see how far the embankment fell, but Justin was careful to stay several steps away from it at all times. It was still raining, and the ever-present white noise of water crashing through the trees had been the only sound for hours, which made the noises Justin heard now all the more disconcerting.

Some of the noises sounded like guttural grunts, and others, low, whooping whistles accompanied by the swishing and crashing of disturbed undergrowth.

Justin rubbed his left shoulder. Something was definitely wrong with his arm. His sense of touch in his left hand was decaying at a rapid rate. Until now, his demon arm had always looked odd but functioned properly. Now, it hung at his side like dead weight, overtaxing the muscles of his shoulder and upper back. He tried to open and close his fingers. Nothing happened. They were locked in place. He tapped the fingers with his good hand.

It's like rigor mortis, he thought. *Like it's dead.*

There came a groan from up ahead, followed by a low hoot. Ahlund dropped down lower and pointed.

"Titanbird," he whispered.

Justin crouched and peaked through the underbrush. His eyes went wide.

The outline of a massive shape was moving through the forest. It walked on two giant hind legs and stood three feet taller than Ahlund. It had no feathers or wings, just a dark hide, and arms with tiny, claw-tipped fingers. Its neck was muscular and lean. Most of its head was an enormous beak—a rounded mass of bone, the size of a blue-ribbon pumpkin. Justin had seen finches on nature documentaries that used their beaks to crack open hard seeds. It occurred to him that this animal could do that with about three coconuts at once. And when that beak opened, emitting a baritone hoot that echoed into the trees, it revealed a mouth full of sharp points of jagged cartilage, like serrated teeth.

This thing was no bird. It was more like a dinosaur.

"Flightless," whispered Ahlund, "but a fast runner. Will feed on men, when it can."

Justin watched with mouth agape. The "titanbird" should have inspired terror. Instead, its body language evoked pity. It was stumbling like a drunk, unable to stand correctly. As it limped to the side, Justin saw a jagged gash across its upper thigh.

"It's—"

Justin was going to say, "It's hurt," but he didn't get the chance to finish his sentence.

A mass of grayish, furred muscle flew through the air and connected with the titanbird in a flourish of beating and striking. The titanbird opened its massive beak and bit and tore at the attacker. The assailant let out a roar so loud and low that Justin's gut shook.

The two giant forms went down. They rolled across the ground as they fought.

"What is that thing?" hissed Justin.

"A blue tiger," said Ahlund.

A shiver traveled down Justin's spine as the massive feline sunk its teeth in and tore a chunk out of the titanbird's back.

To call this newcomer a tiger was like calling the titanbird a parakeet. It met the requirements of a tiger: a feline body, a long tail, a flat, square face, and tiger stripes. But this oversized variant was something else entirely. Tufts of fur, matted by the rain, ringed its neck like a lion's mane. Muscles rippled beneath the skin. The individual vertebrae of its spine could be seen shifting up and down as it lunged and rolled. Its fur color was not really blue, but rather, slate gray offset by black stripes.

Ignoring a giant beak clamped onto its shoulder, the blue tiger sunk its claws into the titanbird, riddling puncture holes the size of quarters into its hide. The bird hooted. The tiger slammed it against a tree.

The wounded titanbird could barely stand. The tiger laid its ears back and bared its teeth, twitching its tail as it circled in for the kill.

The tiger stopped. Its nostrils expanded and contracted.

Its head turned to look over its shoulder. Its eyes fixed on the humans.

CHAPTER 41

It took the blue tiger seconds to close the gap. In three lunges, it pushed through the trees and jumped with claws outstretched.

Justin, frozen in shock, would have been killed if not for Ahlund. The tall Guardian planted his boot against Justin's hip and kicked hard at the same moment, simultaneously pushing Justin forward and himself backward. Justin tumbled headlong into the ground as the tiger crashed through the foliage.

Before he even stopped rolling, Ahlund drew his sword, set it ablaze, and brandished the flaming weapon at the tiger, trying to ward it back. The tiger hesitated, sizing Ahlund up for a weakness. Retractable claws the size of a man's fingers sheathed and unsheathed within the toes of its massive feet as it pawed the leafy ground in anticipation.

Justin scrambled to his feet. Only now did he begin to grasp the size of the tiger. It was a cat as big as a rhinoceros.

A purr rumbled from its throat. Its lips pulled back, and its tail twitched as it watched Ahlund. It raised a paw to bat experimentally at its prey. Ahlund shot a jet of flame. The tiger's paw was doused in the napalm-like manifestation of Ahlund's aurym, and it hopped back, startled, thumping the paw against the ground to bludgeon out the fire. The animal growled at Ahlund in annoyance.

Then, with terrifying deduction, it turned to face the easier meal: Justin.

The tiger stepped toward him, ears pinned back. Justin tried to take a step backward but suddenly realized the rocky embankment was directly behind him.

Justin took a deep breath, pushing back the panic. He searched his soul for the place where the peaceful knowledge of his aurym resided. The tiger got down on its haunches and wiggled its rear, preparing to pounce. Justin reached over his shoulder to draw his weapon—

A blinding burst of flame erupted from behind the tiger. The animal's yowl was ear-splitting. The tiger turned partway around but lunged forward to evade. Its flank struck Justin with the force of a furry truck.

Justin's feet left the ground. His body flew backward, and he and the tiger tumbled over the side of the cliff.

CHAPTER 42

Justin reached for something—anything. His fingers found purchase in a cluster of gnarled roots, and he grabbed hold.

There was a nasty wrenching in Justin's arm as his body weight pulled against it. He shouted as the pain cut through his shoulder but managed to hold on. After a moment of confusion, Justin realized he was hanging from the roots, with his body dangling over the edge of the embankment. Rocks dug into his hips. Rain pelted his eyeballs.

There was a snapping, crashing sound below him. Justin looked down. The tiger's enormous body lay cradled in the branches of trees protruding from of the hillside. Beneath it was a fifty-foot drop.

The tiger roared. It looked up at Justin. And it started climbing.

Ribbons of wood spiraled from tree trunks beneath the tiger's claws. A massive claw swiped up at Justin, passing inches beneath his feet.

Justin tried to dig his feet into the side of the embankment to climb up, but rocks slid free beneath his boots. A clump of black, fertile soil, slimy from the rain, was pulled up as the roots in his hand unreeled out of the ground. His body slipped farther down, closer to the tiger.

Justin searched for the peace inside him. There had to be something he could do. But panic overrode all else. Calling on aurym was impossible.

Ahlund jumped over the side of the embankment and landed on top of the sideways trunk of a slender tree. With a swing of his sword, the air split open. A sizzling arc of fire cruised like a boomerang and hit the struggling tiger across the face with full force.

A fiery explosion destroyed several of the surrounding trees. Flaming splinters and balls of fire rained down as the animal flipped backward and dropped. Justin heard one last yowl, then only the crashing, thumping impact of its body bouncing off trees and branches. It disappeared in the foliage and smoke, and he heard no more.

Justin breathed a sigh of relief just as the roots in his hand snapped.

Ahlund dove, landed on the rocky ledge, and grabbed Justin by the wrist. Justin's body swung inward, bouncing painfully off the rocks. Ahlund lay on his stomach, his sword in one hand and Justin's wrist in the other. Rain streamed through the stubble on his face.

"Climb up!" Ahlund shouted.

Justin tried to raise his left arm.

Nothing happened.

Justin gritted his teeth and growled with the effort, trying to command his arm to reach for Ahlund. His shoulder only shrugged pitifully. The blackened hunk of his demon arm hung there like an anchor.

"I—I can't!" said Justin.

Ahlund was halfway over the edge himself, with his sword still in his other hand. If he grabbed for Justin, he would drop his sword. If he didn't drop his sword, Justin would fall. He felt his wrist slide through Ahlund's hand, lubricated by the rain.

Ahlund hauled back with his weapon arm, pitched his sword like a javelin. He reached forward, grabbed Justin with both hands, planted his feet, and pulled him up. Justin's body was dragged over the edge.

Justin fell to the ground. He lay motionless while the rain poured down on him. Not for the first time, he could hardly believe he was still alive, and, also not for the first time, all he could think about was how quickly it had all happened.

Ahlund walked back to the edge of the embankment, got down on his knees, and reached over the edge. He had speared his sword into a branch. He yanked it free and sheathed it. Returning to where Justin lay, he looked down at the boy.

"Your hand," he said.

Justin turned his head and realized that he was lying on top of his numb arm. He arched his back and had to use his good hand to pull it free. He held his dead arm up to look at it. The bone armor looked the same, but the flesh of his hand seemed to have lost its color. The skin was pale gray, and around the edges, where it was connected to the demonic chitin, it looked purple, as if bruised or infected. But it was not the color that worried him. An almost bone-deep gash ran across the top of his hand, across his knuckles from the pinky to the middle finger. Whether it had been cut against the rocks, on a tree branch, or by a tiger's claw, he did not know. But his hand was so numb that he couldn't feel the injury. More alarming still, it wasn't bleeding. The flesh under the wound looked like a rare steak. But there was not a single drop of blood.

A snapping of branches off to the side brought him up to a sitting position. Ahlund wheeled toward the sound, one hand on the hilt of his sword.

"That dinosaur thing," said Justin. "Damn. Almost forgot about him."

Ahlund snuck forward to peer through the brush.

"It's gone," he said. "Let's get out of here."

CHAPTER 43

It was late at night as they approached, unarmed, on foot, their hands at their sides. They flew no flags of peace, but they walked in the middle of the road, clear of any cover, and for all to see: Leah, Olorus, Hook, and Worth.

The light of double moons illuminated the sentries atop the walls of Cervice watching their approach. The main gate's doors were closed—very odd. In the days of her grandfather's youth, barbarians attempted to pillage some of the outlying neighborhoods. Citizens were pulled back to the interior of the city while the army was dispatched against the raiders. To her knowledge, that was the last time those gates had been closed.

It was said that, originally, the whole city had fit within the ring of the fortified walls. Since then, Cervice had grown, spilling out beyond its barricades so that the streets outside the walls were nearly as urban as the interior. It was one of the most populous cities on the continent—larger than Hartla by several thousand souls. But Leah's warning to Worth that Cervice might be overcrowded was starting to feel ironic, bordering on tragic.

The farmlands were empty. Knee-high weeds grew in the fields as if no one had tended them all season. In these normally thriving neighborhoods on the outskirts of the city, the silence was unsettling. No smoke came from the chimneys. Windows were not just dark; they were boarded up. Doors were fastened with padlocks. No guards patrolled the streets. There was no one to be heard, indoors or out.

Leah looked around the East Quarter, remembering market days held here during her youth. Tradesmen, farmers, and merchants brought their wares from all over the country, some all the way from Worth's homeland of Endenholm. In the evenings, competitions were held, and at night, near the memorial fountain, bards recited poetry and sang songs.

But there were no songs today. The only inhabitants were a few wiry dogs whose eyes shone no longer with the friendliness of companionship but with the desperation of scavengers on the verge of predation. They panted at Leah and her bodyguards as she passed.

Has everyone been moved to the interior? wondered Leah.

"Can you see their uniforms?" asked Olorus.

Hook shook his head to the negative.

"I can't tell from here," said Worth.

Leah assumed the guards on the walls were Nolian soldiers. But she also had assumed Asher would never evacuate the capital city, and after witnessing the state of things outside the walls. . . .

Passing by locked and boarded storefronts, Leah felt like a trespasser in her own home. The innocence of youth on market days seemed a very distant memory. And being here also had the unexpected side effect of bringing up the haunting memories of her last night here.

That night, soldiers had burst into her room without warning, weapons drawn, and set up defensive positions around her door and window. As she had frantically asked them what was going on, alarm bells had begun to toll. Outside her door, she had heard someone yell, "They've killed the king!" Dread had gripped her then, the likes of which she had never experienced, before or since.

For what felt like a long time, those soldiers, members of the High Guard, would tell her nothing. She shook them, pounded on their backs, and demanded to be told if it was true—was her father really dead? But they only looked at her, grim-faced, and spoke to one another about things like defensive perimeters and hunting down intruders. She remembered eventually giving up, sitting on her bed, and weeping.

At some point, Olorus had come to the door. She would never forget his words: "The assassins have been driven out. The city is being searched. Come quickly, Lady Leah. Your brother needs a healer's touch."

Even then, Leah had known Olorus well enough to recognize that his deadpan delivery of the news held terrible implications.

As she was escorted through the palace, she found herself panicked, stumbling, and on the verge of hysterics. They took her to her brother's chambers. There, she was met with royal blood splattered across the bedcovers. Her brother's frantic eyes turned to her, his trembling hand reached out for help, and she fainted. When she woke up, minutes later, he was dead.

The soldiers tried to convince her that he had been beyond saving—that the wounds were so severe, even the best efforts of an expert healer would not have been enough. She tried hard to convince herself of the same thing, but she would always believe that if she hadn't fainted, if she had only been strong enough, then perhaps more than one Anavion would have survived that night.

In the following hours, she became keenly aware that she was watching her life fall apart. She had gone to bed that night worried about a patient at the academy, a man stricken with an unidentified ailment. She'd retired to her quarters earlier than usual and had spent hours scouring old medical volumes for clues before finally falling asleep.

The story of what had really happened that night would take weeks to piece together. The assassins had broken in, killed a dozen or more guards, and, with terrifyingly methodical timing and precision, murdered the king, the queen, and their four sons. At the very same hour, in their countryside plantation on the outskirts of the city, the king's sister and her husband were also murdered. As were the two offspring of the king's late brother—Leah's cousins—at their estate a mile away. Every possible successor to the throne had been killed in a single hour. All but one survivor. Leah.

Men of the High Guard had rushed her through the city streets, telling her that the assassins were still at large and she was not safe in Cervice—not until the roots of this plot could be uncovered. Prime Minister Asher would conduct the investigation with the aid of the High Guard. But as the sole surviving heir to the throne, Leah's immedi-ate protection was paramount. She was to go into hiding, somewhere beyond Nolia's borders. To help ensure her safety, the people would temporarily be allowed to believe she had died along with the rest of her family.

Asher. The man who had been behind the plot all along.

How differently things might have been, thought Leah, *if I'd possessed the courage then to challenge Asher's plan.*

As she later learned, she had not escaped at all. Asher had allowed her to live so she could later take the blame.

She remembered Olorus leading her through the streets that night. When a tall man had stepped out of the shadows beneath the cathedral near the edge of the city, Leah had cried out, thinking it was one of the assassins.

"This is Ahlund Sims," Olorus had told her. "He is a sword for hire without ties to the government. Under his care, you will go more easily undetected."

"But why can't you take me somewhere, Olorus?" Leah had begged. "Why can't it be you?"

"I'm so sorry, child," Olorus had said, tears in his eyes. "These are my orders. In the event that this was an inside job, the prime minister insists that no one affiliated with the crown be trusted. I'm sorry, my lady."

Then Olorus had hugged her, and despite her tearful objections, left her.

"I have two steeds ready," Ahlund had said. "Come, princess. We ride for the Grave-lands."

Presently, Leah took a deep breath as she passed by the solemn edifice of that very cathedral. Its windows were boarded up, and through a gap in the planks, she saw that several of its stained-glass panes were shattered.

The loss of everything that night had, in a strange way, made the death of her family seem wholly unreal. There had been no goodbyes. No funerals. A part of her still thought it hadn't really happened—as if she'd simply been gone on a long trip away from home, and her mother, father, and brothers were alive and well and waiting for her to return.

But, looking around, she realized not even the city had survived her absence. And maybe neither had she. Not entirely.

Hook touched her shoulder to get her attention and signed, *"They carry halberds."*

Halberds. Long, bladed weapons like spears, topped with the heads of battleaxes. The halberd was the traditional weapon of Cervice City Watch. If the men on the wall carried them, it was a strong indication of their identity.

"That's far enough!" a voice rang out.

Leah stopped. Olorus, Hook, and Worth came to a halt beside her. They were fifty feet from the walls.

"You are on foot," the voice shouted again, "without weapons or supplies. Clearly, you are part of a larger force. Tell me now who you represent."

Leah cleared her throat. "True enough!" she shouted. "A force of ten thousand is presently camped in your Borderwoods, six thousand of whom are soldiers."

Leah could not hear the voices from here, but the heads of the soldiers on the walls turned to look at one another. She could see arms and shoulders moving with conversational gestures, some quite animated. She did not wait for their response.

"When did it become so easy," she spoke up, "to invade Nolia?"

The reply was low and deadly. "Step forward, and let my archers show you how easy it is."

Beside Leah, Olorus growled his disapproval. A tingle ran down Leah's spine as she wondered who she was speaking to. Was it Asher? Surely there hadn't been time for someone to run and fetch him in the middle of the night like this. . . . Unless her approach had been spotted much farther out than she'd thought. More likely, it was an officer of the City Watch. She ran through a mental list of names, trying to remember the sounds of their voices.

"You speak to Leah Anavion!" she yelled. "And I have returned to Nolia not to invade it but to save it."

This time, she could hear some of the voices despite the distance. She even heard the command telling them to keep silent.

"Your city is ruled by a false leader," Leah continued. "A man who would have others believe that I killed my own family. To what end? To be reduced to this? Did I kill my family because I grew weary of a life of ease in my homeland? Did I do it because I desired poverty, hunger, and camping in the savage wilds?"

She paused at exactly the place where she had planned to pause, for she had practiced this speech many times in her mind. She had never done all that well in her oration studies, but she understood the importance of knowing when to blaze ahead when to let a point simmer.

Taking a step forward and pushing her voice louder, she directed her words to the soldiers assembled up and down the wall.

"Who is the one who has prospered from all this?" she yelled. "Who has the wealth, the power, and the influence to devise such a scheme and fool an entire nation? Nolia is being held hostage by a tyrant! I have come to free it!"

Silence followed. Her last words echoed through the abandoned streets, bouncing over cobbles and off boarded storefronts. She could see soldiers on the wall conversing with one another.

Suddenly, there was a jolting sound, a thud, and a cranking of chains. The gates began to swing outward.

"Come in, then," the unidentified man on the wall shouted.

Leah looked at the gates, hesitated.

"We are here as a diplomatic envoy," she called.

"Of course," replied the man. "You have my word that no harm will befall you."

Leah turned to look unsurely at her men. Hook's eyes were dark. Worth was biting his lip and only shrugged at her. Olorus stepped forward.

"*Whose* word?" Olorus shouted.

The answer came promptly. "Captain Cimon Endrus."

"Endrus?" whispered Leah. She recognized the name, but he was not a City Watchman. Cimon Endrus was captain of the High Guard—the elite bodyguards of the royal family. Olorus and Hook's unit.

"Anybody we know?" whispered Worth.

"My former commanding officer," said Olorus.

"Does it sound like his voice?" asked Leah.

"So far as I can tell," said Olorus. "He was always a trustworthy enough man, I think, but I do not know if we should trust *anyone* so far as to walk into enemy-held territory unarmed."

"We left standing orders for the army to march if we don't return," said Leah. "He probably thinks we're bluffing about our numbers. Let him try something. Ten thousand of our people will be here within the hour to help us."

"Little good to us if we are dead by then," Hook signed.

A fair point. Nevertheless, Leah took a deep breath and started walking toward the gate. Olorus, Hook, and Worth followed as she passed between the doors. She crossed the threshold, into the inner realm of the city.

Her feet faltered. She felt Hook's hand grip her shoulder to steady her.

The streets were empty. The gardens were uncared for. The houses were boarded up. She looked around, confused. She had feared that she might find an occupying army. Instead, the soldiers on the walls were the *only* souls to be seen whatsoever. There was barely anyone here. Like the outskirts, the inner city was abandoned.

CHAPTER 44

The jungle had done such a thorough job of reclaiming the ruins that it took Justin several minutes to recognize them for what they were. Only after he let his eyes relax and unfocus did the shapes begin to take form—the geometry of arches and domes wrapped in vines and roots, with scattered, dislodged blocks half-hidden beneath leafy undergrowth.

The sun had gone down. The rains had stopped. The matted, disturbed clearing where the titanbird and the blue tiger had fought was hours behind them, and Justin and Ahlund had made camp here, near these ruins. The outlines of the hidden constructs were so shrouded by the dark of night that Justin might never have noticed them—if not for what he felt from them.

The invisible force was so strong that after a few seconds standing close to it, Justin was starting to imagine he could see it. He "saw" waves and vapor trails of energy rising out of the ruins, fluttering like ghostly apparitions.

Daemyn, he thought.

His injured hand was covered with medicinal salves and wrappings. It still didn't hurt, and it still hadn't bled a drop, either. The only feeling in his hand at all was a slight tingle in the tips of his fingers. Ahlund did not know what was wrong or what was causing it. It was not the symptom of any tropical disease he knew, nor the toxin of any jungle plant.

At first, Justin had walked with the dead arm hanging at his side, but Ahlund had since fashioned him a sling. He wore it now, sitting by the fire, watching those ruins and feeling the energy they pumped out. Esthean was only a few hours away, but for some reason, Ahlund had wanted to stop here. Justin was starting to wish he hadn't.

The daemyn emanating from this place put him on edge. It chilled his blood. Ideas and images kept popping into his mind that seemed irrationally fearful. And very dark. He thought dreadful things, and every time he blinked, he saw scenes from childhood nightmares. No matter what he tried to think about, his imagination turned his thoughts twisted and grotesque.

"You are upset," Ahlund said suddenly.

"Huh?" Justin said. He looked up at Ahlund for a second, then turned his eyes back to the ruins without saying anything else.

"I told you," said Ahlund. "The state of your soul causes ripples of aurym. I can tell you are upset."

"Yes, I'm upset," Justin said.

"About your arm?"

Justin's cheek twitched. *Of course* he was thinking about his arm. Somehow, he had gone from one hundred percent health to crippled practically overnight. And what if this was just the beginning? What if this unknown ailment continued to eat away at him like frostbite, ceasing blood-flow, killing cells, until his arm just rotted off?

Or what if it was Avagad? In the five days since Justin had returned to the Oikoumene, the man with the crown hadn't attempted to contact him once. The deadline for Avagad's proposal was over, and now, Justin's arm was dying. Was it a coincidence? Or a message?

Or was this the next step in his devolution brought on by the cythraul's touch—his metamorphosis into a demon?

"About your arm?" repeated Ahlund.

"Yes! Yes, about my arm!" Justin snapped. "About my arm, about this jungle, about fasting—about this whole damn safari. My body's falling apart, I'm starving, I have no idea where we're going, and now, these ruins are. . . !"

Justin trailed off. He closed his eyes, trying hard to fight a swell of irrational anger and fear.

"Can't we go somewhere else?" he said.

"Why?" asked Ahlund.

"Because there's something here," said Justin. "Something bad. Daemyn."

As soon as he uttered the word, he wished he hadn't. His voice seemed to echo through the clearing. But instead of fading away like a natural echo, it grew louder instead, dropping several octaves until it sounded like a voice other than his own.

"Daemyn . . . daemyn . . . *daemyn* . . . DAEMYN . . . *DAEMYN.*

The echo stopped abruptly.

Justin spun around, trying to figure out who had said it, but he found no one but Ahlund, tall and still, watching him.

"These ruins are called the Treasury," said Ahlund. "The Ru'Onorath have never cleansed this haunted place of its daemyn presence. Intentionally."

"Why?" demanded Justin.

"One of the final trials for young Guardians is to face the Treasury, a hive of daemyn, alone," said Ahlund. "For most people, the power of this place is too strong. Many initiates, even after their training is complete, cannot stay conscious within this glade for longer than a few minutes. You, on the other hand, have faced down High Demons. You have spoken to the enemy face-to-face. You have experienced evil that most veteran Guardians could scarcely imagine."

Justin shook his head. "There's no way I can sleep here tonight. It would drive me crazy."

"Even I could never sleep here," said Ahlund.

"What?" said Justin. "Then why did we stop—?"

"I brought you here to prove a point."

"Okay," said Justin. "Point proven. Can we move on?"

"Not to prove a point to you, Justin," said Ahlund.

Suddenly, the shadows surrounding the glen were moving.

Justin stepped back. Bodies took form, emerged from between the trees, and converged. Justin tried to reach over for his sword, momentarily forgetting the state of his arm. All he managed to do was shrug his shoulder and accidentally pull his arm out of its sling. Remembered the hatchet in his bag, he rushed for it. Maybe Ahlund could hold them off by himself until he could. . . .

To Justin's horror, Ahlund was raising his hands into the air—in surrender.

Several men grabbed Ahlund. They took his sword from its sheath, threw him to the ground, and tied his hands behind his back.

"Get off him!" Justin growled as he grabbed the hatchet and charged.

He'd hardly taken a step before he felt his sword wrenched from its sheath behind him. Someone struck his hand, knocking the hatchet from his grasp. Then he, too, was slammed against the ground. A boot stepped down on the back of his neck, pinning his face into the leaves.

Justin turned his face, trying to look up as he shouted, "Let go of me! Ahlund!"

"Ahlund is already gone," said a man's voice.

Justin raised his head from the leaves to look around the glade and realized the voice was right. The bodies that had materialized out of the woods were gone, and Ahlund with them. The man pinning him to the ground was the only one left.

"What did you do with him?" yelled Justin. He thrashed and kicked. "I swear, I'll kill you! I'll *kill you all*!"

"I don't think you will, Justin Holmes," said the voice, calmly. "You are coming with me."

PART V

MILES AWAY

FROM

ALL ETERNITY

CHAPTER 45

Several soldiers came down from their places atop the walls. Along with the halberds, a few carried kite shields like Olorus and Hook. Others had spears or short swords. Most wore the blue of the City Watch. Only one wore the traditional red-trimmed, red-caped armor of the High Guard.

Captain Cimon Endrus was old enough to have been Leah's grandfather. His gray hair was wavy and thick, save for a shiny, bald patch on the height of his head. Leah had always thought the curled, bushy, white mustache on his upper lip made him look like a river otter.

Leah saw Endrus twitch a bit as she approached and realized he had just overridden the instinct to bow to her. Instead, he straightened his back and stood even straighter. Then he turned, blinking in surprise as if seeing a ghost, but he wasn't looking at her. He was looking at Hook. Hook was looking back at Endrus and grinning.

"Where has everyone gone?" Olorus blurted before Leah had the chance to ask for herself.

Leah remembered Cimon Endrus as a formal man, but he gave no introduction. His voice was rich in timbre, deep like a baritone singer, but defeated as he said, "Evacuated. Weeks ago."

Leah opened her mouth to speak, realized a moment too late that she had nothing to say, and shut it again. She looked around at the soldiers.

"Before you are twenty-four soldiers," Endrus said, in answer to her unspoken question. "Twenty-four others are inside the barracks."

"Forty-eight men?" Olorus said. "To protect the whole city?"

"There are fewer than one hundred civilians to protect," said Endrus.

"That's fewer than Ronice!" said Worth. "Where did your prime minister send them—doesn't he feel vulnerable here with such a small force?"

"He is not my prime minister," said Endrus with a bite. "This city no longer pays allegiance to Illander Asher."

Hook signed, *Since when? Since Lady Leah walked through the door?* and Olorus translated the words.

"No," Endrus said. "It was by his orders that the city was evacuated, and we who stayed did so against his wishes. Some of us disobeyed him on principle, others to protect the civilians who refused to leave. There *were* more of us. But with bad news coming in every day, including the loss of communications with other cities, most of those who stayed behind have gradually packed up and migrated eastward. Now, barely anyone remains."

"Where is the prime minister?" Leah said venomously.

"*That*, my lady, is his ultimate betrayal," said Endrus.

He paused to look up at the wall with an expression of disapproval. Leah followed his gaze to a young City Watchman with an arrow still nocked to his bowstring. The archer reluctantly lowered the bow, removed the arrow, and returned it to his quiver. Leah could not blame the man for being on edge. Nothing was for certain, these days.

"It seems you are already aware of Asher's plan," said Endrus, "to evacuate western Nolia."

"Aware, yes," said Leah. "But baffled."

"The strategy was introduced when it became clear how formidable the demon armies in Otunmer and Endenholm had become," said Endrus. "Our western populations, including the people of Cervice, were steadily relocated to eastern cities as a temporary emergency measure. . . . The cities that host these refugees, it is said, are running low on resources. There is waste in the streets, and crime is rampant. Utter chaos. All thanks to Asher's orders."

"Coward," said Olorus.

"I do not think so," said Endrus.

His tone piqued Leah's interest.

"By now," said Endrus, "everyone knows you must have been falsely accused, my lady."

About damn time, thought Leah, but what she said was, "Correct."

"Worse still," said Endrus, "everything Asher has done since taking power seems to have been a means of sabotaging this country."

"Sabotage?" said Olorus.

"Asher is not here—has not been in Cervice for a long time," said Endrus. "He is not even in Nolia. With a force of personal guards, friends, and advisors, he left Nolia and crossed the Gravelands. From what we have heard, he has gone to the city of Isabelle."

Leah felt her hands clench into fists. Isabelle. The capital city of the monarchy of Darvelle, an enemy of Nolia for centuries.

That was it, then. Proof that Asher's betrayal went deeper than a grab for power. Darvelle was larger than Nolia in size but smaller in population. Through high taxation and frequent seizure of private property, they kept their citizens in perpetual destitution, and they sapped anything they could from Nolia. It was a well-known fact that Darvelle funded raids on Nolian trade caravans and outposts. A few groups of bandits managed to make a profitable living out of it, though Darvelle denied any culpability for the raids. The buffer zone of the Gravelands was all that had kept the cold war between Nolia and Darvelle from turning hot for all those years.

That's why Asher's decisions seem so erratic and illogical, thought Leah. *He wasn't inept. He was actively trying to tear Nolia apart. He's not a power-hungry madman at all. He's an instrument of the enemy of my forefathers.*

Which meant her family hadn't been murdered by a traitor. They had been executed according to the orders of a foreign power—the first casualties of war.

"How long?" Leah wondered aloud. "Has Asher been the minion of Darvelle his whole career? His whole life?"

"Long enough to fool us all," said Endrus.

"Darvelle managed not only to kill the king," said Leah, "but to sever the people's loyalty to nobility by inventing a villain out of the heir—me." All at once, the entirety of the plan became clear to her. "Then Asher could steer the country downward, eventually allowing Darvelle to come to the rescue, not as an invading army but as liberating heroes."

Endrus nodded. "That may have been the plan all along. And the rumors of war and demon armies allowed Asher to draw an even tighter grip on the people."

"It's slightly more serious than rumors," said Marcus Worth. "The enemy is closing in, in the west. They invaded my country, razed its cities, and exterminated the Enden people like vermin."

Leah shook her head. "Doesn't Asher—doesn't Darvelle—realize they will be next? Sabotaging our country only makes it easier for invasions to spread to Darvelle and the rest of Athacea!"

Endrus furrowed his brow. "Even if the rumors are true, could roaming coblyn hordes to be *that* great a threat?"

Leah exchanged a frustrated look with Olorus, Hook, and Worth.

"My people are coming in," said Leah. "Tonight. All ten thousand of us. Any objections, Captain Endrus?"

Endrus blinked in surprise. Leah did not wait for a response.

"Thank you," she said. "This madness ends now."

As she turned to gaze upon the empty city, she found herself thinking about Justin again. She had envisioned sharing her triumphant return to Cervice with him.

Welcome home, Leah, she thought.

CHAPTER 46

Fireflies glowed through bioluminescence—a chemical reaction in their bodies resulting in the emission of light.

It was something Justin had learned a long time ago, in the classroom of Jeff Emerson, his next-door neighbor and high school science teacher. For whatever reason, it was one of those things that had stuck in his head. Maybe it was because, at the time, he'd hated Chemistry class with a passion, and the idea of chemicals making a bug's butt turn green was, to him, the coolest thing the subject had to offer.

He remembered learning that bioluminescence was also found in some marine bacteria, and deep-sea fish used it to lure in prey. And who knew? Maybe the aurstones in Justin's sword went through some sort of unequal but related process to create their natural glow. After all, even without aurym power, the stone called a'thri'ik, or cat's eye, glowed naturally—but only in the absence of sunlight. Experience had taught Justin that a'thri'ik did not glow in the presence of moonlight, either—which had seemed strange, until Justin considered that moonlight was really nothing but the reflection of sunlight to begin with.

Still, out of all these light sources and chemical reactions, he had never heard of bioluminescent mushrooms before.

During the day, he probably would have passed right by these little life forms without a clue what marvels they were. But now, in the dead of night, the glowing fungi were beautiful and alien. Toadstool-like species grew out of the soil like little green light bulbs. Others, clinging to the trees, were arranged in shelves like coral, plastered to the bark, and shining with a slightly darker variant of light.

The colorful light put off by these biological wonders were almost enough to distract him from the fact that he was a prisoner.

The stranger walking ahead of him was the only person in sight. Justin was allowed to walk unrestrained, but with his demon arm numb he was basically helpless.

He followed his captor not out of submission but because all other options seemed to have been erased. Attempting to escape would not have been wise. This jungle had already proven itself quite capable of killing him. Facing another blue tiger or a titanbird—while crippled, unarmed, starving, and lost—was an encounter he would not likely survive.

The bioluminescent mushrooms faded with the morning. Justin's captor turned to check on him, and by the light of the morning sun filtering through the trees, Justin got his first clear look at him: a clean-shaven face with thick, severe eyebrows the same goldenrod yellow as his shoulder-length hair. He wore a cloak with leaves sewn into the fabric for camouflage, which made him blend into the jungle around him. A slender sword hung from his belt. Justin could still see no one else. Where the others had gone—the ones who had taken Ahlund—he could only guess.

"Where's my sword?" said Justin, not for the first time.

"We have it," said the golden-haired man, and he kept walking.

"You going to give it back?" Justin asked.

"I would not think so," he said.

"What about Ahlund?"

"He is alive, if that is what you mean. That is the most positive thing to be said about his condition."

Justin squeezed his good hand into a fist. He kept following but casually slowed his pace.

Okay, he thought. *The sun's finally coming up. Time to give this a shot.*

He raised his right arm, opened his hand, and cleared his mind of all the lingering questions and uncertainties, focusing only on the peace and knowledge of aurym. He squinted, trying to envision his cat's eye blade somewhere out in this jungle, in someone's hands. Just like at Hartla, when he'd taken it from Yordar at a distance, all he had to do was call, and it would come to him. It would be airborne before they even realized what happened. He took a deep breath. He flexed his fingers.

The man in front of him abruptly stopped walking.

Justin missed a step as he pulled his hand back down to his side, his concentration lost. The man turned and looked at him with a thoughtful face.

"Far be it from me to pose threats," said the man, "but Ru'Onorath patrols are never out of communication with one another, and if anything were to happen to one of us, it would not take long for the rest of us to react. Ahlund will be dead before you can capitalize on . . . whatever you are doing."

Justin tried to maintain a defiant expression, but the faltering of his resolve probably showed. The man grinned, turned, and kept walking.

"So you *are* Guardians," said Justin, hurrying to catch up. "I thought you were supposed to be good guys. Ahlund was just trying to lead me to—"

"I know what he was trying to do," said the man. "It is a very serious offense. You two are trespassers, although it must be conceded that you are exceptional trespassers."

"Ahlund a trespasser? He's one of you."

"No, he is not."

"But isn't he, like, a former member or something?"

"There is, like, no such thing, I'm afraid," the man said. "One who takes the Ru'Onorath vows takes them for life. He who abandons the vows abandons his life also."

"Abandons his. . . !"

"A Ru'Onora who betrays or deserts the order does so with the understanding that they must never again return to these lands, or use the aurym power of a Ru'Onorath weapon for personal gain. For both of these offenses, the penalty is death. And of both of these offenses, Ahlund's guilt is in abundance."

"You're not a Guardian," said Justin.

"I am Kallorn Rhodos," the man said. "And I am a Ru'Onora obeying my orders."

For a few moments, Justin focused on just putting one foot in front of the other. There was a weariness, almost a sense of lament in the man's speech that seemed to Justin too deep to be a deception.

"You're making a mistake!" Justin said. "Ahlund brought me here because he thinks—"

"I sense that you are upset with me," the man called Kallorn interjected, still walking, still not looking at Justin. "Before you say something you regret, you should know that your anger is misplaced. If anything, I have shown Ahlund mercy. The mandates are very clear, the nature of his return does not change the nature of his offenses. He not only forsook his vows but defiled the gifts of the spirit by using its power indiscriminately. And as a mercenary, no less."

Without warning, Kallorn whipped his slender sword from its sheath and hacked down a branch in his way. The sword had been returned to its sheath before the branch even hit the ground. As Justin passed by the place where the branch lay, he caught a momentary whiff of ozone.

"Ahlund knew the risk he faced by coming back here," Kallorn continued. "I took him prisoner instead of having him killed on sight—which I would have been within my rights to do—out of respect for the man he used to be, not the man he is. The elders will judge the degree of his guilt and determine the manner of his punishment, but even an outsider to our ways must understand that Ahlund Sims has made his choices. The laws prescribe his fate."

"So, you're telling me," said Justin, "that Ahlund brought me here, knowing this would happen to him?"

"A bold sacrifice," said Kallorn, the lament returning to his voice. "He always was bold."

CHAPTER 47

Several hours after sunrise, the monotony of the journey was broken by a sensation Justin had almost forgotten. Wind.

Warm air hit him full in the face. The scenery was changing. Trees were still everywhere, but their trunks weren't as wide, allowing for the passage of breeze. The undergrowth was less formidable here, and high above, he saw larger and larger patches of blue sky as the canopy thinned. Ahead, he could see so much sky that it seemed as though the forest abruptly ended altogether, and he wondered if they were about to descend a steep slope.

So intent was Justin on the apparent cutoff of the jungle that he missed a step. His ankle rolled on a knotted root. As he tried to adjust his footing, the pull of his left arm sent pain flaring through his shoulder. It felt as if it his shoulder had been doused with boiling water. He shouted involuntarily and hit the ground on his backside.

Kallorn knelt beside him, reaching for his shoulder to examine it, but Justin pulled away. Unfortunately, that only made the scalding pain worse. A jolt of nerves shot all the way up through his neck to his brain, dotting his vision with black spots.

"You are ill," Kallorn said.

"Just help me up," Justin said.

Kallorn hauled Justin to his feet. "Can you keep going?"

Justin sneered. "I'll manage."

As Kallorn started walking again, Justin tenderly pulled back the edge of his shirt and craned his neck to get a look at his shoulder. At the place where the flesh of his shoulder met the non-flesh of his arm, the skin was red, swollen, and stretched tight. He could feel it pulsing with every heartbeat. Heat radiated from it, and whitish fluid was collecting around the edges.

The effects are spreading, thought Justin. *This is how Avagad finishes me off.*

Emerging from a clutch of giant ferns, Justin realized the opening in the jungle was no hillside.

The trees ended abruptly at a vast, open space. Rocky cliffs cut straight down, creating a gap that in the jungle that must have been a mile wide. But it was not a canyon; the gap was circular. They were at the edge of a great, misshapen hole in the world—a giant crater at least two hundred feet deep. Thin, azure ribbons of waterfalls spilled down into it from multiple sides.

Kallorn gesture toward the edge. Justin, eying Kallorn, inched toward the edge and looked down. Deep within the crater were the stone-block ruins of an ancient city. The colors of the structures ranged from dark, cinnamon brown to rusty red. Much of the stone was draped in vines. He could see even from here that the multistoried buildings were carved with intricate designs, but the architecture seemed to rely less on geometry than it did to paying homage to the constructs of nature. A pair of white and gray marble towers rose up from the center of the city. To Justin, it looked as if two of the jungle's giant had been turned to stone. The waterfalls spilling in fed pools and streams that flowed through the city.

"Esthean?" said Justin.

Kallorn nodded. "Esthean. City of the Ru'Onorath."

Kallorn stepped forward. Carved into the rock, nearly hidden, was a stone stairway cut into the side of the cliff. It wrapped around the curve of the crater wall, gradually winding all the way to the bottom.

Kallorn started down the stairs. Justin looked over his shoulder back into the jungle, then followed Kallorn.

CHAPTER 48

Leah stood at the top of the walls with Endrus, Olorus, and Hook, hoping that her visibility might lend morale to the two thousand soldiers of Endenholm, the four thousand of the Athacean League, and the refugees of Ronice as they filed in through the open gates of Cervice.

The few civilians left in the city had turned out to welcome them, and the forty-eight soldiers of the City Watch directed the new arrivals to suitable quarters with the help of Marcus Worth. Endrus had spent over two hours briefing Leah on the state of the city. So far, there was no good news. Her disbelief continued to escalate.

"I do not understand why no one stood up to Asher!" Olorus growled at Endrus. "Hook and I deserted our unit out of loyalty to this country. Did *no one* else act? And how was he not indicted for his policies?"

"At first, the people had faith in him," said Endrus, directing his response to Leah. "As far as the public knew, the royal line was broken. Only a few people, myself included, knew that you were alive, but we thought Asher was going to send for you once things were safe." Endrus smoothed out his mustache. "One night, a rather vocal representative who opposed some of Asher's policies was found dead. Soon after, a few other dissenting legislators mysteriously retired from their positions and departed Cervice for the countryside. Asher handpicked their replacements."

That snake, thought Leah.

"And then, one day," continued Endrus, "Asher called a public forum and announced that you had not only survived the regicide unscathed, but had been the mastermind behind the plot all along. We few insiders knew it was a contradiction of the evidence, but anyone who rose in defense of the truth . . . disappeared. Olorus, you ask why no one took action, but some of us did. I was part of an underground group intent on removing Asher from power, but our rebellion was put on hold when a coblyn horde nearly overran Panum. Only after Panum, Asher told us he had received communications from Lundholm and Endenholm indicating that similar assaults had been happening for weeks.

"We were at a crossroads. With war brewing and the people fearful, rising against Asher in a bloody change of regime no longer seemed wise. Though now I wish I had led the rebellion myself. Soon after, he ordered the evacuation of the west."

Endrus shook his head, making a pained face. "The evacuation was an awful affair. And the result? Cervice and other abandoned cities are reduced to what you see here: fortresses manned by a precious few. Even now, Asher occasionally sends us orders by messenger. I think he hopes we will serve as advanced warning for Darvelle, should the danger come further eastward. We politely ignored the orders."

"He is the one who will receive the next message," said Leah. "Anavion blood has been reestablished in Cervice, and Nolia's true heir will defend this land to her dying breath."

"And your League?" said Endrus.

"This army has been entrusted to me," said Leah. "Nolia is and will always be my first priority."

Endrus's curled, white mustache tilted with a smile. "Those are the words I was waiting to hear, my lady," he said. With a formality that belonged in the land's noblest court, he bowed low to Leah. "So long as you have need of it, by life or by death, consider my sword your own."

When he stood again, Leah smiled. Her words were a much bolder statement than he could have possibly understood. The rest of the Athacean League had expected her to return, in a timely manner, with Nolian soldiers to aid in the war. Instead, she was staying here—at least for the time being—effectively reducing their numbers in the Raedittean. She hoped Ahlund, Gunnar, and the Von Morixes in Hartla would understand. They would have to be flexible. Surely, there were still many people out there loyal to Nolia, perhaps stranded, lost, or in need of rescuing like Ronice. By reestablishing herself in Cervice, she could create the safe haven they needed.

"Perhaps you would like to properly take your throne, my queen?" said Endrus.

"No," said Leah. "No, I would not. Olorus, I need messages sent to Hartla and Castydociana to brief the League on our situation here, and to inform them of our intentions. Ask them to send any aid they can spare."

"Yes, my lady," Olorus replied.

"Captain Endrus," she said. "There is work to be done. But before we discuss anything further . . . I would like to see my family, please."

CHAPTER 49

Endrus led the way, a torch in hand, and Leah and Hook followed through dark rooms of the palace. Everything was plastered with dust. When she had asked to see her family, she had expected to be led out beyond the city walls to the Downs. Instead, as Endrus led them deeper and deeper into the palace, Leah had trouble reconciling herself to the realization that her family were not resting in peaceful, open-country graves. They lay deep under her feet, down in the palace catacombs.

Endrus halted at the top of a dark set of stairs leading down, deep into the recesses beneath the castle. Leah took a torch from a sconce on the wall and lit it with the torch Endrus carried.

"I'll proceed alone from here," she said.

Endrus hesitated but said, "As you wish, my lady."

Leah looked at Hook. He frowned. He clearly didn't like the idea of letting her out of his sights, but he nodded. Endrus's body language said something else. He did not seem thrilled at the prospect of being left alone with Hook.

With the torch to guide her steps, Leah proceeded down. The stairs ended in a dank, narrow passageway. Her footsteps gave off wet-sounding echoes as she moved forward.

Burying Nolian royalty in the catacombs beneath the castle was a tradition from a wilder, more perilous age. In those days, interment in open-country barrows had put bodies and grave goods at risk of raiding and desecration, so the bodies of kings and their families were put down here. But that tradition had not been observed for almost one hundred years. Her grandfather and even his father had been buried in peaceful, beautiful, open-country grave-sites, surrounded by expertly tended gardens and shaded by flowering trees. The sudden return to an otherwise discontinued tradition was undoubtedly Asher's doing. Sticking the royal family down here was his final insult.

The catacombs had always been a haunted and terrible place, in her mind. Growing up in the castle, she thought of it as a pit full of ghosts and monsters and maggots eating dead flesh—a place her nightmares had taken her many times as a girl. The oldest of her ancestors were buried in the very deep places. Her father had taken her all the way to the end of the catacombs once so she could pay her respects to the first king of Nolia— a forefather who was so far removed from her that to visit him had been eerie rather than profound.

Even now, as Leah descended another short set of stairs, memories of her nightmares of this place played out in her mind.

At the bottom of the stairs, she came up short. Her torch brought into view a layer of powdery rubble on the ground: residue from freshly cut stone. She braced herself and raised her torch for a better look.

The outlines of several large, stone boxes came into view. The first of the sarcophagi bore the name of her youngest brother. He had clung to life the longest that horrible night. Tears filled Leah's eyes. He was only a year older than her. Due to a birth defect, he had been unable to walk without the aid of a cane, and his love of quieter, more intellectual pursuits had made him an ever-forgotten member of the family. But he had preferred it that way. He had been her closest friend for her whole life.

Numbly, she passed by three more stone caskets. Her other three older brothers, all soldiers and heroes of the nation, lay in order of age. She reached out for the next one and placed a hand on its cold, dry stone. She ran her fingertips over the freshly cut inscription: *Helena Anavion.*

"Mother," she breathed.

The word was too much. Sucking dank air in through her mouth, Leah tasted the tears dribbling over her lips. She stumbled forward. Beside her mother's casket, set upon a dais etched with symbols and words in many languages, sat the sarcophagus of the king. Stone eagles stood watch upon its corners. Her vision was too blurred to see the inscription. She wiped her eyes and held her torch forward for a better view.

> Here Lies King Darius Anavion
> Unequaled Among Men
> Unrivaled Among Kings
> Killed in the Night by a Betrayer

Leah's knees hit the floor. She pressed her forehead against her father's casket and tried to imagine it was his hand on her head. Choked noises escaped her clenched throat despite her efforts to keep them there. The noises echoed through the corridor, deeper into the catacombs, along rows of boxes containing the great men and women of ages past—in the presence of many, heard by none.

CHAPTER 50

As he was led through the city of Esthean, Justin tried to take everything in, but all he could focus on was the agony in his shoulder. Men and women in cloaks stood still as statues and watched silently as he and Kallorn passed. Others wore robes that reminded Justin of Zechariah. None of them approached. All watched from a distance as Kallorn led him under stone arches and beneath ancient edifices. No one said a word.

Crossing a small bridge, they were met by several silent, hooded men standing guard before the doorway of a round, stone temple. He heard a rustling overhead and looked up to see several dark-haired primates sitting in leafy nests on the rooftops of the ruins. Their human-like eyes watched him calmly.

"The council is waiting for you," said Kallorn. He waved his hand, indicating that Justin should take the lead.

Justin looked at the four guards by the door. Hard eyes stared out at him from beneath their hoods. All four held long spears. Justin cleared his throat and gingerly adjusted his sling before walking between the guards.

The doorway opened into a large, oval-shaped room. The domed ceiling was built of overlapping stone archways that, at some point in the past, must have supported a roof, but now, the arches and the spider-webbing vines hanging from them were all that separated the room from the blue sky above.

On the walls were carvings of multi-headed, anthropomorphic deities. Upright, columnar stelae represented men and women in military regalia and headdresses. The individuals represented looked ancient, even by Oikoumene standards. They held royal staffs, weapons, or the severed heads of enemies, and their faces were decorated with designs—war paint or tattoos. Some had fangs for teeth, and all had wide, staring eyes, without pupils.

Ahead of Justin in the room, ten people sat in ten unremarkable wooden chairs. Their skin colors ranged from dark brown to the whitest white. Some of the faces were long and narrow. Others, wide-set and flat. Some had dark, sad eyes, and others' were pale and rimmed red with age. Nine of the ten were men, most of them with beards or curly, pointed mustaches. Some had long, braided hair. Others, no hair at all. Some wore ceremonial armor. Others, robes, togas, or dirt-stained traveling gear, as if they'd just gotten in from the road. The lone female among them looked younger than the rest by at least three or four decades. She was brown-skinned and dark-eyed, clothed in flowing, gray robes. Her black hair had a streak of white running back along the forehead, over her left ear, like half a halo.

Justin stood before them. He heard Kallorn approach and stand behind him. The ten people in their ten chairs watched him. They said nothing.

"Where is Ahlund?" said Justin. He might have expected his voice to echo in a large room like this, but the open ceiling prevented it. "What have you done with him?"

An old man in the central chair stirred. His frail body, sunken into his seat, leaned forward. Wiry, nearly imperceptible white hairs clung to his chin like the tuft of a wilted dandelion.

"Much can be ascertained about you, young man, based solely upon the choice of your first words spoken to us," said the old man. His voice was a weak crackle, like a small frog. "But it is what you did *not* ask first that says the most about you. You did not ask why you were taken prisoner. Why we have brought you here. Or what we want with you. Nor did you ask who we are. You could have requested medical attention for that arm of yours, or food for your empty stomach. You could have asked for your sword. Or, perhaps the wisest option of all, you could have remained silent. Instead, you ask—no, you demand—to know the whereabouts of your mentor. The fact that you asked about your mentor instead of who we are, tells me that you live in the present. That you have not requested food or medical aid, indicates either a degree of noble selflessness, or a devil-may-care disregard for your own well-being. You are not quick enough to wrath that you would threaten us outright, but neither are you wise enough to opt for silence in a situation where you are clearly at a disadvantage."

Justin blinked in surprise.

"As for your mental state. . . ." The ancient man closed his eyes. "You regret much of what has happened. You blame yourself for things, even things beyond your control. *That*, it would seem, is the reason you are not concerned with your physical state. Your afflicted arm is failing you and turning diseased. For all you know, it could kill you or turn you fully into a demon, yet you have not made it a priority. I do not think this is done out of selflessness or disregard. I think, deep down, part of you believes that you deserve it, perhaps as punishment for everything you consider to be your fault."

Justin swallowed hard. He had to moisten his lips before he was able to speak.

"If you can tell all that," Justin said. His voice sounded bigger and stronger than usual after the speech of the old man. "Then maybe you can tell that Ahlund didn't come here because he was trying to break any of your rules. He wanted to ask for your help. Whoever you are, whatever you want with me, if you kill my friend, you are my enemy."

"Headstrong, too, I see," the old man croaked. "Rebellious and overconfident. . . . So overconfident that you have not even considered an alternative to your first assumptions. You have not left any room for the possibility that not all systems are corrupt— that not every structure is in need of toppling—that in some establishments, it is the rebel who is in the wrong." He smiled, revealing many missing teeth in his lower jaw. "Ah, youth!"

Some of the people in the chairs seemed to laugh at this, their shoulders bouncing up and down quietly. Justin felt a surge of annoyance, but before he could say anything, the old man continued.

"We are the elders of the Ru'Onorath," he said, "the spirit warrior Guardians of the Oikoumene, gathered from across this world. Seekers of the will of aurym. I am this council's orator. I would ask who you are, but your reputation quite precedes you, Justin Holmes, fallen angel. You have faced great evil time and again, and, according to Kallorn's reports, you showed extraordinary resilience to daemyn's influence at the Treasury. Even as I now speak, I can feel bolstered spiritual defenses within you, built up over exposure to. . . ."

The old man trailed off as the dark-skinned woman beside him placed a hand on his shoulder and leaned over, whispering something into his big, hairy ear. Justin took the opportunity to turn around and look at Kallorn. The yellow-haired man stood at attention with his arms behind his back.

I've been with him this whole time, thought Justin. *When, exactly, did he have time to report anything to them?*

"Much of your story is known to us," the old man continued when the woman was done speaking to him. "Much more than you might imagine. But even without this prior knowledge, we could have recognized your wounded arm for what it is. You have been touched by a High Demon. Your arm is no longer functioning, yes?"

"Kallorn could have told you that, too," said Justin.

"He could have," agreed the old man. "But he did not. The current state of your arm is but a symptom of a greater problem, one that we can treat. But first, tell me this. What would you say if I told you that Ahlund has already been executed for his crimes?"

Justin felt the pores on his forehead opening up.

"Then you'd better execute me, too," Justin announced. "And you'd better do it before I find my sword."

"Oh, dear," said the old orator in mock concern. "And what if I told you we have ways of *making* you behave?"

Justin shrugged. "Bigger men than you have tried. But have at it, if you want."

The old man leaned forward, squinting at Justin. His lips were drawn into a tight line. "We were under the impression that you came here to train as a Ru'Onora, to learn the ways of the spirit warrior and protect this world. Would you abandon your mission and betray the world out of loyalty to a single friend?"

"Loyalty to your friends is the only thing that makes the world worth living in," said Justin.

The brown-skinned woman beside the old orator stood from her chair. Her gray robes brushed the ground as she walked toward Justin, and he suddenly felt nervous despite his resolve.

The woman didn't stop until she stood directly in front of Justin, only about a foot away from him. Her shoulders were slightly hunched, subtracting from her height, making her at least twelve inches shorter than Justin. Below the half-halo streak of white in her hair, her dark eyes looked up into his.

"Did you really kill Ahlund?" asked Justin.

To his surprise, the woman raised her hand and touched his cheek, sliding a finger along the contour of his jaw. He involuntarily withdrew from her touch.

"After all these years," she said. Her voice was low and rather sweet. "It really is you. You really are Benjamin's son."

CHAPTER 51

The breath left Justin's lungs.

"What did you. . . ?" he said.

But he couldn't finish the sentence. He felt the quiver of his own brow as he stared down into the bottomless pools of the woman's eyes. The lines of her face were difficult to read.

She turned her gaze downward to the dead demon arm. Her hand left his face, and she touched the arm. Her fingernails made tiny, grinding sounds as she scratched the bone-armored surface through the fabric of the sling.

"It happened the same way with your father," flowed the cadence of her voice. "His legs functioned normally, for a time. But, gradually, he lost all use."

"No," said Justin. It was all he could think to say.

"We can help you, Justin," she said. "But you must let us."

"No," Justin said, more fiercely now, taking a frightened step away from her. "No, I see what's happening, here!"

The woman looked compassionate—almost pitying. Justin attempted to take a second step away from her, but Kallorn slid a hand over his shoulder and held him in place.

It's Avagad, again! thought Justin. *He's finally contacting me, fabricating another fantasy to try to trick me.*

When had he gone under? How much had been an illusion? Had it happened at the daemyn-rich Treasury ruins, or before that?

Was this island even real? Had the ocean voyage on the *Gryphon II* been real? And what about Hartla? Had anything he'd experienced since returning to the Oikoumene really happened? Had he ever gone back to Earth at all?

"I'm not even standing here right now, am I?" Justin said, nearly shouting. He looked up through the stone arches above him. "Nice try, but you took it one step too far!"

He felt Kallorn tighten his grip. The woman in front of him was trying to put her face in front of his, to get his attention. "Justin," she was saying. "Look at me, Justin."

"No!" Justin shouted.

He threw his good elbow to hit Kallorn in the face, but before he knew it, he was flat on his back. Pain exploded in his shoulder, making spots dance before his eyes again. Several sets of hands grabbed him and lifted him off the ground. He struggled against them, yelling, thrashing like an animal, but it was no use. They were carrying him. The faces of monstrous stone deities watched from their mounts on the walls. Archways passed above him like rolling clouds.

CHAPTER 52

Since the fall of Hartla, the coastal city of Castydociana, capital of Castydocia, had become the unofficial command center for the Athacean League. The small republic of Castydocia was larger than most Mythaean city-states. Its people were dairy farmers, and their cheese was traded for as far off as Lundholm away in the west.

Gunnar looked out across the city. Its primary fortress was situated upon a rocky promontory jutting into the ocean. Castydocia's characteristic architecture—white-washed brick structures topped with overhanging, sawn-log roofs—was claimed to have been handed down all the way from the Ancient Elleneans. It gave the urban center and its surrounding neighborhoods, rising and falling upon the coastal foothills, a distinctive look.

Gunnar waited onboard the flagship of Count Wulder Von Morix. The *Gryphon II* was moored nearby and easy to spot, being the only set of black sails in a harbor blanketed with white ones. A thousand ships from every member-nation of the League were assembled here, and it was only a portion of their growing numbers. Much of their manpower was currently engaged in a ground war with a demon army near Skyre. Another part of the fleet was fighting some of Yordar's forces off the coast of Ginaska. Two days had passed since Gunnar had found his brother's body at Hartla. He hoped that once news of Yordar's death spread, his confederacy would fall apart, and at least some of the fighting would stop.

You did it, thought Gunnar. *You got what you wanted. Right?*

He sighed, trying not to think about it.

Upon arriving at Castydociana, Gunnar had personally overseen the safe delivery of the Hartlan refugees, keeping an especially keen eye on Feliks Evins and his grand-daughter Maera. They'd been put up with a nice family with several other children for Maera to play with. Gunnar's greatest wish was that they would find peace here, and that nothing like the disaster at Hartla would happen to anyone ever again. But that wish felt more like a fantasy, these days.

He had given the rest of his crew a recess in the city. Lycon, Adonica, Pool, and Borris were probably off having a drink or two right now, celebrating a reunion with some of their brothers-in-arms. He wished he could join them, but there was still too much work to be done.

Gunnar heard footsteps behind him and took a deep breath. He was not looking forward to this conversation. Upon turning around, however, Gunnar realized that the person approaching him was not who he was waiting for. Instead of Wulder Von Morix, Gunnar was looking at a small man, less than halfway between five and six feet. He was dressed in a plain, hessian tunic, giving him the look of a market vendor or a servant. His face was pale and marked with lines of middle age. His hairline had receded on both sides, leaving a sharp widow's peak of pitch-black hair that came down to an arrow-shaped point above the center of his forehead.

"I'm—I'm sorry," the little man said, raising his hands as if to indicate he was unarmed. Gunnar knew that wasn't entirely true. The bulk of a knife could be seen beneath the tunic, above his belt. "I didn't mean to sneak up on you, admiral."

"You one of Wulder's men?" asked Gunnar.

"Sort of," the little man replied. "Not really."

"A volunteer fighter, then?"

"Not really that, either," he said. "Nothing so important. More of a support unit, I guess. I'm a cook."

"Well then, your modesty is misplaced," Gunnar said. "Essential personnel, if there ever was, my friend." He pointed at the bulk beneath the man's tunic. "I guess that means you're armed with, what, a ladle?"

The little man reached into his tunic and pulled out a knife. Not the cooking kind, either. He started to offer an explanation, but Gunnar cut him off.

"What's your name?" asked Gunnar.

"Ragny, admiral."

"Well then, Ragny, I apologize, but I'll have to ask you to leave. I'm waiting to have a private word with the count."

"Well, uh, admiral," Ragny said, putting his knife away and taking a few steps forward. "That's why I'm here, actually. I'm a cook by trade, sir, but I had volunteered hoping to fight. I worked in a little kitchen in Skyre before the war, but when I heard about Justin Holmes. . . ."

He trailed off, seemingly trying to gauge Gunnar's reaction.

Ragny cleared his throat nervously. "You see, sir, I'm part of what some people call the Holy Army. I joined together with some others in upper Athacea and made our way here to volunteer for the war, hoping we could be of some help. There are only about twelve hundred of us here, but I know there are more followers all over the place. Count Wulder says he will put us into the action, but, well, I guess I had it in my mind that the joining the war against the demons would mean fighting for the fallen angel, not cooking below deck, or trying to run that dirty Yordar out of the Raedittean."

Ragny tensed as if remembering to whom he was speaking. "I mean, I'm—no offense meant, sir. I—"

"None taken, friend," Gunnar said.

"Well, anyway, when I saw you, sir—a personal friend to Justin Holmes, as I understand it—I was hoping maybe you'd have some idea of where we of the Holy Army might do best to serve the fallen angel, is all."

"Rather bold of you to step up and take the initiative," said Gunnar. "A cook appealing to an admiral. Almost brazen, even."

"Brazen, sir?"

"It means ballsy, Mr. Ragny."

"Oh." He laughed. "Not enough to ask the count directly, though. He can be cruel at times, sir."

"Do you believe all twelve hundred of you feel the same way?"

"Yes, sir."

Gunnar nodded. "I'll mention it to the count, then. He's due here any minute."

"Thank you, sir," said Ragny.

"No . . . problem?" said Gunnar. By the time he'd said it, Ragny had already scurried off the ship. Reaching a hand up under his hat, Gunnar scratched his head, mumbling, "Wulder must really be doing a number on these poor volunteers."

It was to be expected, though. After losing Hartla, Wulder had become a count without a city, so he had thrown one hundred percent of his efforts into the League. He'd become its central figure, coordinating troop movements, organizing defensive strategies, and planning attacks. He still went by the title of "count," even though, at this point, he was closer to "commander in chief." It put Wulder under excessive stress, and he had never been an even-tempered man to begin with. Thankfully, Wulder showed no ambitions beyond that of his role as coordinator. All nations within the League were free and independent, and his only wish was to organize and coordinate their efforts toward winning the war. The League was an alliance; it was not a military dictatorship.

Gunnar returned his gaze inland, where the coastal plains met wooded hills covered with evergreens. If he wasn't mistaken, he was directly north of his former home, Lonn. It was the closest he had been to his old tavern, Gunnar's Brig, since leaving it behind to ferry a few misfits downriver—a venture that would become the start of an unexpected new chapter of his life.

Thoughts of the Brig brought up memories of Samuel and Vick. Both had been killed in *his* service, far from home.

"Maybe I should arrange a convoy, while I have the chance," Gunnar whispered, thinking aloud. "Send Borris and Pool back to Lonn before something happens to them, too. They don't deserve what I've put them through. They—"

"Ha-*ha*!"

Gunnar turned. The fat frame of Wulder Von Morix strode across the deck with arms wide and a smile lifting his chubby cheeks. His gray-streaked beard was braided and almost reached his belly. He wore orange and white-trimmed furs that brushed the deck as he walked, and atop his head was a helmet adorned with the curled, ivory tusks of a sea beast.

Here goes nothing, thought Gunnar.

CHAPTER 53

"Gunnar, my friend!" Wulder roared. "Finally, you return to us alive and well! Though I catch you talking to yourself! Perhaps too much time spent at sea has. . . !"

As Gunnar turned full around to face the count, Wulder's jubilation wilted. His eyes found the horned helm in Gunnar's hands, so similar to the one on his own head. It was Drexel's.

Wulder stopped. His outstretched arms fell slowly to his sides.

"Dead?" he asked.

Gunnar stepped forward. Silently, he offered Drexel's helm to Wulder. Wulder's head drooped. His eyes were downcast as he accepted it.

"I had held out hope that, somehow, he. . . ." said Wulder. "How?"

"Not demons," said Gunnar. "It was in the same manner as the other counts and admirals who have been executed by Yordar's hand."

Wulder shut his eyes. Yordar had adopted the policy of personally beheading all the figures of authority he deposed. Wulder squeezed his late brother's helm.

"If it brings you any solace, Yordar is dead, as well," Gunnar said. "Whether by demons or something else, I do not know. What matters is that he is a corpse. I saw the body myself. Wulder, I pray that the sins of my family against yours are not so great that—"

"Do not even think it," Wulder said, quickly looking up at him, his face stern. "I do not know whether house Nimbus was more accurately exemplified by you or your brother, and it does not much matter to me. You shall not be held accountable for the actions of your brother. In my eyes, ever will you be Admiral Gunnar, friend of Hartla and defender of all noble-blooded Mythaeans."

Gunnar smiled. "Thank you, my friend."

Wulder nodded. He walked heavily to the deck's railing beside Gunnar and looked out over the sea. "I have already heard rumors that the young ethoul has returned," he said.

"Good news travels quickly," said Gunnar.

"It's true, then? Justin is here with you?"

"Well, no," said Gunnar. "We did get him out of Hartla, but he's with Ahlund, now. They're seeking the council of the Ru'Onorath. I believe Ahlund's hope is to hone Justin's skills for battle against the enemy."

"He is far from here, then." Wulder let out a noise that was half sigh and half grumble. "I'd prefer to have him here, with *un*-honed skills. We need the help. Against men and coblyns, our forces stand some chance. Against cythraul, that is another matter entirely."

"Cythraul can be beaten," Gunnar said. "It's not easy, but it's possible. I've even been developing a little something for the next time I see one of their ugly faces."

"A secret weapon?" said Wulder.

"More like a secret ingredient."

Wulder shook his head, clearly not in the mood for guessing games. "Gunnar, you do not understand the position we are in here. The news you have brought me concerning my younger brother is only the latest in a series of bad tidings. Demon fleets and armies press down on our allies across the entire Raedittean—even from the south, now! And as for Yordar's forces, the man himself may be dead, but some underling general will rise to take his place. They always do. His regime will continue shedding blood, even as it topples in on itself. But I digress. The latest bad news arrived not six hours ago. Just in time to meet you, it seems. A message from Nolia."

"Nolia?" said Gunnar, furrowing his brow. "Is Leah all right?"

"The princess is in good health, it would seem," said Wulder. "She has regained her throne. But she reports that during her absence, population movements were initiated to flee from a demon army amassing in the west."

"In the *west* now, too?" breathed Gunnar. "Tides be merciful. . . ."

"We expected her to send us reinforcements," continued Wulder. "Instead, she is asking that we send troops to *her*! She is trying to make her capital city into a sanctuary for refugees in the region. And judging by the tone of the letter, she is yet oblivious to our disasters on the frontlines, including the sack of Hartla. Bringing Nolia into the League was supposed to *increase* our numbers." He shook his head. "Our reply will be a sad one, indeed, having to inform her of Hartla's fall, in addition to denying her request."

"Denying her request?" said Gunnar.

Wulder looked confused. "Of course."

"You can't be serious," said Gunnar. "You can't spare anything?"

"None. It would weaken us too much. The best she can do is pull back from Nolia and rejoin us here."

"I really don't think she'll do that. Not if there are refugees like she says, or other people in Nolia who need her help."

"She must. Gunnar, I know the princess is a friend of yours. You and your companions are, of course, the ones we have to thank for starting all this. The League owes you a great deal." Wulder paused, his nostrils flared, and his tone abruptly changed. "But while you have been gallivanting about, following your own aspirations, I have been here, fighting battles on multiple fronts. All day, every day, coordinating troops on land and sea, struggling just to hold our own!"

"But you're also gaining more and more support, aren't you?" said Gunnar. "I just spoke with one of the twelve hundred Holy Army volunteers—"

"I am grateful for them, of course!" Wulder snapped. "But it is a delicate balancing act! We're spinning plates just to defend ourselves. I don't know how the enemy can coordinate such numbers so flawlessly, I really don't. But they do. They always manage to hit us just at the right time, just at the place where it will hurt us the most. The smallest mistake, and they pounce. We simply can't spread ourselves as thin as Princess Anavion is asking."

Gunnar could feel *his* nostrils flaring, now. "So what will you do?"

"I will apologize to the princess for my inability to act," said Wulder. "And I will inform her that she must either hold the line with what she's got or fall back to Castydocia."

"She'll never agree to that. Would you? If you were in her shoes, wouldn't you do everything in your power to protect the Hartlan people?"

Wulder looked down at his brother's empty helm. "What do you think I am doing right now?"

For a moment, neither spoke. There was only the sound of lapping waves against the hull, and the cawing of seabirds above.

"I hate to make her choose between the League and her own country," said Wulder, "but it is the only way. I'm sorry."

Gunnar sighed. *This is how it ends. Wulder sees his rejection as what's best for the League, but Leah won't see it that way. She'll see it as Mythaeans taking care of Mythaean interests first. She'll see the obvious contradiction—that we have never hesitated to use our forces against Yordar, yet we choose not to help her people. That makes it look like certain members of the League take priority over others. And once that sort of precedent is set, there will be no going back. If there's even a whiff of corruption, true or not, everything we've worked so hard to build could fall apart. Countries won't be so keen to join us. The volunteers will dry up. . . .*

Gunnar clapped his hands. "The volunteers!" he said.

"Volunteers? You mean that Holy Army lot?" said Wulder. "What about them?"

"They're untrained and untested in battle, right?" said Gunnar. "That's why you haven't sent them out. They'd do more harm than good. Well, maybe this is their chance to prove themselves."

"Are you saying," said Wulder, "that you want to send *them* to Nolia? That is a greater insult than sending no one at all! They're a bunch of runaways and farmers!"

"And cooks," said Gunnar. "And no, I don't want to send them to Nolia. I want to *take* them there."

CHAPTER 54

He was flung into darkness, and he landed hard on his back. He scrambled against the floor, trying to turn around, but the door slammed behind him.

"No!" Justin screamed.

He stood and hurled himself unthinkingly toward the door. His body hit it at full force. He didn't know what it was made of, but all his weight at a sprint didn't so much as jiggle the hinges.

He bounced off and reeled backward. He screamed. It felt like a lightning bolt had hit his infected shoulder, searing, cutting, and electrifying all at once. Back down on the floor again, his right hand curled into a furious fist. The fingernails bit into his palm. The pain in his shoulder made rational thought almost impossible, but one thing was clear: He was in a prison cell. A dungeon.

He punched his knuckles against the stone floor.

"Damn it," he said. "Damn everything!"

"Justin," someone said.

He turned toward the sound. As his eyes adjusted, he could see a bit of light streaming through a hole in the wall. In its glow, he saw that his cell offered nothing to sit on or to sleep on. Only a small, empty room with a wooden bucket in the corner. He was alone.

"Justin," the voice said again, coming from the hole in the wall.

"Ahlund?" said Justin, moving toward it. "Thank God you're alive! What's going on? How are you making that light? A gauge-stone? Give it to me, and I can—"

"It's a candle," came Ahlund's voice through the hole.

Justin hissed in frustration and smacked his hand flat against the stone wall. "My dad, Ahlund. That woman up there said she knew my dad! But it's a lie. This is all a trick!"

"Calm down."

"You don't get it. This place *isn't real*!"

"You are delirious. You're—"

"Listen to me! I've been through this before!"

"Then which is it?" Ahlund spoke up. "Use your head. Have the Ru'Onorath locked us up, or is none of it real? Are you talking to me, locked in a cell, or am I an illusion? It can't be both."

"I. . . . I don't know. She said she knew my dad. She knew his name!"

The door to Justin's cell suddenly opened with a loud creak, and a white glow shined from the doorway so brightly that it hurt his eyes.

Two people stepped inside. One was a hunched, old man. The other was Kallorn, holding a shining gauge stone. He had his sword drawn with the tip pointed at Justin.

"Your arm is badly infected," Kallorn announced. "Ezon is our most skilled healer. If you can *restrain* yourself for a moment, he will take a look."

Justin was too weary for words. He nodded and sat down on the floor.

As the little man shuffled over, Justin realized he recognized him.

"Healer?" said Justin. "I thought you were the leader of the council."

"Oh my, I'm no leader!" the old man croaked—the same man who had spoken to him in the room above, with the others. "As I told you, young man, I am the council's orator. Perhaps you don't know what that means. It means I am the mouth of the council. I am only a representative of our collective authority. If there's a leader amongst us, that would be Cyaxares, the woman you spoke to."

Ezon raised his hand, and Justin felt a tugging sensation beneath the skin of his shoulder. He bit his lip to stifle a cry. In the light of Kallorn's gauge, a glimmer of fluid ran down the fabric covering his demon arm.

Kallorn kept his sword trained on Justin as Ezon worked.

"I had thought that I understood your motives, Ahlund," Kallorn said, directing his words not toward Justin but toward the hole in the wall. "Bringing him here, under penalty of death, seemed noble. But I did not know that this ethoul suffered from such volatile madness. It brings the logic of your sacrifice into question."

"He is not mad," said Ahlund through the wall.

"I'm sure," Kallorn said, unconvinced. "I am not well-versed in fallen angel legends myself, but Cyaxares says that an ethoul, even a well-meaning one, is like an open flame near a barrel of oil. Sooner or later, everyone nearby will pay the consequences."

Justin was grinding his teeth. The pain in his shoulder was dissipating, but aurym-healing was always a difficult business. From time to time, it felt as if he were beneath the very saw of the surgeon. Ezon grabbed the edge of the fabric wrapping his demon arm and unwrapped it, exposing the blackened, bone-armored appendage beneath. Kallorn shifted his gauge to get a better look.

"Justin was injured by a High Demon," said Ahlund. "But what you may not know is that he has also killed several of them. He has looked into the eyes of the enemy. He has defeated evil the likes of which you have never even seen, Kallorn."

Kallorn made a thoughtful noise in his throat. "Impressive, no doubt. But, prior experiences notwithstanding, his behavior before the council of elders was a disgrace. Utterly unbecoming for one in whom so many have placed so much faith. Thus far, the simple idea of a fallen angel has been enough to garner devotees from across the Oikoumene. But if any of those followers were to see a childish outburst like the one he displayed up there. . . . I think he would better serve this cause if he *remained* an idea, and stayed locked up down here, where he can't cause any harm."

"Then let us be glad that your idle musings have no bearing on the decisions of the council," replied Ahlund.

Kallorn frowned.

CHAPTER 55

When Ezon concluded his work, Justin's shoulder throbbed from the trauma, but most of the pain had melted away. He tried to move the arm. Still nothing. Still numb from the shoulder down.

"The infection is cleansed," said Ezon. "So far as I can tell, your blood is not poisoned. You should recover."

"Why can't I move it?" asked Justin.

Ezon considered. "If you do not know, then it is not my place to tell you." And with that, he shuffled over to join Kallorn at the door.

Justin tried to follow, but Kallorn's sword suddenly lit up. The slender steel became wreathed in dancing, blue and white electrical energy like a science fair exhibit. Justin stepped back, smelling ozone and feeling the hair on his arms stand up. Kallorn kept his electrified blade pointed at Justin as he and Ezon backed out of the door.

"Tell the council that Justin requests another audience," Ahlund said through the wall. "Tell them he wants to share his story."

"I will do as you ask," said Kallorn. "I shall consider it your final request. I pity you, Ahlund Sims. I pray your soul finds mercy."

The door closed with a bang, and the only sound was Justin's breathing. Ahlund must have blown out his candle because even that light was gone.

"He really hates you," said Justin.

"He has his reasons," replied Ahlund. "They all do."

"Why did you come back here?" said Justin. "You must have known they were going to kill you for whatever you did. If I really needed to be here, couldn't you have just brought me close and sent me off in the right direction or something?"

"So, you've made up your mind, then? This is a real place, after all?"

Justin sighed. "I don't know. I just. . . . How can they sit up there and judge us like this? They don't know what we've been through."

"True. But you also don't know what they have been through. These are bad times. For everyone. When they call on you again, tell them your story. All of it. And remember what I told you. Rise above self-preservation."

"Ahlund, when did you turn into such a pacifist? You *let* them capture you out there! You didn't even try to resist, and look where it got you. They're going to kill you over a stupid technicality!"

"Justin," said Ahlund. "After everything we've been through, after all you've seen me do, do you really think I have been defeated by a locked door?"

There was a long pause. Justin wasn't sure what to say.

"If I wanted out, I would be out," Ahlund said. "A prison break is not so difficult a thing. It is far more challenging to obey the command to wait, imprisoned, and have faith in the will of aurym."

"*Faith?*" said Justin. "Come on."

Ahlund paused a moment. "Mock me like that again, and you will find out how far from a pacifist I am."

Justin swallowed hard. "I'm, uh, sorry."

"You are making a dangerous assumption, Justin," said Ahlund. "You assume faith is a crutch. Logically, then, the more capable a man is, the less he needs to rely on faith.

Look at me. Rarely must I rely on anything other than myself. That is why I left the Ru'Onorath. I respected the power the Guardians wielded, but I thought their faith in aurym, as a belief system, made them weak. To me, it was like they were praying to the sun; aurym was a powerful entity, no doubt, but that didn't give it a *will*—didn't make it a conscious being to be worshipped. I saw it as misplaced reliance on an imaginary force, to explain the unexplainable, to make up for their stupidity and weakness. If they were strong enough or smart enough, they would realize their beliefs were just wishful thinking. . . . But now, I realize they were the stronger ones. They were able to do what I was not: to have faith even when human pride told me I didn't need it."

"But I don't—"

"Listen to me. All the things you rely upon—your weapons, your friends, your abilities, even the use of your own body—you can lose them all. Anyone who lives long enough does. Trusting in something other than your own methods and abilities, even when you *could* prevail on your own—*that* is what it means to rise above self-preservation. It took me my entire life to realize that. But you do not have the luxury of a lifetime spent learning this lesson.

"Today, you are faced with an inconvenient circumstance: I might be killed. You don't want me to die. You would rather be killed along with me. You might think that's a selfless gesture, but it isn't—not entirely. You're frightened they'll kill me because then, who will you have left? The answer is aurym. Even when everything is taken from you, you will never be alone. I do not expect you to understand or accept this. So long as a spirit of prideful independence persists in you, my words will sound like foolishness. Put away pride. Have faith. And get some rest while you can."

"Ahlund," said Justin, "I understand what you're saying. I just don't know if now is the right time for all this."

Ahlund said nothing.

"That woman up there was talking about my father, Ahlund! *My* father! That's impossible, isn't it? Ahlund?"

But Ahlund wouldn't say another word.

CHAPTER 56

The throne room of the Nolian royal palace was a far cry from the grand hall at Hartla. Nolia was more modest. Its throne room was a smaller, auditorium-style venue. Two hundred people would have been hard-pressed to fit inside. The walls were white. The floors were polished granite. A blood-red carpet ran from the doorway to the throne: a chair upon a raised platform. The platform was a black hunk of basalt from the Orlia Flats.

Seated on the throne, Leah looked around and lamented the condition of this place. Having not been entered for over a month, the room was dusty, and the air was stale.

Upon her request, the torches in the sconces along the walls had been lit, but the light only drew attention to the cobwebs forming in the corners.

The throne was made of wood, cut stone, and fine fabric. But even through the cushions, it felt hard and unyielding beneath Leah's bottom. She felt too small for this giant seat intended for large, overfed kings—not young women of her size. She sat perched forward with her hands on the armrests, trying to look dignified despite her discomfort. Endrus, Olorus, Hook, and Worth stood on the floor beneath her, at the base of the throne's platform.

"It's a larger force than usual," said Endrus. "An ambassador and a cavalcade of fifty armed guards."

"You did say you'd been ignoring him recently," Marcus Worth offered. "Maybe your former prime minister means to scare you into complying."

Olorus chuckled. "Imagine their surprise to discover an army awaiting them this time!"

"How do these meetings usually transpire?" asked Leah.

"An ambassador brings us sealed orders from Asher," answered Endrus. "Usually it is just a reiteration of the importance of providing advanced warning of any danger that could spread east."

"Nolia will be his warning system no longer," said Leah. "Bring the messenger to me. Put the rest of them under heavy guard."

A smirk made the side of Endrus's white mustache tilt upward. "Yes, my lady," he said with a bow, and he marched to the door.

"You are much like your father," said Olorus.

Leah turned to look down at her lieutenant from her throne. He remained at attention, staring forward.

"Thank you," Leah said, and then added, "How so?"

He peeked over his shoulder at her. "Your grandfather was one of the wisest men I've ever known. Wise, stern, unyielding . . . and merciless. In a situation like this, your grandfather would have sent this messenger's head back to Asher a box. You are more like your father. He was no less wise, but of one-hundredfold compassion. I will never forget what he once told me concerning a thief we caught trying to flee through the Borderwoods. 'A man's greatest strength lies not in his ability to lift the sword, but—'"

"'But in his mercy to withhold its sting,'" Leah finished.

Olorus smiled. "He would be very proud, Leah."

A slight blush came to his cheeks, and he quickly turned back around again. Leah could not even remember a time when Lieutenant Olorus Antony had called her by her first name.

At the sound of approaching steps, Leah straightened in her seat, making—sure her feet were touching the ground. Endrus came in through the doorway with a group of guards. Forced to march in front of them was the ambassador, who looked indignant at his treatment. He was clad in purple with a decorative cap atop his head, and a tiny, arrow-shaped beard adorned his chin. Leah glared at the man. Everything about him was Darvellian. Her father and grandfather would be rolling in their tombs if they knew Nolia had suffered so much from Darvellian sabotage.

No more, she thought.

A rough knock from behind almost put the Darvellian ambassador on his knees. He managed not to fall and hurried up the carpeted aisle toward the throne, dusted himself off, and was still walking as he blurted out, irreverently, "What a surprise! The prime minister will be thrilled to know that the former princess of Nolia has finally been located. Less thrilled, perhaps, to learn that Cervice is being held captive by the swords of foreign invaders."

The irony of the statement—that this man, a foreigner himself, would condemn "foreign invaders" in her city—was something Leah was not willing to dignify with a response. She waited for him to reach the base of the throne. Guards stepped up to flank him, each with a hand on his shoulder.

"Do you know what they call you?" said the ambassador with a grin. "The Oleander of The West. Delicate. Beautiful. Toxic and *deadly*. I am—"

"State your business," Leah said. "Quickly."

The ambassador blinked in mock surprise. "So high and mighty upon your stolen throne. No matter. Asher will see that you pay for your crimes in full. I have come bearing orders for this outpost from the prime minister—"

"*Outpost?*" Leah cut in. Despite her attempt to keep a straight face, she felt her lip curl with a sneer. "This is the capital city of Nolia, and you are trespassing in the heart of enemy territory, Darvellian. Whatever message you carry, you can keep it. Tell Asher this city is not his outpost. Nolia will be a victim of foreign sabotage no longer. Leah Anavion reigns in Cervice. And unlike the prime minister who had my mother and father killed in their sleep, *I* will not flee into the wind like a coward. If he, or anyone else, would like to challenge me in that regard, let them come and see for themselves how deadly the Oleander of the West can be."

The ambassador forced a congenial smile. "Very well. I will deliver your words. But know this. Darvelle will not allow you—"

Leah waved her hand. The guards began hauling him away.

"Wait, *wait*!" cried the ambassador.

The guards paused.

"A token from Darvelle," the ambassador said, reaching into his breast pocket.

The guards grabbed a tighter hold on him, but he came out only with a sealed envelope.

"Asher's letter," he said. "It may prove helpful to you, my lady—"

The ambassador was in mid-sentence when he acted. In a flash, he brought one elbow up into a guard's face, knocking him back. He threw the other's grip off his shoulder, and a glint of steel emerged from his sleeve. He leaped at the throne with a dagger raised and primed to kill.

He didn't come close. Hook Bard was in front of Leah with his shield raised before the attacker had taken a single step. Worth drew his sword and joined Hook. Endrus, too, moved to intervene, but Olorus got there first. Olorus hit the Darvellian ambassador like a charging bull. In one fluid motion, he wrapped his arms around the man, turned, lifted him, and slammed his body into the floor. Leah heard the man's head smack against the stone.

"Assassin!" Olorus shouted, keeping his full weight on top of the ambassador and his knee pressed into the base of his spine. The limp Darvellian, either concussed or dead, offered no resistance as the guards converged on him and pried the weapon from his grasp.

Olorus stood. He adjusted his neck with an audible crack, brushed himself off, and started walking back toward the throne.

"Good work, Lieutenant Antony, as usual. . . ." Leah started to say, but she trailed off at the expression on his face.

Instead of looking satisfied, Olorus seemed confused and bleary-eyed, almost as if he were drunk. His first few steps were sure-footed, but then one leg suddenly gave out. He tried to adjust by favoring the other side, but he overcompensated. The Darvellian ambassador was being hauled out of the room as Olorus tripped and fell. His body hit the ground awkwardly.

"Olorus!" Leah cried.

She left the throne and rushed to him. Hook was already there, rolling Olorus over to get a better look. Olorus's eyes darted from one person to another, blinking rapidly. His face was contorted in agony, but Leah could see no sign of any injury.

"We need help!" yelled Worth.

"Get the medics in here, now!" shouted Endrus.

"Olorus!" Leah said.

The lieutenant raised one hand. She thought at first he was reaching for her, but instead, he turned the hand over, indicating his wrist. A tiny cut—a nick of fresh blood as thin as a strand of thread—had lanced the bare flesh between his glove and bracer. It had barely even broken the skin.

"Poi—son," Olorus breathed.

His body convulsed. A noise came out of his throat like hiccups. His teeth were clenched. Spittle formed at the corners of his mouth, foaming in his beard. Hook grabbed his friend by the hand, squeezing tightly for courage. Leah's fingers were trembling as she held them over the cut. She tried to focus her energy and feed her aurym through her ring to find the source of the poison, praying it hadn't yet reached his heart.

"Stay with me, Olorus!" said Leah. "Olorus?"

"Tell . . . mother," Olorus gasped. "Love."

There was one last hiccup. Olorus's body slumped.

PART VI

EARTHRISE

CHAPTER 57

Justin woke with a start. He didn't know what had woken him, and he didn't know how much time had passed since being placed down here in this dungeon. There was no light or sound.

And yet, there was something.

He lay, unmoving, trying to focus on whatever it was. It was so faint that if there had been anything else down here for his senses to focus on, he might never have noticed it at all. Focusing harder on it, he adjusted his perceptions, like tuning a radio, and realized it was coming from the wall that separated his cell from Ahlund's. The only comparable feeling he could think of was when he'd been in the cellar in Hartla, feeling Ahlund signaling him.

It . . . is Ahlund, thought Justin.

In the past, Justin had been able, through some sort of spiritual sixth sense, to feel the presence of cythraul, coblyns, and daemyn energy sources even at a distance. Daemyn was easy to feel. He had been told that even individuals not particularly sensitive could feel the cold, haunted feeling that accompanied daemyn, regardless of whether or not they knew it by its proper name. Aurym was subtler. It required far more effort to detect, but now, tuning out all else, Justin realized that he could feel—could almost see—Ahlund's life force through several feet of solid rock.

"Ahlund," said Justin.

At the sound of his words, the sensation dissipated like a vapor on the wind. It was gone.

"Yes?" said the gravelly voice on the other side of the wall.

"I. . . . Never mind."

"I hope this cell has cleared your mind," said Ahlund. "When the council calls on you again, you must be prepared."

"That woman," said Justin. "She's the leader of the Ru'Onorath?"

"Cyaxares," said Ahlund. "Yes."

"Is there any way, any means that you can think of, that she could possibly know my father?"

"I don't know," said Ahlund. "This bargain that Avagad proposed to you. You said he gave you until winter to decide."

"Yeah," said Justin. "He said, after that, he couldn't be held responsible for what would happen to me or my friends."

A moment of silence passed. Justin opened his mouth to say something else but stopped short when a strange, metaphysical sizzle drew his attention toward the door. Somehow, he knew it was about to open and that Kallorn would be on the other side.

Light spilled in, challenging his vision to the point of agony, and he raised his good hand to shield his eyes.

"If you are ready to conduct yourself accordingly," came Kallorn's voice from the light, "you have been invited to speak with Cyaxares. She has agreed to listen to your story."

Justin stood.

"A word of advice," said Ahlund. "The old man. Don't mention him."

As Justin stepped out, Kallorn placed a hand on his shoulder and directed him up an adjoining hallway.

CHAPTER 58

Justin stood before the council's chairs, but this time, they were empty.

Cyaxares kneeled on the floor alone, meditating, with her chin downturned and the hood of her robes draped over her head. Kallorn stood behind Justin with his sword still drawn. Evidently, the yellow-haired Guardian was taken no chances.

While he waited for someone to say something, Justin went inward, trying to tune the radio frequency of his aurym to sense the life forms around him as he had in the dungeon. But things were too chaotic up here. There was so much aurym. So much life. In the trees. In the vines draped overhead. Creatures crawling on the walls. Birds flying over the city ruins. It was overwhelming. To pick out a single individual was like finding one, specific grain of sand on a beach.

Kallorn sheathed his sword and walked away. When he was gone, Cyaxares spoke.

"Was it the man with the crown who transformed your arm?" she asked, her face still hidden within her robes.

Justin ran his good hand over the bone armor of his demon arm. The pain had subsided thanks to Ezon's healing touch, but the hand at the end was still pale and ragged like a corpse.

"One of his cythraul did it," said Justin.

"The High Demon's most horrible ability," she said.

She stood and turned to face Justin. Her dark eyes studied him. Then she folded her hands into the sleeves of her robe, turned, and began walking away. Justin grumbled in annoyance and followed.

"The transformative powers of the High Demons are not fully understood," she said. "Very few opportunities have arisen since antiquity to study the effects."

"Is it going to kill me?" Justin asked, picking up the pace to walk alongside her.

"It could, but it won't," she replied. "I will show you a way."

They left the council chamber and entered an empty hallway. Ivy blanketed the walls, climbing toward the sunlight streaming in through the open-ceilinged roof.

"You are not in the Kharon," she said.

"In the what?" said Justin.

"When last we spoke, you believed that the things around you were not real," she said. "You thought you were being tricked into seeing them. It sounded like you had experienced it before. There is only one place that matches that description—though it is not really a *place* at all. The Kharon is not a physical plane; it is a spiritual reality. Through it, faraway souls can come in contact with one another. Their minds can connect, communicate, and interact while their bodies stay in place. And, in line with your concerns, some elements of the Kharon can be manipulated to take on specific appearances. Until now, it was my understanding that connection through the Kharon required the willingness of both participants. But you indicated that you were tricked into it. Was it forced upon you?"

Justin hesitated, unsure of how much he should share with her. "The first time," he said, "I didn't even know I was there. It was like a bad dream I couldn't wake up from. He had created this entire illusion, and even after I escaped, it was hard to distinguish the dream from reality."

"If Avagad has harnessed the ability to force his way into the minds of unwilling people. . . ." Cyaxares trailed off and walked silently.

"So," said Justin. "What about my arm?"

"A cythraul's concentrated daemyn touch has the power to transmute living flesh. No amount of healing can reverse the affliction, nor is there any known aurym-based process to counteract it. In other words, it is irreversible. Your arm stays that way. For good."

Justin felt the blood drain from his face. Cyaxares seemed to notice.

"Don't fret," she said in a tone that was almost scolding. "We may not be able to reverse it, but that doesn't mean we can't control it. How long has it been since your arm was exposed to daemyn?"

"You mean since was it turned?"

"No. How long since exposure to daemyn? Of any kind."

Justin's brow furrowed. "Well, I used it to, sort of, absorb a cythraul attack a couple of days before we got here."

"And it's had none since then?"

"*Had* none?" said Justin. He turned to look at her as it suddenly dawned on him what she was trying to say.

"That's right," said Cyaxares. "Living flesh needs blood-flow to sustain it. In the same way, demonic material like your arm requires a regular infusion of daemyn energy to remain vital. Therein lies the true curse of a cythraul's touch. It makes the host a slave to daemyn. Without regular exposure, your arm will not function. It was the same way with your father's legs."

Justin missed a step at the mention of his father. He and Cyaxares were at the end of the hallway, about to emerge into a courtyard. The ruins rose up around them, but in this squared, central area, there were only ferns, vines, and short, young trees allowed to grow wild. It was a patch of untamed jungle right in the middle of the city ruins.

"That was what made me believe this was all an illusion," said Justin. "You saying you knew my dad. It's impossible."

Cyaxares turned to face him. She drew back her hood, revealing the half-halo of white hair wrapping around her forehead.

"Impossible?" she said.

Justin thought about that. "Okay, improbable."

"Now we are getting somewhere," said Cyaxares.

Justin started to say something, but she raised a hand, silencing him.

"By now," she said, stepping into the jungle courtyard, "you must have learned the irony of the Low Demon, the coblyn. It is a life *form*, but it has no life *force*. Coblyns have no spirit energy, but they still need aurym to survive. Thus, they must feed on it, from man or beast, for sustenance. The High Demon is different. It, too, is without spirit, but cythraul do not feed on aurym. They feed on daemyn. They do not hunt for it, however. Instead, daemyn is constantly being channeled to them . . . by their master."

"Their master," said Justin. "You mean Avagad?"

Cyaxares sighed heavily. Her dark eyes were sad, almost pitying, as she said, "No."

A silence followed in which neither seemed ready to pursue the subject further. In the end, it was Justin who spoke.

"I want to believe you," he said, "about you knowing my dad, but I just don't see how that could be."

Cyaxares reached into her robes and drew forth a small, wooden box with a glass lid. "Nothing I could tell you would convince you of what you cannot see with your own eyes," she said. Opening the box, she took out a small scrap of paper. She looked at it for a moment, then looked up at Justin. "Come to your own conclusions, then, son of Benjamin."

She held out the scrap of paper, and Justin recognized it. It looked a hundred years old if it were a day—faded, damaged, dull, and frayed along the edges. But it was not a piece of paper at all. It was Justin's tenth grade school picture.

CHAPTER 59

Justin took the glossy, wallet-sized photo from Cyaxares, but he could summon no other words. He stared at the photo of himself—hair carefully styled, a collared shirt, posed before a blue, marbled background—in a photo that looked like it had been in storage for a lifetime.

"To explain the existence of what you hold in your hand," Cyaxares said, "I must start with the story of Avagad himself." She took a deep breath. "You asked me if he was the one whom I referred to as the master of the cythraul. Avagad is a dangerously powerful man, but he is still just that. A man. His roots can be traced back to a group of warrior-monks devoted to aurym, who harnessed the Ancients' power of unlimited years."

"You mean he was one of the Brethren?" said Justin.

"You've heard of us, I see."

Justin's eyes snapped up at her.

"Yes," said Cyaxares. "Us. . . . Avagad and I were both members of the Brethren. Our order was founded by a scholar named Amphidemus who had devoted his life to the study of spirit energy—aurym and daemyn. He taught the Ancients' secret of long life to a sect of devoted followers. At the core of Amphidemus's teachings was the belief that either side of the energy could be used for righteousness and evil alike; neither was inherently good or evil. Amphidemus was wise in many things, but in that theory, he was wrong. It would prove to be a costly mistake.

"The methods Amphidemus taught us for harnessing immortality were rigorous. It took years of study, and, after that, years more training and practice, sometimes decades, before the effects could be properly exploited. Amphidemus knew that in the wrong hands, immortality could be a terrible thing. Thus, he retreated into the ice-packed south and built a sanctuary far from the inhabited world. Few found their way there to learn the secrets of immortality. I was one of them. But perhaps I should start the story prior to that, at the true beginning of all this.

"Nine thousand years ago—four thousand years before my birth—the Ancients fell. Demons invaded and overran the Oikoumene. Mankind was enslaved. Daemyn reigned supreme, and the voice of aurym faded to a whisper. It was only with the arrival of the first fallen angels that humans were able to rise up and wage war against the demons. Over the course of a thousand-year-long war, humanity took back their homeland. By the time of my birth, mankind was at war with itself in many places over many things, but we were safe from the demons, at least. That did not last.

"I was still a young woman, just an initiate striving to learn the ways of the Brethren, when a new demon invasion threatened the Oikoumene. Amphidemus, myself, and the rest of the Brethren led the free people of the world in a counterassault against the demons. We were strong and united, but even our combined efforts were not enough." Cyaxares smiled. "And then, a warrior appeared to us. His name was Benjamin Holmes."

Justin realized his tenth grade photo was quivering in his hand. Cyaxares reached out and gently took it back from him. He rubbed his fingers together to try to control the shaking.

"My dad," said Justin. "You're telling me he was a fallen angel?"

"He arrived at the height of the war," she said, putting Justin's photo back in the box. "Amphidemus trained him in the ways of aurym, honed his skills until he was ready, and then, we fought a war together."

"But, wait," said Justin. "You said you were a young woman when this happened. That would mean it was at least—"

"Five thousand years ago."

"That. . . ." said Justin. "Now, that definitely is impossible."

"With Benjamin's power," she continued, "we were able to drive the demons back. But when ultimate victory was finally within our reach, the demons set a trap for Benjamin. Your father escaped with his life, but he was badly wounded by a cythraul's transforming touch." She touched Justin's demon-arm. "Your father's legs were turned, like your arm.

"Benjamin was still able to help us win the war and drive out the demons, but we soon realized that without a regular, almost constant infusion of daemyn energy, Benjamin could not use his legs. Amphidemus tried various sources of daemyn, but the prolonged exposure took a toll on Benjamin. It made him angry, irrational, and tempted by dark forces. He was withdrawn and . . . unstable. He soon became a danger to himself and others. Sometimes, it bordered on madness. And when dealing with the aurym power of an ethoul, madness becomes an indescribable peril. In the end, Benjamin decided to leave the Oikoumene forever. A self-imposed exile to forgo the danger he posed to others. Your father's story ended in sorrow, but he was a hero to this world, though none now live, save myself, who remember his name."

CHAPTER 60

Cyaxares gave Justin a moment to absorb her words.

"Unfortunately," said Cyaxares, "our present problems stem from the heroes of the past. Not your father, in this case, but the Brethren. In the beginning, the Brethren were devoted to the peaceful study of the spirit. In your father's time, we became warriors out of necessity, but in the following ages, Amphidemus's belief that aurym and daemyn could coexist led to increasingly . . . radical practices. Aurym was, and is, the natural life force of the world. The Brethren believed that daemyn was just as natural. I, however—having seen the way the demons worshipped daemyn, and the effects daemyn had on your father—began to question the concept. Daemyn seemed far too unnatural to be of this world. It felt more like a perversion of the organic. A disease. A blight upon nature. Then, twenty-five hundred years after Benjamin Holmes saved the Oikoumene, an ambitious young man named Avagad was initiated into our ranks."

Justin squeezed his good hand into a fist.

"By that time," said Cyaxares, "some of the Brethren had begun . . . dark practices. I saw that they were devoting themselves to daemyn, so much so that aurym was largely abandoned. This, to me, was confirmation of my suspicions about daemyn. So blinded were my brothers and sisters by the darkness that they could not see how far they had fallen. Try as I might, I could not convince them to turn away from it. Avagad, as he grew in power, made me especially nervous for the future of our order.

"Knowing I could no longer be an accessory to their dark arts, and realizing that it was too late to convince them to turn away from this path, I left. I stole away in the night and left the Brethren behind forever. For a while, they hunted me. I have no doubt that they would have killed me for my betrayal, but I fled north and managed to elude their pursuit. For several years, I wandered. Directionless. Hopeless. Heartbroken. Surviving but not living. Lamenting the fate of a world where daemyn had grown so strong in the hearts of humanity.

"Finally, the spirit convicted me. I realized that aurym had led me out of that darkness for a reason. I had been entrusted as the bearer of aurym's beacon. It was my task to rectify the Brethren's mistakes. I committed myself—*submitted* is perhaps a better word—fully to this most holy mission. Aurym led me here, to the hidden ruins of Esthean. After years of solitary study and preparation, I began taking initiates of my own. Not to use aurym or daemyn to our own ends. Not to become immortal. To be devotees of aurym. To make the spirit our eternal ally. And to fight daemyn wherever we might find it. To become Ru'Onorath: Guardians of the Oikoumene, committed to the preservation of the light."

Cyaxares paused, then looked hard at Justin.

"The true nature of daemyn would, ultimately, be revealed to the Brethren all too late. Daemyn is not a natural part of this world but a creation spawned by an unholy creator. And that creator uses it to control, and bend to his will, everything daemyn touches. Amphidemus and the Brethren thought that aurym and daemyn were two equal and exact aspects of the same spirit energy—a cohesive oneness that spanned the world—and that by observing both sides of the energy, they were serving the singular totality of the spirit. They were wrong. Daemyn corrupted the Brethren. They became puppets dancing on the strings of a hidden master worlds away. They did not even know that this master existed. Yet he ensnared them. Toward the end, some of the Brethren did begin to see what was happening to them, but, as I said, it was too late. The hidden master finally showed his hand. He revealed himself to the darkest among them, who would destroy the rest and take his place as the most powerful living soul."

"Avagad," said Justin.

Cyaxares nodded. "It has taken me generations of gathering information to learn the full story of what happened during the Brethren's final days. From my understanding, the master of daemyn communed with Avagad through the Kharon—the same spiritual realm through which Avagad contacted you—and commanded him to carry out his terrible will. When inner conflicts caused the Brethren to splinter, Avagad made his move. With a host of High Demons at his command, he slaughtered his brothers and sisters, thus purchasing, in immortal blood, his place at his master's side. All but Avagad were killed. Not even Amphidemus survived."

Justin pretended to look at something on the ground but was really trying to hide his face, fearing that Cyaxares might discern, from his expression, the thoughts racing through his head.

If Avagad killed all the Brethren, thought Justin, *how did Zechariah escape?*
Ahlund's words echoed in Justin's mind: *Don't mention the old man.*

"In many ways, Avagad is only an instrument," said Cyaxares. "As an aurstone is a conduit for spirit energy, so is Avagad a conduit for the will of his master. When he gave in to the lure of daemyn and took the ultimate step no other among the Brethren had yet taken, he became its willing and eager slave."

"But who is the master?" asked Justin.

Cyaxares sighed. "Where to begin?" she said. After a moment, she continued. "The place we refer to as the Oikoumene is the ancestral homeland of the ancient Elleneans, but it is only a small part of our world. The Oikoumene is made up of a group of closely packed continents surrounded by vast oceans, across which exist other such inhabited places—some perhaps even more populous than our own—all part of a great globe the Ancients called Eo. Further, the Ancients believed that Eo was only one of many worlds. Other realms. The world of you and your father, I believe, is one such other realm. And your father once explained to me that your world was but one small stone suspended in a vast void, infinitesimal within the encompassing expanse. . . . Perhaps I will live long enough to study such a concept. For now, I can only approach it as a curious observer from a distance.

"One of the many realms the Ancients theorized about was a place called Mu . . . the dark world. Home of demons and monsters, ruled by a dark god: a giant wielding a sword made of living fire, with a blade so large it could level a city with a swing. In their writings, the Elleneans referred to him only as the Nameless One. He was the immortal god-king of demons. The father of the cythraul. The creator of daemyn and the wellspring from which it flows."

"He *created* daemyn?" said Justin.

"And controls it. And through it, he can manipulate everything it touches." Cyaxares took a deep breath. Her slightly hunched shoulders rose up, then came slowly back down as she released the breath. "Your father won us a great victory against the demons, but since then, the Nameless One has built up his armies yet again. The demons are strong now. Perhaps the strongest they have been since the age when they conquered and enslaved the Ancients. And mortals have such short memories! They believe only what they can see with their eyes. A hundred years pass, and kings and countries forget about threats from beyond the Oikoumene. They become more concerned with fighting one another over minutiae. A *thousand* years pass, and what was once regarded as knowledge becomes fable. History is downgraded to fiction, and our sworn enemies become the stuff of fairy tales." Cyaxares shook her head. "The Nameless One uses Avagad. Avagad uses his worldly influence to set the table for the demons' feast. Although most of the western world remains oblivious to this threat, the eastern continent of Erum offers a preview of what is to come. Its once mighty empires are falling to demon invasions even as I speak. As the enemy presses in on the central landmass of Darsida, still more demons terrorize parts of Athacea and the Raedittean. The master of daemyn failed in his previous attempts to take this world. This time, he has spent millennia surrounding us on all sides. The Oikoumene sits within his grasp. Now, all he has to do is squeeze."

Cyaxares started walking again, out into the overgrown courtyard. She ducked beneath some low-hanging tree branches as she made her way toward the opposite end. Justin shivered, then followed.

"What you have just heard," she said, "is a story that few souls, even among the Ru'Onorath, will ever know. Common warriors like Kallorn and Ahlund. . . . I keep them in the dark about such things. This is not done out of deceitful intent, I promise you; it is simply because the lives of mortals are so very brief in the course of eons-spanning conflicts. Men like Ahlund and Kallorn are here today and gone tomorrow, and hardly a thing has changed. It is almost unkind to trouble them with it. The people of this world cannot fathom what is happening, and they won't—not until they are under Avagad's heel. By then, it will be too late. The Nameless One's demons will enslave mankind again and drive us to the brink of extinction, keeping only enough of us alive to feed upon. Unless you and I can stop it."

"You and I?" said Justin.

"I hold the knowledge," she said, "and you hold the potential for great ability. If your power can be properly honed, we could give this world a fighting chance, at least. . . . I'm sure you have many more questions. Sleep on them. Meditate on what you have learned. I will see to it that you are accommodated with private chambers. Tomorrow, we can begin the process of restoring your arm. Then we will discuss how you wish to proceed."

"I already have private chambers," Justin said.

Justin had been hoping to evoke a response with the comment, but Cyaxares only waited for him to continue.

"As long as Ahlund is a prisoner," said Justin, "so am I."

"You realize that, by law, he should be dead," she said.

"So they tell me," said Justin.

A small smile crept across Cyaxares's face. "But he who makes the laws can also break them. Or, rather, *she* who makes the laws. I will release Ahlund. His crimes are remembered. But they are hereby forgiven. Consider yourselves our honored guests."

Cyaxares started to walk away, back the way they had come.

"Wait," said Justin.

She turned.

He squinted at her, thinking of the soft-spoken, bespectacled man who had raised him. "My dad was a *warrior*?"

Cyaxares looked at him, seemed to consider for a moment, then reached into her robes and pulled out the small wooden box again. She opened it, and Justin thought she was going to hand him back his school photo. Instead, she took out something else: a brown envelope sealed with hardened wax.

"What's this?" asked Justin.

"Perhaps you can tell me," said Cyaxares, and she turned away.

As she left, Justin slipped his finger under the envelope's flap and broke the seal.

CHAPTER 61

"It's bad luck to set sail at night," said Adonica. "You do know that, don't you?"

Gunnar, raising his hands to cup his mouth, shouted, "Hey, be careful with those supplies!"

The recipient of this sentiment was a beanpole of a man wearing overalls, visible within the lantern light of the dock. He and another man—an even more accurate caricature of a farmer than the first—were doing their best to haul a crate into the open cargo hold of the *Gryphon II*. In response to Gunnar's orders, the beanpole raised one hand to give a salute. It was a hand that would have been better utilized holding the crate he was carrying, for the shift of weight not only caused him to immediately lose balance, but it also sent the crate toppling over the side of the pier—along with the second farmer, still doing his best to carry it. As the heavy crate pulled Farmer Number Two over the side with a yelp of fright, Beanpole was left standing flat-footed, alone on the pier, a look of surprise on his face. A half-second later came the splash.

Gunnar turned away, removing his hat and gripping a fistful of his hair by the roots. He couldn't bring himself to even look at Adonica Lor as he said, "Private, if you are honestly under the impression that bad luck is the worst of our problems, I'd say you are being very optimistic."

He heard the splashing of Farmer Number Two treading water below. "Get 'im a lifeboat!" someone shouted.

"Just throw down a bloody rope!" someone else argued.

"Don't make me *climb* up!" Farmer Number Two yelled from the water.

"I see your point," said Adonica.

Gunnar was having a hard time remembering why he'd ever thought this was a good idea. In addition to the *Gryphon II*, Wulder had placed five ships and their crews under Gunnar's command. The twelve hundred volunteers who self-identified as the Holy Army were in the process of boarding these ships. They were men and women from across Athacea and the Raedittean who had pledged their support to Justin the ethoul. It had been Gunnar's idea, inspired by the little cook named Ragny, to recruit these people to sail to Nolia's aid under Gunnar's command. Strange as it seemed, Borris and Pool were now two of the highest-ranking individuals serving under Gunnar. Thankfully, Lycon and Adonica had volunteered to join them.

The big, solid frame of Lycon approached him and saluted. Gunnar tried to summon the decency to salute back, but it came off more like swatting a fly. "How are things on the other ships, major?" he asked, cringing in preparation for the answer.

Another yelp of fright and another splash told him, without looking, that gravity had claimed another victim. Maybe Beanpole himself, this time.

"As good as they are here, sir," Lycon said.

"That bad?" said Gunnar.

"On the plus side," said Adonica, "if these tenderfoots keep on pitching supplies in the drink, it'll be dawn by the time we set sail. Won't have to worry about that bad luck."

"What'd I tell you?" said Gunnar. "An optimist, deep down."

"Admiral, I was wondering if I might I have a word with you," said Lycon.

"You are, aren't you?" asked Gunnar.

Lycon started to say something, then blinked, unsure how to proceed. Gunnar seemed to have that effect on him a lot.

"Lycon, if you want me to scram, just say so," said Adonica.

"No, private," said Lycon, "this concerns you, too. But I'm not so sure we should discuss it around unfamiliar ears."

Gunnar furrowed his brow, but with the sound of the splashing increasing behind him and the first responders still arguing over what to do, anywhere was better than here. He nodded and led Adonica and Lycon below deck. One of Wulder's advisors was in Gunnar's quarters when they entered, updating his war maps by moving pushpins from one place to another. Gunnar told her to finish later and shut the door behind her as she left, leaving Gunnar, Lycon, and Adonica alone.

"Do you remember what that old man said, in the island village?" said Lycon, without preamble.

"Hyd, Inn—o—cen," said Adonica.

"Yes," Lycon said. "Those words have not been far from me since. I spent our interim here seeking out locals with knowledge of the tribal languages of the Raedittean. I consulted the city librarian. I talked to some merchants who do business with native populations throughout the archipelago. I spoke with several islanders we liberated from slavery under Yordar's yoke. None of them had ever heard those words before. None of them."

Gunnar ran a hand through his hair. "I wish Zechariah were here right about now," he said.

"I never met him, personally," said Lycon. "Do you think he'd have known what the words meant, sir?"

"You'd probably have a hard time getting him to shut up about it," said Gunnar. "Even if he didn't know, he might at least have had some sort of theory about what happened to those people."

Gunnar thought about his brother pinned beneath fallen rubble in the palace of Hartla. He had been defenseless against whatever came and ripped his arms from their sockets.

I'm starting to think we picked a very bad time to split up.

"I need to ask both of you a question," said Gunnar. "A question that cannot leave this room. First off, Private Lor, whoever you heard it from was right. I *have* gotten by on luck more than anything else. I don't have the discipline of a soldier or the leadership of a general, and I realize that my judgment can be questionable at times. I need you two to fill in for my weaknesses. That's why, as of right now, the two of you are as much in charge of these hooligans as I am. Consider it a promotion."

"You said you had a question, admiral," said Lycon.

"And now that we're equals, I expect a damn straight answer," said Gunnar. "Is this mission a mistake? Because I'm not so sure anymore."

A long pause followed. Lycon was stern, as usual, and Adonica seemed for once to be following the major's example.

"These volunteers are coblyn fodder," said Lycon.

Gunnar and Adonica both looked at him in surprise. The bristles of his beard lifted in a smile.

"But we'll make soldiers out of them," he said.

CHAPTER 62

Leah stood before the tomb with tears in her eyes.

How could this happen? she kept wondering. *How can he really be gone?*

He had come so far. He had survived so much. To think that a life such as his would end not in glorious battle, nor peacefully in the night as an old man, but by the blade of a cowardly assassin. It was criminal. It was unfair.

You deserved better than this, Leah thought. *You* earned *better than this.*

She thought back to all the dangers she had faced and had managed to live through—a young woman with no military background or experience in battle, until recently. All she had was a bit of self-defense training . . . and some bodyguards willing to give their lives for her.

If anyone should have been in the ground, it was her. And yet, she was allowed to live on while he. . . .

Tears blurred her vision. She ran her hand over the tomb. It just didn't seem possible that he was dead. Not for the first time, shock threatened to overtake her ability to comprehend the full scope of the tragedy. She didn't want to leave him behind like this. She wanted to stay here, or if she had to leave, to come back tomorrow and the next day and the next. She wanted to stay here and never leave his side, to be as stalwart and resolute for him as he had been for her while he was still alive. Though it pained her—though it felt like a curse to be alive while he was dead—she knew she was needed among the living.

Leah closed her eyes and gripped the edge of the tomb tightly.

"I have to go," she whispered. "But I'll never forget. I promise. I'll remember every-thing you did and said. Everything you taught me. Thank you."

A gentle hand touched her shoulder. She winced at it, not because of the touch, but because it was a reminder of the work that needed to be done. Work only she could do.

"Goodbye," she told the tomb. "I love you."

She blinked away the tears and turned around. Behind her, Olorus stood with his arm in a sling. Beneath his beard, he wore a sad frown.

"I'm sorry, my lady," he said. "But we must go."

Leah nodded. She turned back to the tomb, running her hand over the inscription of her father's name one last time. She looked at the others around it, the stone boxes that held her mother and four brothers, and burned the images into her memory.

After retrieving his torch from the nearby sconce in the wall, Olorus led the way back up through the catacombs. Leah followed. Neither said a word.

Olorus was not a tall man, but he was stocky, with a solid build. That was lucky, as his body weight had probably saved his life from the poisoned blade that had been meant for her. Had the same poison gotten into her bloodstream, as intended, it would have killed her in seconds. It might have killed Olorus all the same, had an exceptionally talented healer not been there to intercede. Olorus's body weight, along with the loca-tion of the wound, had allowed Leah to isolate most of the poison before it could be pumped into his heart. A little had made it in, spreading into the rest of his body and causing a series of seizures. But by slowing his blood-flow and strategically clotting areas to partition the poison, Leah had gotten him out of it alive.

Now, he was up and walking, wearing a sling to limit movement. The injured arm troubled him with stiffness and bouts of hot, searing pain in the tendons. If he had listened to her at all, he would still be in bed right now, but he'd insisted on remaining by her side, even just to visit her family's tombs. After what had happened, he was taking no chances.

Leah watched him walking ahead of her. He took the steps carefully, one at a time. Since getting back on his feet, he had been *quiet*—a word that, in all likelihood, had never been used to describe Lieutenant Olorus Antony in his life. Maybe it was just the sickness, but his change in demeanor made Leah wonder if his brush with death had quenched some of the old fire in his belly.

He stopped partway up the steps and took a deep breath. He turned and grinned apologetically for having to rest. His face was stretched and haggard. The hair on his head was neatly shorn, but his facial hair was getting quite long. At the upper reaches of his beard, along the cheekbones, the hair wasn't red but off-white and wiry, almost like Zechariah's. Though it had probably been there all along, Leah had never noticed it before. Now, it seemed to be the dominant feature of his face, framing his old, tired eyes. She had never thought of him as old before.

Once Olorus caught his breath, he resumed climbing the stairs, and Leah followed.

The Darvellian ambassador had survived his encounter with Olorus Antony—albeit with a bad headache, a split scalp, and gaps in his memory—and was currently imprisoned in the castle dungeons. His caravan of guards had been sent back to Darvelle with a message: Princess Anavion had returned, Nolia would rise again, and they would stand against any who opposed them.

Furthermore, Leah had added to the message that Islander Asher, the former prime minister, was wanted by the Nolian government on charges of capital murder, regicide, treason, and a litany of other offenses, and if any state were found to be knowingly harboring him, it would be seen as a direct act of war and retaliated for accordingly. She had a feeling neither Asher nor Darvelle would take kindly to that. She just hoped she would hear back from Hartla soon regarding the additional military support she had requested. With demons in the west and now the impending ire of Darvelle, she needed as much help as she could get, to build defenses and turn Cervice from an urban center into a military base of operations. The future of Nolia depended on it.

I wish Zechariah or Ahlund were here, thought Leah, *to help me make some of these decisions. And Justin. Friends are in short supply, these days.*

Leah had gotten a rare chance for a private word with Zechariah shortly before he left Hartla. His task was to journey into the south as a lone emissary to the empire of Raeqlund. Leah's discussion with him had mostly been about Justin's disappearance. When she approached the subject of Avagad, Zechariah only offered one brief, mysteriously vague comment: "I would have done many things differently, if I had known Avagad was behind all this."

How he knew Avagad, Leah did not know, but it didn't surprise her.

As Leah and Olorus reached the top of the stairs, they found Hook waiting. He and Olorus nodded to each other, indicating wordlessly that all was well, and then took up positions flanking Leah to exit the catacombs into the lower hallways of the palace. In peaceful times, these rooms housed excess food stores, but most of that had either been taken by Asher's evacuating forces or used up by the troops and citizens left here to fend for themselves. The League army and Worth's Enden forces had brought supplies with them, but neither had anticipated the additional four thousand refugees from Ronice, nor an empty capital city with plundered stores. So far, things had been manageable, but finding enough food for the over ten thousand mouths here would soon catch up with them. Supplies would run low, and then what? Would any of these people stand by a leader who couldn't even feed them?

"Remind me where we're going," Leah said, trying to distract herself.

"A briefing with Endrus on the city's eastern defenses," Hook signed.

Leah sighed. "Let's get on with it, then." She turned to Olorus. "How are you faring, lieutenant?"

"Much better, my lady," he said, and kept walking.

"Olorus. Again, I can't thank you enough for what you did."

"Might I forego this upcoming briefing, my lady?" he asked, almost cutting her off. "There is something I wish to attend to."

"Of course," she said. "Take as much time as you need."

Leah stopped mid-step. Olorus and Hook both came up short at her sudden halt. Neither was prepared when she stepped forward and wrapped her arms around Olorus in a hug.

"Thank you," she said.

Olorus was frozen in place for a moment. Then he raised his good arm and squeezed her tightly around the shoulders. His whiskers tickled her face.

CHAPTER 63

Skies were clear over the Nolian countryside, and the air was dry and cold. The red, gold-tipped minarets of the palace reflected the midday sun. To the east, the Cervice River snaked its way through the city districts before disappearing into the Border-woods. Beyond the river, rolling plains stretched out where agricultural fields were overgrown with tall grasses and weeds. The farmhouses were boarded up and abandoned. All these sights were nothing but unpleasant reminders of the happy homecoming that had eluded Leah. The fantasy of home just kept getting shattered.

Thankfully, progress was being made. The walls were now well-manned with guards and archers. Companies of scouts patrolled the Borderwoods and the edges of the Gravelands, and here in the city, daily training drills were being conducted to acclimate troops and civilians for the days ahead.

Leah, Hook, Worth, Endrus, and a few handpicked representatives from their respective camps stood on the wall.

"A few of the storehouses yielded stocks of barley and wheat," said Endrus, gesturing across the plains. "There's plenty of iron and steel left at the smithies—too heavy to carry off during the evacuation. We were also lucky enough to uncover stores of potatoes, spices, and oats, but it still won't be enough to last long, even on strict rations. We may need to search private residences, I'm afraid."

Leah nodded. She had declared that all state-owned properties and storehouses were free for salvage, but she had designated private residences as off-limits. She didn't want anyone to return home to find their houses ransacked. Only as a last resort would such measures be taken.

She leaned against the wall to watch a group of men transporting stone blocks by steed-drawn wagon from a half-deconstructed government storehouse. Even the stones of the buildings were being put to use. It was necessary to complete the newest building project: walls along the main bridge.

There were normally several bridges up and down the river, but now, there was only one. She had ordered the others to be collapsed. Fortifications were being built around the remaining bridge, including a set of zigzagging walls with archers' turrets. Many streets along the outer city were being walled off, while certain alleys would be dotted with fortified command posts and bunkers.

With the lone bridge the only option for invaders from the east, the enemy would be forced into a funnel. And with certain streets strategically walled off, it made Nolia's outer city into a maze. If Darvelle attacked, it would take them time to navigate their way through—all while taking arrows from concealed archers' posts on the rooftops. Even if Darvelle broke through the outer defenses, the forces of Cervice would have plenty of time to fall back to the city's main walls.

"There is no place within twenty miles where the river can be forded," said Endrus. "And the next closest bridge is fifty miles north, through thick brush and difficult traveling in the Borderwoods."

"What about boats?" said Worth. "If they have the foresight to bring some canoes or skiffs, they could ferry soldiers across wherever they please."

"It's possible," said Endrus. "But we'll have plenty of advance warning and time to respond accordingly to that."

Leah turned to look in the opposite direction, across the city proper, to the west. The western inner city was mostly wealthier residential neighborhoods. Outside of the walls were mills, vineyards, breweries, estates, and plantations that might have looked beautiful if there were people left to tend to them. Instead, their fields were browning with the cold.

A chill wind tugged at Leah's dark hair. Surely, the first snows were not far off.

"The western defenses need a lot of work," she said. "That's where the real threat lies. Somewhere out there are the same demon armies that destroyed Lundholm and Endenholm. We must put as much stone between them and us as possible. . . . The prime minister owned a plantation on the western outskirts, did he not?"

"He did, my lady," said Endrus.

"Well, then," said Leah. "Given his voluntary relocation, it is safe to assume he has no further use for it. Consider his home open to the most liberal of salvage."

Endrus chuckled. "Anything that isn't nailed down?" he said playfully.

"If it's nailed down," said Leah, "pull it up."

CHAPTER 64

Justin was not Justin.

He knew this because he should have been in the backseat. It was dark. The roads were slick with rain, and the wipers were going hard. He'd had this dream before. Plenty of times, in fact. It was a dream of a memory, and he knew exactly how it went. But he was supposed to be in the car's backseat. Instead, for some reason, he was driving

He looked at his hands on the wheel and noticed how much hairier they were than usual. The fingernails looked different, and a gold wedding band was on his left ring finger. He tilted his head to check the rearview mirror and saw the silhouette of a sixteen-year-old boy in the backseat, illuminated by the headlights of a passing car—a boy whose arms were still both human. Justin was looking at himself, sitting behind him.

He turned. His mother sat in the passenger's seat beside him. The sight of her alive made his chest hurt.

Checking the mirror again, Justin realized the face looking back at him wore glasses. The skin around his eyes was lined with wrinkles, a five o'clock shadow coated the jaw, and the hairline was receded.

I'm Dad.

Through streaming trails of rain, a green light shone above them. The wipers swiped at the windshield with a dull *thunk-thunk*. It was happening all over again, exactly the way he remembered it, but this time through his father's eyes.

There was no warning, because they never saw it coming. They never saw it coming, because the car had its lights off. The driver had forgotten to turn the lights on, because, as would be discovered later, his blood alcohol content was .27.

The green light hung above them. They were midway through the intersection. For a split-second, Justin saw the outline of the other car coming straight for the front passenger-side door. Then, impact.

Normally, Justin was in the backseat for this dream. He would ride the whole thing out, getting badly cut, bleeding from his arm, hearing his mother's surprised voice one last time before the car rolled, and she died. But this time, in the front seat, Justin was only with them until the roll.

He heard himself shout. His seatbelt either snapped or its mount became dislodged. He shot forward through the windshield. Glass was everywhere. He felt himself being cut. Then, open air. Zero gravity. Cold March rain pelting his face as his body spun head-over-heels.

He leveled out, and he was falling. The ground was racing up at him, but it wasn't a rain-slicked street, strewn with pebbled glass and twisted metal. Instead, it was a forest floor covered in leaves and lit by a midday sun. He landed—

Justin turned from the landing so violently that he almost fell out of bed. His hand was latched in a death grip on the sheets. He was gasping for breath, and for a moment, he thought the dampness of his shirt was from the driving rain coming down on a state road in mid-western Pennsylvania.

He dabbed at his shirt with his good hand. *Sweat*, he realized.

He looked around the room. It was a stone box not much bigger than his cell had been. The difference was, this stone box had a window—and a door he could open whenever he wanted. He took in a deep breath and let it out slowly. Sunlight streamed in, illuminating the little room. He sat up in bed.

After waking up in the hospital after the crash, all he'd been able to remember was that first roll. He remembered his father crying out, his arm being cut, and then, nothing. He was on strong painkillers after that and only half-conscious. His first clear memory was almost a full day later, when a doctor came in to tell him that his mother had passed away and his father had been found.

He'd never really thought to question that second part. His mother was dead. Why would it have occurred to him to perseverate on the other piece of news? Even after he was released from the hospital, he and his father barely talked about the crash. They had certainly never spoken about the ten to twelve hours during which rescue crews had been unable to locate Benjamin Holmes.

Justin reached for the tiny bedside table. On it sat an open envelope, its wax seal broken. He took out the parchment, a long, single sheet folded twice, and he read it. Again.

> *To whom it may concern,*
>
> *Once, there was a book. A leatherbound volume in which I shared my experiences of accidentally traveling from Earth to a strange other world called the Oikoumene, on a planet I call Antichthon.*
>
> *In that book, I divulged theories about what this world might be, how I came to be here, and why. But something happened. The book was lost. I do not know if it was stolen, destroyed, or simply misplaced, but I find it imperative to write this letter, if only out of foolish, misplaced hope.*
>
> *No denizens of the Oikoumene, to my knowledge, can read English letters. Thus, I write knowing full well that no one is likely to read my words. But so long as this letter exists, a spark of hope can still smolder in me. I treasure that spark because my soul has become filled with darkness. My name is Benjamin Holmes, an "ethoul," from Earth.*
>
> *Whoever you are, if you can read the words of this hopeless missive, then I can only assume that you, too, come from my world. I must also assume that you are an ethoul. If so, you have my condolences.*
>
> *It is under grave circumstances that I write this. Many people have benefited from my presence in this world, but I fear that a far greater number now suffer because of my hubris. With shame, I communicate my failure to you, mystery reader, and out of all the warnings I could give a fellow ethoul, there is only one that you must know:*
>
> *Resist the darkness.*
>
> *Daemyn is not like aurym. It is the creation of the Nameless One. If you give in to its twisted influence even a little, all light will be doused from your spirit. My spirit is so consumed by the darkness that I have difficulty controlling my actions. It began as a simple lack of patience. Frustration coupled with impulsiveness. I told myself it was stress. But*

soon, I became like an angry drunk. I couldn't control my reactions to the things around me. Gradually, it was not just my reactions that I lost control over. It was my actions as well. I became a slave to a strange and powerful force that wrested an increasing degree of control over me. I do things I do not want to do. I black out and wake up to see that I have done something horrible. It is daemyn. I am consumed by it, and the Nameless One uses me to do his bidding. I see now that he has been for a long time.

He has almost full control over me now, which is why I write this letter quickly (in one of my few, brief moments of clarity) in the hope that I will be able to go ahead with what I plan to do, and to leave a warning to others. I am too weak to fight against daemyn's hold, so my only recourse is to retreat. I am leaving the Oikoumene forever.

I will leave instructions for this letter to be given to a trusted friend. A friend whom I have hurt and betrayed. She will know what, if anything, to do with it. I pray that, whoever you are, you heed my words. Crave the light. Flee from dark things. Resist evil. Perhaps you can succeed where I have failed.

Justin turned the letter over to check the back, but it was blank, just as it had been the first time he'd checked. No closing, no signature, no date, and no postscript. The letter simply ended.

Benjamin Holmes. His father. An ethoul who had traveled to the Oikoumene, just like Justin . . . five thousand years ago.

Justin tried counting on his fingers. He had spent a couple weeks in the Oikoumene the first time, then returned to Earth to find that only hours had passed. Then, after just five Earth-minutes, he'd returned to discover that over a month had passed here. The ten to twelve hours his father had been missing after the car accident would have been enough to have spent years in the Oikoumene.

But his legs . . . thought Justin.

Now that Justin really thought about it, he couldn't think of a single time he had actually seen his father's bare legs after the crash. With his mother's death, there had been so much else to focus on that it never really occurred to Justin to ask for many details about Benjamin's injuries. He just knew his dad couldn't walk since the crash.

Justin scanned the piece of parchment up and down, taking in the shapes of the words and letters. It did not surprise him that he hadn't recognized Benjamin's handwriting when Avagad allowed him read—briefly—from what he'd called the Book of Unfinished Dreams. This letter, like the book, had been written using a quill and ink, which required careful strokes, more like a paintbrush than a pen or pencil, resulting in a very different technique. But now that Justin was aware of what to look for, he noticed the place where his father had written his name. The way the writer wrote the capital letter *B*—with the top swoop extending back and curving so far down that it nearly dipped below the line. . . . It was just like how his father signed his name.

"Are you okay?"

Justin looked up, startled. Ahlund stood in his doorway. How long he'd been there, Justin did not know.

"Huh?" said Justin.

"I heard you from the next room," said Ahlund. "You shouted."

"What did I say?"

"'Mom.'"

"Oh," said Justin. He placed his father's letter back on the bedside table and adjusted the sling holding his bad arm. His thrashing had loosened it. "Bad dreams."

Ahlund nodded. "Kallorn tells me I have you to thank for my freedom."

Justin shrugged. "I don't think Cyaxares ever really intended to kill you."

"Really."

"You knew all along she wouldn't, didn't you?"

Ahlund said nothing.

"Well, you're welcome, anyway," said Justin.

"Did she offer to train you?"

"Kind of. She had stuff she wanted to talk to me about, first. And she wants me to rest before I make any decisions. I didn't make a very good first impression, and I think she's worried I'll go bonkers again."

Ahlund lowered his voice to a whisper. "Did you mention the old man?"

Justin hesitated. Cyaxares, it seemed, thought that she and Avagad were the only Brethren still living. She either didn't know that Zechariah had survived, or she had intentionally kept him out of her story. Either way, something was off. But odder still was the fact that Cyaxares had shared things with him that even Ahlund knew nothing about. Things she admitted that she hid intentionally from mortals and "common warriors."

Justin wasn't sure he liked this new dynamic. He felt more comfortable being the one in the dark. At least it was honest.

"I didn't say anything about him," Justin whispered back. "But why didn't you want me to mention—?"

Justin closed his mouth at the sound of footsteps in the hall outside. A robed Ru'Onorath man strode past the doorway behind Ahlund and kept walking. Justin decided not to pursue the topic further. For the moment, anyway.

"If Cyaxares offers to train you," said Ahlund, "there will be a test."

"What kind of test?"

"There is no way to know. It is different for everyone. Created uniquely for every new initiate based on their weaknesses and strengths."

Justin stood from the bed. His gaze wandered to the letter on the table again.

"Are you sure we can trust her?" he said quietly.

"If we cannot trust Cyaxares," said Ahlund, "then I do not know who we can trust."

CHAPTER 65

"We call it 'the Well,'" she said.

At Cyaxares's cue, Justin stepped forward in the late-morning sun. They were on the outer edge of the ruins of Esthean, near one of the walls of the crater. A sparkling waterfall came down nearby—a ribbon of blue stretching all the way from the jungle above to a pool at the crater bottom.

But that wasn't what they'd come to see.

Instead, they stood before an unremarkable hole in the ground. There was no water in this "Well," but something was coming up from it. A cold, invisible aura rose from it and assaulted the extrasensory perceptions of Justin's spirit.

Daemyn.

"We do not know why the Well radiates daemyn so," said Cyaxares. "It rises through this vent like smoke from an underground fire."

"I couldn't feel it until we got close," said Justin, "but, now." He cringed at the daemyn slithering hungrily through his brain.

Crave the light, thought Justin, harkening to the words of his father's letter. *Flee from dark things. Resist evil.*

Perhaps you can succeed where I have failed.

"New Ru'Onorath are brought here to test their endurance against the effects of daemyn," Cyaxares said. "Most cannot even approach the Well. You, however, showed resilience to the Treasury, a place that most aurym-sensitive people have difficulting passing within half a mile of. We keep guards posted there to prevent inexperienced initiates from being drawn in, to their doom."

They keep guards at the Treasury, thought Justin. *So, that's why Ahlund took us there. He wanted them to see my abilities. That was the "point" he had been trying to make.*

"I don't get it," said Justin, looking back toward the outer buildings of Esthean. "You talk about the Ru'Onorath as if you've got Guardians and new students everywhere, but this place is practically empty."

"Only the council elders, myself, and about a hundred others are currently stationed in Esthean, and many of those spend their time on patrol in the jungles or gathering food. Much of a Guardian's life is spent on the road. Especially in these times. We act in secret to guide the will of aurym. That often means operating in the shadows. Infiltrating governments or guilds to subtly help guide them toward the light. There are Ru'Onorath who give up their very identities and spend decades—sometimes most of their lives—on assignment. It is an act of utmost devotion to the will of the light. But enough questions. It is time for you to regain the use of your arm. Walk to the Well. Sit before it."

Justin looked at the Well. Although he hated the feel of this place, he felt strangely drawn to it. He edged closer and sat down.

The Well was hardly six inches across—less a well than a burrow, really. Dark, freezing energy moved around him, seeping into him. It felt paranormal. Haunted. It was as if all the creations of his nightmares—all the ghosts in his grandparents' attic, all the monsters that had ever hidden under his bed, in the basement, just out of view, or silhouetted by strangely shaped shadows cast on his bedroom wall—all of them were here. And they were delighted to see him again.

"It may take a while," Cyaxares said from behind him. "Try meditating."

"*What* may take a while?" asked Justin.

Cyaxares made a noise in her throat. Justin turned to look at her and found that she was shaking her head in frustration. "You may have the look of your father," she said, "but you are nowhere near the student he was."

"You sound like my elementary school teachers," said Justin.

"Your transformed arm needs daemyn," she said patiently. "Here at the Well, it will receive it. Now, sit and wait. I will send for Ezon."

"Ezon?" said Justin. "The healer? Why?"

But Cyaxares had already turned and was walking back toward the city ruins.

No sooner was Cyaxares out of sight than Justin realized why she was fetching the healer. As his demon arm absorbed the daemyn, a tingle manifested beneath the bone armor and moved downward into his wrist.

Soon, he began to feel his hand. And it was horrible.

The wound from his battle with the blue tiger had never bled a drop, but suddenly, blood began to pour from it. He had to tear off his sling and wrap it around his hand to staunch the bleeding, and in the process, he noticed he could lift his left arm again, for the first time in days.

When Ezon finally arrived, Justin was leaning over the Well, holding his demon arm above it like he was roasting a hot dog over a fire. After Ezon stopped the bleeding and closed the wound on his hand, Justin practiced flexing his fingers, feeling the daemyn being drawn into the demonic chitin like metal filings to a magnet. The cold, dark presence was terrible. And yet, there was something about it. . . .

My spirit is so consumed by the darkness that I have difficulty controlling my actions. . . .

"Dad. . . ." Justin whispered.

At the sound of footsteps, Justin turned. Cyaxares stood behind him.

"I believe you," said Justin. "About everything, I think."

"You should," said Cyaxares.

"How do we stop Avagad?"

"Come with me, and I will show you."

"Can I have my sword back first?"

"No. For now, you fight without it, son of Benjamin."

CHAPTER 66

Justin slipped the jab and circled right, keeping his guard up as he went. Ahlund threw an elbow. Justin blocked it with a forearm, then counter-struck—easily blocked, of course—and backed away.

"There!" panted Justin. "Got it!"

Sweat poured down his face. His clothes were drenched with it. For hours, he and Ahlund had been fighting in the courtyard near the main hall. Beneath the shadows of Esthean's millennia-old stone towers, the two clashed in hand-to-hand combat. Deities carved into the edifices watched with unseeing eyes.

"Hours to learn one simple maneuver," said Ahlund, "and you celebrate this fact?"

Justin's lungs ached. After the prolonged effort of attacking, defending, and evading Ahlund for hours on end, his muscles were somehow both stiff and burning at the same time. "I'm better with a sword," said Justin. "Can't we fight with swords?"

"There are warriors who train their entire lives in unarmed combat," said Ahlund. "If your weapon is taken from you, a man like that will kill you in seconds. Unless you—*learn*."

Ahlund rushed him. Justin tried to evade, but Ahlund's hand shot forward. His fingers jabbed Justin beneath the ribs. A chop with the flat of his hand hit Justin behind the knee, making it impossible to support his own weight, and he barely caught himself as he started to fall.

Both strikes hurt worse than Justin would have expected. He reacted instinctively, throwing a powerful uppercut at Ahlund's face. Ahlund sidestepped it and pushed Justin's arm aside like swatting a fly.

"Will we never break you of that habit?" Ahlund said.

Justin looked down at his hand. It was curled tightly into a fist. Ahlund had already called him out on that several times.

"You aspire to be a spirit warrior of the Ru'Onorath," Ahlund said. "Yet you fight like a country drunkard."

"I can't help it," Justin said, uncurling his fingers. "It just feels like I should be making a *fist* if I'm trying to hit someone."

"You keep saying that, and I keep telling you, you aren't strong enough for that," said Ahlund. "Use the heel of your hand."

Justin grumbled under his breath as he put his guard back up with his hands open. Ahlund's instructions seemed counterintuitive. On TV and in the movies, people always fought with their fists. You never saw competitive fighters hitting with open hands. Yet Ahlund kept insisting that Justin strike with the heel of his hand instead of with a closed fist. It made haymaker punches look like karate chops and jabs look like high-fives, and Justin felt silly doing it. At first, he'd been naïve enough to think that the rule of open-handed fighting was to keep them from hurting one another, but that clearly was not the case. Ahlund hit hard, and the strikes were brutally painful.

Ahlund jumped forward. Justin tensed, ready to defend.

Ahlund stopped before he reached him. He pointed at Justin's hands, and Justin realized he had clutched them into fists automatically.

"Have it your way," Ahlund said. He stepped forward and placed both arms behind his back. "Punch me."

"Huh?" said Justin.

"With a closed fist," Ahlund said. "I want you to punch me. In the face. As hard as you can."

"Yeah, right," said Justin, laughing. "You're going to dodge it or flip me or throw me or something."

"I won't dodge," said Ahlund. "And I won't counter. Free shot. Punch me in the face. Hard."

"Look, I'll stop using my fists—"

"There's a healer standing by," Ahlund cut in. "What are you afraid of?"

"I'm not afraid," said Justin. "I'm just not going to—"

"You coward, I'm asking for it! Make me regret it. Are you a man, or aren't you? Do it!"

Justin closed his hand into a fist, hauled back with his right arm, and punched Ahlund straight in the face.

Ahlund was true to his word. He didn't dodge. He didn't counter. He didn't use aurym or any other sort of tricks. All he did was tuck his chin into his chest. And instead of Justin's fist connecting with Ahlund's face, it hit him squarely in the center of his forehead.

Pain erupted in Justin's hand and shot up his arm. Somehow, he managed not to cry out, but he couldn't keep from pulling away and cradling his hand to his chest. The blow knocked Ahlund back a step, but that was all. He was still standing. The skin above his brow was split. Blood flowed freely, framing his eyes and dripping off his nose, but he seemed unfazed.

Justin looked down at his hand. The knuckles of his ring and pinky finger were in the wrong place. His hand trembled. The pain was deep and throbbing, and his fingers wouldn't move.

Justin heard a low hooting from overhead. Looking up, he spotted a few of the dark-haired primates lounging spread-eagled in their leafy rooftop nests, watching the humans fighting below. Their curious hoots almost sounded like laughter. Justin glared at them.

"Anyone, even a country drunkard, will duck his head automatically if you try to punch him in the face like that," said Ahlund, wholly unconcerned with the blood streaming down his face, running through his beard, and soaking the front of his shirt. "Let us now assess your situation. You have given your opponent a small cut, and you have broken your own hand. Now he is angry, and you are crippled. Well done."

Justin was tempted to say something snarky or at least to tell Ahlund to hurry up his lecture. His hand was hurting badly and already swelling up. But he bit his tongue, literally, and decided to wait until Ahlund was finished.

"A human skull is much, much stronger than a human hand," said Ahlund. "A little logic should tell you which will come away better off when they meet. And while there are methods used by warriors to build up their bone strength for striking, *you* are not one of them. Until then, we do it my way."

"Loud and clear," said Justin. "Can I go find the healer?"

"I'm here," came a voice from the doorway. Little Ezon shuffled into the courtyard. "Cyaxares said I'd likely be needed. You require an awful lot of attention, don't you, Justin Holmes? Were you so prone to injury as a child, as well? The kind of boy who's always falling out of trees, I suspect? Hmm?"

Justin started to reply, but Ezon grabbed his hand to examine it, causing him to hiss painfully through his teeth. The swelling was already so bad that he could hardly see the individual knuckles. Amazing how the body responded to these things so quickly.

Justin didn't *think* he was particularly injury-prone, but it was true that he was becoming a connoisseur of pain these days. He had experienced enough by now to have developed a refined palate. The sharp stab of a broken bone in the moment actually wasn't all that bad, but the hot throbbing that followed—the body's defense against the injury—was thoroughly disagreeable.

"Want my advice?" asked Ezon. "You *can* hit a man with a closed hand, you know. Hammer-fist." He balled one hand into a fist and hit it against his opposite palm as if beating a drum. "Aim for the cheek. There's a bundle of nerves at the jaw—let me show you."

Before Justin could stop him, Ezon reached up with one hand and pressed his thumb into the hinge of Justin's jaw, between his cheek and his ear. With very little pressure, the old man made Justin yelp and jump back. His palate had just tasted a new breed of pain. It was sharp and immediate—like a live wire had just been grounded—sending jarring, intense signals to his brain. Instantly, there were spots before his eyes. It was surprisingly unpleasant and enduring for such a small amount of pressure, and it didn't so much as leave a no mark.

Ezon laughed. "Sorry! But it might come in handy, someday. Let me see those knuckles."

"Pressure points, Ezon?" said Ahlund. "I'd have thought you were above such things."

"I admit, it's a parlor trick," said Ezon. "But get enough nerves firing all at once, and it creates sensory overload. The brain can't keep up. It blacks out. With a couple of light strikes in the right places, a little old man like me could drop a Rorrdvuuk barbarian—without even hurting him."

Ezon set his healer's aurym to work, and Justin bit his lip as the knuckles went sliding and grinding back into place.

"Would that really work?" Justin asked, trying to distract himself from the pain.

"Oh, it works," said Ezon. "But I wouldn't recommend trying anything like that when it counts. It's tough to find the right spot in the middle of a life-or-death struggle. And demons don't *have* pressure points, as far as I know."

"Fortunately, Avagad does," said Ahlund. "He's the real enemy."

No, thought Justin. *He's not. . . .*

Justin looked away, not wanting Ahlund to read anything on his face.

The Nameless One, thought Justin. *He uses the cythraul, the coblyns, and Avagad as his servants. Daemyn is an extension of his will, but there's a limitation to his power—there must be. Something must prevent him from entering the Oikoumene himself. Otherwise, why would he need Avagad at all?*

When the bones were mended and the swelling reduced, Ezon left Justin and healed the cut on Ahlund's head. Then he shuffled off to watch from a distance.

"Ready?" said Ahlund.

Justin raised his hands—palms open. "Ready."

CHAPTER 67

Atop her favorite spot on the walls before the sun came up, Leah handed the letter back to Hook. He looked at her questioningly, then lowered his dark eyes and to read it in the torchlight for himself. Worth watched with a questioning look.

Though the sun had not even risen on this day, crews had already been hard at work for hours. Cimon Endrus was orchestrating the digging of trenches running through the former plantation fields along the western edge of the city. Until a few minutes ago, Worth and some of his soldiers had been conducting training exercises in the ways of the Endenholm phalanxes. As for Olorus, Leah didn't know where he was. She hadn't seen him for some time.

Hook finished reading the letter and lowered it, gazing out at the countryside, the wind tugging on the long, dark hair that the headband around his forehead held back. Leah took the letter from him and handed it to Worth. It was written in the hand of Count Wulder Von Morix himself.

"*I do not like the implication,*" signed Hook as Worth read.

"Implication?" said Leah.

"*You requested reinforcements. By what authority does Wulder determine the quality of those reinforcements? His words imply that he has final say. He thinks us beneath him.*"

Worth finished reading. "Well, at least this friend of yours, Gunnar Erix Nimbus, is coming. And with twelve hundred volunteers, sailing this way as we speak. Er—well, not *speak*, necessarily. But, uh . . . converse. Communicate."

Hook looked at Worth. Worth turned away, scratching his chinstrap of red facial hair awkwardly.

"Twelve hundred will help," signed Hook. *"No thanks to Von Morix."*

Leah was tempted to agree. It sounded as if the whole thing had been Gunnar's idea.

The bad news was that Hartla had fallen to enemy invaders. It seemed impossible. She could only imagine the size of a demon army able to sack such a well-defended city. Wulder's brother Drexel had been killed in the assault. She would have to send her condolences.

On the positive side, Yordar was dead, which was a great victory in the Raedittean. And there was one other piece of good news in the midst of all the troubles.

Justin was back.

That news had been little more than an afterthought in Wulder's letter, but to Leah, it was everything. Justin hadn't been killed or captured by Avagad after all; rather, he had turned up in Hartla a long while after the League's forces had moved on. He and Ahlund, unfortunately, would not be coming to Nolia because of other matters, of which Wulder seemed either unaware or uninterested, but the fact remained. Justin was alive. Alive and fighting. It sparked a fire of hope in Leah.

"Endrus will want to know," said Worth.

Leah nodded, forcing herself back to the present. "Right. He'll know best where to put the volunteers when they arrive."

Hook smirked, and, not for the first time, Leah got the feeling there was some sort of unfinished business between him and Endrus. Endrus seemed to intentionally avoid Hook, and Hook was unapologetically derisive toward just about anything Endrus had to say.

"The 'Justin' mentioned in this letter," said Worth. "He's not *that* Justin, is he?"

"That Justin?" asked Leah.

"The one they say is an ethoul."

"You've heard of him?" said Leah.

Worth looked astonished, "You mean to tell me," he said, "that the fallen angel everyone has been talking about—he is part of your League?"

Leah started to reply but was cut short when Hook's hand touched her shoulder. The smirk he'd been wearing a second prior had been replaced by a frown. He pointed to the east. At the heights of the watchtowers on their newly built fortifications along the river, a great flame burned in the early morning darkness.

"The signal torch is lit?" said Worth. "But, that means. . . ."

"We're being attacked," said Leah.

CHAPTER 68

The eastern sky was navy blue with the coming dawn as Leah directed her steed down the road at a trot. Flanked on either side by Worth and Hook, she was careful not to seem nervous or hurried. Too many eyes were watching her.

The twilight of dawn prevented her from seeing anything yet, but her scouts told her that an army two thousand strong had assembled across the river. It was not Darvelle; that much was clear. Some of the scouts had ventured to guess that they were barbarians. In any case, Leah would address the matter in person, along with her bodyguards, Worth and Hook.

Where in blazes is Olorus? she wondered.

Lines of archers were assembled atop the walls on the bridge, with arrows already nocked, prepared to fire at the first sign of trouble. Several companies of Cervice's forces were gathering on the city side of the river with weapons drawn, ready to charge across the bridge. As she, Worth, and Hook rode by them, they remained silent and ready.

They entered the bridge fortifications: a narrow, zigzagging canyon of stacked stone. On the other side, they passed through a set of wooden gates cobbled together from scrap wood and barn doors and bound with salvaged iron. Leah could see her breath as she and her bodyguards rode. Though no snow had yet fallen, winter was here in earnest now, and it was shaping up to be a harsh one.

They stepped out onto the opposite side of the river where Endrus and a company of Nolian soldiers stood in ranks, opposing the much larger group assembled only a couple of hundred yards ahead, silhouetted by torchlight. For how far they stretched out, she could only guess. Leah had learned from initial reports that they wore no armor, carried few weapons, and had as many women and children with them as men—and twice that many animals. Though no communications had yet been made with this unknown army, she had ordered her forces not to engage, hoping they might be wandering refugees. Now, she was told, the leader of the group wanted a word with her. And he refused to speak to anyone else.

This may have been a mistake, thought Leah as she brought her steed to a halt. It seemed a recurring thought, these days.

From what she could tell, most of them sat astride steeds, bareback. She could hear the barking of dogs, the bleating of sheep, and the mooing of cattle. The men at the front of the procession wore thick furs, and their skin color was the deep brown, almost black, of fertile soil. Their heads were shaven. Thick, black beards adorned their faces.

"Hook," Leah whispered. "These people are Cru."

In confirmation of Leah's words, a man stepped from the midst of the lines. Like the others, his head was shaven, and a wooly beard hung from his face. His large eyes glistened in the torchlight as if close to tears, and as he smiled, bowing deeply to Leah, she recognized him.

"It's Sif, isn't it?" she said.

"I am humbled that Leah Anavion remembers me," Sif said, adding a second bow. "It is wonderful to see you again."

"The feeling is mutual," said Leah. She had met Sif when she, Olorus, Hook, Zechariah, and Justin had passed through a Cru village in the Shifting Mountains. It all seemed so long ago, now. "This is . . . a surprise."

"I hope our visit this morning is no trouble to you," said Sif. "The Cru are here. All shall be explained, if my lady would be so kind as to come with me. I have been instructed to invite you before our council of elders."

Leah furrowed her brow, confused. "I'm flattered, of course, but Sif, I cannot visit your elders. I must not leave my city."

Sif smiled, bowing yet a third time. "My apologies, my lady. I should have been clearer. You need not travel far to visit our elders. A few steps are all that will be required. As I said, the Cru are here."

As Leah looked out at the mass of humanity before her in the half-light of dawn, the truth of Sif's words hit her. They *were* here. All of them. The entire Cru nation was at her doorstep.

PART VII

SAIL ON

CHAPTER 69

Leah, Worth, and Hook stood before a long, wooden wagon with several oxen hitched to the front. They were in the middle of thousands of Cru people—an entire mobile society, right here at the gates of Nolia.

Sif drew back a curtain on the wagon. A man sat cross-legged in the doorway, looking at Leah. Deep lines marked his face, and his head was spotted with age. His body was bent and contorted with the hardship of age, and a thin, long, ghostly-white beard seem hung in his lap and draped over his feet.

With a gnarled hand, the old man grasped Sif's shoulder to steady himself, and with the audible creaking of joints, he stood and stepped down from the wagon. Leah was amazed to see that he exhibited so few signs of the common maladies of age other than his shrunken posture and the whitening of the eyes.

"Leah Anavion," said Sif. "May I introduce you to our head elder."

"Call me Thid, please," the old man said. His voice was deep but frayed.

"Greetings, Thid," said Leah, bowing.

"And greetings to you, Lady Leah," he said. "It was a long journey out of the mountains, with our ancestral path closed, but travel to your country has thankfully been less perilous than we feared."

"To what do I owe the honor of your visit, so far from home?" Leah said.

Thid smiled and made a humming sort of noise in his throat. He said nothing.

Leah looked nervously at Hook. The ancestral path to which Thid referred, an ancient gate through the mountains, had been closed—violently—when Leah and her companions had fled through it to evade a group of cythraul. She did not know if the Cru harbored resentment toward her for this, but they certainly would have been justified to do so.

"The *home* of A'cru'u'ol is deep beneath the mountains," Thid said. "But it is the curse of *the trapped people* that we lost our way home many generations ago. Until the day when we finally find our way back, our home is wherever we are." Thid paused, cleared his throat, and then recited, "'Seek not the return to old ways. For the coming evil will sever you from your traditions. The strong must forge, instead, a new path.' That is a prophecy that was delivered to us two cycles of the moons ago. And one cycle ago, we shared those same words with your friends, Justin and Zechariah."

Leah shifted uncomfortably. She and her friends had stayed in the Cru village as guests not long after closing the gate, but they had left by sneaking away rudely in the middle of the night—conduct unbecoming of a guest. Another reason for the Cru to think less of her.

"It is a great blessing," continued Thid, "that our prophets receive these revelations—branches of possible futures—on which we, the council, determine how to act. We live on but one branch of a great tree of time. Behind us are many pasts. Ahead, many possible futures yet to grow. The prophets have told us that the days are filled with evil, and still a more terrible evil approaches. As I shared with your friends, on one branch of the future, A'cru'u'ol will be destroyed. On another branch, we will find our way to our ancestral home, and there, hidden deep in the mountains, we will be safe from evil while the rest of the world perishes. But, on a third prophetic branch, it has been foretold that A'cru'u'ol will do something that we, as far back as our longest stories can remember, have *never* done before. It states that the Cru will pledge their allegiance to an outsider and fight in a war under the banner of a king."

"A king. . . ." said Leah. "I apologize if you haven't yet heard the news, but there is no king in Nolia anymore. He was killed by—"

"We know what happened, my child," said Thid. "We are a peaceful nation. Rarely are we ever forced to bloody our axes on anything but sheep and aurochs. This council was inclined to seek out any branch of the prophecy but the one that led to war. But, as the severity of current events becomes clearer, we have decided that the proper course of action is not to hide, nor to be wiped out, but to stand against it. . . . I tell you these things so you may understand what we are about to do."

Leah looked at Hook and Worth.

"Interpretation of prophecy is a difficult business," said Thid. "Especially across cultures. Some words do not always translate neatly into their intended meaning. For instance, the word that we take to mean 'king' can also mean, 'son with authority,' implying, less specifically, not the title of king, but the leadership a man has. The prime minister who took his authority from your father qualifies, under this definition."

Leah hoped Thid, Sif, and the other Cru around her didn't notice as she quietly sucked in a long, cold breath.

"If you have come here to threaten us. . . ." said Worth, leaving the rest of the sentence unspoken.

Thid smiled. "No. But you can learn much about a person, and their chosen company, by observing how he—or she—responds in such situations. I should go on to mention that the A'cru'u'ol word for 'king' does not carry with it the same . . . biological implication that your word does. Pardon my thick tongue if I confuse any terms. What I mean is that gender does not play a role in the word. It could be translated in your language as 'king' *or* 'queen.' And 'son with authority' can also mean 'daughter with authority.'"

Thid paused. He smiled widely, revealing a mouth that was mostly pink, smooth gum line with only a few teeth remaining.

"I am afraid," he said, "that this old body of mine would be quite unable to rise from any bow I might attempt to perform. You will have to take me at my word when I tell you that A'cru'u'ol have come to pledge our allegiance to you, Lady Leah, Queen of Nolia, Daughter with Authority."

Worth laughed aloud in relief. Hook's shoulders visibly relaxed.

"In these troubled times," said Thid, "we cannot remain fractured."

"Look at all the livestock they've brought," Leah heard Worth whisper to Hook. "Plenty of fowl and dairy bison. With the eggs and milk alone—no more food shortage!"

"Th—this comes as a. . . ." Leah stammered. "I can hardly find the words, elder."

"As we have seen," said Thid, "words are often inaccurate, anyway."

"Then permit me to shake the hand of a newfound ally."

Thid grasped her hand, and his bony grip was hard and strong. "Not an ally," he said. "A subject. And your loyal servant in these troubled times."

CHAPTER 70

Justin ran hard, ducking beneath a giant fern frond, then hopping over a fallen tree branch coated in moss and fungus. With every breath of steamy, jungle air, moisture coated the inside of his lungs.

A sudden noise made him dig the heels of his boots into the ground and skid to a halt. He stood quietly, his bare chest heaving with the effort of drawing breath.

He wore only a pair of high, loose-fitting trousers and boots. Even his bone-plated demon arm was uncovered. The only item he carried was a long bolo knife in a scabbard at his belt—a machete-like blade, more a tool than a weapon.

He took another deep breath and this time held it in for a moment before letting it out slowly through his nostrils, grinning a bit. Not so long ago, he would have needed his inhaler to run like this. He didn't quite know what had changed. Maybe it was the air of this world. Maybe it was his diet. Maybe it had something to do with aurym.

Whatever the reason, it was far from the only major change in his body. He had been training with the Ru'Onorath for two weeks now, and he was leaner and more muscular than he had ever been before. Hours of combat training had increased not only his endurance but also his skill with a sword. Or a knife. Or a stick. Or his bare hands. It depended on the day.

He listened carefully, trying to find the sound again. Kallorn Rhodos was out there somewhere, hunting him, just waiting for him to make a wrong move.

The sound came again: a low, guttural hoot that echoed high above the treetops. The call was answered by another, several hundred yards away, and Justin let out a sigh of relief. He rarely saw them through the thickness of the jungle canopy, but the loud, persistent hooting that was often heard high in the trees belonged to the same species of primate he had seen nesting on the ruined rooftops at Esthean.

He wiped the sweat from his brow and squatted on his haunches. A familiar, scaly, coral-like fungus clung to a rotting stump beside him. He ran his finger over the fungus and smelled the residue. Satisfied, he snapped off a portion, put it in his mouth, and chewed, savoring the watery, honey-sweet juices it produced. He closed his eyes and listened to the birds, the dripping branches, the howl of the monkeys—

The slight tug of his hair trying to stand on end was all the warning he got.

Still propped on his haunches, Justin leaped sidelong. He crashed sprawling into the nearby undergrowth as a white light flashed around him, and a miniature bolt of lightning struck the ground behind him with a sizzling crack. The impact zone erupted in a shower of blue and white sparks.

Justin rolled through the brush, shot to his feet, and pumped his legs, propelling himself backward. Another bolt of lightning, half-shrouded by the smoke from the first one, hit the ground in front of him too close for comfort. He pivoted on the balls of his feet and slipped behind a tree.

Justin chewed the fungus in his mouth a few more times, then spit it out. Leaning behind the refuge of the tree, he waited, listening. The howling monkeys had gone silent. It was just quiet enough for Justin to hear the rustling of branches. Something was moving.

He dropped to his hands and knees, peeked out from behind the tree, and scanned the jungle. To his side, a half-rotten tree stood with vines wrapped about its deteriorating trunk. The base looked weak. He followed the vines across the ground with his eyes. One was just a few feet away.

A tiny movement in the branches caught his eye, no more than twenty feet from his present position—roughly the point of origin of the attack that had nearly fried him. He focused on it, watching. A branch twitched as if burdened with weight.

Justin looked at the vine on the ground running to the half-rotten tree. Pressing his body flat against the forest floor, he inched out from cover, moving slowly and carefully beneath the fronds of the undergrowth. Kallorn claimed to be a master at sensing life forces, but the volume of living aurym pumped out by the jungle made it tough even for an expert. If Justin kept low enough, the underbrush would mask his presence. Or at least he hoped it would.

Justin knew that in the event of another strike, the nearly imperceptible tug of his hair was the only warning he would get. That tingle was Kallorn honing in on his target—drawing the line that its electrical current was about to take. In close-quarters combat, Kallorn had demonstrated the effectiveness of his power by zapping Justin with low-intensity jolts. The only way to avoid the attack was to move *before* it was unleashed. Because once Kallorn drew his aim, the attack was instantaneous: a fully formed bolt, reaching from end to end faster than human mental faculties could process. If you saw it coming, it was too late.

Those lightning attacks were like a high-powered rifle; there was no defense once the trigger was pulled. Which meant, in a world of swords and shields and bows and arrows, Kallorn Rhodos was one of the deadliest men alive.

Justin crept forward, feeling the leaves above him sliding across his bare back as he went, trying his best not to disturb them. His only advantage was that on the other end of those lightning bolts, the shooter was still human. With all the usual limitations and shortcomings. He may have wielded superior weaponry, but he still could be tricked, distracted, and outwitted.

Justin reached one of the vines connected to the dead tree. Carefully, slowly, he grabbed it with both hands and reeled it in until it was taught. The sound of it dragging across the ground seemed deafening. Testing the vine, he took a deep breath and pulled backward.

The vine trembled in Justin's hands, but it held firm. There was a squishy, cracking sound from the other end. The vine slackened in his hands, and the dead standing tree began to topple.

CHAPTER 71

Crashing resounded everywhere. Dislodged branches broke and slammed into the ground as the bulk of the tree tilted farther and farther, faster and faster, falling toward Justin. He dropped the vine and scrambled to his feet. A shot from Kallorn landed near his feet, but he ignored it. He ran, ducked beneath a group of large fern fronds, hopped a creek bed, and swung wide, all the while watching the place in the branches where he'd seen Kallorn move. He heard the dead tree slam against the earth behind him. He grabbed the lowest branch, started to climb toward Kallorn's hiding place—

A hand slipped up under his armpit from behind and yanked him backward out of the tree. Justin didn't have the luxury of being surprised. He knew he would hit the ground square on his back—knocking the wind out of him and maybe knocking him unconscious entirely—if he didn't act fast. He grabbed the arm that was pulling him and twisted hard to the side, throwing Kallorn off-balance. The Guardian lost his footing. Both fell and tumbled across the forest floor.

Justin got to his feet with his knife drawn, but somehow, Kallorn was already standing. His green cloak, with sticks and leaves sewn into the fabric, gave him a degree of camouflage even in plain sight. His short sword was drawn and pointing at Justin. Kallorn had a peculiar method of aiming; he held the sword horizontal and used his offhand to steady it, letting the blade rest in the crook of his thumb and forefinger. With one eye closed, he aimed down the length of the blade as if it were an arrow nocked on a bow.

"A bold distraction," said Kallorn, his blade aimed at Justin's face. "But not as economical as my own."

Justin frowned, not understanding his meaning. Kallorn shifted the aim of his sword to point at the tree Justin had previously been attempting to climb. The leaves in the branches bounced slightly. Justin made a face, realizing that the same static electrical charge that made his hair stand on end was being used to intentionally trigger movement in the branches.

"You've got a whole bag full of tricks," said Justin. "But you'll use them all up sooner or later."

Kallorn turned the sword on Justin again, and Justin felt a strange pressure—a change in charge in the electromagnetic field surrounding his face.

"You made clever use of your surroundings," said Kallorn, "but your follow-up was flawed. It would have been far more prudent to utilize the distraction for an escape."

Justin shrugged. "Fortune favors the bold, right?"

Kallorn cocked a yellow eyebrow at him. Justin tensed, preparing to dive for cover again. He'd been out here with Kallorn all day, running, being hunted, sometimes escaping for a while before getting caught—usually getting shocked in the process. He had learned never to let his guard down.

Finally, Kallorn lowered his sword and sheathed it at his side. "You have spent too much time with Ahlund," he said. "Those who gamble with their life as the wager, their *fortune* doesn't last long."

"Ahlund's hasn't run out," said Justin.

"Some beat the odds longer than others," said Kallorn. "Ahlund defies logic. It is . . . irritating."

Justin scratched his neck and wiped the sweat from his forehead. "Would you have really killed him just for coming back here?"

"Yes," said Kallorn.

"But you were friends," said Justin. "Why do you hate him so much?"

"I don't hate him," said Kallorn. "I pity him."

Kallorn might have said more, but his gaze suddenly went distant, as if he were seeing through the trees.

"Cyaxares wishes to speak with you," he said.

Without waiting for a response, Kallorn turned and started off through the jungle. Justin put his knife away and followed. He had to learn how they did that.

CHAPTER 72

The return to Esthean was uneventful but for a short downpour, and an hour later, Justin was led into the council chambers. Cyaxares and Ahlund were waiting. Cyaxares nodded to Kallorn. He turned wordlessly and left.

Cyaxares folded her hands in her robes. "We three must discuss an unpleasant matter," she said.

She let the words hang in the air for a moment before continuing.

"Your deliberate deception," she said, "regarding your partnership with a certain immortal man from the Gravelands."

Justin's stomach dropped.

"I have never met Zechariah personally," Cyaxares continued. "I first learned of his existence only one hundred years ago, when he became the advisor to the boy-king of Raeqlund. I surmised that he was only an imposter posing as one of the Brethren. But as time passed, and I continued to receive reports from the south about this immortal man, I became convinced that he was genuine, likely accepted into the Brethren after I departed from their order. Imagine my surprise to learn that Avagad and I were not the last living immortals after all."

"Avagad?" said Ahlund. "He is one of the immortals?"

"Do not interrupt me, Ahlund," said Cyaxares.

She said it almost sweetly, yet the air seemed to sizzle with the rebuke. She did not so much as look at Ahlund.

"This man, Zechariah," Cyaxares said. "He would have been but a recruit to our order at the time of Avagad's betrayal. Young—comparatively speaking. Untested and unlearned in the lore of the Ancients. A novice to our ways. A weakling compared to Amphidemus and the rest. Yet he apparently prevailed where the rest failed." She looked hard at Justin. "Remarkable that he, alone, survived Avagad's betrayal."

Justin's brow furrowed. "You mean you think. . . ."

Cyaxares said nothing.

"No," said Justin. He looked at Ahlund but found no help there. "No. Zechariah's done nothing but help me *fight* Avagad and the demons. There's no way he would—"

"You mistake my musings for an allegation," Cyaxares said. "I am not accusing this man of anything. I do not know him. My agents told me that after leaving Raeqlund, he took up residence in inner Athacea. Naturally, when I sensed your arrival, I ordered some of my Ru'Onorath to investigate. Reports circled back to me that an ethoul, a young boy, was rumored to have appeared in Athacea and was traveling with some odd companions. One of whom was an old man rumored to be one of the immortal Brethren. I surmised that it must be this Zechariah I had heard about . . . and the look on your face confirms it. It is disturbing that you intentionally kept his existence hidden from me, even after I have shared so much with you and given you ample time and opportunity to tell me about him. Someone who was a prudent judge of character would wonder about the nature of your presence here—and who it is you really serve."

Justin tried to swallow, but his throat was dry.

"Cyaxares," said Ahlund. "Honored elder. Do not blame the boy. I was the one who told him to—"

"He is not a boy," Cyaxares snapped, turning on Ahlund so quickly that it made Justin flinch. "Justin's *ineptitude* and general *lack of sense* are either a clever ruse, or you and your secret ally have coddled him too much. You have treated him like a child, and in response, that is how he behaves. I may have spared your life, Ahlund, but do not confuse amnesty for forgiveness. You are still the same man who abandoned this order and betrayed everything we stand for. You gave up your right to a voice in these chambers long ago. You are not a Ru'Onora, Ahlund Sims, and you never will be again."

In his peripheral vision, Justin thought he saw Ahlund's hands tighten into fists.

"That said, our laws no longer apply to you," Cyaxares continued. "I can't rightly harbor ill feelings toward an outsider for deceiving me." She turned her dark-eyed gaze on Justin. Her face hardened. "But you."

Justin had to resist the urge to retreat a step. He felt exceedingly small despite his much greater physical stature.

"Even after I answered your questions, restored your arm, and honored your request to spare Ahlund's life," said Cyaxares. "Even after everything I shared with you about your father and about yourself. Even after I agreed to help you and train you in the ways of the spirit warrior. Even after all that, deceit still rules your heart. Your actions can be excused no longer.

"You claim to desire the light, but there is darkness in you. I will imply no more about your possible allegiances to other parties, but I *will* remind you that when you first arrived here, you expressed astounding loyalty to your friends, going so far as to prioritize their well-being above the good of the entire world. One of those friends, Ahlund Sims, betrayed this organization, indiscriminately bloodied his sword for any who would pay, and has avoided execution for his crimes by mercy alone. Another, the man called Zechariah, has a shadowed past. Maybe he escaped Avagad's assault on the Brethren, and maybe he now mentors you with righteous intent. Or, considering the trickery that this enemy is capable of, maybe the apparent opposition between Avagad and Zechariah is nothing but their greatest stratagem yet."

CHAPTER 73

Justin started to open his mouth, but the look on Cyaxares's face made him think better of it.

"If Zechariah's intentions are pure," she went on, "then why has he not sought me out in all this time? He surely knows of my existence. Between us, we could have become the Oikoumene's greatest protectors. I don't expect you to answer these questions, but they must be asked. I do not doubt your intelligence, Justin, but even I, with the wisdom of many lifetimes, cannot perceive Zechariah's agenda or make sense of his actions. How can you, having known him for less than a season's harvest, hope to understand what he does in secret and in shadow? I ask you, where is he now? But do not answer that question, either! You do not—cannot—know the answer, not beyond reasonable doubt."

She stepped closer, extended her arm, and placed a gentle hand on Justin's cheek.

"You can only walk one path, Justin," she said. "To follow one is to destroy another. Will you proceed in the ways of the Ru'Onorath, following the selfless and noble path, as your father did? Or will you pursue the ambitions of the self: emotions, comfort, and friends?" She removed her hand and stepped back. "You place so much importance on a few fleeting lives. But think of them in contrast to all the souls of the inhabited world, some born and many yet unborn, whose lives may depend on you. Ask yourself, what would your father do? I'll hold no ill will against you, no matter your decision, but I refuse to be deceived. No one can serve two masters. I will not teach you the sacred secrets of aurym just so you may use it for your own gain.

"To become a Ru'Onora is to adhere to our tenets. These past weeks have been a prelude to your real training. To learn more will mean joining our order and devoting yourself to our ways. Only then will I take you on as a student. Youth and inexperience will never again be viable excuses for deception or irresponsibility. Those are my terms. If you accept, the next step of your journey awaits. If you refuse. . . ." She shook her head. "Then we are done here."

Cyaxares paused. Justin didn't know what to say.

"Think hard on this decision, but do not fret, either," Cyaxares said. "It will be as it is with all the greatest choices in life: When the time comes, your spirit will know the way that is right, and the path will illuminate itself so naturally that it will be as if no decision was made at all. That is how you will know you have made the righteous choice. I'll expect an answer after your trial. Assuming you pass."

"Trial?" said Justin.

"I'm sure Ahlund warned you there would be a trial. A test. Yours will be a simple matter. An experience to teach you how to find your own way. When you have completed the trial, I will accept your answer."

CHAPTER 74

They traveled like ducks in a row, single-file, up the foggy river. All sails were down. The repetitive grinding of oars rotating in the rowlocks was music to Gunnar's ears, and the smacking of their paddles against the water echoed off the sandy, rock-studded riverbanks. It was a fond reminder of simpler times. Times when his father still lived, his brother was only just becoming a promising political player, and Gunnar was a lad with adventure on his mind—and two eyes in his head.

After a week spent skirting the northern coast of Athacea, Gunnar's six ships rowed against the current, journeying up the western branch of the Cervice River. The waterway was narrower than usual here, but the river ran deep. As long as they traveled in single file, even these large, ocean-going vessels could make it up the river all the way to Cervice.

Gunnar squinted his single eye. In the gray half-light of morning, mist rose from the river in fat, ghostly fingers. The fog on the banks was thick as cloud cover. Though he couldn't see it, he knew he was close to the fork where the river split and its eastern and western branches diverged.

Rowing upstream was no one's idea of a good time, but it was the most direct route to Nolia's capital. These twelve hundred volunteers had a long way to go to prove themselves, but Gunnar had the equally difficult challenge of proving himself as their leader. Which was why, despite having spent all night at the helm, he was making it a point to be present and visible for this particularly difficult leg of the journey. He was even considering taking a turn at the oars. Solidarity and what-have-you.

"Nice and easy, Captain Pool," Gunnar said. "Light to starboard as you take this bend. We'll reach the fork in a moment."

"Aye, aye, sir," Pool replied from the helm.

Pool piloted the *Gryphon II*, the lead ship of their procession. Borris was stationed on the next, and Lycon and Adonica were on other vessels. Gunnar hoped their distributed expertise would make up for the overall lack of it.

"Begging your pardon, admiral."

Gunnar turned toward the voice only long enough to identify the speaker. Ragny. The cook and Holy Army volunteer who'd made all this happen.

"I see this probably isn't the time, sir," said Ragny, "but I promised some of the others I would speak to you. I think the journey has been hard on them, and some are worried about whether this is what Justin would have us doing."

Gunnar kept his gaze on the river as he spoke. "I believe he would. And I understand, you and your friends are due some assurances. If it helps, I have it on good authority—my own—that the princess of Nolia is one of Justin's closest friends. Maybe a little more than that."

At the wheel, Pool smiled.

"And *maybe* I shouldn't have said that," said Gunnar. "It's only a guess, mind you. My point is, she's no casual acquaintance or distant relation. She's high on Justin's list of priorities, and, by association, so is Nolia. If he weren't tied up halfway across the Oikoumene in other affairs, you'd best believe he'd be high-tailing it to Nolia alongside us. Could already be on his way there, for all I know. So you tell your friends. . . ."

But Gunnar lost his train of thought as his singular eye caught a glimpse of something ahead.

Through the fog, Gunnar could see the place where the Cervice River split, but something was there that shouldn't have been. Some sort of geometric pattern was directly in front of them.

"What in blazes?" said Pool.

The boxy shape gained detail. It was the front of a ship. And then another. And another. And another. The *Gryphon II*, coming up the western branch, was suddenly only three hundred yards away from about fifteen ships moored along a wide elbow of the adjoining eastern branch. Thanks to the low visibility of the fog, it had been impossible to see them until now, and they were right on top of them. A few were galleys like the *Gryphon II*, but most were fat, hulking cargo ships so big it was a wonder they could fit in the river at all. Gunnar couldn't see any crews or passengers yet, but he could see their flags.

"Darvellian ships," said Gunnar. "Enemies of Nolia."

"Waitin' for us?" asked Pool.

"I don't think so," said Gunnar.

"Those aren't warships," said Ragny. "I think they're troop transports. Heading to Cervice up the river like us, admiral?"

Gunnar frowned. "Rascals stole my idea."

The smacking of the oars against the surface of the river suddenly seemed as loud as thunder.

"Should I sound the alarm, admiral?" asked Pool.

"Hell no," Gunnar replied.

"Even if we could turn around, they'd run us down all the way to the ocean!" said Ragny. "What'll we—?"

"Shut up," said Gunnar, whispering now. "Get below deck, Ragny. On my mark, I want you to give the order: All oars at full speed."

"Oars at—?"

"Do as I say, sailor," said Gunnar.

"Your, uh, *mark*, sir?"

"You'll know it when you hear it!" snapped Gunnar. "Now go!"

Ragny hustled to comply, leaving Gunnar flaring his nostrils. These fools would be the death of him—if he wasn't the death of himself, first.

"Cap'n," whispered Pool, reverting to Gunnar's old title from their fishing days. "What are we doin'?"

"Just keep her steady and hold a straight course along the main channel," said Gunnar. "We're going to catch them unawares and bull-rush right by before they can do anything about it. When I give the command, you sound the alarm. We're going to shoot the gap."

Gunnar turned and looked back the length of the *Gryphon II*. Borris, at the wheel of the vessel directly behind them, was watching Gunnar intently. By the look on his face, he saw what awaited them. The *Gryphon II* was already partway through the fork in the river, and there still was no sign of activity from the Darvellian ships, but several lights burned along the shoreline: the cook-fires of a camp.

The silhouettes of seated men materialized before the fires. It was not a question of if Gunnar's convoy would be seen, but when.

It figures, thought Gunnar. *Where's a random demon massacre when you* need *it?*

Gunnar knew it was not a nice thought, but his group didn't stand a chance against trained Darvellian soldiers. Maybe they would let them pass.

There was only one way to find out.

Gunnar set his jaw, took a deep breath, and yelled, "Full speed!"

His voice broke the quiet of the morning. It echoed back at him from the banks. Below deck, Ragny relayed the message, spurring the rowers to action. At the wheel, Pool grabbed the bell and clanged it wildly, crying, "All hands on deck!" To his credit, his voice only cracked a little.

The clanging of a second bell tolled. But this one was in a different key and came from across the river, from the foremost Darvellian ship. It was followed by shouts from the enemy encampment. More silhouettes took shape on the banks and raced for the ships. Onboard, men lined up along the railings with crossbows already in their hands. Judging by the swiftness of the response, it seemed they hadn't been caught as unaware as Gunnar had hoped. And they were not going to allow them to pass.

The *Gryphon II* was almost through the fork to the main channel, but the other five Mythaean ships still had a long way to go. Holy Army soldiers hurried to the sides of the ship in a disorganized horde. Most looked confused; all looked scared. Some had bows. Others had either forgotten them, had neglected to string them, or were under the illusion that this was a drill.

"Form lines!" Gunnar commanded. "Arrows up!"

Borris's ship was an even worse mess. Only a dozen or so of the two hundred onboard had managed to make it on deck so far.

"Ready!" Gunnar shouted.

A foreign voice across the river shouted a command of his own. Gunnar heard the distinctive, mechanical hinging of crossbow levers. Their payload—compact, dart-like quarrels—could not only puncture plate armor but would also be more accurate than the arrows of the Holy Army's longbows.

"Aim!" Gunnar shouted.

Men and women around him pulled back their bowstrings. A longbow may have been less accurate, but its firing rate was superior to a crossbow's by a factor of three— if capable hands were doing the firing, anyway. But most of his archers were still trying to nock an arrow. On Borris's ship, a few more had joined in with the others. Farther back, a female voice shouted orders. Adonica was doing her part to command another unit of novices.

A second foreign command from across the river. Crossbowmen raised their weapons to look down the sights at his ships, at his people. They were so close now that Gunnar could see their earlobes.

Gunnar drew his cutlass and raised it into the air.

"Fire!"

CHAPTER 75

The Darvellian commander gave his command simultaneously.

The high-pitched twang of bowstrings erupted around Gunnar as his archers fired. The crossbows across the river made cracking sounds as they loosed their payloads.

There was a half-second of silence while both volleys were airborne. Gunnar held his breath.

The impact of the projectiles sounded like shuffling cards. Crossbow quarrels stuck the hull of the *Gryphon II* and studded its deck. Several Holy Army archers fell or wheeled around, grasping frantically at the tails of broad-headed darts buried in their chests, arms, or shoulders. Across the river, Holy Army arrows bounced off Darvellian hulls or stuck there like quills. A few crossbowmen cried out. One toppled overboard and smashed into the shallows below.

The foremost Darvellian ship was being pushed back from the shore, preparing to intercept Gunnar's tiny fleet. Oars extended from the rowlocks.

"Ready!" Gunnar shouted. "Aim! Fire!"

As the archers fired another volley, Gunnar gripped Pool's shoulder. "Keep us centered in the channel," he said. He heard the levers of enemy crossbows working new quarrels into place. "Watch those corners! At full speed, she'll turn more quickly than you think. You're in charge, here."

"I'm in charge?" said Pool. "Where're *you* goin'?"

"I'll be right behind you, lad!" said Gunnar.

Without waiting for a reply, Gunnar sprinted across the deck toward the rear of the ship. Holy Army archers nocked fresh arrows.

"Fire at will!" Gunnar yelled as he ran. "Fire, fire, fire!"

As the archers began firing at their own pace, another volley from the enemy came in almost horizontally—hardly a degree of arc. Several of Gunnar's people went down, but the *Gryphon II* was already through the fork to the main channel. Now it was Borris's ship, partway through the fork, who received the full wrath of the crossbows.

Gunnar sheathed his sword, grabbed a line hanging from the mast, and jumped off the stern of the *Gryphon II*. A quarrel whizzed past his head as he swung across the gap and landed on the prow of Borris's ship. He came up running.

Borris's ship was only the second of six, and across the river, the Darvellian ships were all moving, now. At this rate, they would either cut off the Holy Army convoy midway or be right on their tails.

Gunnar jumped, planted his foot atop a supply barrel, hopped up to the helm, and sprinted past Borris.

"You're in charge here, Borris! Follow Pool, full speed ahead, fire at will!" Gunnar spat in one breath without slowing.

People parted to make way. A few feet in front of him, a man fell clutching a quarrel buried in his stomach. Gunnar gritted his teeth and pumped his fists. He was aware that as he ran, he remained stationary in physical space; it was more like the ships moved beneath his feet while he stayed in place.

The third ship in the procession was piloted by a Hartlan captain, or it had been. As Gunnar hopped the gap and cut across the deck, he found the gray-haired captain sitting in a pool of blood and holding a hand to a gash in his head. A volunteer woman—a fierce-faced girl probably younger than Justin—had stepped in and taken the wheel.

"Good work, give 'em hell, soldier!" Gunnar called to her as he ran past.

He saw Adonica Lor among the archers, loading and firing a bow and barking encouragement to her troops. She did a double take as he sprinted by.

"Where do you think *you're*—?" she shouted.

"Can't talk, got a plan, keep shooting, you look pretty," Gunnar rattled off.

The gap between the third and fourth vessels was alarmingly narrow—so close he barely needed to jump. As he ran, he swung close to the open doorway that led below decks, and over the singing of bowstrings, he bellowed down the hatch, "You're coming in too close! Reduce to three-quarter speed!"

The fog of the cold morning soaked his hair and his face with moisture as he leaped from the fourth ship to the fifth. Four Darvellian ships had cast off from shore. Crossbowmen were all over them, now. Other soldiers and crossbowmen ran along the sandy shoreline, shooting at the Holy Army ships fleeing the scene. The *Gryphon II* was almost out of range by now, but the sixth ship, the final vessel in their convoy, was in serious trouble.

Gunnar stepped across the gap to the sixth ship. Quarrels buzzed through the air like mad starlings. A Darvellian ship was right behind them in pursuit. At the rear of the ship, Lycon Belesys and a group of soldiers had created a turtleshell-like phalanx of overlapping shields. Lycon was in the middle of it, shouting orders and holding up the center shield.

It was clear how this would play out. The Holy Army oarsmen would tire and have to be replaced by fresh arms. That could be done three, maybe four times. Darvelle, on the other hand, with their superior numbers, could rotate fresh hands much longer.

Even now, the pursuing vessel was closing the gap—a mere twenty-five feet behind them in the water. The Darvellian commander stood on deck, sword raised to inspire his men as he shouted orders. Pikemen gathered along the rails holding coils of rope and nasty, hooked polearms, preparing to lash the boats together. The pikemen would board, cut down Gunnar's less-experienced people, overrun the ship, and repeat the process until this whole escapade was all for naught.

Gunnar jumped over a fallen body. He felt an arrowhead bounce off his shinbone, causing a jolt of pain, and he slid the rest of the way across the deck to join Lycon beneath the phalanx. The interiors of their shields were riddled with broadheads poking through. A few men lay dead where their shields had failed them.

Bright, red blood flowed from the wound in Gunnar's leg, but he ignored it and grabbed a bow from one of the dead man's hands.

Lycon nodded to him. "Good morning."

"Not really," Gunnar shouted over the impact of projectiles thudding against the shields. "You any good with a bow, major?"

"Some of us might yet escape, if we sacrifice one ship," Lycon said, ignoring Gunnar's question. "The river is narrow enough that scuttling this vessel may dam up the way, which could buy the rest time to—"

"I said, are you any good with one of these, major?" Gunnar said, shoving the bow at Lycon.

Lycon blinked at him. "Proficient, sir."

"Proficient!" said Gunnar. He laughed like a madman. "That'll do!"

CHAPTER 76

As Lycon accepted the longbow, holding his shield up with one hand, Gunnar grabbed his leather satchel from his belt. He opened the pouch, poured out a handful of tiny, brown seeds, and called on aurym. He felt a warm pulsing sensation as the spirit power swirled and coalesced in the aurstone in his left eye socket. He let it flow, willing life into the seeds in his palm. The shells split. Green shoots with spiky bristles emerged.

Gunnar grabbed an arrow and commanded the shoots to grow. They wrapped tightly around the shaft, forming a knot of green ivy just behind the broadhead.

"Give me your shield!" Gunnar shouted, and he and Lycon traded positions. He handed Lycon the arrow, adding, "I intended these little guys for use against cythraul. Not much to look at as seedlings, but full-grown—"

The man behind Gunnar screamed as one too many projectiles hit a weak point in his shield, broke through, and took him down.

"Well, you'll see," said Gunnar. "I hope. Hit the hull, low, beneath the prow."

"Yes, sir," Lycon shouted.

Lycon nocked the ivy-wrapped arrow. Only now did Gunnar notice that the major was wounded. A quarrel had gone all the way through the meat of his thigh and was protruding from the opposite side.

"Ready?" Gunnar said.

Lycon took a deep breath.

Gunnar counted down: "One, two, now!"

Gunnar lowered the shield, and Lycon stood, fired, and quickly ducked back down.

"Direct hit, I think," he said.

Gunnar squinted with his good eye, reaching out through the spirit. It was difficult, across such a gap, to maintain a connection with small, individual plants, but he'd had plenty of practice. He could feel their tiny life forces wrapped around the arrow that was now embedded in the prow of the ship.

"Proficient shooting," said Gunnar. He peeked through the shields. The ship was only half a dozen yards away, the pikemen were too close for comfort, and the Darvellian commander's eyes were bloodshot and gleaming.

Gunnar latched onto the life forces of the plants. He flexed his fingers, raised his arms, and let his power flow, sending it forth to fuel the eager life forces of the young plants. They accepted it gladly. They moved. They crawled. They grew.

A dart passed so close overhead that it would have gone through Gunnar's hat, but his hat wasn't on his head. Apparently, it had flown off somewhere along the way. He kept his concentration on the plants. He wrapped the individual plants—not ivy, per se, but a species of tough vine—around each other as they grew, braiding them until they formed something akin to a wooden rope.

Bright blue flowers blossomed. The vines divided and divided again. Their tiny, seeking fingers slipped between the boards of the prow, then expanded within and tied themselves into knots on the interior walls of the ship. The opposite ends grew out over the surface of the river, floating and slithering like water snakes as they searched for solid ground.

For Gunnar, it was like a little of himself had been imparted into every plant. His consciousness became many—his mind partitioned into dozens of autonomous pieces, each controlling an individual life form, coordinating them toward a singular goal.

The anchor-points were secure, grown nearly to the size of adult tree roots on the ship's interior. And finally, the ends of the vines reached the eastern shoreline.

"Got it," said Gunnar.

Gunnar drew both hands into fists and unleashed the full force of his aurym. The vines on the riverbank burrowed down through the sand, through a foot of soil, and into wet, hard clay beneath. There, they spread outward horizontally, forming into a spider-webbing root system.

The distance between Gunnar's convoy and the pursuing ship was now negligible. What the Darvellians did not know was that there was a long, braided coil running from the prow of their ship all the way to shore—a mooring line, whose slack was quickly unreeling.

The gap narrowed to a couple of feet. The front line of Darvellian pikemen hopped the gap and charged. Men and women of the Holy Army rushed to meet the attackers. Swords clashed with pikes. Knives flashed at throats. Men grappled and pounded with weapons and fists alike.

And then, Gunnar's vine-rope went taut.

With an audible twang, the forward momentum of the Darvellian ship—now fastened to the riverbank by a living anchor—was yanked suddenly and violently sideways. Twenty or more soldiers waiting their turn to board were thrown by the change of momentum and toppled into the water. The oarsmen in the guts of the ship, still none the wiser, kept rowing, propelling the vessel along its presumed course. The bulk continued forward, but with the prow tethered, the ship only pivoted on its axis. It swung sideways in the river.

The crossbow quarrels stopped falling as panic began to spread among the Darvellians' ranks. The waters of the narrow, swiftly moving river—previously cutting to either side of the sleek prow—now hit solidly against the broad side of the exposed hull. The water had nowhere to go but up. And in. The river entered the open ports of the rowlocks. Oars went limp as the oarsmen inside were flooded.

The next Darvellian ship in line, moving just as quickly, had no time to adjust. Its full-speed chase became ramming speed, and its prow slammed into the exposed opposite side of the anchored ship.

The impact was loud as thunder. The whole ship tremored. The sound of snapping boards echoed up the river as the collision split the first ship's deck down the middle. Crossbowmen were knocked flat or pitched overboard. For one brief moment, Gunnar saw the Darvellian commander waving his sword frantically, still trying to give orders. Then a splintery fissure opened beneath him, and he plummeted into a churning pit of grinding wood and crushing debris.

There was a flash of flames, and Gunnar realized an overturned lamp had sparked an oil fire. The mainsail caught fire instantly. The blaze spread along the rear of the broken ship. The sailors and soldiers still on their feet abandoned ship, diving into the river. A third Darvellian ship added its bulk to the pileup, compressing the wreckage of the second ship and further choking the river.

Gunnar's people cheered in triumph. The Darvellian pikemen unfortunate enough to have boarded early were either finished off or kicked overboard. And meanwhile, the distance between the pileup and the Holy Army convoy grew.

Gunnar mopped his brow with his handkerchief. For a moment, he considered preparing a few more arrows for Lycon to fire, adding more plants to help strengthen his makeshift dam. But it seemed unnecessary. Excessive, even. From shore to shore, the Cervice River had become a wall of flaming wreckage.

Gunnar turned to Lycon. The big Hartlan stood staring at his handiwork in disbelief.

"Dam up the river," Gunnar said. He patted Lycon on the shoulder. "Very good idea, major."

As the sights and sounds of the wreck faded away behind them, Lycon shook himself from his stupor. He kneeled, reaching for Gunnar's injured leg, preparing to use his healing power to close the wound, but Gunnar blocked his hand.

"Leave it," said Gunnar. "Let me feel it a minute longer."

Lycon grinned. "Yes, sir," he said, and he turned his attention to his own injury.

Gunnar watched Lycon snap off the fletched butt of the crossbow quarrel in his own leg, grab the shaft behind the broadhead, and, with hard, steady pressure, pull the quarrel the rest of the way through his thigh and out the other side. The man painted a beautifully vulgar word picture as he worked. When it was out, he calmly placed his hand on the leaking puncture and called on his healer's aurym. He healed the wound only enough to stop the bleeding. Then he set out looking for others more seriously wounded.

"No warning shots."

Gunnar turned. Standing behind him was Ragny.

"No questions, either," said Gunnar. "They didn't care who we were. Just wanted us dead."

"We were fortunate to escape," Ragny said.

"Fortune favors the bold, Ragny. *And* the simple. Which is why simple plans are always the best plans. But you, my friend—you are not so simple, are you?"

"Sir?" Ragny said, confused.

"I ran back here, jumping over ships like a madman," said Gunnar, "and you followed me."

"I felt I was needed, sir," said Ragny.

"A cook *and* a madman," said Lycon, rejoining them. "The world could use more of both."

Ragny blushed a little. "But, sirs, why do you think they were guarding the river?"

"I don't think they were, lad," said Gunnar. "If they were guarding anything, or expecting anybody to come up the river, their ships wouldn't have been beached as they were. They would have blockaded the river's fork. They'd have had scouts posted downriver to warn them of our approach. And they certainly wouldn't have left the western branch open long enough for us to slip by. What I think is that we just happened to be in the same place at the same time. . . . And the fact that they were so keen to eliminate us without any questions implies that they don't want anybody to know they're here."

Gunnar looked back down the river. They had rounded a bend and he could no longer see the wreck, but black smoke rose above the trees, mingling with the dissipating fog.

"I think that fleet was meant for a surprise attack," said Gunnar. "Darvelle is going to invade Nolia."

CHAPTER 77

Olorus entered and closed the door behind him.

The room, on the third floor of the palace of Cervice, had once belonged to the second-in-command of the High Guard, but it had served as Olorus's private quarters since the League arrived, weeks earlier. Its single window let in only a small cone of light. The bed was made. It hadn't been slept in for days.

His arm no longer required a sling, but it clearly pained him. He used his opposite hand to undo his sword belt and let it fall to the floor. He started to cross the room to the washbasin, then stopped suddenly. His shoulders slumped.

"My age is telling," he said, without turning around. "Only a foolish old man would let an intruder get the drop on him like this."

Leah stepped out from the corner. Olorus turned to look at her. His gray-ringed beard pulled up with a smile.

"Never thought I'd see the day when the whippersnapper who adventured with a toy sword in the gardens would get the best of me!" he said.

Leah tried to smile, but she couldn't. His expression fell.

"What is it?" he said.

"Olorus," she said. "Ever since those adventures in the gardens, you've been a protector to me. In the months since my family was killed, you became more than that. More than an ally or a friend. More like a father."

Olorus's brow furrowed, not out of confusion but to mask other emotions threatening to reveal themselves. He opened his mouth to speak, but Leah cut him off.

"Things made so much more sense when the adventures were imaginary," she said. "Not like now, when everything is cogs within cogs, moving mechanisms behind an ever-shifting veil. I trust you with my life, but Olorus . . . where have you been?" She gestured to the bed. "Why have you let me believe you've been staying in these quarters when it is clear no one has slept here? Why have I not seen you in days? Where have you been going?"

Olorus looked at the floor. His cheeks were red.

"How did you know I would be here, now?" he asked.

"Hook told me," said Leah, "but that's all he would tell me. . . . You haven't been present for a briefing in days. Are you even aware of what's been happening? The fortifications on the river are complete, but our walls along the western front are nowhere near ready. Word of what we're trying to do here has spread across Athacea. Isolated populations from some of Nolia's last bastions of defense have joined us. In the past two days alone, a thousand new Nolian soldiers pledged their allegiance to the city and the League, plus three times as many civilians. They bring reports of injustices, battles, raiders pillaging vulnerable villages, and barbarians *allying* themselves with demons marching this way. And in the midst of all this, one of my most trusted friends, a lifelong military man and seasoned strategist, is sneaking around behind my back."

Olorus still wouldn't look at her.

Leah frowned, further disappointed by his silence. Hook was good at what he did, but he could not be everywhere at once. Cimon Endrus was dependable, but Leah did not always see eye-to-eye with his priorities. Marcus Worth was lionhearted and quite intelligent, but he was too cautious and not always eager to work alongside anyone he viewed as outsiders—especially, for whatever reason, the Cru. As for her newest advisor, Sif, he had an uncanny ability to see situations from every angle and objectively weigh advantages and downfalls, but he was still no Olorus Antony. Leah needed someone wise enough to know when she was wrong and bold enough to call her out. Olorus was integral to her war council. He knew this country and its military, and he was unabashedly blunt. He and Hook were also the closest thing to family she had left, and as much as she tried to suppress her feelings, it was distressing to feel abandoned by someone who had until now so vehemently refused to leave her side even for a moment.

"You are entitled to your privacy," she said just to break the silence, "but please help me *understand*, Olorus."

Olorus was not a man prone to introspection, and he was far from eloquent. She hardly expected a soliloquy out of him, but she deserved something.

Finally, he cleared his throat.

"It's my mother," he said.

CHAPTER 78

Leah's lips parted in surprise. "Your mother? I didn't realize she was still. . . . Is she in the city?"

"No," Olorus said. He plodded to the bed and sat heavily upon it, rubbing his injured arm. "And that's just it, my lady," he said. Only now did he look her in the eye.

"I'm . . . so sorry," said Leah. "You mentioned your mother when you were afflicted by the poison, but it slipped my mind until now. I'm ashamed to admit I didn't know you had any family."

"I'm not sure I still do," Olorus said. "And I may never know. My father was killed in a border skirmish when I was a lad. Mother has a small place in the North Quarter. She's lived alone there since the day I enlisted. She always understood that there was a chance, someday, that I might not come home. Like my father. But on the day Hook and I deserted the army, I. . . . I couldn't leave without telling her what I was about to do. I felt she needed a fair warning in case word reached her that her son was, well, a traitor. I wanted her to know I was acting out of loyalty to the crown. It was difficult to leave her here, and I have wondered for months about her well-being. I'd hoped that, returning to the city, I would find her well. But she's gone. Some of her things are missing. Maybe that's a good sign. Maybe she evacuated to the east with the rest. But she is frail. I was not here to help her. *No one* was here to help her. To make sure she understood what was happening, to help her pack her belongings, to see that she made the journey safely, or to make sure she drank enough water along the way. She doesn't always remember to. . . ."

Olorus coughed. It sounded as if he'd choked on his own spit.

Leah had never felt so low. While she was fretting over her war council, Olorus was searching his home city for the woman who'd given him life.

How could she have been so blind? Somehow, it had slipped her mind that, in the process of supporting her, men like Olorus, Hook, Worth, and the rest were placing her needs above their own. They were always there for her when she needed them. The moment one of them wasn't, her response was to rain accusations upon him.

Olorus and Hook had been friends to her. But as she listened to Olorus's story, saw his worry, sensed his sorrow, and felt his pain, she realized how little she knew about these men who continually sacrificed so much for her. She knew their positions and their capacity to perform them, but did she know *them*? As people?

He truly is like a father to me, she thought. *But if there is a distance between us, it's nobody's fault but mine. How can I expect him to treat me like a daughter when I haven't even been a proper friend?*

She turned away from Olorus, wondering what his mother looked like. The city evacuations were a troubling thought, but when she *pictured* it, the scene was even more worrying. Families being displaced was bad enough. But what about those without any family? What about the old, the sick, the weak, and the disabled? She prayed that their neighbors had been kind enough to tend to them.

Leah, you fool, she thought. *You are not the only one who lost their family in this country's downfall.*

She looked around the unkempt room. Without the resources for regular upkeep, the palace felt dark, dreary, and haunted. It was very different from the warm, safe home she remembered, but at least she still had a home. Sleeping in her old room at night had been unfulfilling—a dusty, taunting reminder of everything she'd lost—but the familiarity of old surrounding did offer a small degree of comfort. And not everyone had that luxury.

Suddenly, the truth of Olorus's absences dawned on her.

"You've been staying in your mother's house," she said. "That's why you haven't slept here."

"When we first arrived and found the city abandoned," said Olorus, "I put off going to look for her. I don't know why. Maybe I didn't want to face it. Maybe I already knew she wouldn't be there, and I was afraid. . . ." He rubbed the tiny scar on his wrist. "I've had brushes with death before, but never like this one. It made me think about my mother and the sort of son I've been to her. I needed to know where she was and what happened to her. The unintended result is that I've been abandoning my duty to search for the answers. Becoming almost as sorry an excuse for a soldier as I was a son."

Leah started to say something—to apologize, to empathize, to vow to help him find his mother again—but Olorus cut her off.

"I can't imagine you've seen much of Endrus lately, either," he said, changing the subject. "Not with Hook around, at any rate."

Leah smiled. "He does act strangely around Hook," she said. "When we first arrived in the city, you could have cut the tension with a knife."

"A knife is probably exactly what Endrus is worried about."

Her smile disappeared. "You mean he fears for his life? From Hook?"

"Maybe not his *life*," Olorus said. "Just his dignity. When Hook was promoted up from the falconers in the south to join the High Guard, he and Endrus bumped heads."

"They fought?"

"Yes. And bumped heads—I didn't mean it figuratively. You know Endrus. Good fellow, but thick as a stump sometimes. If given the opportunity, that man would follow regulations until it killed him and his corpse would still be standing at attention. At the time of Hook's promotion, Endrus had just been made captain of the High Guard, and he ran a tight ship. We had been warned in advance about this new lad being brought up, Hook Bard. It was said he could be . . . a handful. But when Endrus saw him standing in line on his first morning of drills with that strip of cloth tied around his head—*quite* against standard issue High Guard uniform—well, he saw it as a personal offense and a challenge. When Hook refused to remove it willingly, Endrus tried to take it off of him."

Olorus paused, looking into the distance almost wistfully.

"By the time we managed to rescue Endrus, Hook had broken his wrist, bloodied his nose, and—well, have you noticed that golden tooth of his? The real one went through his lip when Hook head-butted him in the mouth." Olorus laughed at the look on Leah's face. "Hook spent a whole week in the dungeons for that one! He'd have topped it off with a flogging and probably a dishonorable discharge, if not for your father. When King Darius saw Endrus's face and heard that a *recruit* had done it, he just had to hear the story. Your father went, in person, to visit Hook in the dungeons. I don't know what sort of discussion they had, if any, but the king granted Hook a royal pardon, absolving him of his crimes. If I had to guess, I'd say the king did it because he saw in Hook exactly the kind of man you'd want to have your back. Maybe he even learned of Hook's past life as a slave. Or maybe he just thought Endrus was so full of excrement that he liked the idea of someone beating a little of it out of him."

Leah tried not to laugh but couldn't help it.

"In any case," continued Olorus, "the king reinstated Hook in the High Guard, and Endrus never bothered him about his headband again—or anything else. In fact, he showed such deference to Hook that he often asked *me* to oversee the lad instead, which is how Hook and I first became friends. The rest is history."

Leah was still smiling. She had never heard that story. It was amusing to think that Hook and her father had been friends, and she had never known it.

"At least one nice thing about being home," said Olorus. "Reliving the good old days."

"Yes, but I have a strange feeling about it," Leah said. "Like we won't be in Cervice much longer. Like our days here are numbered."

"That's because this is the longest you've been in one place for months!" Olorus stood and placed a hand on her shoulder. "No one is going to run us out of this city.

We're not going anywhere until you say so!" He squeezed her shoulder for good measure, then stepped back, winking and growling with a little of his old fire, "And Olorus Antony's spear will be at your side! Just like the good old days!"

Leah stepped forward and leaned her head into his shoulder. Olorus didn't do anything at first. Then he placed a hand on her head and ran it over her hair.

"It's hard, sometimes," she said.

"I know," said Olorus. "I'll be with you."

"I know," said Leah.

CHAPTER 79

On this tiny corner of shoreline, there were no white sand beaches. Instead, the jungle ended abruptly at a jagged, rocky embankment that hung out over the sea below. From up above, Justin could hear the sloppy, hollow churning of waves sloshing beneath the overhang. Somewhere out over the ocean, the sun was sinking behind rain clouds. Night was upon him, but his journey had only just begun.

"This is where I leave you," said Kallorn. "Do not bother trying to retrace our trail. By the time the sun rises, our tracks will be gone, anyway. Just watch your step and keep your wits about you."

"So, this is it?" said Justin. "You just leave me here? That's my final test?"

"Your final test?" said Kallorn. "By the spirit, no. It is your *first* test. If you pass, that is when the hard work starts."

Justin looked out into the shadowy jungle. Kallorn had been leading him around in what felt like illogical circles for the past several hours. Finally, they had arrived here, and now, there was nothing but miles of jungle between him and Esthean. All Justin had to do was find his way back. Somehow. Alone.

"I don't understand the point of this," said Justin.

"Which is the truest indication that the lesson is needed," said Kallorn.

"What lesson?"

"Indeed."

Justin sighed. He looked up. Above him, the clouds had not yet rolled in, and the sky was steadily transforming into navy blue with the coming night. A few stars were already visible. The moons were slivers. Two days ago, Ahlund had pointed out several constellations to Justin and had explained how to use them as a compass. With the exception of those few words on the subject, Justin had no idea how to navigate in the wilderness. And even if he did know the way, he didn't know how he was expected to make it through unfamiliar territory, alone, with only the supplies in the small pack they'd given him. The only encouraging thing was that Kallorn was carrying Justin's cat's eye claymore on his back. It was the first time he'd seen it since it had been taken from him in the jungle. It seemed he might finally get it back.

He turned to face Kallorn, but Kallorn wasn't there. Instead, the cat's eye claymore lay on the ground, in its sheath, where he'd been standing. Justin looked around, but there was no sign of him.

"See you later, I guess," Justin mumbled.

He took the pack off his shoulder to examine the contents: a portion of dried meat, a chunk of flint, a hatchet, a spool of thread, and a needle. No more.

He picked up his sword and strapped the sheath to his back. He lowered his hands to his side. His demon arm had been fed with daemyn at the Well before leaving the city, and it felt strong.

Closing his eyes, he took a deep breath, then, quick as a flash, reached over his shoulder with both hands and whipped the claymore from its sheath in a practice-draw. It felt lighter than he remembered it. He flexed his fingers around the hilt, called on aurym, and fed a tiny jolt of power into the sword's blade. The veins of a'thri'ik glowed with green brilliance. The power was coming to him more easily than ever, now.

I wonder what kind of weapon Dad used, thought Justin.

Then he slipped his sword back into its sheath and stepped into the jungle.

CHAPTER 80

He walked for only an hour, most of the time with his sword drawn and a constant influx of aurym feeding it, using it as a torch. He might have pressed on through the night, but Kallorn had marched him in circles for the better part of a day. As it stood, he needed to rest, and now was as good a time as any.

Having Ahlund around had spoiled Justin; he wasn't used to having to make a fire himself. He used his hatchet to strip the bark from some branches, then piled them and struck the flint against his sword to produce sparks. After many tries, and with help from a piece of the parchment his dried meat had been wrapped in, he managed to get a flame going. He cared for it like a precious life form, feeding it tiny scraps of wood until it grew large enough to take full branches and fend for itself.

After eating some of the meat, Justin climbed into the crook of a branch over the fire. Its heat was unwelcome but would keep away the bugs, and the elevation protected him from other creeping things on the ground.

Sleep was elusive. The underbrush moved all around him with the passing of unseen creatures. Alone in the jungle, knowing dinosaur-birds and giant tigers were out there somewhere, it wasn't easy to shut his eyes. Especially with no one to watch his back.

That's probably what Cyaxares wants me to learn, he thought. *She didn't like that I cared more about my friends than the Oikoumene. Maybe this is supposed to teach me self-reliance . . . but while I'm up a tree, how many people are in danger? How many lives has the war claimed since Ahlund and I left Gunnar, Lycon, Adonica, and the rest?*

How many people have died . . . who I could have saved?

He sighed. He turned to look at his sword, hanging by the strap of its sheath from a branch beside him, easily accessible in case he needed it quickly. Thanks to training sessions and conversations with Kallorn, Ahlund, and Cyaxares, he had a stronger grasp on aurym than ever. Still, the last time he'd used his power through his sword in earnest had been in Hartla, against the cythraul. Justin wondered what would happen if he had to use it now. If a prehistoric creature attacked, would he be able to dial down the power enough to avoid alerting every demon in the hemisphere to his presence? Cyaxares had promised to train him in the use of his power but only after he returned from this test, and even then, only if he accepted her conditions.

"Dad," whispered Justin, picturing his face through the kitchen window, the way he'd last seen him. "I wish I'd gone in to talk to you. I wish I'd had more time."

Time. That was a funny concept, these days. Not only did time pass at different ratios between the worlds, but he has been running the numbers in his head and had realized that the math didn't work. The ratio of the passage of time appeared to be variable.

The book said there was a terrible price when using the Keys of the Ancients, thought Justin. *I thought it meant the time difference, but maybe it's worse than that. Maybe the time difference is random. I was on Earth a few minutes and came back five weeks later in Oikoumene time. Maybe that was just the luck of the draw. Maybe it was just as likely that I'd come back in five years or five hundred years. Or, who knows? Maybe backward. In the past.*

Justin pulled himself up and climbed higher into the tree, craning his neck to see the moons and stars through the canopy. Thankfully, the rain clouds were moving off into the distance. Using the position of the stars as Ahlund had taught him, he picked out a tree to the southwest: a reference point to get him started in the right direction.

He grabbed his sword and climbed down to the forest floor. It seemed a shame to stomp out his fire after he'd worked so hard to get it going, but if he couldn't sleep, he might as well walk. The sooner he got this over with, the sooner he could do something productive.

He closed his eyes, feeling the aurym flowing around him—an eternal song sung by every plant and animal in the jungle. A memory came to him of Zechariah, telling him about aurym for the very first time. The words were as clear as if he were speaking to him now.

"We are all born with a spark already in us. As we grow, live, learn, and love, our spirits flower and bloom, and the power grows stronger."

In the dying embers of his fire, Justin drew his sword and set it aglow. He fixed his pack over his shoulder and set out into the jungle.

"Aurym, Justin, is the measure of a person's inner strength. Their will, their faith, their compassion. If a person can tune in to his own aurym, he can learn to listen to the aurym around him. And feel it. . . ."

Zechariah. . . .

Suddenly, something was coming right at him.

Justin felt its aurym before he saw it: a giant flash of life force bearing down on him like a train. He braced himself and gripped his sword with both hands. He couldn't see it or even hear it, but he knew through the clairvoyance of aurym that something was racing toward him. Was it Kallorn? Was this part of the test, sent by Cyaxares to—?

The flash of life force appeared in physical form. A giant shape lunged out of the shadows of the trees. Justin jumped sideways, raising his sword. Claws swiped at him as he hacked his sword in defense.

A massive paw batted him. His feet left solid ground, and he flew through the air.

Justin hit the ground, tumbled, and gained his feet with his sword still in hand. He looked up at the thing.

"Didn't think I'd see you again," said Justin.

The gray, black-striped body looked even more enormous than the first time he'd seen it. The tiger crouched on all fours before him, big as a truck, looking at him with its ears pinned back and lips curled. Justin's wild swing with his sword had landed a lucky shot to its forequarters. The fur was matted sticky and red, but the tiger did not seem to notice.

It flicked its tail, only three-quarters of the correct length. The rest had been lopped off by Ahlund's sword. No doubt about it. It was the same blue tiger. The very same one.

Claws unsheathed from its toes, and it growled at him, baring teeth the size of bananas.

PART VIII

COSMIC

MESSENGER

CHAPTER 81

Without the clairvoyance of aurym to sense it coming, he would have been dead already. And without the light of his cat's eye sword, he wouldn't have been able to see it as it prepared to tear him apart, bite by bite. The blue tiger seemed to understand that there was something different about him. It took a few seemingly casual steps, circling Justin for another attack.

Wonder if Dad ever had to deal with anything like this, he thought.

In the green light of his sword, Justin saw something black trailing from the tiger's front paw like a tiny banner. It was a piece of the new fabric from his left arm. He realized that the wrappings now hung in tatters, and beneath, three parallel trenches were carved through the blackened, bone armor. He had seen his demon arm break through stone and stop sharp, heavy blades, and this was the first time anything had left a mark. He could only imagine the state he would have been in if his *other* arm had suffered the same attack. Dead from blood loss in a few minutes, probably.

Justin pulled free the rest of the wrappings and let them fall to the forest floor. He stepped backward. At his movement, the blue tiger made a noise in its throat that sounded eerily like an inquisitive purr. It advanced on him.

Effortlessly, Justin called on aurym. His sword increased from a jade glow to a dazzling, emerald beam so bright it hurt his eyes.

The tiger stopped in its tracks and waited on its haunches, squinting at the sword's light. Justin took a deep breath. The adrenaline of the surprise attack was wearing off, and the reality of his situation was sinking in. He was alone in the jungle, and a carnivore the size of a minivan was about to tear his muscles off his bones like a chicken wing. He didn't doubt that he could use aurym to kill it; he had seen his aurym cut a building in half. The question was, could he control it? And who would sense it?

It'll be like putting up a signal flare, thought Justin. *Avagad will feel it. Cythraul will feel it. Demons will come this way from every direction, and the same thing that happened to Hartla will happen to Esthean.*

The tiger bared its teeth at him. The bony ridge of its spine could be seen in the shadows from his emerald sword. The vertebrae shifted as it readied itself to pounce. Instead of the vertically slit, almost reptilian pupils of a housecat, it had big, round ones, more like a dog or a human. But in its movements, its mannerisms, its playful ruthlessness—in almost every other way, it was a house cat. A really, really big house cat. And Justin was a mouse.

And finally, tired of waiting, the tiger roared, and it attacked.

CHAPTER 82

Leah woke to the sound of raised voices and fists pounding on her door.

Sitting up, she realized that she'd fallen asleep with the candle on her bedside table still burning. Its tiny flame flickered upon a lump of wax that had melted down almost to the base, leaving a hard puddle on the tabletop. Her clothes lay draped over the chest of drawers in the corner.

"My lady!" someone shouted.

The pounding increased. Her bedroom door bounced on the hinges. For a moment, she thought it was a dream—a retelling of the night her family was murdered, but in that dream, the door was usually flung open. Guards came in telling her she was in danger, and she was whisked off to try, and fail, to save her brother.

On the other side of the door, Olorus Antony shouted, "Invaders, my lady! Darvelle attacks!"

Not a dream, she realized. *Not this time.*

"Give me just a moment!" she shouted, throwing off the covers.

"They'ee coming in at a full charge," Olorus continued. The floor was cold beneath Leah's feet as she rushed to the chest of drawers and began dressing in the candlelight. "Our guards posted in the northern Gravelands along the Borderwoods were attacked and driven back. They retreated to the city, but Darvelle is right behind them! No ambassadors—no attempt at negotiation. They are attacking, my lady."

A surprise invasion in the night, thought Leah, wrenching the shirt down over her head and buckling her belt.

"Bastards!" she hissed, unable to contain it.

Darvelle didn't know what they were getting themselves into. If they thought they could attack and kill her people, and siege her walls without repercussions, they were sorely mistaken.

She strapped the saber to her belt. Her enemies would bleed for this.

She threw her cloak on over it all, crossed the room, and opened the door. On the other side, Olorus and Hook were waiting.

"All forces to the walls," she said. "And find me some damn armor."

CHAPTER 83

There was no mindless bull-rush charge for Justin to dive away from. Of course there wasn't. This was a master killer. It came at Justin not with reckless abandon but with meticulous, calculated movements. Fast enough that he couldn't get away, but slow enough that an unexpected evasion wouldn't spoil the beast's aim. Justin only had time to take one step back before it got to him. Its paw came at him in a careful, grasping reach—to grab him and pin him down for the first bite.

Out of desperation, Justin swung his sword at the paw. It hit so solidly that he felt the blade bounce off the bone. The tiger didn't make a sound as it pulled away, sat down, and raised its paw. A thin, neat slice had split the pad of its foot, bringing a flow of blood to the surface. With ears pinned back, it kept a watchful eye on Justin as it licked the cut.

Testing me, thought Justin. *It won't make the same mistake twice.*

The tiger came at him again, this time so quickly that he wondered if it had been trying to fool him into letting down his guard. Its eyes were wide in the green light of his sword. Its ears were up. If he hadn't known better, he'd have almost thought it wanted to play. As before, he had time only to back up a single step, getting ready for another swing of his sword—

His hips hit something solid. A second too late, he realized he'd backed himself against a tree. Nowhere to go. A paw came down at him.

Pressing against the tree, he rolled sideways, following the curve of its trunk. He threw himself sidelong, but searing hot pain erupted in his lower leg.

Justin clenched his teeth and hopped, swinging his sword behind him in a wide arc as he turned to face the tiger. The animal pulled up short, easily avoiding the sword. It lowered itself into a crouch, watching him yet again.

Blood ran down Justin's leg. A claw had caught him in the calf. It wasn't deep, but it hurt like hell and it was a sobering wake-up call. This wasn't a sparring lesson with Ahlund or hide-and-seek with Kallorn. This was a game of life and death, a game his opponent had practiced since birth.

Luck only lasts so long, he thought. *I'm going to get tired or make a mistake before this* thing *does. It knows that. That's why it's in no hurry. It'll wear me down, and then it'll be too late for me to use aurym.*

It's now or never. I have to risk it.

Justin called on his power and fed it into his sword. It bloomed brighter than ever, and he visualized the wave of aurym energy that would shoot forth from it at his command, tearing through his foe like a carving knife through tender meat.

The tiger watched with interest as Justin hauled back to swing his sword.

Justin hesitated, thinking back to Hartla and how quickly the demons had come down on the city after his arrival. He remembered how little time it had taken them to feel his power, locate him, and—

The tiger jumped at him, and Justin lost his nerve. He closed the flow of his power and instead stabbed his sword forward like a spear, catching the animal in the shoulder before its claws could land. It roared and jumped back but pounced again. Justin brought his left arm up. Claws raked through the demon armor as he wheeled away from the creature.

He looked at the demon arm. More trenches had been gouged through it, but it neither bled nor pained him. The tiger wanted him. It would go to any lengths to take a bite out of him. So, maybe he should let it.

Justin let go of his sword with his left hand. He raised his left arm toward the tiger, presenting his elbow to it. The tiger didn't move.

"Come on, you big, dumb animal," Justin whispered, taking a step forward. "Open wide and see what happens."

The tiger blinked at him. It lowered its big, gray head. The giant nostrils opened wide to sample the air. Its eyes darted one direction and then the other. It seemed almost suspicious—as if it sensed a trap. Justin knew this plan would probably hurt, but it was the best idea he could come up with at the moment. He would let the tiger would clamp down on his demon arm, and while it had him, he would plunge his sword into its neck.

He realized, in all likelihood, that just as many teeth might enter his real flesh as his demon-bone armor. The tiger might grab onto his chest with both claws at the same time that it bit him. And there was also the possibility that even if his plan worked, the tiger might not immediately die. A lot of damage might be done during its death throes. Still, it was a better plan than bringing the demons down on Esthean.

As the tiger moved a bit closer, Justin tried to focus on the living aurym around him. He tried to feel the spirit of the beast before him. Maybe there was some way to make sure it went only for his demon arm. Through the clairvoyance of aurym, despite the abundance of other sources of energy threatening to override it, Justin realized he could feel the roaring heat of the life force of the tiger before him.

Justin's brow furrowed. He would have expected simmering fury from this thing. Or a sort of bloodthirsty, angry intensity. But what he found was not sinister or evil; it was intelligence and hunger. And that was it. There was not a trace of anger. It was a strange contradiction. This creature, even as it strove to kill him, had no anger within it. No ill will against him. Even as it inched its way forward, sizing him up for the best way to tear out his throat, there was no anger.

It would have been easy—and convenient—to paint the tiger as a wicked killing machine, especially given that the animal's zeal to feed was in direct conflict with Justin's desire to live. But when Justin really thought about it, this animal was doing nothing wrong.

The tiger was dangerous, but it was not evil. It was less evil than any human who had ever lived; it was incapable of evil. Even in the most shadowed recesses of its heart, it carried no sinful desires, no malevolent intent. It was just hungry. This creature was the embodiment of strength, insight, and instinct being utilized to satisfy a primal need. There was nothing remotely insidious in trying to eat.

So, what do you call that? thought Justin.

The answer seemed clear.

Innocence, he thought. *You call it innocence.*

There was nothing wrong with killing Justin. He was meat in the jungle—fair game. Justin was the one to blame for stepping willingly into the food chain. And because of his mistake, *he* was now going to have to do something deplorable. He was going to have to kill an astounding creature whose innocence he could literally *see*, thanks to the clairvoyance of aurym.

Justin's left arm was still raised, egging on the tiger to take a bite. He tightened his grip on the sword, already regretting what he was about to do.

"I'm sorry," Justin said. "I don't want to do this."

From somewhere deep within his soul, the silent voice of aurym answered.

So don't.

Justin uncurled his fingers. He dropped his sword, leaving himself defenseless.

CHAPTER 84

Adonica pushed the first one forward. His hands were bound, and he tripped and fell before Gunnar. The second stood in front of her. His hands were also bound. Terror showed in his eyes despite his best attempts to hide it.

"Far as we could tell, there were only two of them," said Adonica. "Didn't take much pressure to make them talk. The trouble is figuring out what they're saying."

Gunnar scratched the back of his neck. The men had been picked up just off the banks of the Cervice River. Ragny, of all people, had spotted their fire through the fog. They had actually approached the ship, waving. It wasn't until they'd been close enough to see Gunnar's archers aiming at their faces that they had realized their mistake. They had surrendered without a fight.

Given the encounter the previous morning, it wasn't hard to guess who they were. The Darvellian fleet Gunnar had left trapped downriver would have relied on scouts to determine when and where to unload their troops. Adonica's men had found no one else, but there would be others—runners placed throughout the woods to relay messages for Darvelle's plan of attack. If these two went missing, it wouldn't take long for the bulk of the army to find out.

Gunnar looked from the prisoners to Adonica, then to Lycon a short distance away. Other soldiers had gathered around, too, including Ragny, probably eager to see for the first time how their admiral would deal with prisoners of war.

"Well, then," said Gunnar. "Let's see if we can't figure out what these fellows were up to."

Gunnar kneeled before the man on the ground. He cleared his throat before saying, in the Darvellian language, *"How we doing, blokes? You'll have to excuse my associates. I think binding your hands was overkill, don't you? Considering there's two of you and a few hundred of us. But, hey, social niceties are the first casualties of war. Am I right?"*

"You speak Darvellian?" said Adonica.

"Had a lot of rich travelers from thereabouts when I ran the Brig," said Gunnar.

"The Brig?" said Adonica.

"Never mind," said Gunnar and turned his attention back to the prisoners. *"How's my speech? Thickly accented, I'm sure, but understandable?"*

The one on the ground said, *"Passable."*

"Don't talk to him," scolded the Darvellian still standing. *"Don't give him the satisfaction."*

"You're Mythaean, aren't you?" said the man on the ground. *"What are you doing here? With all these people?"*

"Not sure you'll like the answer," said Gunnar. *"But before I tell you that, I think you ought to know that we ran into some of your friends on the river. Seems like they're invading Nolia. So tell me, just how stupid can you Darvellians be?"*

Both men looked confused.

"Isn't it enough that we've got demons running loose and wreaking havoc, leaving their stink all over the place?" continued Gunnar. *"I ain't Nolian. Maybe you're invading their lands for a good reason. But is now the right time? Your people have the wrong enemy in their sights. Whoever's in charge of your fouled-up country must have a head full of loose shug monkey excrement."*

The man on the ground glared at Gunnar. *"How dare you speak of my nation in such a manner. . . ?"*

But he trailed off, because his partner started laughing.

The man on the ground turned and glared at him, snapping, *"Pull it together!"*

The standing prisoner shrugged. The fear had left his eyes. *"He's right. We're all thinking the same thing—why are we even here? Some uppity statesman's vendetta? You prepared to die over it? Not me."*

"Me neither," said Gunnar. *"That's why I'm pissed at you guys."*

"You don't know these lands!" said the man on the ground. *"You don't know the history of our countries!"*

His partner ignored him, opting to speak to Gunnar instead. *"That Nolian prime minister. Asher. He cut a deal with Darvelle, but now his knickers are twisted because the princess came back. She's reuniting the country, spreading rumors about a murder plot, and making Darvelle look bad. So our leaders thought we should send good soldiers to their deaths just to save face."*

"So you are *invading Nolia,"* someone said.

Gunnar looked up and realized it was Ragny, also speaking in Darvellian.

"I'm not," said the standing man. *"I can think of better things to die for than rich geezers with bees in their britches."*

"Coward!" said the man on the ground. He sneered up at Gunnar and Ragny. *"It doesn't matter. Before you showed up, we received word that the bulk of our army has already reached Cervice. Once our transport ships make it to them, they'll unload our soldiers right into the city. This changes nothing, you ugly, one-eyed son of a—!"*

"Well, Ragny," said Gunnar. "I think we've heard enough."

"What'd they say?" asked Lycon.

"Darvelle's invading, all right," said Gunnar, raising his voice so that all assembled, and maybe even some on the other ships, could hear him. "They're attacking even as I speak, and they'll be expecting reinforcements to come up the river. Instead, they'll get us! Prepare yourselves! We're going to war!"

To Gunnar's surprise, cheers went up from the crowd. He started to turn to walk away, but Lycon grabbed him by the shoulder.

"What should we do with them, admiral?" he asked.

Gunnar looked at the Darvellian scouts. The standing one seemed unconcerned, while the one on the ground glared nervously.

"Eh, let them go," he said. "They can't cause any. . . ." But he paused, chewing on a loose strand of his mustache and thinking. Then he pointed at the one on the ground. "That one called me ugly," said Gunnar. "Untie his hands, then make him walk the plank."

"Untie his hands?" said Lycon. "Sir, in these shallow waters, it really won't do him any harm."

"Yeah. But he'll be all wet."

As Lycon followed his orders, Gunnar found Ragny and pulled him aside.

"Sir?" said Ragny.

"We're going to need some defenses made," said Gunnar. "If an army really is waiting up the river, like these men said. . . ."

Gunnar paused mid-thought to watch Lycon push the Darvellian onto the plank. The man stepped into position with all the gravitas of a martyr, but he refused to jump, so Lycon nudged him overboard with his boot. The prisoner managed to retain his dignity until he landed in the river. Then he yelped, and Gunnar heard him cursing the water's temperature as he waded to shore. The other Darvellian watched, laughing.

"If all that's true," said Gunnar, "we could be walking into a slaughter."

"What do you suggest, sir?" asked Ragny.

"You ever build a fort as a kid, Ragny?" said Gunnar. "I'm envisioning something like that." He pointed to his left, indicating the eastern side of the river. "Unless I'm very mistaken, the enemy will be on our port side. So we barricade that side up as best we can. Gather every man and woman who knows how to use a hammer, and every piece of scrap wood you can find, and build me some walls. Doesn't have to be pretty. Use tables and chairs for all I care. Take down the sails if you have to."

"The sails?" said Ragny, incredulous.

"Our priority is to get into the city," Gunnar said. "The ships are of secondary concern. Can you manage it?"

Ragny saluted. "Aye, aye, admiral."

"Good," said Gunnar. "Because this may get well and truly messy."

CHAPTER 85

"Battle stations!" yelled Olorus as he jogged. "To your posts!"

"Battle stations!" echoed a dozen cries around them.

In the dark of early morning, torches were lit all along the city walls. Beneath the red minarets of the palace, booted feet clanked against the brick of the streets like hammers to many anvils. Above it all, alarm bells gonged. Leah followed Olorus and Hook. Just getting through the streets was like running a gauntlet. All around them, armored men hurried to obey commands.

Hundreds of archers were already in position on the walls. Leah prayed they would not be needed, and that the company of troops situated on the eastern front, and the fortifications along the river, would be enough to hold back Darvelle's advance. Only time would tell.

She was outfitted in a suit of chainmail with a steel breastplate and gauntlets. Over it, she wore her mother's powder blue cloak, a symbol of Nolian royalty. Hook had procured the armor for her in advance. She had little doubt that it had been forged originally for either a young boy or a rather dainty-figured man, but it fit her quite well.

As she ran, she found herself marveling at the people she passed in the streets. Cervice, once home almost exclusively to Nolians, had become a blend of many people and many cultures. She saw Nolians, Enden people, Castydocians, Mythaeans, and Cru.

And now, all her preparations and promises to protect them would be put to the test.

She followed Olorus and Hook up the stone stairs and took her place at the command post along the eastern walls. Cimon Endrus, Marcus Worth, and Sif of the Cru were waiting for her, as well as several ranking officers of the League, the mayor of Ronice, and representatives from other Nolian populations who had made the journey to Cervice and pledged themselves to her cause.

Leah looked down from the command post. Stretched out across the countryside were the countless torches of enemy soldiers.

"How many?" she asked no one in particular.

"We don't know," said Endrus. "They *were* at full charge, but now they seem to have halted."

"Mind games," said Olorus. "Hoping that in our haste to respond, we would reveal a weakness."

"One of their battalions has split off from the main division and appears to be moving north," said Endrus soberly, pointing across the battlefield.

"A two-pronged attack?" asked Sif.

"Won't amount to much," spoke up Marcus Worth. "When the sun comes up, that second battalion will realize the bridge at the woods has been felled. They'll have to turn back."

"But if the main army has halted, perhaps they mean to negotiate after all!" said the mayor of Ronice from somewhere behind.

An argument followed, but Leah and her real military advisors knew better than to even dignify the mayor's unfounded optimism with a response. Reports indicated that this army had already attacked League platoons stationed in the Borderwoods and along the eastern road. Their intentions were clear. There would be no negotiations.

"Get me down there," Leah said.

"Down *there*?" said Endrus. "Outside the city walls?"

"Outside the city walls," said Leah, "outside the new fortifications, outside it all. Get me across the river, to the front lines."

CHAPTER 86

Justin's sword hit the ground, wobbled, and settling into place in the undergrowth.

The tiger seemed suspicious. The lingering aurym power in the cat's eye claymore kept its blade alight for half a second before the a'thri'ik shards went out entirely, dousing the jungle into total darkness. Justin could not see the tiger. He could not see anything.

He closed his eyes and called on aurym.

Suddenly, the energies of a million life forces around him could be sensed—and seen through his closed eyelids. Their combined, overlapping presences formed a great blur at first, and finding the spirit energy of the tiger was like trying to see a light bulb against the sun. But, like tuning a radio, Justin adjusted his senses. Some of the lesser life forms were reduced in intensity. The trees faded and became the backdrop to brighter spots: animals. Most of them were far away—he was seeing them *through* the trees and the foliage, he realized.

But the biggest was the tiger. In the blackness left by the doused light, it had soundlessly crept forward, crouched low, only a few feet away from Justin.

Justin raised his hand. He opened his palm, and through closed eyes, he saw the outline of his own hand, glowing with life force. His demon appeared as an empty void.

The tiger stepped toward him, and Justin took a frightened step back. His hand quivered involuntarily. His stomach felt hollow. He didn't know if what he was about to attempt was even possible, but he had to try.

He remembered how he had been able to call to his sword in his time of need against the cythraul. Later, he had used the same trick to call it to him from out of Yordar's hands. He remembered how it had felt to use aurym *without* channeling it through a stone, calling on a force outside of himself.

"Aurym, Justin, is the measure of a person's inner strength," Zechariah had once told him. "Their will, their faith, their compassion. If a person can tune in to his own aurym, he can learn to listen to the aurym around him. And feel it. . . ."

He felt the tiger's life force. The silent voice of aurym, outside of him yet somehow also within him, added to Zechariah's explanation:

And speak to it.

The tiger was within arm's reach now, but Justin wasn't paying attention to its warm breath or its heady musk. He focused on its life force and pressed in further, listening. It was hungry. It was calm. A killer without anger—to Justin's human understanding, the ultimate contradiction. He could listen to it. But he could also speak to it.

With a subtle push of aurym, he opened up his soul, showing his spirit to the tiger, telling it that he was not for eating. Not right now.

Something changed. The blue tiger sniffed at the air, and Justin felt his sandy-blonde hair lift slightly—pulled forward by the inhale. He pushed deeper.

The tiger had fought well, he told it. But this time, it was not allowed to win. It was not allowed to hurt him. Maybe they would fight again another day. But tonight, it would have to find something else to eat.

The tiger grunted in its throat. It flicked its half-tail, turned, and slipped away into the jungle, silent as a ghost.

All this, Justin saw as spirit-auras behind his closed eyelids. He was afraid that he would open his eyes to find it had all been a vivid hallucination and that the tiger was still there, about to bite off his head.

It was half a minute before he worked up the courage to open his eyes. Slivers of moonlight were streaming through the canopy, but they offered little visibility amid the shadows. He had to grope around on the ground to find his sword. He set it aglow and looked around. The tiger was nowhere to be found. It had left.

Justin's legs went numb as the full gravity of what he had just done began to sink in. He fell to the ground, landing hard on his rear end. His whole body trembled. He couldn't seem to get enough breath into his lungs. He closed his eyes again and sensed—no, *saw*—the tiger several hundred yards away. It was sitting on the ground, licking the minor wounds Justin had inflicted upon it.

I better get out of here, he thought, *before it changes its mind.*

He opened his eyes again and had to push the light of his sword quite bright in order to recalibrate his direction, then he started walking.

Death and destruction are the easy way, he heard spoken, deep within his mind. Maybe it was something he'd been told before that he was remembering, or maybe it was that small voice of aurym again; it was getting difficult to tell the difference.

Anyone can kill something, came the words. *Far fewer learn how not to.*

He shut his eyes and listened to the life forces in and of the jungle all around him— every tree, every plant, even the ground beneath his feet. After a few moments, he withdrew the power from his sword until its light was completely out, and he walked with his eyes closed. He didn't need to see anymore.

CHAPTER 87

The rising sun was visible for only a few seconds before slipping behind the clouds. It was the coldest day yet. So cold that Leah wasn't surprised when the snow began to fall. Tiny pellets pitter-pattered against sword, shield, helmet, and armor, creating a sound like many toy drums.

Leah stood with Olorus, Hook, Worth, Sif, and two thousand other soldiers on the front lines. She would have preferred to have been on steedback, but with fewer steeds than soldiers, all the fighters around her were on foot, and it was better to stand beside them than over them. She had lost count of how many troops she now commanded in Cervice, but she knew it was over nine thousand.

Ahead, across half a mile of abandoned, overgrown farmlands, a host of Darvellian cavalry and infantry was approaching. Hook had estimated their numbers to be around five thousand. The second Darvellian battalion, which had split off and marched north to where the Cervice River flowed into the Borderwoods, seemed to have come to a halt along the river. Leah had thought they would turn about when they realized the bridge had been destroyed, but they hadn't. They seemed to be waiting.

There didn't appear to be any catapults or siege engines; surely Darvelle hadn't expected to encounter deconstructed bridges and newly built walls. Part of Leah was tempted to muster the full force of her numbers and hit this Darvellian advance head-on with everything she had. To not just beat them, but to crush them. To humiliate them. To route them and drive them fleeing across the Gravelands in a retreat that would demoralize a nation and go down in history. But that wouldn't do. Her people had worked hard to construct the city's new fortifications. Best to use them to their advantage instead of charging out like barbarians—as satisfying as that would have been. When Darvelle finally charged, they would face Leah and her infantry, as well as a barrage of arrows from the walls.

"Patience, Leah," Olorus whispered beside her, as if reading her thoughts.

Her hands were clasped behind her back in a show of confidence, but they were shaking. All was quiet as she and her soldiers waited for the bloodbath to begin. Her dark hair was tied back. She took a deep breath, feeling the way the breastplate of her armor rose up with it and rubbed against her neck.

Then, amidst the quiet, Leah suddenly heard her name being called from behind her. She turned. The crowd was parting for someone to pass through—a teenaged Nolian girl, out of breath from running.

"A message from Captain Endrus," said the girl.

Leah only nodded, afraid that if she spoke, the nerves would be audible in her voice.

"Ships are coming up the river!" the girl said.

CHAPTER 88

Justin woke with a start, pulling violently away from something that was not there. A quick hand-hold on the knob of a branch was all that kept him from falling out of his tree.

For a moment, he sat there panting. About an hour after his encounter with the tiger, he had stopped to make camp. He must have been sleeping for several hours, because the sun was rising and the sky through the canopy was clear and blue as sapphire.

Readjusting himself in the tree, he wiped at his brow with the back of his hand, peeling off a thick, dripping layer of sweat.

A nightmare, he thought. *Can't remember it, though.*

But that wasn't entirely true. An image remained stuck in his short-term memory while all the rest faded away. It was a face. A face on fire.

No. It was a face *made* of fire.

The image was trapped in his head. It had a head like a man, but not. Four horns jutted out of its head. Tusk-like fangs protruding upward from the lower jaw. It had no eyes. Just empty sockets looking at Justin. A sword made of fire rose high over its head.

The Nameless One. . . ?

It was all he remembered of the nightmare, and for that, he was grateful.

Grabbing his sword from where it hung nearby, he slipped down from the tree. His campfire had burned down to gently smoking coals, but he still spread them before setting off.

He limped slightly as he walked. The scratch from the blue tiger hadn't been deep, but even the smallest of wounds was cause for concern in a place like this. He had a needle and thread in his pack, but he didn't think he had the stomach to stitch his own flesh, so he'd wrapped the cut tightly with a piece of cloth, hoping that would be enough to stave off infection until he made it back to Esthean.

Justin stopped, looking up. He recognized the species of a narrow tree in front of him. The same kind grew in one of the courtyards in Esthean. He left his pack and his sword on the ground, grabbed one of the lower branches, and started climbing.

A shiver ran down his spine. He couldn't shake the image of the horned head and the flaming sword. He shook his head. There was nothing to be afraid of. It was only a nightmare.

In the higher branches, Justin found what he sought. The round, maroon-colored fruits were the size of his fist, and he plucked three, using his shirt as a pouch to carry them back down the tree.

Had it really been a nightmare, though? Was the flaming face the product of his subconscious, created by the description given to him by Cyaxares? Or was it some sort of vision?

Or, worse still, had he momentarily slipped into the dream-world Cyaxares called the Kharon?

Justin reached the ground. He used his hatchet to break through the tough outer rinds of the fruit and peel off the inner skin. He ate the fruit one by one, letting the juice dribble down his chin. There wasn't much meat to them, but they were rich and sweet. More than anything, they were a source of clean water.

These lonely hours made him long for days gone by. Being Lisaac's prisoner had been a terrible experience, but it had been during in those days that he had grown close to Leah. They'd had no one but each other.

I miss her, thought Justin, tossing a fruit rind over his shoulder.

He missed the others, too, of course. But Leah was something else.

An unwanted feeling suddenly crept through Justin's left arm like a worm. A numbing, little tingle went all the way up to his fingers. He grumbled. It had only been a day since he last sat at the Well to absorb its daemyn and fuel his arm, and already he was feeling the need to recharge. His arm hungered for it, and as a result, his soul hungered for it, too.

Sitting at the Well, absorbing daemyn—he hated it. The only thing worse was going without it.

I'll get there soon, at least, thought Justin. *I bet I can make it to Esthean by midday.*

Once the fruit was gone, Justin gathered his things and started moving. He closed his eyes, calling on aurym to feel the life forces of everything around him. Far off in the distance, he saw and felt something that did not match its surroundings. In the bright blur of life forces, it was a dark void—just like his arm. It was the absence of life; it was the absence of aurym. Daemyn.

The Treasury.

CHAPTER 89

"Blast!" said Marcus Worth. "I can see them now!"

Now that Leah redirected her attention, she could see them, too. There were ships coming upriver through the Borderwoods, and the thousand or so Darvellian soldiers along the edge of the forest were waiting for them.

"Ah, so that is their plan," said Sif. "Ferry their soldiers across the river."

"Never mind that," growled Olorus. "Who knows how many more they're transporting within the guts of those ships!"

Leah could already see three vessels so far, and more were coming. She looked at Hook, whose eyes were sharper than the rest, and she was surprised to see that he was grinning.

Hook looked at her and signed, *"They are war galleys. The first is a demon ship. The rest are not."*

"A demon ship," Leah said. She squinted toward the river. "Leading Mythaean war galleys! It's Gunnar!"

No sooner had the words left Leah's mouth than the truth appeared to be confirmed. There was a visible change in the Darvellian lines on the riverside. Suddenly, they were backing away from the river, forming ranks, drawing bows and crossbows and hurriedly preparing to fire on the ships.

"I don't believe it," said Olorus.

"An ally of yours?" said Sif.

"An ally," said Leah, "but with those Darvellians there to meet them, they will be killed before they can unload. We have to attack them."

Hook tapped her shoulder to get her attention. *Too risky. The main army would move forward and cut us off.*

Leah's teeth were grinding as she watched the river. She saw the *Gryphon II*, oars rising and slamming into the water to power it upstream. It was hugging the opposite side of the river, but the waterway was narrow. They were well within range as the Darvellians launched their first volley. Arrows and projectiles rained down on the League ships.

"A'cru'u'ol will ride."

Leah turned. Sif watched the river with determination in his round, teary eyes.

"You can't attack them," said Olorus. "You'd be cut off."

"But we can approach from the city side and provide cover as the ships unload," said Sif. "Our mounted archers can be there in minutes."

"You would place your people in direct fire, to help them?" said Leah.

"Your people are our people, princess," said Sif. "And we will save our own, any way we can. You have only to say the word."

She did not have the luxury to hesitate. Every second lost meant more arrows raining down on Gunnar's people.

"Hook, will you go with them?" said Leah. "You can find Gunnar and get him up to speed, and move his people inside the city walls. Any of them who can fight can report to Endrus."

Hook saluted, and he and Sif hurried off. Worth moved in to take Hook's place at her side.

"My lady," said Olorus. "The enemy is charging."

Leah turned. Like a great wall, Darvelle was coming forward. Several lines of cavalry led the way, followed a battalion of infantry. The snow was falling harder now, evolving from pellets to thick, heavy flakes swirling wildly on the breeze.

CHAPTER 90

All was mayhem. They had known it would be mayhem, but no amount of mental or physical preparation could have prepared them for this.

Gunnar was fairly sure it was snowing, but the air was so thick with projectiles that it was hard to tell. Whether word had gotten out about their plan or it was just an unlucky coincidence, enemy soldiers were everywhere.

The *Gryphon II* had hardly even broken from the edge of the forest when the first arrows and quarrels started falling. They whizzed past like swarming hornets, plunked into the river, hit the hull, and slammed into the ship's newly built makeshift fortifications with the incessant pounding of a hailstorm. Barrels, beds, boxes, tables—every object that could be spared had been stripped for parts and nailed together, creating ramshackle walls along the sides of each of Gunnar's ships. The sails had been stretched across the vulnerable side to serve as netting to help catch, or at least slow, the missiles.

Saner men might have turned back. Saner men certainly wouldn't have mutilated their own ships to serve temporary purposes. And that was why Gunnar had never gotten along very well with sane men.

The thudding of strikes against the hull was unending. Gunnar watched from the stairwell that led below decks as pieces of the improvised fortifications broke loose against the pummeling quarrels and swayed on their supports. Adonica and Pool were beside him on the steps. The crew, the passengers, and the oarsmen were crammed in the holds below. On deck, a hunched helmsman steered according to the directions of a barely protected navigator perched low upon the bow, gesturing over his shoulder to indicate their distance from the banks.

Everyone was suited up. Even the oarsmen rowed in battle gear. Now, it was up to Gunnar to decide what happened next. The ships would have to be abandoned, he knew that. The best-case scenario was to tie off somewhere and unload his men at the soonest opportunity. They would have unloaded in the Borderwoods and marched the rest of the way, but knowing that Darvelle was primed to attack Cervice, Gunnar hadn't wanted to risk the time it would take to lead poorly trained volunteers slogging through thick woods in the cold. And it was a good thing he hadn't. Darvelle was already here. Nolia needed their help.

Still, as the arrows fell, it was hard not to wonder if he'd made a terrible mistake.

The battery of projectiles finally became too much for a section of wall at the front of the ship. The nails gave. It toppled inward. The navigator narrowly dodged the falling debris, only to be turned into a pin-cushioned by half a dozen arrows at once. The blunt force sent him stumbling backward and over the opposite railing. His cry was drowned out by the splash of his body in the river. It wasn't fun and games anymore. People were dying. Because of Gunnar.

Gunnar started to head out to take the navigator's place, but a hand grabbed his shoulder and pushed down hard. It planted him on his rear, and Adonica sprinted past him, legs pumping, her helmet on her head and a circular, wooden shield held up in defense. An arrow hit the shield and stuck there. She jumped, landed on her knees, and slid across the deck into position at the bow of the ship, where she began shouting orders back to the helmsman with her shield still raised against the onslaught.

"Blimey," said Pool, still ducked on the stairwell behind Gunnar. "I think I'm in love."

"She's too much woman for you, lad," Gunnar said. He craned his neck to shout down the stairwell. "We're getting close! Everyone, get ready!"

"Hey, *one-eye!*"

Gunnar turned his attention back to the bow. Adonica had about a dozen quarrels stuck in her shield already. Tiny tongues of fire climbed the shafts. The Darvellians were shooting flaming arrows.

That's not good, thought Gunnar.

"Look starboard!" Adonica shouted.

Peeking out from his hiding place, Gunnar saw the walled city of Cervice and the surrounding countryside. The snow was driving in sharp, diagonal trajectories, occasionally swirling on updrafts in complete circles. And charging through the snow, across the field, straight for them, were what appeared to be hundreds of barbarians on steedback.

"Oh, come *on.* . . ." said Gunnar.

They were bearded and clad in furs, riding bareback with stout recurve bows in hand. Even from here, he heard the whooping and screaming of war cries as they charged at the Holy Army ships.

Gunnar had almost resigned himself to the inevitable end when he recognized the soldier leading the charge: a man with long, dark hair tied back by a headband.

"Hook, you beautiful son of an aurochs!" Gunnar shouted, laughing. He turned to face the man at the wheel. "Hard to starboard! Run us aground!"

The frantic helmsman spun the wheel full around to the right. Gunnar braced himself as the gray sky shifted overhead. The *Gryphon II* slammed into the river's banks with a grinding lurch. Gunnar drew his cutlass and turned and shouted into the hold, "Everyone over the side! Abandon ship!"

CHAPTER 91

Pool led the way. Throwing caution to the wind, the portly little sailor hustled up the stairs and made a break for the starboard railings where he unrolled each of the prepared rope ladders over the side in succession. Sailors and soldiers followed as Gunnar waved them on.

The Darvellians' flaming arrows were taking their toll. The *Gryphon II*'s sails—draped over their portside fortifications—had caught fire. Under ordinary circumstances, a relay of water buckets could have prevented the flames from spreading, but ordinary circumstances, these were not. Gunnar waved to the helmsman, who abandoned his post with pleasure.

Hook and his company of bearded wild men were returning fire across the river at the Darvellians. Pool climbed down the rope ladder for the banks below, and men and women of the Holy Army followed his example. At other points along the river, the scene was repeating itself. The rest of the ships in Gunnar's convoy had followed the *Gryphon II*'s lead and were crash-landing into the shoreline as sailors and soldiers threw down ladders or nets to climb down. Gunnar saw one of the wild men abandon his mount, help a woman onto his steed, then slap the animal's rear to send it racing back toward the city with her safely aboard. But Gunnar's gaze was torn from the scene by the sudden realization that his ship was moving.

People were still streaming up from below deck on the *Gryphon II*, but the combination of the abandoned oars, the unmanned rudder, and the river's current was causing the ship to drift—to rotate in place.

Gunnar cursed. The makeshift fortifications were already on fire and falling apart, but if the ship kept turning, their exposed side would be facing the enemy. The people still trying to escape would be left out in the open. Directly in the line of fire of enemy crossbows.

A rush of air whizzed past Gunnar's face like a low-flying bird so close that it made him shrink back involuntarily. He heard a meaty thud, and an oarsman rushing past shouted out in pain. A crossbow quarrel was buried up to the fletching in his arm.

"You'll be all right, lad!" Gunnar shouted. He helped the injured man across the deck to one of the ladders. "Hurry, now!"

The flames on the fortifications had spread, creating a wall of fire. The ship was still spinning, and Gunnar could now see the Darvellian crossbowmen and archers on the bank. Some of them had clear shots now. The bodies of the unfortunate littered the *Gryphon II*'s deck.

Finally, the flow of people from below decks ceased, and the last of the oarsmen hopped over the side. Only Gunnar and Adonica remained. Adonica had retreated to the center of the deck but was pinned down behind a chunk of dislodged fortification. Flaming quarrels pounded down around her relentlessly, splitting and shattering into splinters and shards of barbed metal. As the river continued to push at the ship, Gunnar knew that Adonica's position, and his, were just moments away from being completely exposed.

"Lor!" Gunnar shouted. "Now or never! Come on!"

Adonica inched from cover. She was met almost immediately by a glancing shot from a quarrel. She cried out in anger and retreated back into cover, a deep gash carved across her upper arm. A loud ping resided as another shot hit the top of her helmet and was deflected to the side.

"Just get out of here!" she shouted at him.

"Nothin' doin', private!" Gunnar yelled.

A stray arrow coated in flaming pitch hit the deck near the toe of his boot. The burning drops splattered, spreading flames across the boards, and Gunnar stomped his foot to bludgeon them out, shouting, "Why does this keep happening to my ships!"

CHAPTER 92

Justin stood before the ruins of the Treasury.

The fact that he had made it here was proof that his amateur navigation skills were at least moderately effective, but he owed most of it to aurym. He had been able to feel the Treasury—and see it when his eyes were closed—from miles away.

Standing in the same spot where Kallorn had taken him prisoner not all that long ago, Justin was again amazed at how the jungle had reclaimed these ruins. Vines, flowers, giant ferns, and even entire trees grew out of the top of the structures. He had to unfocus his eyes to see the patterns of doorways, arches, and caved-in roofs. The pits and hollows were like the orifices of a skull.

He had been told that this place was a ceremonial proving ground for newly initiated Ru'Onorath. He tried to imagine Ahlund as a boy his age or younger, standing right here, taking on the challenge of facing daemyn. How, Justin wondered, had Ahlund come to be part of Cyaxares's strange brotherhood of warriors? And where had he come from, and who had he been, before that?

Justin squinted at the vine-draped stone doorway. The Well was nothing compared to this. This place stank of evil. Daemyn oozed from it like fluid from a punctured sore. And maybe it was just his imagination, but it seemed even more sinister here than it had during his first visit.

So why do I want to go in?

It didn't feel like any malevolent temptation luring him. It was more like curiosity. Maybe part of him wanted to prove he could do it. Or maybe it was his arm.

Even now, he could feel the demon arm recharging, sucking in the daemyn that seeped from the Treasury. But the *source* of energy was down there somewhere, within the ruins. A bigger, more potent version of the Well, perhaps? Whatever it was, it was strong. Maybe strong enough to keep his arm satiated for a long time.

Justin hardly even thought about what he was doing as he stepped forward. The curtain of vines over the doorway was stiff and strong. They creaked in protest as he pushed them aside, drew his sword, and stepped into the darkness of the Treasury.

CHAPTER 93

It felt more like a dream, or a nightmare, than reality. Olorus and Worth were at her sides, but here, on the front lines, there was only so much protecting they could do. Her life was in her own hands.

Killing her first Darvellian—parrying his sword strike before running him through with her saber and throwing him to the ground—had inspired a strange reaction in her soul. It was a combination of horror, surreal awe, and glory all at once. Snowflakes clung in her eyelashes as she fought. When the next enemy came at her—launching a clumsy strike with his axe at her upper body—her hands responded automatically. She deflected the blade and sliced horizontally below the attacker's helmet. Her aim was perfect. Her saber cut through his neck as cleanly as a butcher's knife. Even as the life poured from his throat, he raised his axe to strike at her again, forcing her to slice a second time and finish the job.

She heard a hollow clang and turned to see an enemy footman's face bloodied by a strike from Olorus's shield. On her other side, Marcus Worth grabbed a Darvellian soldier's weapon-arm with both hands and knocked him to the ground.

The necessary detachment of Leah's emotions from her actions verged on an out-of-body experience as she turned and cut another man down with one swift stroke. A few yards away, a Darvellian charging toward her went down with a set of arrows buried in his chest courtesy of the Nolian archers atop the bridge fortifications. All around her was crashing, smashing, screaming, bleeding, shouting, and slashing, but Darvelle hadn't gained an inch. Cervice's lines were holding. Her forces hadn't even needed to fall back to the bridge yet.

And suddenly, over the din of battle, Leah heard a bell.

Worth had just stabbed a man through the stomach when he dropped back, taking Leah by the shoulder and leading her back through Cervice's defenses, away from the front lines.

"Do you hear that?" he said, shouting to be heard.

"They're sounding the alarm on the city walls," said Leah. Sheathing her sword, she realized that her hands were covered in blood—none of it her own. Almost a quarter-inch of snow already lay on the ground, and she scooped up a handful of it to scrub off the blood. "More trouble along the river?"

"Or a second Darvellian wave," said Worth. "Let's get you to the command post and find out."

"Not without Olorus," she said.

On cue, the lieutenant came shoving through the Cervice lines. He had started the battle with a spear, but that had evidently been lost or broken. Now, he had his shield in one hand and a short sword in the other.

"Bells?" he growled. "Or are my ears ringing?"

"Captain Worth, I'm leaving you in command here," said Leah. "Unless you hear otherwise, the contingency plan stands. Any difficulties and you pull back, drop the gate, assemble your phalanx on the bridge, and await orders."

"Of course," Worth said. "And Leah, if anything happens to me, I want you to know, I. . . ." He swallowed hard, and a look of embarrassment crossed his face.

"Off those steeds, soldiers!" Olorus was shouting to some nearby cavalry.

Worth was unable to finish the sentence. Leah gave him a fleeting glance as Olorus pulled her to the waiting steeds. The two of them mounted up and set the steeds galloping into the zigzagging bridge fortifications, back toward the city proper.

CHAPTER 94

The deck rocked beneath Gunnar's feet. Looking aft, he realized the *Gryphon II* had slammed into the next ship behind it in the convoy. Both were on fire and floating aimlessly as the survivors raced toward the city. If Gunnar and Adonica were to count themselves part of that group, they were going to have to do something fast.

Gunnar grabbed hold of the open door that led below decks, threw his body weight back, and ripped it off its flimsy hinges. He hauled back and tossed the door sliding across the deck to where Adonica was crouched, pinned down and now almost in direct line of Darvellian fire. Adonica grabbed the door. It took a good deal of effort to lift, but once it was up, it shielded her entire body. Putting it between her and the enemy-occupied shoreline, she backpedaled toward Gunnar. It rattled with the impact of enemy arrows as she went, but it held firm.

As soon as Adonica was close enough, Gunnar jumped out from his cover and joined her behind the door-shield, helping her carry it toward the side of the ship.

"Not a bad little bit of improvisation, if I do say so myself," said Gunnar.

A sharp cleft in the top of Adonica's helmet marked the place where the glancing shot had hit. Blood snaked down her forearm from the gash across her bicep, but, amazingly, there was a smile on her face as they reached the railings.

"I owe you one, admiral!" she said.

She slapped Gunnar in his rear end, then grabbed the closest rope ladder and hopped over the side. Gunnar stood there for a moment, still holding the door in shock—until an arrowhead burst through inches from his head, shaking him from his daze. He propped the door up to cover him as he reached for the ladder, but he couldn't resist one last look around before abandoning ship. The *Gryphon II*'s fortifications had become an inferno. Fires raged across the decks, and flaming arrows were still raining down. He hastily saluted the ship that had been so good to him, grabbed hold of the rope ladder, hopped over the side—

And almost landed on top of Adonica.

"Nowhere to go!" she yelled up at him.

Looking down, Gunnar saw she was right. It was a drop of fifteen feet to the shallow waters below. The ship had pivoted so far around that even here, on what was once *opposite* the enemy side, a few fire arrows had hit the hull. As luck would have it, one had found the rope ladder. The bottom half was already missing, and Gunnar could feel the heat of the flames that were eating away at what remained.

Most of the wild riders and Holy Army fighters were halfway to the walls of Cervice by now, but directly below, Gunnar spotted Hook Bard on steedback, wading out into the river to position himself beneath the ladder. Adonica was looking up at Gunnar.

"Let go, private!" Gunnar said.

"What're you worried about?" shouted Adonica with a smirk. "Aren't you supposed to go down with the ship?"

Gunnar let go with one hand and drew his cutlass. "Stupid rule."

He swung his sword, and it chopped cleanly through the ropes below his feet.

Adonica's smile disappeared. He thought he heard her saying something inaccurate about his mother as she plummeted downward. Half a second later, she landed squarely in Hook's outstretched arms.

Gunnar sheathed his weapon and jumped.

He aimed for the shallows near Hook, prepared to tuck and roll, just hoping the fall wouldn't break his ankles. Arrows and quarrels plunked down all around him as he hit the water. Instead of his ankles breaking, his feet sank in thick mud, and he fell forward. He swallowed about a quart of river water and came up coughing and sputtering, half-crawling up the bank.

Hook's wild men on steedback used their recurve bows to provide cover for the Holy Army stragglers. They loosed volley after volley of arrows across the river. Some of their archers, one steed, and at least two dozen of Gunnar's oarsmen lay facedown in the snowy grass, arrows in their backs. The rest were making their way toward the city. Hook rode with Adonica on the back of his steed. Gunnar saw no sign of Pool, Borris, Lycon, or Ragny.

"Do you need assistance, my friend?" someone called.

Gunnar turned to answer but realized he wasn't going to be given the chance. A bearded wild man on steedback leaned down, grabbed Gunnar by the arm, and pulled him off the ground with frighteningly little effort. As the steed accelerated, Gunnar scrambled the rest of the way onto its back. Arrows whizzed by, but he and his rescuer were steadily moving out of range.

Gunnar looked back. The *Gryphon II* was engulfed in flames. With no one left to propel it upstream, it was drifting back the way it had come, downriver, floating aimlessly into the Borderwoods. It was already tilting slightly to one side—the first sign of the sinking process. If Gunnar hadn't lost his hat a few days before, he would have removed it.

CHAPTER 95

The hallway inside the vine-curtained door led to stairs the descended downward. The majority of the Treasury, it seemed, was a dungeon leading deep underground.

No sunlight could penetrate through to illuminate his surroundings. The a'thri'ik shards of Justin's cat's eye blade—which glowed naturally in the absence of sunlight—gradually came alight even without the help of aurym. The jade fluorescence of his sword revealed carvings on the walls. But instead of the motif of animalistic yet dignified deities common in the city ruins of Esthean, the walls here were lined with writing. Strange glyphs and pictographs ran in rows on either side of the hallway.

Moving forward, Justin found that the lines of writing came together ahead of him at a large, stone stela mounted above stairs leading deeper underground. It was a carved depiction of a monstrous creature. Some of it had crumbled with age, but the image was clear.

A cythraul.

Justin raised his sword like a lantern to get a better look. The image was far from photo-realistic; it had a disproportionate body. Like the medieval artwork in his high school history books on Earth, it stood in a strangely one-dimensional pose, looking a bit smashed together. Somehow this imperfection of design only made the creature more terrifying. Its arms and horned head were too big for its body, and there were strange, wavy lines coming out of its mouth. Justin wasn't sure what to make of this last feature until he saw what the High Demon was holding in its hand: a disproportionately small human body. The head was missing, and the same lines that poured from the cythraul's mouth also sprouted from the human's headless neck.

Justin kept moving, passing beneath the image of the cythraul. He wondered if the stela was a depiction of a battle from antiquity. Was it the account of some great tragedy committed by an ancient enemy? Or, given the daemyn that dominated this place, was it a glorification? An object of reverence.

Maybe these ruins were a temple devoted to the worship of demons. The thought made Justin shudder, yet he still felt himself being drawn deeper.

The daemyn grew stronger as he went. The air was thick with it. He closed his eyes briefly, trying to call on his aurym senses to see via life forces, but it was no good. Like the hollow darkness given off by his arm, this place was as black as ink in a bottle. Even in the short time since he'd learned how to sense life forces, he had grown accustomed to it. Without it, even *with* physical sight, he felt like he was flying blind.

He reached a room at the bottom of the stairs. The ceiling was only a few feet above his head, but the walls extended far off to either side. He couldn't tell how far they went.

The floor and ceiling were mirror images of one another, with stone blocks so perfectly laid that they were without visible seam. He moved to the side and finally found a wall. There were a few doorways, but most were caved in. A few opened into shadowed, unknown destinations. But he knew where his objective lay. Directly ahead. At the opposite end of this great hall.

Justin's throat was dry. If the darkness and the daemyn weren't enough, the silence rounded it off. He slid his foot against the floor just to make a sound. The scraping noise sounded loud, but it was there and gone again in an instant, leaving not even the whisper of an echo in the low-ceilinged room. It was like being in a coffin.

His demon arm tingled fiercely. It was hungry.

CHAPTER 96

As she climbed the stairs toward the command post on the eastern walls, Leah caught a glimpse of the aftermath of the battle that had taken place along the river. The dark humps of corpses could be seen on both sides of the river, still warm enough that the snow that fell on them melted. The fire on the sinking *Gryphon II* had spread to other ships, and, having run aground at the entrance to the forest, its flames had ignited the low-hanging, leafless branches of the Borderwoods. Several trees were already blazing, pouring smoke into the sky. The snow was picking up. Leah hoped it would be enough to quench the flames before they became a wildfire.

"What's all this?" said Olorus, behind her.

The command post was crowded with people. She recognized Pool and Borris—crewmen of the original *Gryphon*, since promoted to captains in the Athacean League. There was Cimon Endrus, as expected, as well as Hook with a shallow cut across his lower jaw. Standing beside him was Sif of the Cru.

And there, in the midst of them all, and escorted by a big Hartlan man and a female soldier in a helmet, was Gunnar Erix Nimbus.

Leah marched forward, parting the crowd. She embraced Gunnar, but he returned the embrace only halfheartedly. When she let go of him, she found a strange, shocked expression on his face.

"Good to see you, princess," he mumbled.

"What is it?" asked Leah. "What's wrong?"

Gunnar put on a brave face and pointed.

Turning to follow Gunnar's gesture, Leah was confused to realize he was pointing not toward the Darvellian front, but toward the opposite side of the city.

Across the western farmlands, some of Cervice's forces were rushing to join the skeleton crew of guards on the fortifications. Beyond, beneath the snowy skies, out over the fields, and past the outlying plantations and long-emptied storehouses, the entire horizon looked like it had been blotted out by black ink.

And the black ink that was moving.

For as wide as her field of vision allotted, the horizon was covered with moving blackness, as if all the shadows in the world had coalesced into a singular mass. Tall, terrible shadows waded through oceans of smaller, child-sized ones. A demon army stretched across the fields for miles. It engulfed the land like a deluge, flooding the world.

Advancing on Cervice.

CHAPTER 97

There were three-dimensional carvings along the walls here, too. More cythraul, disproportioned like the one upstairs and committing similarly bloody acts.

The shadows cast by the carved cythraul in the light of Justin's sword made the creatures look like they were stepping right out of the stone as he walked by. He half expected them to.

Daemyn soaked through his demon-arm and into his heart. He felt fear knocking at the barriers of his will—unnatural fear that was uncanny, terrible, and wrong. It was more like panic than fear, a phobia threatening to overwhelm his fortitude. Many before him, he'd been told, had been driven to unconsciousness by such fear, some to the brink of madness. Even his own father, if Cyaxares's stories were true, had suffered from paranoia and violent outbursts due to his prolonged exposure to daemyn. In his letter, Benjamin had confessed to becoming a slave to a strange, powerful darkness within him. It was a feeling with which Justin was becoming increasingly familiar.

But I can do it, thought Justin. *I might need daemyn to keep my arm functioning, but it won't overwhelm me. I can resist it.*

Dead-eyed stone cythraul watched him from the walls, wreathed in lines of ancient writing. He passed multiple doorways leading who-knew-where, but he kept going. The daemyn here had a source, an abyss that was as deadly midnight black as a demon's heart, and he was going to find it.

The room ended abruptly. Ahead was a wall with an arched doorway leading deeper into the ruins. He couldn't see through it, but he knew he was close to the source. He called on aurym to try to sense something of what lay beyond, but again, the haze of daemyn drowned out everything around him.

When he reached the doorway, he leaned in with his sword raised, tentatively willing a bit of aurym through the blade to brighten its glow. Little by little, the green light revealed a room.

The room was smaller than he might have expected but no less extravagant. Scattered across the floor were coins, plates, jewels, and bars of silver and gold. It seemed the name "Treasury" was no accident.

The brighter he willed his sword, the more gold he realized there was. Piles of it lay feet deep in some places. It wasn't a fortune. It was a hundred fortunes. Piled on top of the other, protected for eons unknown by an aura of daemyn so strong. . . .

Justin froze. Amid the piles of gold, his probing light landed upon a pair of booted feet.

He pushed forward, increasing the light from his sword. The booted feet became armored legs. Still farther, and the legs connected to hips seated in a massive, gold-encrusted throne. Draped over the armrests were hands—hands that did not belong to any statue.

Justin took another step, pushing the shadows back to reveal an armored torso. Then shoulders. Then a neck.

A sharp, clean chin. A man's face. A diamond-studded crown.

"Hello, Justin," said Avagad.

PART IX

ACROSS

THE

STYX

CHAPTER 98

Justin's body stood frozen in place, but he was adrift on an ocean, pummeled by waves of confusion, anxiety, terror, regret, and uncertainty. His mind was a net, capable of holding only one of them at a time before it slipped through to be replaced by another. Amid the turbulence, one thought broke through and took precedence above the rest.

I was wrong.

The Kharon. The spiritual realm Avagad had used to forcefully communicate with him—first in the Drekwood and multiple times after that. According to Cyaxares, it was the same process used by the Nameless One, the god-king of the demons, to enforce his will on his servants. And Justin was in it. How long he had been in the Kharon—and how much of his experiences had been illusions—were questions he hardly dared ask. This strange dreamworld was a place where terrible deceptions could be enacted, where illusions became real, and reality was subjective.

Avagad stood from the gold-encrusted throne. His ceremonial plate armor was white as snow, and Justin wondered what sort of metal it was. The shoulder guards were curled upward like talons. A diadem sat on his head, set in the center with three diamonds in triangular distribution. A silver scabbard was at his belt, containing a dagger, and upon his back was what appeared to be a sword as long as a spear. Even in the dark, his eyes pierced like cold needles.

"Did you think I would just forget about you, Justin?" he said.

Justin's breath came in rapid gasps. How could he have been so careless? So arrogant? A few personal victories, and he thought he understood? Justin had suspected he was in an illusion back when he'd first encountered the Ru'Onorath council. Cyaxares had managed to convince him otherwise. But had his first instinct been correct?

Avagad bent over and scooped an armor-plated hand through the gold coins at his feet. He stood and uncurled his grip, letting them fall through his fingers. They jingled and pinged as they landed.

"All a man could ever want, right here," said Avagad. "Such vast riches, lost to time. Forgotten by the world."

With one coin left in his palm, Avagad closed his fingers around it, forming a fist.

"For most of human history, we have willingly killed for this," he said, squeezing it in his hand as if testing its weight. "Nothing but some shiny metal. A silly thing, really, to lose one's life over, when, like everything else, it all just turns. . . ." He opened his hand, but instead of a coin, his palm contained only a bit of crushed, lustrous powder fine as table salt. He sprinkled it on the ground before him. "To dust."

Justin's throat was dry as sandpaper. He had to swallow hard before he could speak. "What are you doing here?"

Avagad looked at him and dusted off his hand, frowning. "I shouldn't even dignify that question with a response. I told you what I wanted, Justin. I made it very clear what I'd do if I didn't get it and what you needed to do to avoid forcing my hand. I won't pretend your decision disappointed me. Like most great men, the only thing I enjoy more than the victory is the fight to get it."

"My decision?" said Justin. "I didn't make any decision."

"In that way, you did," said Avagad. "The rules were clear. I gave you a generous timeframe to decide. Did you think if you ignored my offer it would just go away? Negotiations are over. I've come to collect, Justin Holmes, the progeny of the legendary Benjamin."

Avagad put his hands behind his back. He strode forward, wading through the piles of gold as effortlessly as if they were water. Justin took a step back.

"My boy, I knew who you were from the very beginning," said Avagad. "Not many alive today know the name Benjamin Holmes, but in my position, I am privy to a great deal of otherwise unobtainable knowledge. The moment I saw you, I knew you were the offspring of Benjamin, one of the most powerful fallen angels to ever live. And I knew you would be formidable if you survived long enough to discover your true power. From then on, my mission was to provide you with the necessary push for your aurym abilities to catalyze. I knew it would take a gentle touch to push you in the right direction without breaking you. With legions of soldiers and demons at my disposal, why would I entrust the capture of an ethoul to some oafish brute and his thugs? Lisaac was disposable. You were *meant* to kill him—and to escape my cythraul in the Athacean wilderness. I was counting on it. I also never doubted you would become a great leader among the people. A hero of Hartla. A founding member of the Athacean League. The inspiration behind the volunteers who call themselves the Holy Army. That is why I have allowed you to remain free all this time; the greater the following you build up, the greater the schism when you join my cause. I made you an offer, Justin. I had faith that, whether in prudent acceptance or noble defiance, you would rise bravely to the occasion. I assumed that if you accepted, you would seek me out, and if you rejected my offer, you would lead the charge against me."

Avagad shook his head, making a *tsk-tsk* sound with his tongue and teeth.

"Imagine my disappointment to learn how critically I overestimated you. You chose neither. Instead, you let your allies fight and die while you hid from it all. I wonder if the great Benjamin would be proud of his sniveling bitch of an heir."

Justin felt his throat clench.

"So, here we are," said Avagad. "By now, you must understand what happens next."

"You can't make me do anything," Justin said. "I've learned about the Kharon. It's a spiritual plane, not a physical one. You can talk to me in this world. You tried to get me to walk through a doorway once, but even that was something you couldn't *force* me to do. You can't make me. . . ."

Justin trailed off at the wry grin on Avagad's face. The grin morphed into a giant, toothy smile, which evolved into laughter. Deep, halting, and derisive.

"Little boy," said Avagad. "You have fought cythraul. You have harnessed the aurym power of a fallen angel. And now, you are training in the ways of Cyaxares's Ru'Onorath. You have progressed too far to be ensnared by such a primitive device as the Kharon."

Justin gritted his teeth. "What do you mean?"

"If you were in the Kharon," Avagad said, "I would not be able to do—*this.*"

Avagad's foot shot forward and stomped the ground. The impact zone erupted in a flash of light, driving a shockwave tunneling forward through the piles of treasure. Twin sprays of coins jetted to either side in the shockwave's wake as it tore across the floor and hit Justin. The invisible force that slammed into him felt like a slab of ice. His feet left the ground with a gut-wrenching impact. Somehow, he managed to keep his sword in his hand as his body sailed backward, through the antechamber doorway, and out into the main hall. While still airborne, Justin realized the meaning of Avagad's words.

He wasn't in the Kharon. He was in the Treasury. And so was Avagad.

CHAPTER 99

"Full retreat," said Leah.

"What!" cried multiple voices.

Her makeshift war council—Olorus, Hook, Sif, Endrus, Gunnar, Pool, Borris, and a few others—all stared at her.

"Pull everyone back from the bridge," she said. "Get all our people, every sword and shield at our disposal, to the western walls."

"Battle still rages on the eastern front, my lady," Endrus said. "If you order a retreat, Darvelle will be emboldened. They will attack with full force, and our gate won't stand for long if no one is there to defend it. There will be nothing between our enemies and the city's inner walls."

"Then we will surrender," Leah snapped.

"My lady!" Endrus fumed. "You are raving mad if you think I will stand idle as you—!"

"Darvelle attacks with an army," said Leah, stepping aggressively toward Endrus. "But they are at least humans. Humans who acknowledge surrender and know mercy."

"You would beg for their mercy?" Endrus spat.

"You misunderstand me," said Leah. "Even when men do not choose to exercise mercy, they at least *know* it." She flung a hand westward, toward the horizon, where the black ocean of the demon army was growing larger and nearer by the second. She raised her voice for all to hear, saying, "Demons do not acknowledge surrender—they have no concept of mercy! Some of you have seen your friends, family, and countrymen torn open to be feasted on by these animals. To fly the flag of defeat to Darvelle would make this a bleak day, but at least some of our people would survive, if not myself. Such a humiliation would be far more preferable, I think, than allowing every soul entrusted to us to be consumed by these beasts even as their lungs still draw breath." She turned back to Endrus, lowering her voice. "*All* of our people would die. Do you understand? Everyone. Even if it means losing to Darvelle, we need every soldier we've got fighting to keep the demons out of this city. So order the retreat, Captain."

Endrus's mustache twitched. "This is a mistake," he whispered. But at full volume, he said, "At once, my lady!" With a quick salute, he raced down the stairs from the command post, mounted up on a steed, and took off toward the eastern front.

The rest of Leah's war council stood and watched. Soldiers, archers, and cavalry were assembling along the western front, but at the moment, Leah did not have the heart to order her friends to join them.

Finally, one of them broke the silence.

"A word comes to mind," Sif said. "Serendipity. I have been told it means a happy, unexpected circumstance. It occurs to me that we are experiencing the opposite."

"Those are called catastrophes, friend," said Gunnar. "And I, for one, am starting to feel like they're following me wherever I go. Olorus. Hook. Mighty fine to see you boys, by the way."

"You as well, gardener," growled Olorus. "Reunited in the midst of bloody conflict, as usual."

"Right," said Gunnar. "Lycon. Adonica. Either of you see if Ragny made it out?"

The female soldier only shrugged, and the big Hartlan shook his head, saying solemnly, "I haven't seen him, sir."

Gunnar hesitated, then turned to face Leah. "Well, princess, we lost a few, but I've got roughly twelve hundred soldiers suited up and ready to serve. You just tell us where to go and when."

Leah stared out at the demon army covering the countryside. She tried to remember what the land had looked like during happier times, not so long ago, but it was hard to picture it, now.

"Leah?" Olorus said.

"Olorus, please see to it that every able body we have is positioned along the western fortifications," she said. "As for anyone who is less than able or less than willing, if they can shoot a bow, get them on the walls. Anyone who is absolutely unable to fight, Hook, please see to it that they are safely within the palace. Station some of the High Guard at the doors. Sif, please get your soldiers ready. You can escort their families to the palace. Gunnar, take your people to the western walls, too. If they have bows, I want them firing. And you—Lycon and Adonica, was it? For now, I could use your help setting up a command post."

Leah hardly heard their acknowledgments. Instead, she found herself deep in thought, trying to estimate how few daemyn blasts it would take for the cythraul to destroy the city's shoddy fortifications. But defending those fortifications was their only hope. Coblyns were nearly as fast as steeds. Even abandoning the city wouldn't do them any good. They would be run down. She and her people were trapped here.

CHAPTER 100

Justin hit the ground. His neck snapped back, his skull cracked against the floor, and he saw stars.

He heard his sword clatter across the stone as he rolled and realized he must have lost his grip on it. When he finally stopped rolling, he had trouble standing. The floor seemed to tilt beneath his feet. The only light was the green glow of his sword lying partway across the room. He shook his head, trying to steady the dizziness, but it only made things worse.

From the shadows ahead, he heard footsteps and a dull jingle of boots wading through coins.

"You must be a very distant relation of Benjamin Holmes," came Avagad's voice from the doorway. "He was before my time, but I heard many stories about him. A powerful warrior. An expert in the command of aurym. After he was injured by a cythraul's touch, he became a slave to daemyn. Instead of being a savior of the Oikoumene, he became its tyrant. He drove the demons out and set himself up in their place. They say the atrocities committed during his reign were abominable enough to rival the demons. Finally, Cyaxares and Amphidemus forced him to abdicate his throne."

Justin crouched on his knees, fighting the dizziness. He curled his hands into trembling fists.

Don't listen to him, he told himself. *He's a deceiver, you know that.*

"Do you remember my promises, Justin?" said Avagad. "The things I said I'd make you do to your friends? Those promises were not made out of hubris. I took a lesson from the history books, you see. What worked on one Holmes would surely work on another. I ordered the cythraul to turn your arm. Tell me, have you felt it yet? The darkness calling to you? The same dark power that enabled your predecessor to save a world—and then rule over it?"

Justin shot to his feet. He pumped his legs, darting across the hall to retrieve his sword—

A screaming, roaring sound drew Justin skidding to a halt. Through the shadowed doorway of the Treasury antechamber came a flash of cobalt blue light. The light grew, and suddenly, chilled air came racing from the doorway—a visible blue wind. And then, with an audible *snap*, the blue wind turned into a slicing gale. Justin jumped back with hands raised to protect his face. Even from several yards away, the freezing cold seemed to sear his skin. The ground beneath seemed to grow several inches, and Justin realized it was a layer of ice like a frozen river, formed over the floor in an instant.

Flashes of indigo strobed from the doorway, silhouetting Avagad's armored body as he stepped out into the main hall. One hand pointed at the ground in front of him. From his finger, purple flames intermittently shot forth and licked the floor, melting the ice as he advanced.

"Still think you're in the Kharon?" said Avagad. With every word, cobalt-blue flashes seemed to emanate from between his teeth. "Still think this is all just an illusion?"

He swung his hand, and parallel blasts of liquid, indigo fire went uncoiling from his fingertips, forming a horizontal tornado of purple flame that shot up the middle of the room. The ice melted instantaneously, and a suffocating wall of heat pushed Justin still further back from his sword. The peripheral temperature alone was enough to singe the hair off his arm.

"You thought you could hide you from me?" Avagad shouted in a voice that seemed to shake the room. "No one hides from the will of daemyn! Not the mercenary. Not the princess. Not that ship captain. Not Cyaxares in her jungle citadel, either. And certainly not you! I see all. I know where all of you are at all times—and I know exactly what you are doing. Each of you continues to exist *only* because my master has, thus far, willed it to be so."

"The Nameless One. . . ?" breathed Justin.

"Yes," said Avagad. "The father of the cythraul. The creator of the black aurym. Ever has he reigned as god-king of the demon realm of Mu. Once, his children overran the world of men, enslaving the Oikoumene. But fallen angels overthrew the demons. The Nameless One has made multiple attempts to retake the Oikoumene since then, each time thwarted by ethouli sent from beyond this world. Last time, it was Benjamin Holmes who bested the demons. . . . Then took their place as overlord."

"No!" said Justin.

"Have you ever heard the Tale of the United Planet?" said Avagad, pausing to admire the indigo flames dancing from his fingertips. "Two armies of men engaged in a great battle, utterly destroying themselves, only to learn that defeat and despair are the only ways humankind can ever be truly united. Humans are warlike creatures. They will always find a reason to fight one another—until an *outside* force presents itself, that is. Then, they band together out of necessity. Therein lies the problem. Each time the Nameless One and his demons have attempted to take back the Oikoumene since the days of the Ancients, aurym has sent a fallen angel to defend it. It is a repeating cycle. An ongoing struggle between light and darkness that began the day the Nameless One gave birth to daemyn. My master realized that for his next attack to be effective, he needed mankind to do what they do best. To fight one another. Weaken themselves. He needed a human element on his side."

Justin took a step toward his sword but quickly stepped back again when Avagad threw a hand backward in a bored sort of way. Flames shot into the gold-filled room from which he had emerged. Indigo light raged as the room was turned, in an instant, from a treasury into a smelting furnace. Rivers of molten gold snaked out from the doorway.

"I was part of the Brethren when the Nameless One contacted me through the Kharon for the first time," said Avagad. "He made me his disciple. He taught me the ways of daemyn, and with each lesson, I devoted myself more and more to my new master. When the time came to destroy the Brethren, I wiped them out with joy. And for the next five hundred years, I ruled in the east, influencing kingdoms and empires. I was to use a combination of subterfuge, aggression, and deception to inspire the nations of humankind to maintain a constant state of war with one another. To keep them all weak enough so that when the time came, it would take only the *slightest* pressure for all the blocks to tumble.

"Not long after the Nameless One unleashed his armies in the east, you arrived, just as predicted. Aurym always sends a champion. But this time, things would be different. For one, my master has placed his forces under my command. Who better to exploit the weaknesses of the world of men than one who has lived in it for a few thousand years? The other difference. . . . This time, he will *end* the struggle between light and darkness forever. Permanently. He once enslaved the Oikoumene, yet aurym still prevailed. This time, he will stand for nothing less than complete victory over aurym. This time, he plans to destroy it. All of it."

"Destroy all aurym?" said Justin. "But that means . . . destroy all *life*?"

Avagad's only response was a smile.

"But thats mean you, too!" Justin shouted. "Why would you—?"

"Dear boy," said Avagad. "You, of all people, should know by now how narrow the gulf is between the living and the dead."

Justin looked down at his demon arm. "You would let yourself be turned?"

"It is the greatest blessing my master can give! To survive the purge of all living things and become his devoted servant fully. . . ." Avagad took a deep breath, and the flames dancing from his fingertips seemed to glow brighter than ever. He stared at Justin's arm. "I will not deny my envy for you, that you were gifted a taste of the turn before I was. But all is in accordance with the master's plan. It is not yet time for me to join the ranks of demonkind. He still has need of me in this lesser, human form."

"You don't really believe that, do you?" said Justin. "If this Nameless One of yours cares so little for life—hates aurym so much—what's to stop him from just killing you, too, once you've served your purpose as the 'human element' in his plan?"

Avagad sighed and hung his head. "Your stupidity astounds me, Justin. It truly does."

While Avagad's eyes were turned to the ground, Justin took the opportunity to check the position of his sword across the room.

Avagad looked back up at him. "Think of all the resources that have been expended for the sake of your capture. Think of how much trouble my master has gone through to keep you alive rather than simply snuffing you out while you were still a weakling. Think of the web we have worked to weave just to help you discover your power."

"What are you talking about?" said Justin.

"*I* am not the human element, Justin," said Avagad. "You are."

Justin gritted his teeth. "I would never do that."

"Ah, but you would," said Avagad. "And you will. Benjamin Holmes drove back the most recent demon invasion, but because of his wound, he became a slave to daemyn. He established himself as the absolute ruler of the Oikoumene. And, as I said, what worked on one Holmes will work on another. Your arm was turned so that you, too, would become a slave to the Nameless One's will. *Nothing* has happened that has not been part of my master's plan. Not even your choice of company. . . . Only Cyaxares, hiding in the wilderness, managed to survive the breaking of the Brethren. None of the fabled immortal men were left alive—none but those who committed the betrayal, that is. I did not act alone, you see. I had a partner. I still have a partner. A fellow member of the Brethren who worked with me to destroy the rest of them. And has continued to work with me in service to our master. Keeping a close eye on you. Protecting you, when necessary. Teaching you. You know of whom I speak."

CHAPTER 101

The blood had drained from Justin's face. "No," he said.

Avagad smiled. "Remarkable, isn't it? Zechariah has always been so adept at bending people to his will."

"No," Justin said again.

"Oh, dear," said Avagad. "What's the matter? Your wise teacher who just happened to be in the right place at the right time to take you under his wing—is he not the unassuming, kind old hermit you thought he was?"

Justin shook his head. "You're a liar. I don't believe you."

"Why ever not?" laughed Avagad. "There's no point in deceiving you any longer. We knew aurym would send a fallen angel to stand against the Nameless One. But this time, instead of fighting that angel, we would simply control him. So we created a ruse in which the angel became our ally instead of our enemy."

Avagad sighed. "However. We ran into a problem. We were dealt an inferior specimen." He sneered, his words brimming with disgust. "Your initial resistance was promising, but as things have progressed, you've proven yourself to be nothing a dull-witted, ignorant brat. We had hoped that you would inspire and lead a great portion of humanity, and that when you joined us, they would follow you. But you lead no one. You have no followers. You only follow others. It is all you seem to know how to do.

Worthless boy. Time after time you have disappointed. You're not enough of a threat to be killed outright; your innate abilities, at least, are still desirable. That is one of the reasons I'm here. It's time for you to be turned. To make you into the weapon you were always destined to be. And, naturally, to destroy the Ru'Onorath once and for all."

"There's too many of us," said Justin. "You'll never—"

"I'm not alone, you dunce," said Avagad. "An army of men and demons surrounds Esthean. They are attacking the city even as I speak. It took a great deal of concentration to mask their presence from the Guardians' senses, but I appear to have been successful. My master has allowed Cyaxares and her bastion of aurym to survive long enough. There will be no survivors. None but *you*, anyway. But I daresay you'll hardly recognize yourself after today."

Justin's rage boiled over. He raised his hand, and aurym flowed through him like a river, pushing back the darkness, calling for his sword.

The cat's eye claymore lifted off the stone floor and flew through the air, quick as a flash, into his grasp. Justin saw, for a split-second, a look of surprise on Avagad's face. Justin hacked his sword in midair, summoning aurym and pushing it through the aurstones in the blade.

Emerald aurym energy rent open the air. Light exploded from the blade, manifesting in an energy wave far too large for the low-ceilinged room to contain. The aurym blast gouged trenches through the floor and the ceiling alike as it raced toward the man with the crown.

Avagad raised his hands in defense. Indigo flames clashed with Justin's green energy. There was a violent crack like thunder, and before Justin could see more, half the ceiling caved in.

Shards of broken stone whizzed outward from the point of impact. A piece slashed Justin across the cheek, and he fell back. Looking up, he realized that cracks were spreading across the ceiling directly above him.

CHAPTER 102

Justin scrambled backward as a piece of the ceiling landed in front of him big enough to have crushed his legs. Debris rained down around him as he stood and ran. Falling stones pelted his shoulders and bounced off his sword.

Justin hit the stairs, taking them three at a time, but the cave-in was spreading behind him. The entire Treasury rumbled and shifted as if caught in an earthquake. He reached the upper level and raced toward the light of day at the end of the hall. He had almost reached the doorway when a smashing sound prompted him to look back.

The stela of the cythraul, which had previously been mounted over the staircase, came flying halfway down the hall as if launched from a cannon. It shattered against the ground.

Behind it, at the far end of the hall, through the dust and falling rubble, a flickering, indigo shadow was growing.

Justin stabbed his sword forward, firing a green spear of energy down the hallway, toward the source of the indigo light. It sliced through stone like butter, but he didn't wait to see the impact. He turned and sprinted toward daylight.

Justin ran through the Treasury doorway, through the hanging vines, out into the light.

He felt a pulse. A shockwave rippled through the air, knocking him to the ground.

Behind him, the tunnel collapsed in on itself, bringing down what must have been thousands of pounds of stone. Clouds of dust reached out after him as he got to his feet. He paused only to sheath his sword. Then he sprinted into the jungle without looking back.

An army of demons. Surrounding Esthean.

Ahlund, Kallorn, Cyaxares, and all the others, thought Justin. *If Avagad really managed to conceal their presence somehow. . . .*

But another thought wriggled into his mind.

Zechariah. . . . No. It's a lie. It can't be.

CHAPTER 103

Gunnar squinted against the driving snow. He could feel it clinging to his mustache as he hurried along the lines overseeing the distribution of his people on the walls.

Calling them "walls" was a bit generous. Some of the fortifications on Cervice's western front were stacked, mortared stone, but most seemed to have been cobbled together from scraps of deconstructed houses. In some places, the builders had incorporated existing standing buildings. Leah's new command post was on top of a stone guardhouse, a once freestanding structure now part of the walls.

It was along these ramshackle defenses that the forces of Cervice lined up, waiting for the fighting to begin: Mythaeans, Nolians, Endens, Cru, Holy Army men and women, and other fighters from all over Athacea. There were thousands of them. The eastern front had been abandoned by order of the princess, and all forces were gathering here, in defense against an army of demons beyond count.

Yet, despite their numbers, it was deadly quiet.

These shoddy walls wouldn't hold long, thought Gunnar. *A couple of cythraul blasts will punch holes straight through them. The coblyns will pour through, and that'll be the beginning of the end.*

He exhaled sharply, hoping his feelings didn't show. Leah's orders were logical. If they weren't, he or someone else would have told her as much. But that didn't mean he disliked this any less. It was almost worse to know that even if they did everything right, the outlook was still so bleak.

Ladders were leaned against the walls for archers to climb into positions. Gunnar pushed his way to the front to climb up. He didn't like the way the ladder swayed under his weight. He reached the top and found himself on sets of planks hardly a yard wide. Ahead, rolling forward over the countryside, was an ocean of black.

"By the seas. . . ." Gunnar breathed.

There must have been forty to fifty thousand of them. Most of the black army was made up of coblyn bodies, but others, to his surprise, were men. Who they were, he didn't know. Not for the first time, Gunnar wondered how wicked a man's heart had to be to willingly side with such monsters.

Several cythraul were spread out among the hordes. Relatively few, given the size of the force, but that wasn't surprising. A single cythraul was enough to wipe out a village. Five or six of them as generals, leading these numbers, was more than enough to take a large city.

Gunnar watched as the front of the black army reached a storage silo on the outlying farmlands. The men on the front lines spread out to go around it, but the coblyns slammed mindlessly into it like raging waters. The silo shuddered, tilted, bowed, then went down and was swept under and lost in the black. A few seconds later, the sound of its collapse reached Gunnar's ears. And through the whistle of the cold wind, he could hear the first distant murmurings of the hoots, grunts, screams, and caws of coblyns.

Gunnar thought about Pool and Borris, somewhere among this army. He thought about Lycon and Adonica with Leah at her command post. He thought about the men and women of the Holy Army—people like little Ragny the cook—brought halfway across the continent to fight here, in a battle that would likely be their last. Nobody had seen Ragny since the arrows started falling on the river, but that was sometimes the most difficult part of the chaos of all-out war. Not every casualty received a proper send-off.

Not every soldier killed in battle got the honorable end, or the burial, that he or she deserved. Gunnar had only learned secondhand of the death and burial of Samuel, one of his oldest friends. It had happened on a small island battleground in the Raedittean—hit by a stray arrow fired by one of the archers serving in Yordar's confederacy. A one-in-a-million shot, right in the heart. Maybe Ragny had been dealt a similar fate, hit by an arrow and knocked overboard. Or maybe his was one of the bodies on the shoreline, presently being covered by falling snow. That was the way of war. Sometimes you befriended allies whom you never saw again and whose fates you would never know.

In the end, what difference does it make? thought Gunnar. *In a few minutes, the rest of us will receive the same.*

And this time, would there be anyone to tell the tale? Anyone still alive to wonder what happened to them?

At the sound of a whistle, Gunnar looked up, squinting his single eye against the snow. Leah, Lycon, Adonica, Olorus, and Hook were assembled at the command post along with a few others he did not recognize. All were staring out over the field of battle except for Adonica. She faced Gunnar. One hand was waving his direction, and the other was pressed to her lips, whistling.

CHAPTER 104

"The gate has fallen," said Cimon Endrus.

Leah turned her attention to the east. Her heart grew heavy. Darvellians were pouring through a broken section of the gate, funneled through the zigzagging walls that lined the bridge. Soon, they would cross the river. An enemy army would be within the outer city of Cervice, something that had not happened since the time of Leah's great-grandfather. Now, all that separated them from the heart of the city were the main walls, which were easily scalable, unguarded as they presently were.

But Leah found herself barely interested in the Darvellians at the moment. Because a new arrival on the scene had her full attention. It was a *fourth* army.

The unknown force was materializing out of the wooded marshlands south of the city. The lookouts had seen them first. The initial report was that large "creatures" were emerging from the marshes, surrounded by foot soldiers. She had assumed that this was an extension of the demon force. But now that she saw the creatures, she wasn't so sure.

Gunnar hopped over the waist-high stone barricade that separated the roof of the guardhouse from the rest of the fortifications.

"All right," he said, his breath producing vapor in the cold air like smoke from a chimney. "What's everybody looking at?"

Without word or sign, Hook handed the spyglass to Marcus Worth, who in turn passed it to Gunnar. Gunnar looked at Leah and the others once more, trying to read their expressions before accepting the spyglass. He steadied himself against the roof's barricade and raised the glass to his single eye.

Leah watched Gunnar as he scanned the southern wilderness where the creatures had emerged. It was clear by his body language when he spotted them.

Gunnar our down the spyglass, turning to look at Leah.

"War elephants?" he said.

CHAPTER 105

Leah didn't have any response. She took the spyglass from Gunnar's limp hands and looked again. Even at the height of summer, most of the trees on the marshlands south of Cervice remained bare. A Nolian settlement—abandoned, like many others now, according to her scouts—was situated along the edge of the marshes. Wildlife flourished there.

But not usually elephants.

Through the spyglass, Leah saw the brownish-gray, hulking bodies lumbering out of the marshlands and across the fields. Trunks hung from their faces. Tusks protruded from their upper jaws. Childhood memories of seeing the great creatures at city festivals filled in the rest of the details for her: skin as tough as tree bark, bristled with wiry hair. Giant ears. Human-like eyes. In days of old, they had commonly been used in battle, but she had never seen such a thing in person before. The geometric shapes of platforms and towers were mounted on their backs. There were at least fifty of them, and clustered around their legs were legions of footmen and cavalry.

Leah saw no demons among this force yet, but there could be little doubt. These were the front lines of another army coming for Cervice.

"Darvelle is retreating," said Olorus.

Leah turned and realized he was right. Despite their progress, the Darvellian army was turning about. Apparently, they too had seen the newest arrival to the battle and were not keen to try their luck against the other two armies attacking Cervice.

Our enemies are so many that they flee from one another, thought Leah. *Like scavengers fighting over a carcass.*

She suppressed a shiver. The analogy was too accurate for comfort.

Three invading armies or two, it hardly mattered. The demons' forces would be the end of Cervice.

Gunnar suddenly wheeled from the scene and started to marched away.

"Where are you going?" Worth demanded.

"I'm gathering my people," said Gunnar, "and I'm charging."

"You can't be serious," said Endrus.

Gunnar raised both hands in the air, one toward each army. "Why not?"

Without another word, he hopped over the side of the wall to climb down the ladder. After a short pause, Adonica Lor turned to give them all a grin and an informal salute before following Gunnar over the side.

"With all due respect, my lady," Endrus said. "You cannot let your subordinates display such impudence—"

"Gunnar is not my subordinate," said Leah.

"Yes, and with all due respect, Endrus," Olorus said, "shut your mouth before Hook shuts it for you."

Endrus's face turned red. As for Hook, he had gotten the spyglass back and was leaning forward intently, studying something far ahead. At first, Leah assumed he was counting the numbers of the newly arriving army. But there was something about the way he stood.

"What is it, Hook?" said Leah.

Without looking away from the spyglass, Hook raised one hand and made a series of signs that were so quick that Leah missed them.

"What?" said Olorus. "Are you certain?"

Still not looking back, Hook signed, *"Yes."*

"Ha!" barked Olorus, a smile spreading across his face. "Ha-ha!"

"What is it?" Endrus said with a scowl. "What did he say?"

"Yes!" Olorus yelled. He turned to look at Leah with glee on his face and fire in his eyes. "Ha-ha-*haaa*! Yes, yes!"

"The man has . . . *lost* it, it seems," Sif said almost reverently.

"Olorus?" Leah said, gently.

"Yes, that explains the elephants!" Olorus yelled, swinging his arm toward the advancing army. "Why didn't I think of it before—it's obvious!"

"Our impending doom," Endrus snapped. "Yes, quite obvious—"

"Doom? Doom!" Olorus bellowed. "I think not! Leah! That is Raeqlund!"

"Rae. . . ?" Leah breathed.

Finally, Hook turned from his spyglass to look over his shoulder at her. This time, she had no difficulty in reading his hands, nor the smile on his face, as he signed, *"The old man leads the charge."*

CHAPTER 106

Zechariah!

The name repeated in Justin's head as he sprinted through the jungle.

Everything had changed; when the Treasury ruins collapsed behind Justin, it was as if a great veil had suddenly lifted. An army of demons was surrounding Esthean. Until now, Avagad had kept its presence shrouded, somehow.

Now, Justin could feel it—could see it, miles away, when he closed his eyes—the dark auras of demons beyond count, surrounding the crater that hid the city ruins. As he sprinted through foliage and hopped over logs, he began to hear the thunder-cracks of cythraul unleashing daemyn blasts to rain hell down on the city.

Justin forced his legs to pump harder. Deception was the most consistent weapon in Avagad's arsenal, but this army had not been a bluff. It made Justin wonder how much more of what he said was true.

The mid-morning sky was cloudless and sunny, but ahead, Esthean was darkened by storm clouds of the metaphysical variety. He saw cold, black lightning strikes clashing with bright sunspots of their antithesis: expelled aurym energy. The Ru'Onorath were fighting back. But there were too many demons. It wouldn't be enough.

A swelling of aurym power erupted close by. Skidding to a halt, Justin squinted through the underbrush in its direction. Through a break in the trees came a flash of orange and red. Flames cut through the jungle like napalm. A sound hit his ears that was like the roaring of an entire pride of lions. A cythraul. Very close.

Justin drew his sword and sprinted for the source of the commotion as more flashes lit up the forest. Between the trunks and almost impenetrable vegetation, he glimpsed Kallorn, his sword raised in defense, then Ahlund, with flames sputtering from his blade. Then the cythraul. It was a small one, only ten feet tall, but instead of two eye sockets in its fleshless skull, there was only a solitary, abnormally large one set in the center of its head. The body was armored with rock-hard bone plating. It held no weapon, but a black axe was wedged in a giant tree nearby with the blade sunken halfway into the trunk—apparently the monster had gotten it stuck there and hadn't been able to pull it free.

The cythraul spun toward Ahlund, bringing down a giant fist he narrowly avoided. At the same moment, it shrugged off a bolt of lightning from Kallorn's sword. It raised its hand toward Kallorn, producing a ball of daemyn energy.

Justin rushed in, sword held low. There was little margin for error. Kallorn and Ahlund were so close that if Justin's attack went wide, they would be hit by the aurym blast just as surely as the cythraul. Justin crow-hopped, let his aurym flow, and hacked at the air in a quick, downward chop.

A narrow, arcing plowshare of emerald energy sizzled through the jungle like an extension of his blade. It cut between Ahlund and Kallorn.

The cythraul saw the attack coming and raised its hands to defend itself, but the aurym-blade hit it fully down the middle and kept going into the jungle, splitting the monstrous body in half from cranium to navel. Its single eye socket cracked in two like a broken egg, spilling black goo as the halves dropped away from each other.

Purple energy discharged from the falling body. Ahlund and Kallorn dove for cover as it imploded. Giant fronds of vegetation wilted instantly within the blast. Trees caught ablaze with black and purple flames. Bone plates crunched and collapsed inward until there was nothing but a pile of dust, flashing and crackling with the final remnants of its energy.

"Incredible," Kallorn said before he had even gained his feet. His clothes were scorched—by fire or daemyn, Justin did not know—but he seemed otherwise unharmed. "Truly, you are an ethoul."

"A rather convenient time to become a believer, Kallorn," said Ahlund as he, too, stood.

Ahlund's long hair was soaked with sweat. Blood dribbled down his neck from a cut behind his ear. Justin didn't know how long they'd been fighting that monster, but it was a testament to their strength that they had put up such a fight.

"What are you two doing out here?" asked Justin.

"Last night, I . . ." said Ahlund, but he hesitated before proceeding. "Aurym spoke to me again. I sensed that a dark entity had taken up residence at the Treasury. I tried to sneak away to investigate, but I was followed." He shot a look at Kallorn.

"You should count yourself lucky you were," said Kallorn, sheathing his sword.

"What you sensed was Avagad," said Justin. "He's here. For me."

Ahlund's brow hardened into a scowl.

"I fought him in the Treasury," said Justin. "I got away, but he told me that an army of demons is surrounding Esthean."

"So, that is what I am sensing," said Kallorn, turning in the direction of Esthean. "There must be thousands of them."

"Avagad used some sort of trick to hide their presence from detection," said Justin, "so he and the army could march right to the city without being noticed." He looked at Ahlund. "But you still felt it."

"I tried to warn Cyaxares," said Ahlund. "I told her something was coming, but she trusts no one but herself, least of all an exile like me."

"Avagad lured me to the Treasury," said Justin, "and I was stupid enough to come running. I managed to escape, barely. I can't sense him now, but he could be using that same trick again. He plans to destroy Esthean and everyone in it. . . . Is there any quick way off the island?"

"Our boats are kept in the bay along the southern shoreline," said Kallorn. "On foot, we can make it there in an hour's time, perhaps."

Justin looked at Kallorn. He had not missed the inflection placed on the word we.

"Surrounded as it is, that city is as good as a sealed tomb," said Ahlund. "There is no way out."

"No alternate escape route?" said Justin. "No secret tunnels? Caves?"

"Only the stairs," said Kallorn. "And a ladder hidden behind the waterfall that empties into that small stream in the crater. It offers a bit of cover but not enough to conceal a mass evacuation."

"Where does the stream empty, then?" asked Justin.

"It seeps into a series of pits like the Well at the opposite end of the crater," said Kallorn. "Esthean was built as a sanctuary to stay hidden from the world. It was never meant to defend against an attack. My brothers and sisters are outmatched, outnumbered, ambushed. . . . Many have surely been killed already. It feels as good as betrayal to leave the rest, but even with our help, what chance would they have?"

"Whatever we are going to do," said Ahlund, "we must do it quickly."

Both men looked at Justin. Justin blinked, suddenly realizing they were waiting for him to decide.

CHAPTER 107

Justin's throat tightened. His gaze wandered to the giant demon axe stuck in the tree nearby. He closed his eyes. In the distance, through the bright and colorful life forces of the jungle, he saw the great, hulking shadows of cythraul—dozens upon dozens of them—surrounding Esthean, launching bursts of blackness down into the crater. Spears of light shot back up at them. Justin was *seeing* the battle in real-time. As he watched, he heard a chorus of hooting overhead, followed by a rustling in the trees. Without looking, he knew that the primates he had seen nesting in the ruins of Esthean were fleeing through the jungle. At least someone had made it out.

"How many people are in Esthean?" asked Justin.

"One hundred and twenty, at most," said Kallorn.

Justin squeezed his hands into fists. His aurym power was strong, but couldn't fight a demon army. By grace alone he had escaped Avagad's trap at the ruins. For what? To run headlong into another? He, Kallorn, and Ahlund wouldn't do anybody any good by charging into a battle they couldn't win.

One hundred and twenty people. Far fewer than the soldiers lost at Gaius because he wasn't there—or in any number of other battles fought in the interim, while he was gone. This was war. And in war, people died. The effort of trying to save them sounded quite noble in theory, but hopping atop the funeral pyre wouldn't help those who were already dead. Cyaxares wouldn't want that. She would want him to escape. So long as *he* survived, hope lived on. War wasn't about winning battles. It was about doing today what would make the world safer tomorrow. And today, it was more prudent to retreat, regroup, and face the enemy again another time. Escape was the only viable option, for the sake of the greater good.

Escape. The logical course of action. Keep hope alive. The greater good. So why did it feel so wrong?

Rise above the self.

"Justin," said Ahlund. "You know what you have to do."

It was true. He did.

CHAPTER 108

"Raeqlund!" Leah said.

It seemed too much to hope for. But as she stared through the spyglass at the elephants, the cavalry, and the ranks of soldiers, the truth was undeniable. She saw men on steedback in colored robes, with flowing dark hair and long, curled beards. They wielded crescent-shaped scimitars and pole-mounted glaives. Atop the elephants were archers. Flags flew over their platforms—banners as red as blood with a slashing, white line through the midsection. The flag of Raeqlund.

On the platform atop the lead elephant stood a figure in gray robes. His white beard hung past his sternum. In his left hand was a sword. His sharp-featured, ancient face was contorted in a rallying cry as he raised his right arm to order a full charge. A buckler shield was mounted to his forearm, and where a hand had once been was instead a gleaming, metal hook. Zechariah was leading the charge.

He had been gone for so long—the immortal man who'd played such a pivotal role in mustering Leah, Justin, Ahlund, and the others to this fight—that Leah had nearly forgotten about his mission in the south: to journey to Raeqlund, to present himself before a king whose father he had once served as a royal advisor, and to bring one of the world's largest military powers into the Athacean League.

They were still coming out of the woods. Several hundred war elephants led a charge of what must have been twenty thousand soldiers marching through the driving snow. Their lines were shifting. They weren't marching on Cervice. They were marching on Nolia's enemy. And Darvelle's forces were still retreating.

"You're right, Olorus," said Leah. "It is Raeqlund, and they are turning to attack the demons."

"They've come to aid us?" Worth said.

"But Gunnar and Adonica!" said Lycon. "If they open the gates to charge out now—!"

A booming crash like thunder cut him off. Leah turned to see the aftermath of an enormous explosion along the walls. Bricks, rubble, and bodies rained down. A black spheroid of daemyn was still visible, with sizzling, purple energy dancing in the aftermath. The front lines of the demons were only a few hundred yards away, and the first of the cythraul had just blown a hole through Cervice's wall with a single shot.

The same cythraul, sitting astride a massive, eight-legged mount, raised its hand again. Another daemyn blast shot from its palm and hit the same section of wall even as survivors of the first strike attempted in vain to flee. Men were swallowed up or burned alive.

A building-sized chunk of wood and stone broke loose from the fortifications and toppled. At an order from the cythraul, the charging coblyns formed an arrow-headed attack pattern and rushed for the opening. The coblyns responded faster to orders than even the most disciplined human army, almost as if they shared a singular consciousness with their masters.

"Merciful spirit . . ." said Cimon Endrus, and Leah was reminded that he, like many others here today, had never seen one of these creatures before, had never witnessed what they could do.

"Even the strongest walls cannot hold back High Demons," said Leah. "Raeqlund comes to our aid, but we will still be destroyed if we do not act, now."

"You mean—?" said Sif.

"We follow Gunnar's lead," she said. "We charge out."

"*Yes!* Ha-ha!" shouted Olorus. "Let us polish our spears with demon blood!"

"Olorus, Hook," said Leah. "Hurry down there and tell Gunnar to hold off his charge for a minute. We'll all go out at once. Marcus, I need you and Sif down there, too, leading your people."

"Yes, your highness," said Worth.

"Understood, princess," Sif said.

As they left, Leah looked around. She had assigned her junior officers and officials like the mayor of Ronice to oversee the safety of civilians falling back to the palace. It left only Lycon Belesys and Cimon Endrus remaining at the command post with her.

"Shall we coordinate from here, then, my lady?" asked Endrus.

"Only until I am certain everyone is where they need to be," she said. "Then I will charge out with the rest. You gentlemen are welcome to join me."

Lycon's bird-nest of a beard shifted as he smiled. "Good," he said. "It has been too long since my demon blade has been dulled on coblyns."

Leah turned back to face the battlefield. The demon army was adjusting to the encroaching threat of Raeqlund. A portion of the demons were turning to face them. At the walls of Cervice, the cythraul in the lead launched another daemyn attack that took a bite out of the fortifications so close that she felt the shockwave ripple through the walls and shake the rooftop beneath her feet.

The coblyns raced for the hole in the wall. The gate dropped outward, and the forces of Cervice charged to meet them.

CHAPTER 109

"What did you say?" asked Kallorn.

"I said," said Justin, "we have to go to Esthean."

Kallorn made a face. "But we will be killed."

"And if we run away and let our friends die here, we will live," said Justin. "But if we have to set aside our humanity to save the world, we'll be left with a world I wouldn't care much to live in."

Ahlund looked at Justin. His face might not have shown much, but Justin thought he saw something in his eyes—something that looked almost like pride.

Justin took a deep breath, adjusted his sword on his back, and started walking. He knew without looking that Kallorn and Ahlund were following him.

He had very nearly decided to flee. Not for the first time since discovering his aurym abilities, his mind had almost tricked him into a course of action his heart knew to be wrong. That ever-present enemy, daemyn, had a subtle presence in the thoughts of men, and it had *almost* convinced him that escape would be a noble course of action. How easy it was to convince yourself you were doing the right thing when that thing meant saving yourself. Allowing people to die when it was within one's power to save them was worse than wrong. It was reprehensible. That was a hard truth to reconcile. But there it was.

For a moment, abandoning Esthean had seemed like a necessary evil, but when Justin really listened, he knew the truth. There were no necessary evils, and there were no greater goods. No evil was ever necessary, and all good was great.

"We will probably die," said Ahlund.

Justin picked up the pace, closing his eyes to navigate by aurym alone.

"I know," he said.

CHAPTER 110

The guards kicked loose the winch levers. The chains whizzed free as the gate fell outward. It went down like a tree—slowly at first, then gaining speed with the descent. There was a sound like thunder, along with the cold, dark sensation of daemyn followed by bricks and bodies falling from the walls.

Gunnar, on foot, raised his cutlass and shouted, "Charge!"

The fall of the gate revealed a countryside covered in black. A roiling sea of coblyn bodies, their numbers beyond count, with the giant forms of cythraul intermittent throughout, was all Gunnar's eye could see. The gate crushed some of them, causing it to lie lopsidedly. Lines of coblyns loped and galloped over it, and the human forces ran to meet them.

"Charge!" echoed Adonica Lor, racing forward to lead the charge herself.

To Gunnar's surprise, Pool and Borris were right behind her with weapons raised. Then Sif of the Cru on steedback, leading a cavalry of mounted warriors. Next was Hook Bard, leading League and Nolian soldiers.

Gunnar watched as the first line of coblyns was chopped to pieces under sword, axe, and spear. The Holy Army gave a collective war cry as they, too, charged into the fray.

"My old friend!" growled Olorus as he came up beside Gunnar and grabbed him by the shoulder. "Another battle in which I may call you *brother*! Let us charge out together!"

Gunnar smiled. He gestured regally toward the fighting, with a flourish of his hand, and said, "Age before beauty."

Olorus let loose a nonsensical growl of glee as he ran for the gate, and Gunnar ran right alongside him.

The two of them pushed through to the front lines, where humans and demons fought atop a growing pile of bodies. Child-sized animals sprang forward with long limbs swiping and slashing.

"Through wind and tide!" Olorus shouted. "And squall and foe! Eh, gardener?"

Together, Gunnar and Olorus raced past Hook, past Sif, past Pool and Borris, past Adonica, over the pile of corpses—and into the mass of leathery demon bodies. Gunnar hacked the head off his first kill. Olorus's spear picked off two at once, and his shield swung in brutal arcs, cracking skulls like melons. Black blood shot skyward like spurting ink.

Rage and glory filled Gunnar as he sliced a coblyn in two. He felt claws sink into his back.

"We shall. . . !" Gunnar shouted, stabbing a face. "Ever. . . !" Teeth punctured his arm. He grabbed the coblyn by the head and twisted, snapping its neck. "*Journey . . . on!*"

CHAPTER 111

Ducked low in the underbrush alongside the creek that flowed into the Esthean crater, Justin watched as half a dozen cythraul raised their hands, summoned blacked spheres of daemyn energy, and launched them down into the crater. The demons were not invading Esthean. They were bombing it.

Coblyns at the cythraul's feet jumped up and down, giggling with delight. To Justin's regret, he realized that there were some humans standing alongside the coblyns, too. Some fired arrows into the crater. Others threw rocks. To think that men and women were actually fighting *for* these creatures, killing their fellow human beings, made him sick.

Every so often, a blast of aurym power—flame, lightning, or other varieties—came up out of the crater directed at the demons, sometimes hitting a few coblyns. The Ru'Onorath were fighting back. But it wouldn't be enough.

"That hidden ladder is behind the waterfall ahead, right?" asked Justin.

"Yes," Kallorn replied. "But I don't see how we make it there without being noticed, first. If they see us, they'll know where to fire those daemyn attacks, and we'll be at their mercy while we descend. But why enter the city at all? We should do our fighting up here."

"Fighting them isn't the goal," said Justin. "There are too many cythraul. We need to get our people *out*. And the only way to get anyone out is if we get in first."

"And what route do you propose for getting them *out*, once we're *in*?" asked Kallorn in a patronizing whisper.

"Kallorn, until a few weeks ago, my biggest problem was my Chemistry midterm, and I didn't even have an escape plan for that."

"What are you talking about?" Kallorn demanded.

"I'm doing my freaking best—that's what I'm talking about!" hissed Justin. "You got a better idea?"

Ahlund whistled like a songbird to get their attention. Justin turned to look at him. The tall mercenary said nothing, he only gestured to the creek beside them. Then, wordlessly, he pivoted his head, following its path toward the edge of the crater. To the waterfall.

"Oh, no," Kallorn.

"How deep is the pool?" asked Justin.

"You cannot be serious," said Kallorn.

"How deep?"

Kallorn sighed. "Probably deep enough, if you hit the right spot. But that is a big 'if.' The bottom is uneven. Twenty feet deep in some places, five or six in others."

"As long as we keep to the center," said Ahlund, "we should slip down into the deeper, main channel."

Kallorn pointed to the cythraul ahead. "There's still the problem of getting past them."

"If we remain hidden below the water," said Ahlund, "perhaps use logs or branches to hide our—"

"Leave them to me," said Justin.

Justin crept forward. Ahead, six cythraul were packed together around the waterfall's crest. The hooting and howling of coblyns sounded a bit like a mixture of wild dogs and elementary school recess. The human fighters with them shouted in strange languages as they fired their bows down at the city.

Justin swallowed hard against a dry throat. His own death was a sobering concept, but it was with an anxious heart that he assessed the killing of human beings. Destroying a monster was one thing. Killing a person was another matter.

Like it or not, he thought, *this is war, and you're a soldier.*

Justin looked over his shoulder at Ahlund and Kallorn.

"Get ready to jump," he whispered.

Kallorn nodded. Ahlund touched his forehead, then his shoulder, then his heart: mind, body, spirit.

CHAPTER 112

Gunnar ducked beneath a handful of razor-sharp claws and stabbed his cutlass into the attacker's body. He, Olorus, and Sif fought within view of one another. Not far away, Hook and Adonica fought side by side, and Borris and Pool were somewhere behind them.

Four more coblyns came at Gunnar at once, and he drew a pouch of seeds from his belt and tossed them to the ground. A quick flow of aurym was all it took. The seeds burst into life—splendidly colorful tufts of flowering greenery came into being among the never-ending blackness. The plants moved according to Gunnar's command and grabbed the coblyns. They wrapped around their necks, broke their spines, and stabbed spear-like branches through their bodies.

"I greatly enjoy watching you do that!" Sif said from beside Gunnar. The Cru man feinted forward, tricking a coblyn into reacting, and promptly sliced its head off.

"I say it's cheating!" Olorus growled from the other side.

"All's fair in war and—something else, I can't remember what," said Gunnar. He turned toward Olorus. "Is that really our old man out there, leading that army?"

"That, or some other one-handed codger," said Olorus. "Either way, he's getting the job done."

The hills south of Cervice were high enough that even from here, Gunnar could see the Raeqlund army as it collided with the demon lines. Elephants stomped through coblyns. Arrows cascaded from archers on mounted platforms. And here, outside the walls, the battle had turned in the humans' favor. In fact, to Gunnar's astonishment, he realized that the coblyn lines were actually receding. For a moment, it looked like the demons were retreating. But then the true reason became apparent.

"Cythraul!" Olorus shouted.

"Fall back!" Gunnar yelled, waving his sword.

The monster came riding straight toward them on a giant, eight-legged mount. Any coblyns that did not part quickly enough were trampled indiscriminately. From its forehead grew two huge, backward-curling horns, like a ram. In one hand, it carried a rusted hatchet with a haft as thick as a sapling. A nearby group of League soldiers were too engrossed in battle to see it coming, and Gunnar could only watch as the ram-horned cythraul cut through them all with a single swing of its hatchet. Then the cythraul bent down and snatched up a Nolian soldier by the waist.

The man shouted in surprise as he was lifted off the ground. The cythraul slowed its advance to a trot, carrying the flailing man like a gaffed fish. It held the soldier up, high above the ground, presenting him for all to see. And then, in one quick motion, the cythraul hauled back and slammed the captive against its own ram-horned skull with a wet crunch.

Several soldiers around Gunnar gasped. The cythraul slammed the poor man into his horns again. And again. Then it pitched the man's broken body aside like a used handkerchief.

A moment ago, Gunnar had been surrounded by comrades bellowing brave war cries. But after that display, there was near silence. He did not have the heart to turn to see how many had retreated.

The cythraul turned. It looked straight at Gunnar. Perhaps it sensed his aurym power. Whatever the reason, it was suddenly as if Gunnar were the only human on the whole battlefield. The cythraul opened its blade-toothed maw and roared at him, but Gunnar felt no fear. Only rage. He did not wait for it to charge him. With sword held low, he sprinted at the monster, and he yelled, "Make me work for it, whoreson!"

CHAPTER 113

All along the walls, coblyns were slamming against the fortifications. Directly below Leah's command post, coblyns broke their claws against the building walls. A hole had been blasted through a nearby section of the wall, but a phalanx of Enden soldiers led by Marcus Worth kept the flow of demons at bay.

"Most of the cythraul have turned their sights on Raeqlund," said Endrus.

"It may give *us* a fighting chance," said Lycon, "but it puts Zechariah and his army in danger."

That was true. Even as Leah watched, a blast of daemyn hit the elephant beside Zechariah's, beheading the magnificent creature and killing many mounted warriors on the ground. The rest kept charging.

And very soon, she reminded herself, *you will be down there in the thick of it.*

Leah turned back to survey the walls. At the gate, Gunnar, Hook, Olorus, Sif, Adonica, and their soldiers had done an admirable job of holding strong against the horde, but now, a ram-horned cythraul astride a giant mount was charging to meet them. The sight was enough to make Leah question her endorsement of the charge. Cythraul were not invincible. They could be killed, but it always came at a great cost, and as her friends stepped forward to meet it, she wondered how many of them would—

"Ragny?" said Lycon.

Leah had been leaning on the edge of the wall, but at this, she turned around. She, Lycon, and Endrus were the only ones left at the command post, but someone else had joined them: a small man with no armor or weapon in sight, clad in ill-fitting and un-remarkable clothing, like a servant. There was a burn mark across the bottom of his shirt, and the legs of his trousers were in tatters. Beneath a severe widow's peak hairline, a matting of scabbed blood trailed from a nasty gash. Most notable was the fact that his right hand was coated in bright red blood, as if he'd been holding a gushing wound.

"I can't believe it! Ragny!" said Lycon, raising his arms and rushing to greet him. "When we couldn't find you, we thought—"

Lycon was in mid-sentence when Ragny dropped low, darted forward, and kicked Lycon in the chest.

What happened next was a violation of both fundamental physics and common sense. Lycon probably outweighed Ragny by seventy-five, maybe a hundred pounds. A man of Ragny's size shouldn't have been able to lift Lycon an inch off the floor. And so, as Lycon's feet left the ground, and his body sailed backward through the air, he was probably just as shocked as Leah at what was happening to him. Lycon didn't even get the chance to cry out before his lower body slammed into the raised lip of the roof's edge. He flipped backward and plummeted from the wall like a brick.

"*Lycon!*" cried Leah.

Cimon Endrus drew his sword, but Ragny was faster. Before Endrus could so much as raise it to strike—probably before Lycon had even hit the ground thirty feet below— Ragny lunged. Effortlessly, he smacked the blade out of Endrus's hand, grabbed him by the upper arm near the shoulder, and forced him to the ground. Endrus made a painful noise. He struggled, trying to pull away. Ragny planted his knee on Endrus's chest, grabbed him by the other shoulder, and pulled. Physics and common sense were vio-lated yet again as Ragny ripped off both of Endrus's arms as easily as pulling apart a soft pastry.

Ragny held Endrus's limbs, one in each hand, as he turned to face Leah. From the disembodied arms, the blood fell and dribbled. From Endrus's empty shoulder sockets, it flowed like rivers, but not for very long. Too terrified to run, Leah could only watch Endrus and hope the shock was enough to dull some of the pain as he lay, silent, mouth agape beneath his otter-like mustache, blinking rapidly at the sky.

Ragny looked at the pale arms in his hands as if seeing them for the first time, and dropped them with disinterest. He blinked at Leah.

"What are you. . . ?" she breathed.

She was going to say, "What are you doing?" but the words got caught in her throat. Ragny answered, "Innocen."

PART X

LAST

STAND

CHAPTER 114

Justin drew his sword, called on aurym, and set it alight. With a horizontal swipe, he pushed the power through. A shimmering jade disk erupted from the blade. Its first victims were the trees. Centuries-old giants were severed through the trunks and started to fall.

Justin replaced his sword in the sheath and yelled, "Jump!"

He didn't bother to watch what happened to the enemies ahead. He leaped from the bank, falling feet-first into the creek. Water in his ears muted all sound, and he struggled to get his head above the current. Even behind closed eyes, the sight-sensation of his own attack was almost blinding as it collided with the dark daemyn shapes at the edge of the crater.

He swiped hard at the water, trying to reposition himself at the center of the creek. The gap in the trees—the opening that marked the waterfall's drop—approached must more quickly than he'd anticipated, and with it, the chaos and destruction his power had caused. Everywhere was the cracking, banging, and smashing of trees chopped down by his incorporeal blade. Of the six cythraul, only one turned in time to defend itself, but its efforts were wasted. While the others were torn apart, it was blown backward, chest smashed flat as if caught between a hammer and nail. Black blood spewed from the punctures of its own ribs as it spun and toppled over the cliff. Child-sized coblyns died by the score without ever knowing what hit them. As for the human soldiers, they had time only for a moment of confused terror before the blast either consumed them or carried them over the edge.

The green aurym-wave continued out, over the crater. Bodies were boiled to steam within its glow. Black, purple-fringed eruptions marked cythraul deaths—if they could be said to have ever been alive in the first place.

One of the fallen trees slammed down in front of Justin and bounced against the raised embankment only a few feet above his head, and he floated beneath. Black, demonic ichor dribbled into the creek and clung to the water's surface like oil. Some of the luckier soldiers fled through the collapsing forest while coblyns stood staring, his power having blinded them into a stupor.

And suddenly, the creek disappeared. The bottom dropped out.

Blue sky. The city of Esthean a hundred feet below him. The water stopped flowing and hung alongside him like a viscous curtain. Partially blinded by foamy spray, Justin watched the crater bottom zoom up to meet him.

CHAPTER 115

Where is Justin when you need him? Gunnar thought as he ran.

The cythraul spun its hatchet with the dexterity of a carnival performer and hacked at him. Gunnar jumped back to avoid being cut in two.

Beneath the ram horns on the monster's head, empty eye sockets flashed red. The hooves of its eight-legged mount sank into ground and corpses alike as it advanced. Behind it, the army of coblyns watched from an obedient semicircle, screeching, hissing, barking, clambering manically.

Gunnar dared not look behind him. He could hear grown men cowering to the point of whimpers—and those were the ones who hadn't run. Not that he blamed those who had.

The cythraul yanked on the reins, causing its mount to pull up short and rear, four front legs kicking at the air. It pointed its hatchet at Gunnar.

"I. WILL FEAST. ON YOUR *FLESH*!" boomed its halting voice.

Some of the whimpers behind Gunnar became unashamed wails of terror. Nearby, Olorus shouted orders, commanding the lines to stand fast.

Gunnar pulled a pouch of seeds from his belt and rubbed the fabric between his fingers, feeling the many potential life forces within: vessels waiting to be filled with spirit. He had developed the concoction specifically for use against cythraul. It had sunk a Darvellian warship. Now, it was time to see how it held up against a High Demon.

Gunnar did not feel fear. He did not muse about the past or contemplate the relevance of death. Those were things he had done too many times before and, in a way, had grown out of. The cythraul opened its tongueless, lipless mouth, baring bony fangs in anticipation. The eight-legged demon mount whinnied eagerly, and Gunnar charged again. He raised the pouch of seeds to his sword, slicing the bag open. He tossed a handful of seeds to the monster's side. Its hatchet came down, and Gunnar dove the opposite direction, feeling the impact of the blade shake the ground behind him. He came up and tossed the rest of the seeds to the monster's opposite side.

Gunnar reached for the aurym inside him, grabbed hold of it, and pushed it through his aurstone—an aurstone approximately the size and shape of a human eye, hidden behind the patch on his face. He raised his hands, found the vessels of the seeds, and transmitted a portion of the spirit within him across the gap, into them. The seeds cracked open, shooting up into plants reaching for the cythraul.

Adonica and Hook raced past. They leaped, slicing at the cythraul's left leg. Then Sif was there, riding sidesaddle on his steed. He reached the cythraul and abandoned his steed, jumping and grappling with the head of the demon mount. He plunged his blade into its meaty throat. Then came a roaring charge of Nolian, League, and Holy Army soldiers all at once. The coblyns came to meet them. Amidst the flurry of lifeforms at his command, Gunnar found the plants he was looking for: two trees, one of each side of the cythraul.

The cythraul kicked Hook and Adonica back. It brought its hatchet down, reducing one armored Nolian to a pulpy mess. The demon mount bit a chunk out of Sif's arm as he worked his blade behind its larynx. A blast of daemyn energy from the cythraul's hand disintegrated a swath of charging soldiers like sugar in water.

Gunnar already had the trees to man-height on either side of the cythraul as it fought. He drove the roots into the earth, tying knots beneath the ground for support. The same rope-like vines he had used to tether the Darvellian warship grew up the trunks of the trees and weaved together over the trees' bark like chainmail.

So focused was Gunnar on cultivating his hostile orchard that he didn't see the coblyn leaping at him until it was too late. The child-sized demon came down on him, claws slashing and fanged mouth agape.

CHAPTER 116

As Cimon Endrus died, Leah backed away from the edge of the wall, toward the set of stairs that led down through the interior of the guardhouse. The little man followed her as she moved. Lycon had called him Ragny. He had called himself Innocen.

Leah made no sudden movements. She had a sword at her belt, but drawing it would bring this man's speed into play, and she had seen how fast he could move. And his strength. He had kicked Lycon off the side of the building with the ease of a child punting a ball, and the way Endrus's arms had ripped from their sockets. . . .

The pool of Endrus's blood spread across the rooftop. It seemed pointless to try to fight him, but there were guards at the bottom of the stairs and outside the building, on the city-side of the walls. She just had to make it to them.

Leah reached the stairs, placed her shaking hand on the railing, and stepped down backward, keeping her eyes on him as she moved. He followed her slowly.

"Wh—why?" she said. "Why would you kill those men?"

She was several steps down the stairs. The man called Innocen followed slowly. His first step down the stairs coincided with Cimon Endrus's blood dribbling over the stone, as if following alongside him. The little man said nothing.

"You. . . ." said Leah. "Don't come any—!"

There was no warning. In a fraction of a second—much, much faster than humanly possible—the little man's body went from several yards away to inches from her face. Their noses were almost touching. She could see the pink capillaries in the whites of his eyes. He whispered, "Boo."

Leah jerked back instinctively. Her foot missed the stair, and she fell.

Leah cleared several steps before landing on her back. For some reason, the fall didn't hurt. She looked up the stairs, but Innocen was gone.

Leah scrambled, trying to get to her feet. The landing hadn't hurt; something soft had cushioned her fall. She started to stand when she noticed that her hand was touching someone's fingers. She froze. A dead soldier lay beneath her on the stairs. His eyes were wide open. His blood painted the walls. She had landed on his corpse.

Leah jumped up, stepped over the man, and raced down the rest of the stairs. At the bottom, she emerged onto the brick-laid street along the interior of the fortifications.

All the air left her lungs. Bodies lay everywhere.

They were soldiers. Some of them had suffered variations of Endrus's fate. Others seemed to have had their necks broken. The closest one lay facedown on the road with a fist-sized hole in his back, slightly left of the spine, about where his heart should have been, and Leah remembered the bright red blood coating Ragny's hand.

The chaos of war was loud as thunder on the other side of the walls, yet here lingered a ghostly silence. A noise from behind caused Leah to wheel around. Ragny, or Innocen, was bent over, examining one of the bodies. He lifted the dead man's sword, studied it a moment, and then let it clatter back down to the street with disinterest. He had taken off his bloodstained, tattered shirt and now wore a sleeveless undershirt. His muscles were pronounced. There was not an ounce of fat on him, but that didn't explain the inhuman strength he had displayed.

She was alone with him. Everyone else had charged out—except for Lycon, Endrus, and the dead guards around her. The remaining occupants of the city were in the palace.

Leah drew her sword and planted her feet, taking a defensive stance.

"Do you know how the admiral convinced all these volunteers to come to Cervice?" Innocen asked.

Leah swallowed, but she couldn't speak. She looked over her shoulder, up the street at the nearest gate. It was several hundred yards away. When she tuned back to Innocen, he was standing completely still, but in the second she'd looked away, he had cut the distance between them in half.

"He told me personally," continued Innocen, "that Justin Holmes cared for Leah Anavion, and we could do no greater service to the fallen angel than to protect someone for whom he cared so deeply. Is that true, princess?"

Leah took a careful step backward, keeping her sword up. Innocen didn't seem bothered.

"I'm always one step behind," he said. "Fortune seems to favor the angel." He smiled. "But not this time."

CHAPTER 117

Moments passed that seemed longer than moments. Justin could see the destruction caused by the cythraul's spirit-bombing of Esthean far below. It looked like he was going to land right in the middle of it. He was going to sail over the water, miss the pool, and crash down into the stone buildings.

His body tumbled. He flailed his arms, trying to adjust, but water was everywhere. His open mouth caught a mouthful of water and he coughed, still flailing, somersaulting as he went. As his body turned, he spotted swirling, white water. He straightened out, straining to enter feet-first.

In his panic, he did not have the presence of mind to take a deep breath before going under, but it would have been a futile gesture, anyway. The impact and sudden pressure of water enveloping him forced all air from his lungs. A great bubble came out of his mouth, and all he knew was chaotic, slamming turbulence as he desperately tried to swim for a surface that seemed impossibly distant.

His lungs felt like deflated sacks of embers by the time his head broke free. He sucked in air just in time to register that giant chunks of rock were falling into the water around him, knocked loose from the walls by daemyn blasts.

A dislodged slab of cliff-side hit the pool so close that the waves crashed over Justin's head and into his mouth, choking him again.

"Justin!" someone was shouting.

He spotted Kallorn and Ahlund ahead, both pulling themselves up onto dry ground. He had entered the water first, but they had evidently been more successful at navigating their way out of the pool.

Cupping his hands around his mouth, Kallorn yelled, "Get out of—!"

A meteor of daemyn slammed into the earth ten feet behind Kallorn and Ahlund, knocking them on their faces. Debris rained down on Justin as he swam. A sound like a volcano erupted from behind him, and the undertow of the water—sucking him *in*, rather than pushing him out—told him that a daemyn blast had hit the pool dangerously close to his position.

His feet reached solid ground. Arrows, rocks, and daemyn came down from all sides, and he felt a trickle of blood running down his jawline from a cut he didn't remember sustaining. Ahlund and Kallorn gained their feet just as the building beside them collapsed. Justin drew his sword and found a target on the crater lip. A cythraul was preparing to throw another daemyn blast. Justin willed aurym through his blade, and he fired.

CHAPTER 118

Innocen walked casually toward Leah. He didn't bother to step over the bodies but instead seemed to go out of his way to step *on* them, balancing upon their backs, stomachs, and ribcages. He hopped lithely from one to another, as if they were stepping-stones in a stream. The childlike behavior drew a stark contrast to the scowl on his face. And the blood on his hands.

"You came to the wrong place," Leah said. "Justin isn't here. Even I don't know where he is."

"I know," said Innocen. "I'm here for you, princess." He hopped off the last body, then nudged it with his foot. "What do you think? Not bad for a cook."

"This. . . ." Leah began, but she choked on her words again.

"It's an aurym ability," said the little man. "A very rare one once utilized by the Cult of the Hyd. Mostly forgotten about, these days."

Leah took a quick step back, preparing to run. In response, Innocen came at her. She remembered, as a child, studying a housefly as it crawled across a table. She remembered being amazed by the way its legs moved—so quickly that she couldn't see its footsteps. Innocen moved the same way. He was so fast that his movements looked instantaneous.

Before she managed to take a second step, Innocen was in front of her, holding the blade of her sword between his thumb and forefinger. She had to look down at him; he was several inches shorter than her.

Leah tried to pull the sword from his grasp. She put her whole body weight against it. His fingers did not budge. Her sword felt as if it had been cast in stone.

Innocen raised his opposite hand and swiped at her blade with a sideways chop. The flat of his hand snapped the steel blade like a cane stalk. As the top half of her sword clanged against the street, Leah let go of the hilt and reatreated a step. Innocen tossed the bottom half of her broken weapon aside.

"Justin is not here," Leah repeated. "And the demons won't take Cervice. Not with Raeqlund here to help us. You can tell Avagad that he. . . ."

Innocen's face broke into a smile that made her forget her words. "Little girl, I don't work for Avagad," he said. "Though, believe me, he's tried. That crazy zealot has wanted to recruit me for years. In fact, he was so offended by my rejection that he tried to take me by force." Innocen cracked his knuckles. "It didn't work."

"Who are you, then?" asked Leah. "Not a cook, clearly."

"I wouldn't go that far," said Innocen, stepping on top of another body. "I can make a decent meal."

"Have you no respect for human life?" Leah fumed, looking at the dead man beneath his foot. "Get off him!"

"I respect human life," objected Innocen. "It's a beautiful thing. So beautiful, in fact, that I strive to take as much of it as I can, as often as possible."

Leah's jaw clenched.

"Feels great to have something go right for a change," said Innocen. "It seems like I've been stuck one step behind, right from the start. I felt the ethoul arrive on the Gravelands, but it took me days to get there. By the time I did, the trail had gone cold. I followed a pack of cythraul around the Shifting Mountains, through Darvelle, into Upper Athacea, and eventually all the way to the Drekwood. They led me to the ruins of Gaius, where Avagad's forces were amassing a coblyn army. There, I waited. I observed your friends' attack. Then I felt the ethoul use his power. I set out to track him down, and I was so, so close. . . . But Avagad was aware of my presence. He sent a pair of cythraul to prevent me from interfering. By the time I dispatched them, the ethoul's trail had gone cold.

"Rumor eventually reached me that Justin was in Hartla. Heavily defended. Despite my abilities, I still have most of the weaknesses of an average man, which means I have to be careful. Diligent. Sneak my way in and leave no one standing when I take what I came for. In the guise of a merchant, I infiltrated Hartla to search for him. Several times, I passed within arm's reach of you, princess. But no ethoul. He had vanished, leaving me no closer to my goal. I waited, but, like everyone else, I was forced to evacuate Hartla during Avagad's heavy-handed attack on the city. I spent the following weeks alone at sea, scouring the Raedittean."

Innocen smiled and shook his head as if remembering a funny story. "Those native islanders are so superstitious. Tear off a few arms, and they'll tell you anything."

Monster, thought Leah.

"I was actually on my way back to Hartla to search the city's ruins when Justin returned there," said Innocen. "That was perhaps the closest I've been. But, alas, by the time I got there, he was gone. I thought the admiral's brother, Yordar, might know where he had gone, but the man was a coward. Invented all sorts of fallacies just to make the pain stop. He was a particularly enjoyable kill. . . . *Ragny the cook* was born not long after that." Innocen bent over slightly, mimicking a submissive posture and shaking his hands in phony fear. "Admiral Gunnar, sir! Beg your pardon! Er—um, I just want to help!" He sneered and made a gagging noise in his throat. "I knew if I stayed with Gunnar long enough, he'd eventually lead me to Justin. But then, my dear, I heard about you. The object of the ethoul's affection. That was when I realized I'd been going about things all wrong. Why chase after the fallen angel when I could make him come to me?"

"A trap?" said Leah.

"Obviously," said Innocen. "I spoke to Gunnar and planted the idea to bring the Holy Army volunteers—and their timid cook, Ragny—to Nolia, to aid one of Justin's closest allies. A companion since the beginning. A friend. A *loved one*?" Innocen cocked his head sideways, trying to read Leah. "I see . . . Too soon to say. That's all right." He looked around. "We should be off, dear, before I have to kill any more of your friends." He turned to gaze off into the distance, looking troubled. "I only wish I'd done something more creative with that insufferable Lycon Belesys. Should have taken my time with him. Kicked off a wall to be eaten by coblyns? It's uncharacteristically passive of me."

"I'm not going anywhere with you," said Leah.

Innocen nodded, putting a finger to his lips and pretending to think it over. "Hmm. Uh-huh. I see. Maybe you're right. Captives are a bother, and killing you might serve the same purpose anyway, so long as I advertised it enough. That would light a fire under Justin's ass, don't you think? Might get him to come running, seeking revenge. He'll be distraught. Reckless. Easily tricked. Yes, perhaps you're right. Perhaps I should kill you. Make it a grand spectacle. Something people will write about for centuries."

Leah took another step back only to find she had run out of room. Her shoulders were against the wall of a building.

A smile crept across Innocen's face. "A joke, princess. Abducting you is the best option. I've learned a lot about Justin. His compassion, they say, is one of his most notable qualities—and therefore, one of his greatest weaknesses. Killing you would infuriate him, but holding you at my mercy, all the time allowing him to think about what I might be doing to you. . . . That, I think, will have a greater effect than even the grisliest of murders. Now. Come along. We're leaving."

Leah felt her way to the corner of the building. She could still hear the sounds of battle outside the walls and thought she could hear elephants. How far was it to the nearest gate? How far would she make it if she tried to run?

"You won't get out of here without being spotted," said Leah, trying to stall for time.

"Obviously," said Innocen. "I'm counting on that. I need witnesses. It wouldn't be a very effective kidnapping if you just up and disappeared."

He took an aggressive step forward. Leah held up her hand.

"Wait, tell me one thing, at least," she said. "You still haven't said what you want with Justin."

"You're a talkative little shrew," said Innocen. "It's not to force him to join me or to use his powers, if that's what you're thinking. That's Avagad's way, that bullheaded bastard. If he weren't so blindly devoted to the tenets of worshipping the Nameless One, he really would rule half the world, instead of by proxy. His religion limits him. Makes him nothing more than the middleman between the demons and their god. No, I serve neither man nor god. I have no tangled web of lies, no hidden machinations. My plan is simpler. And simpler is always better. . . . Do you know how coblyns kill?"

"They . . . eat living human organs," Leah said.

"Do you know the reason why?"

"To feed on aurym."

"And did you know that some humans can gain aurym power the same way?"

Leah felt her lips part. Her mouth hung open.

"I told you I was a cook," said Innocen. His expression did not change as he opened his mouth, showed his teeth to her, and snapped them together, hard. The clack echoed.

CHAPTER 119

It came from his sword like a great, reaching arm: a solid flow of aurym that collided with the crater wall like a battering ram. Justin had been aiming for the cythraul on the crater's edge, but hitting the wall was just as effective. An entire portion of the cliff-side was instantly burned away. More was dislodged by the shockwave, blown outward in a typhoon of rock and earth. Several cythraul were caught in the blast. Others plummeted, and coblyns and enemy soldiers spilled over the broken edge.

It was as Justin watched the aftermath of this attack that he realized how they were going to escape Esthean.

"Justin!" shouted Ahlund.

Justin turned. A ball of daemyn was coming straight for him. He raised his left arm as a shield, and the blast spiraled into him like water down a drain.

"Go!" Justin shouted at Ahlund and Kallorn. "Gather any survivors!"

"And what're you doing?" Kallorn demanded.

"Digging us out of here," said Justin. "Go!"

As Ahlund and Kallorn sprinted up the street, another daemyn blast hit the ground dangerously close to Justin, unleashing a seismic charge that knocked him to his knees. Rubble and debris pelted his back like a dozen punches, but he jumped back up, turning toward the place where his aurym had hit the crater wall. A huge chunk had been blasted cleanly away from the upper lip of the crater. Cythraul were everywhere along the edge. Tens and twenties of them—maybe a hundred. Trying to kill them all would be hopeless. The earth, however, posed less of a challenge.

Justin called on aurym and swung his sword again. Another blast of green energy erupted from the blade and shot forth like an alien sunbeam. It parted the curtain of dust and smoke, hit the wall below his first strike, and kept going, blowing a hole through the rock and bursting forth from the ground above.

The earth cracked and heaved like the upwelling of plate tectonics. Jungle trees flew skyward. He did not bother surveying his handiwork but swung his sword again. And again. And again.

CHAPTER 120

A shield flashed in front of Gunnar and hit the incoming the coblyn with a gong. It hit the ground, and Olorus brought his boot down, crushing its head.

Olorus turned his shield and spear on the horde, putting himself between Gunnar and harm's way. "Give it hell, gardener!" he shouted.

Gunnar redoubled his efforts. Sweat beaded on his forehead as he commanded the trees to reach skyward. They were tall enough, their roots deep enough, and their vine-armor strong enough for the attack to commence.

He shifted his tactics, growing the trees' branches out. They groped at the demon mount, searching for vulnerable spots, and began to bury themselves into its body like spears. A ghostly whinny was cut short as Sif, still clinging to the demon-animal, wedged his blade forward, slicing outward through the throat.

Apparently realizing the intent of Gunnar's attack, the cythraul turned its attention on the trees. It swung its hatchet, lopping off the top of one. Gunnar felt the tree's pain and flinched at the terrible surgery. He shot vines out to clutch at the cythraul and its mount, trying to tie up his weapon arm. And, ever so slowly, he grew the trees inward, twisting them, making them reach for one another.

The vines knotted to one other across the gap. The trees wrapped into a spiral, enclosing the cythraul in an arborescent cocoon. Adonica, Hook, and Sif retreated as Gunnar's vines lassoed the arms and legs of the cythraul. The demon mount was dying beneath it, but the cythraul fought on. It tried to push over one of the encroaching trees but failed. It tore through a set of vines only to have the hatchet pried from its grip in the process. A ball of daemyn appeared in its hand, but it shot wildly to the side, taking out only coblyns.

There was a loud twang, a whistling noise, and a solid *thunk*.

Gunnar looked up in surprise. A spear as thick as a fencepost had hit the cythraul and sunk halfway through its chest. The monster looked down at it in shock. It was not a spear at all, Gunnar realized, but a harpoon.

A noise like a trumpet drew Gunnar's attention around. A war elephant was charging into the battle, trampling coblyns as it came, surrounded by an entourage of Raeqlund warriors on steedback. Their cries echoed across the battlefield.

Mounted atop the elephant was a platform housing a large contraption of levers, braided wire, and pulleys, and men were cranking the gears fervently. It was a mounted ballista—a giant crossbow. Another barbed harpoon was being loaded into place. Aiming the rig was a man with a long, white beard.

C H A P T E R   1 2 1

The ropes of the ballista were drawn taught. The elephant-mounted gunners stepped back.

"Fire!" Zechariah cried.

The gunner threw a lever. The arms of the contraption sprang forward, and its payload whizzed through the air. The cythraul was in mid-roar as the harpoon connected with its head, passed between its open jaws, and jutted out from the back of its skull. It stuck there, leaving the fanged mouth wedged open.

Reinvigorated, Gunnar let his aurym flow. He willed the trees to reach further. A vine-covered branch from each tree reached into the cythraul's open mouth.

"Fire!"

Another harpoon hit the monster's chest, passed all the way through, and out the other side, pinning a coblyn to the ground like an insect on a collector's board. The tree branches reached the cythraul's head. One went down into the throat; the other went up, constricting the upper jaw. Had the monster's face been capable of emotion, it might have looked concerned as the branches pulled, forcing its mouth open wider and wider and wider.

Sweat poured down Gunnar's face. He closed his hands into fists. With all his effort, he pulled them away from one another. The two branches followed his movements, pulling violently in opposite directions.

The cythraul's upper jaw unhinged from the lower. The head tipped back at a nightmarishly unnatural angle. In a panic, the cythraul finally tore one arm free of the vines and reached up, trying to hold its head on, but it was too late. Sharp snaps like the breaking of a crab's shell emanated from within the head cavity. Black blood gushed from its mouth. One last crack, and only soft tissues remained. With a final burst of effort, Gunnar forced the upper branch to yank sideways.

The cythraul's ram-horned skull popped off into the tree like a cork wrenched from a bottle, leaving behind a lower jaw, and a neck hole fountaining as if it had struck oil.

"Get back!" Olorus was shouting.

All assembled did their best to heed Olorus's warning. Gunnar, too, scrambled for cover. He tripped and fell sprawling to the ground, too exhausted to get back up. Bone plates crumpled with an energized implosion. With a sucking bang, the energy whizzed outward, sizzling with violet lightning. The cythraul was no more.

Lying on the ground, Gunnar breathed, "Got the bleeder."

"A team effort, as usual."

Gunnar turned his head toward the voice. A man stood over him. Deep wrinkles lined his bearded face. His eyebrows were like branches laden with snow. In his left hand was a short sword, held upside down. Where his right hand should have been was a steel hook.

Zechariah grinned. "Always happy to lend a helping... well, you know." He winked.

It took until now for Gunnar to realize that the people around him weren't rushing back into the fight. Instead, they were holding their current positions. He readied himself to order them back into the fight, but then realized with astonishment that the demons were falling back.

Gunnar stood to look out over the battlefield. Sif, clutching the bite on his arm, walked up to stand beside him and Zechariah.

"The devils are retreating," Sif said.

Gunnar hardly dared believe it. But it was true. The tides of the black ocean were receding. The combined forces of Cervice and Raeqlund—thirty to thirty-five thousand strong—began to bellow a victory cry at the sight of it. A few other cythraul had been defeated during Raeqlund's charge. Those left were waving the coblyns back, leading them in the withdrawal.

Gunnar edged closer to Zechariah. "Demons don't retreat," he whispered.

"Not lightly, they don't," said Zechariah. "But it seems even cythraul know a lost cause when they see one. They will regroup and return. But for now, we can call the day a victory."

Gunnar shook his head, "One of these days, my luck is going to run out, and it's going to run out *hard*."

"Makes you wonder if it's really luck at all," said Zechariah.

Gunnar cocked an eyebrow at Zechariah. "Guess I'd better get re-accustomed to your riddles and teachable moments. . . . Welcome back." He turned to look back at the command post on the wall, but, to his surprise, it was empty. "That's strange. Where's Leah?"

CHAPTER 122

Green energy exploded from Justin's sword with each swing. Rock and earth blew apart. The daemyn bombs hitting the city were only background noise. Justin defended against the blasts when necessary, but he focused his efforts on cutting down the crater wall.

Sweat coated his face as he pumped out the waters of aurym from the deep, deep well of his soul, steadily carving a trench through rock. It was as if he were watching himself from somewhere outside his body, awestruck and a bit terrified by what he was doing; a seemingly normal teenager with the ability to impose his will upon the very planet, to manipulate and carve it to his liking.

Until now, he hadn't fully comprehended the potential. *This* was the power Avagad wanted. *This* was what Zechariah had warned him about—a weapon that could bring entire civilizations to their knees. And the name of the weapon was Justin Holmes.

No one should have this kind of power, Justin thought as his green aurym energy cleaved bedrock. *It should not exist. I should not exist.*

He wasn't human. Humans were not capable of this sort of single-handed destruction. He was trying to save his friends, but with such power at his command, how long until it corrupted him? How long until he exploited it for other ambitions? How could he retain a sense of reality—a sense of right, wrong, or simple humanity—when his will *was* reality?

Was this what had happened to his father? Had he been driven mad by daemyn, as Cyaxares has said, or had it been his own power that had pushed him over the edge?

Justin's senses flared. A ball of daemyn was coming down on him from behind. He turned, raising his arm. But instead of hitting him, the daemyn stopped in mid-air. It hung there like a small, black sun above his head. Beneath it stood Cyaxares. Both her hands were raised skyward. Her aurym energy took the form of a great, invisible barrier. She clapped her hands together, and the daemyn shattered like a glass marble. Shards of it warped and faded away with heat-shimmering vapor trails. In its wake, Ahlund, Kallorn, and about forty to fifty Ru'Onorath ran toward Justin.

Justin turned back. He called on aurym and let loose a war cry, rending the air with his blade once more. The blast traveled down the trench, hit the end, and arced upward in a slice, leaving a long, sloping canyon that led out of the crater and up into the jungle above. The ground was uneven. The walls were probably dangerously unstable, but it was finished. He had done it.

"Come on!" he shouted. "Let's go!"

Cyaxares nodded. She focused her aurym barrier on protecting the rest of the Guardians as they hurried for the exit. A volley of arrows came down, but they bounced off her shield and dropped to the ground harmlessly. Kallorn retaliated. He took aim with his sword and sizzled an electrical finger along the crater's lip, burning up a batch of coblyns while Ahlund shot fire at enemy soldiers on the other side. With Justin in the lead, they ran for the trench.

CHAPTER 123

Leah looked over her shoulder, hearing triumphant cheers outside the walls. Something fortuitous had occurred. Maybe the battle had been won. But from in here, the rejoicing sounded like a dreadful parody.

"Cheering?" Innocen said, craning his neck to listen. "How gullible you all are. All a victory means is that you managed to avoid extinction for a few more hours. Nothing is won. More battles will be fought, and your numbers will be chipped away while the demons only continue to multiply. The people's morale will decline. How long do you think they will remain willing to keep hurling themselves into the jaws of death like this? Even to an outsider, your looming downfall is obvious: There are no crops to harvest. Once your storehouses are empty, what happens? Once the livestock run out halfway through winter, what will these people eat? Have you thought of that? Humans can weather many hardships, but hunger is the great equalizer. When they must look into the eyes of their starving children, knowing that *you* brought them to this, do you think they will still fight and die for you? No.

"At the moment, you are riding an idealistic high. But the coming famine will break you. Loyalties will be strained until your already flimsy alliance falls apart completely. Coblyns are disposable. Even cythraul are disposable. Humans are not. Avagad will strike again. Harder."

"We'll have more people by then," said Leah defiantly. "We'll find ways to feed them. More cities will join us once they hear of today's victory—"

Innocen laughed. "Your country is held up by plundered nails and barn doors. Oh well. Let the demons wipe humans from the Oikoumene, for all I care. Good riddance. I'll live on. With Justin's help, I'll—"

There was a meaty *thud*, and Innocen dropped to one knee. An arrow had hit him from behind and was sticking through his thigh.

Leah looked up. Behind Innocen stood a young Cru man in the street with his bow still raised. The Cru archer reached over his shoulder to grab another arrow, shouting, "Run, princess! Go!"

Quick as a flash, Innocen ripped the arrow from his leg, wheeled, and threw it like a javelin. With nearly the same force and speed as if it had been shot from a bow, the arrow zoomed back at the Cru archer. Another meaty thud echoed up the street as it struck him in the neck.

Leah turned and sprinted.

CHAPTER 124

They were at the threshold of the trench when a shadow appeared overhead. Justin looked up.

"Uh-oh," he said.

A cythraul was diving down at them. It had jumped over the side of the cliff with disregard for its own well-being.

Justin spun, swinging his sword upward at the descending monster. His aurym shot forth like a rocket, but before it could connect, the cythraul tossed its arm forward, throwing a black ball of daemyn down at the rear of the group. Several of the old, white-bearded Ru'Onorath elders were facing the wrong direction.

"Watch out!" Justin cried.

At the same moment that the falling cythraul was shredded by Justin's aurym, the ball of daemyn hit the ground. The elders never knew what hit them. Daemyn vaporized their bodies, leaving behind only crackling energy and a great, rending hole in the earth.

"Down!" Ahlund shouted.

The tall Guardian threw his body on Justin, forcing him to the ground and covering him.

Justin hit the canyon floor and looked up. Another enormous shadow was above them. Not a cythraul. A boulder the size of a house. But it wasn't falling. It was hovering in mid-air.

Ahlund looked up in surprise. He stood and pulled Justin to his feet. Behind them, Cyaxares had her hands extended overhead. Her small body was hunched as she held the chunk of cliff suspended above them. From the look on her face, it was all she could do to keep it there.

Ahlund, Justin, Kallorn, and the rest of the Ru'Onorath rushed out from beneath the stone. Cyaxares's knees buckled slightly, and the boulder dropped several feet. Justin tried to rush back for her, but Ahlund held him in place.

Cyaxares's eyes found Justin's. Her lips stretched tightly over her teeth. She flexed her fingers, and in response, the boulder above her head cracked up the middle and split into two. She whipped both arms backward over her head, and the two chunks of stone went crashing down behind her.

"We can't outrun them," said Ahlund as Cyaxares rejoined them, "but if a defense can be mounted, some of us might escape."

"I can do it," panted Justin. "Cyaxares. It's Avagad."

"I am a fool," said Cyaxares. "I knew he could mask his presence, but it never occurred to me that he could hide others, let alone an army. I thought I knew his limitations. It seems the peaceful shelter of Esthean has dulled my wits. . . . Ahlund, I should have listened to you."

"You would have," said Ahlund, "if I had not been such a fool myself in the past. All is forgotten, elder."

As they hustled up the slope toward the jungle, the bombing of Esthean grew fainter behind them. The cythraul were abandoning the city in favor of the chase, and Justin knew that the Ru'Onorath would be overtaken long before they made it to the boats unless something was done.

Cyaxares, short in stature, struggled to pull herself over a chunk of uneven ground. Justin grabbed her by the arms and dragged her up.

"You should not have come back here," she said, dusting herself off. "I tried to govern your actions by my priorities, and for that, I owe you—"

"The apologies can probably wait," said Justin. "Ahlund, Kallorn, and I will hold off the cythraul. You lead everyone else to the boats. We'll be right behind you."

Cyaxares stiffened her lip and nodded.

They reached the top of the slope—the exit point of Justin's handmade canyon— and with the surviving Guardians on her heels, Cyaxares jogged off into the jungle.

Ahlund, Kallorn, and Justin stood together, watching Cyaxares and the others leave. Several fallen trees lay around them, smoking from Justin's energy. Justin could hear the approach of cythraul, crashing through the trees to get to them.

Justin closed his eyes and searched with his aurym. Many demonic forces were coming this direction. But there was another, off in the direction Cyaxares and the others were running.

"Kallorn!" Justin said, opening his eyes.

The golden-haired Guardian seemed to know what Justin was about to tell say. "A trap?" he asked.

"A cythraul, I think," Justin said. "Just one. Maybe with your help—"

"That only leaves the two of you to cover our escape," said Kallorn. "I might remind you that this venture is only a success if *you* survive."

"I'll do my best," said Justin. "Just keep them safe. We'll find our way. Go."

Kallorn hesitated. Then he nodded, turned, and ran. His leaf-plastered cloak blended in with his jungle surroundings, and he was gone.

Justin and Ahlund exchanged a look. Neither said a word.

A few moments passed. Movement in the undergrowth ahead announced the arrival of their foes. Justin tightened his grip on his sword, then swung a sideways chop through the air. A blade of green extended outward, slicing through the trees, and he heard the pained roar of a cythraul and an explosion of daemyn. Ahlund shot a jet of flame into the surrounding jungle that caught in the leaves and quickly grew into a wildfire. A clutch of coblyns came streaming through the undergrowth on the other side, and Justin turned his sword on them, moving it as gracefully through the air as if he were signing his name. A spinning, twirling light show tore the creatures apart and sizzled through the foliage behind them.

Justin looked down at the canyon trench before them. If he could widen it into a sort of dry moat, it might slow them down for a while—

Two things happened at once. A cythraul leaped through the trees directly in front of them, and a life force popped up behind Justin: a horrifyingly familiar entity that had managed to conceal itself until now.

No! thought Justin.

He spun, trying to fire off a quick shot at Avagad, but it was no use.

The ground shook with power—the same ground-stomping attack Avagad had used against Justin in the Treasury. The invisible shockwave collided with Justin's body. Resistance was impossible. There was nothing he could do as he was knocked off the ground, tossed backward through the air, and tumbled end-over-end, down into the very trench he had constructed minutes before. His sword was knocked from his hands. He flailed his arms as he fell, trying to find the ground. Seconds passed.

He landed on his back. His neck jerked with the impact. The base of his skull cracked sickeningly against the stone, and the lights went out.

CHAPTER 125

The gate was a hundred yards away. Leah could hear Innocen shouting obscenities behind her as she ran. She hazarded a look over her shoulder. He limped after her, but even on an injured leg, his aurym-fueled speed was inhuman. She would have had better luck outrunning a steed. In seconds, he would close the distance.

Leah turned sharply around the corner of a building. Up ahead was a mass of shields. It was the Endenholm phalanx that had defended the breach in the wall. They stood conversing in the street and congratulating each other. With them was Marcus Worth.

"Enemy!" Leah shouted as she ran. "Enemy in the city!"

Worth drew his sword. The shields of the phalanx went up, forming a singular entity, like a turtleshell quilled with protruding spears. Leah ran past them. More voices shouted the alarm.

Innocen rounded the corner.

"Enemy in sight!" Worth shouted. "Protect the princess!"

Leah turned to watch. She expected Innocen to retreat, but the sight of the phalanx did nothing to dissuade the little man. He limped straight for them. One overly confident Enden warrior at the front of the phalanx broke ranks and shoved his spear at Innocen. Innocen sidestepped the attack, lunged forward, and snapped the soldier's neck with a flathanded chop. He swung his other hand sideways, slapping another soldier cartwheeling across the ground.

Another spearhead jabbed at Innocen. He grabbed it with his bare hand, yanked the soldier bodily from the phalanx, grabbed his throat, and pulled. He came away with a handful of gore that he promptly threw into the face of the next attacker, blinding him long enough to kill him with a punch to the chest—all the way through and out his back.

Worth rushed him, and Innocen launched a fist at him, too. Worth got his shield up quickly enough to block the punch—only to be kicked in the leg. His knee snapped sideways. His lower leg turned at an unnatural angle, unable to support his weight, and he fell with a cry.

As the soldiers closed in around him, Innocen stepped on a shield with his good foot, boosted himself up, jumped over the entire phalanx, and landed on the other side. Eyes fixed on Leah, he sprinted at her.

Leah ran again. She was at the gate, now. The air smelled of blood and body odor. The ground was littered with coblyn bodies. She saw soldiers coming her way, alerted by the Enden's shouts, but they wouldn't get to her in time. Even as she raced over the dropped gate doors, out onto the battlefield, Innocen's feet thudded against the planks close behind her.

A mighty roar erupted behind her. Leah looked over her shoulder. A big man barreled toward Innocen, a giant sword raised high over his head.

Innocen skidded to a halt in surprise. The big man swung his giant, black blade at him, but Innocen spun away from it with the grace of a dancer.

"*You!*" Innocen snarled, hopping on one foot, blood soaking his leg.

Lycon Belesys's beard was plastered with dried blood. With another roar, he turned in a full circle, swinging his black-bladed demon sword in a wide arc. Innocen was forced to retreat a step.

More soldiers were converging to help Lycon. Some were too eager; Innocen kicked a man of the High Guard, sending him flying. His arm darted forward and stabbed another through the chest with nothing but his fingers. He turned, reaching for Lycon.

A loud *twang* erupted, and a huge harpoon shot by, inches over Innocen's head. It hit the wall behind him. There was a puff of dust as it stuck in the stone. Behind Leah, a war elephant with a mounted ballista on its back was charging at the gate. Its gunners worked to reload.

Innocen looked at the harpoon stuck in the wall. He looked at Lycon. He looked at the Enden phalanx moving his direction, boxing him in on the other side. Then turned to glare at Leah.

"Next time," he said.

It was the last thing he did before jumping straight up—higher than any human being should have been able to jump. His hands grabbed the haft of the harpoon stuck in the wall. He swung up and propelled himself to land on one foot atop the fortifications. Arrows fell around him as he took off sprinting across the top of the walls. Another harpoon came sailing after him, loosed from the elephant-mounted ballista, but the shot went wide. Leah could see him running along the wall for several hundred yards. Then he dropped down, disappearing from sight.

Leah let out a long, quivering breath. She might have crumpled to the ground if not for a big hand gripping her shoulder for support. She looked up in surprise. It was Lycon. His face was a bloody mess and one eye was swollen shut, but he was, somehow, alive.

"Thank you," Leah managed.

Lycon only nodded.

Leah was vaguely aware of the familiar faces of Olorus, Hook, Gunnar, and Adonica rushing toward her. Behind them, she thought she saw Zechariah. The battlefield was empty except for the bodies of the dead. The demons had receded over the countryside.

The day was won. But it didn't feel like it.

CHAPTER 126

Blue sky above jungle trees. The sensation of his body moving.

Justin blinked rapidly, trying to take it in. He was still on his back. A hand was clamped tightly to his ankle, dragging him across the stone floor of the trench. He'd been knocked out, but he didn't feel injured. Ahlund must be pulling him to safety. . . .

Looking up, he saw the outline of a body covered in white armor. Avagad had hold of him and was pulling him along the trench.

Justin kicked his foot free and rolled sideways across the stone. He reached out with his hand, calling for his sword—

Avagad grabbed Justin by the arm, lifted him off the ground, and flung him bodily up and over the edge of the trench. Justin spiraled through the air and slammed against the forest floor on his back, the wind knocked out of him. He looked around frantically, trying to push himself up as he gasped for air.

The backdrop was a blazing wildfire, pouring smoke into the air that stung Justin's nostrils as he gained his feet. He saw Ahlund with his sword trailing fire, surrounded by four cythraul. At first, Justin thought he was taking turns attacking each of them. But as Justin watched, he realized *they* were taking turns on him.

Ahlund's clothes were in tatters. He bled from a dozen wounds. He unleashed a torrent of flame at a cythraul who sucked it into its palm without effort. One of the others reached out with its sword, rested it gently against Ahlund's shoulders, and pulled, slowly slicing inches deep into his back. Ahlund shouted in pain, turned, and shot a blast of fire at the cythraul. The blunt end of a spear cracked him from behind, knocking him to his knees. A kick sent him flopping sidelong. Noises bubbled up from the monsters' throats that sounded like laughter.

Justin started toward them, but he made it only a couple of steps toward the fight before his feet suddenly stopped moving. He felt a terrible cold eating at his toes and looked down to find his feet trapped in two cones of ice. He tried to pull free, but the ice grew, encasing his ankles, then his knees. He beat at it with his fists, but it was hard as stone.

He heard Ahlund cry out again. Justin reached out his hand, desperately calling for his sword. Nothing.

Avagad stepped into his field of vision. The sharp face beneath the diamond-studded crown studied Justin. The long, slender sword was still strapped to his back. He held Justin's cat's eye claymore in one hand.

Justin reached for it, calling for it with his aurym. It trembled in Avagad's hand but remained firmly within his grasp.

"Remarkable," Avagad said. "It truly wants to listen to your command, this ancient weapon. Had I known you were capable of such a thing, I'd have been more careful in the Treasury."

Ahlund stood. Like a punch-drunk boxer, he swung his sword in a wild, hopeless attack, only to be batted across the face by a bone-armored backhand. Another demon's blade caught him across the middle. Blood sprayed, and he grunted in surprise, but he managed to stay standing.

"Ahlund!" Justin shouted. "Hang on!" He turned again to the ice at his feet, trying to break through it with his fists. He felt one of his fingers break.

"You are a slippery one," said Avagad. "Too erratic for my master's liking. He has decided you will be turned. Immediately."

Still holding Justin's sword, Avagad approached Ahlund fighting the four cythraul. Ahlund had been cut so many times that his shirt hung off his body like a scarf.

"Behind you!" shouted Justin.

Ahlund spun. Fire blossomed from his sword, reaching out for Avagad, but the man with the crown opened his mouth. Ice crystals sparkled in the air, and the flames died in the cold gust as surely as if he were blowing out a match.

A cythraul cracked Ahlund over the head with the butt end of its sword, knocking him to his knees. Avagad drew with long, slender sword, circled around behind Ahlund, and stabbed.

Ahlund threw his shoulders back involuntarily as the blade traveled through him. The steel tip protruded from his front, beneath his ribcage.

"No!" Justin cried.

Avagad twisted, then withdrew the sword. Blood leaked from Ahlund's side. His limp body started to collapse, but Avagad grabbed him by the hair and lifted him. Ahlund still held his sword, but it only smoked, now. He seemed only partially conscious as Avagad brought him over to Justin—a nearly seven-foot-tall man carried like a kitten by the scruff of its neck.

Avagad held Ahlund up for Justin to see, wrenching his head back by the hair. His eyes were blackened, swollen, and cloudy, and seemed to look at nothing.

"Do you see what you made me do?" Avagad scolded.

"Go to hell!" Justin yelled.

Avagad smiled. "I'm immortal, Justin. I'm not going anywhere, thank you very much, and neither are you. It's time for you to receive the master's ultimate gift. But before you are turned, you are going to help me fulfill a promise I made to you. Do you remember?"

The cat's eye sword was still in Avagad's other hand. Justin reached for it, called to it again, but it was hopeless.

"Let me refresh your memory," said Avagad. "I promised that if you resisted me, I would not kill your friends; I would make *you* kill your friends. So now, let me show you what it is like to be turned fully. Witness the extent of devotion you will have to the Nameless One when your time comes."

Avagad looked over his shoulder at the cythraul. "One of you, come here." He gestured to Ahlund. "Change this man."

"No!" said Justin, reaching out for his sword again. "Stop!"

Ahlund struggled only slightly at Avagad's words—too stunned or too concussed to be wholly aware of what was going on. His sword had dulled from red hot to gray.

Avagad propped Ahlund up on his feet and wrapped his free arm around his neck, holding Ahlund against his body, choking him as he held him in place. Beneath the swelling, Ahlund's eyes rolled in his head.

"You thought I was bluffing about what I could make you do?" Avagad said from over Ahlund's shoulder. "I never make empty promises, Justin. You will kill all of them, eventually, when your will is no longer your own. But this one, you will kill of your own free will. Because at the touch of the High Demon, the man you knew will be just as dead as that arm of yours. What remains will be my servant."

"Ahlund!" shouted Justin.

The cythraul propped its spear against a nearby tree and approached.

"Out of mercy, you will put him down like a mad dog!" yelled Avagad. "Out of pity, you will destroy him. And only then will I grant you reprieve of your human life and give you the gift of the Nameless One's undying servitude!"

The bladed, lipless mouth of the cythraul opened in a growl as it stepped forward.

"Don't!" said Justin. "I'll do whatever you say! I—"

"The time for that has passed," said Avagad. He nodded to the cythraul. "Do it. Turn him."

The cythraul placed its giant hand on top of Ahlund's head.

CHAPTER 127

Ahlund's eyes opened wide at the touch. They locked on Justin—the same eyes that had glared at Justin the night his house burned down on the Gravelands, that narrowed on him with disapproval when he acted cowardly or foolish, and that softened with stern compassion in the rare moments when Justin deserved it. A dark glow appeared beneath the cythraul's hand. There was a hissing sound, and locks of Ahlund's hair fell off trailing smoke.

"Ahlund!" Justin screamed. He threw himself forward, but the ice around his legs kept him locked in place. "Wake up, Ahlund!"

Ahlund's mouth opened, but he made no sound. His cloudy eyes watched Justin. His lips moved, mouthing a single word:

Run.

Ahlund weakly lifted his sword up, turning it toward himself. He rested the tip below his own collarbone, drew a tight grip on the hilt, and pulled. In one swift motion, Ahlund ran the sword through his own body, all the way to the hilt.

There was a crunching noise like folding metal. Behind Ahlund, Avagad's eyes went wide in shock as Ahlund's blade sunk into his chest.

The cythraul took a step back in surprise. Avagad's grip around Ahlund's neck slackened, and Ahlund's previously blank face morphed into an expression of rage. He opened his mouth and roared so loud that it shook Justin's stomach.

A flash of yellow light. A shimmer of heat in the air. Fire erupted behind Ahlund as he shot a burst of flames through his own body. Avagad let out a wail as a ball of fire like an unstable sun enveloped him and blasted him backward.

The cythraul stepped forward, reaching for Ahlund, but Ahlund ripped the sword back out of his own body. The blade was broken. He spun the stump in a low slash, and flames hit the ice at Justin's feet, melting the outer layer instantly. Ahlund leaped at the cythraul and drove the blazing half-sword into its exposed throat. Flames exploded out of the back of its neck. The monster fell back, roaring and gargling black blood.

Justin wrenched his boots free of the weakened ice. As the first cythraul lay dying, the other three rushed forward. Justin reached out his arm, calling for his sword.

"Come on, come on, come on!" he growled, flexing his fingers.

Nothing came.

Ahlund swung his half-sword again. Furious waves of red-rimmed, blue flames smashed against the approaching cythraul. Purple, electrical energy jumped from the dying one's neck. There was a loud *snap* and a shockwave of daemyn as the creature's own energy turned against it. The explosion caught the nearest approaching cythraul and bit through its bones.

Ahlund was knocked to the ground. Justin shielded his face, still calling for his sword, but it wouldn't come.

Ahlund tried to get up, fell back, did not move.

"Run," Ahlund said.

But Ahlund hadn't said anything, and Justin's ears didn't hear anything. He heard it in his mind.

Justin stopped calling for the sword. He ran to Ahlund. The cythraul caught in the daemyn explosion was half-destroyed and leaking black ichor across jungle leaves. As it, too, exploded with daemyn, consuming another of its brothers in a chain reaction, Justin wedged his arms under Ahlund's body. Lifting his seven-foot-tall body was like trying to pick up a fallen oak, but with a howling grunt of effort, Justin picked Ahlund up and slung him over his shoulders. Daemyn explosions erupted from behind as he turned and ran.

CHAPTER 128

Justin's breath wheezed through his clenched teeth. An unknown fluid dribbled in lines down his face. It might have been tears. It might have been sweat. It might have been blood. And any of these three substances may or may not have been his.

His legs burned. It was a struggle just to put one foot in front of the other. Cythraul were close behind him. He could feel them hunting him, could hear them roaring with fury. Soon, they would be on him, but he had nothing to fight with. All he could do was keep moving.

He took another step, and his feet sunk partially into soggy ground. He was wading through a marsh.

"Hang on, Ahlund," he panted. "It can't be much farther. We're going to make it."

Up ahead, he spotted blue sky—a break in the trees.

The bay. It had to be.

Closing his eyes, Justin saw and felt Cyaxares's presence ahead. Kallorn and the others were already sailing away, but they had made it out. Cyaxares had waited behind for Justin and Ahlund.

He waded through scum-skimmed, ankle-deep waters. "Told you," said Justin. "Almost there."

The trees thinned. He found a gap, and he pushed through. Ahead, Cyaxares waited at the edge of the narrow bay—more like a small channel where the swamp drained into the sea. Beside her was a wide canoe with the beam of an outrigger hanging over the side.

Justin tripped and fell to his knees. The extra weight of Ahlund's body made him hit the ground harder than usual. Cyaxares raised one hand, and her aurym power lifted Ahlund off Justin's shoulders. The stump of Ahlund's broken sword fell and stuck in the mud. Somehow, through everything, Ahlund had held on to it.

Ahlund's body floated in midair as Cyaxares guided him to the canoe and gently laid him down in it. Justin tried to tell her they had to hurry, but his lungs labored just to draw breath, and he produced only gasping, empty syllables.

Cyaxares stepped in and took the oars. Justin grabbed Ahlund's sword from the mud, slipped it under his belt, and braced his hands against the edge of the canoe. He waded through the water to push it out, then hopped in, using one of the crossbeams as a seat. Cyaxares rowed, pushing them along the channel, toward the sea.

Carefully, Justin repositioned Ahlund's body into a more comfortable position. Cuts marred his entire body. Most weren't even bleeding anymore. The stab wound beneath his ribcage dribbled watery fluid. The large hole in his chest below the collar-bone, where he had driven his own sword through himself, was wide, dark, and ragged. His face was battered. His mouth hung open, a thin stream of dried blood trailing from the lips. Most of his chestnut hair had been burned away. The top of his head was sickly black. Like Justin's arm, the scalp had been transformed into black bone armor.

"Ahlund. . . ?" said Justin.

Ahlund's eyelids fluttered. His eyes studied the sky for a second. His gaze drifted down and found Justin's face.

"You're alive," Justin breathed. "Thank God you're alive! Just hold on. We made it. You saved us."

Ahlund's right arm stirred, and he raised his hand. The movement was strained as he reached up and touched Justin's forehead. His lips opened and closed like a fish.

"Mind," Justin helped.

Ahlund lowered his hand. His arm was shaking. His muscles were tense. The tendons in his neck stood up. His body convulsed once, sharply, as he pressed his fingers to Justin's shoulder.

"Body," Justin choked out through a clenched throat.

Justin felt his chin trembling. Ahlund moved his hand and pushed his fingers against the center of Justin's chest.

"Spirit," Justin said.

Then, the always stoic, ever expressionless Ahlund did something Justin had almost never seen him do before. He smiled.

Ahlund's hand fell. His eyes closed. He exhaled.

Justin grabbed him by the shoulders. "Ahlund," he whispered. "No. Please."

Ahlund's body was still. Tears turned Justin's vision wavy and blurred. He closed his eyes against them and, through the extrasensory clairvoyance of aurym, watched the light of Ahlund's body fade, dim, and go out.

"Stay with me," Justin begged.

Ripples stretched out behind the canoe as Cyaxares rowed. Ocean breeze tugged at Justin's hair, pushing the tears in sideways tracks down his face. He lowered his head into his hands.

CHAPTER 129

"This. . . ." said Leah. "I'm sorry, but this is a lot to take in all at once."

In the large, circular room that traditionally served as the chambers of the Nolian royal council, Leah sat in one of the lower seats. The high seat was meant for the king, but she felt more comfortable down here.

Days had passed since the Battle of Cervice. The dead had been buried. The wounded had been healed. The newcomers had been housed within the city of Cervice as best as could be managed. With the influx of new forces from Raeqlund, plus Gunnar's volunteers—and new refugees arriving daily from across Nolia—the city was now easily as crowded as it had ever been in its heyday, which presented many . . . *unique* problems.

Surrounding Leah now were the members of her makeshift council of bright minds and, more importantly, loyal friends. Seated on either side of Leah were the recently promoted General Olorus Antony and General Hook Bard. There was Captain Marcus Worth of Endenholm, Sif and Elder Thid of the Cru, the Brethren Zechariah, Admiral Gunnar Erix Nimbus, Captain Pool, Captain Borris, Major Lycon Belesys, and Private Adonica Lor. There were other officials, too, whom Leah knew on less intimate terms: members of the Nolian High Guard who had been here since the beginning, the mayor of Ronice, newcomers from Raeqlund appointed based on Zechariah's endorsement, and more. Noticeably absent from the assemblage was Cimon Endrus, who had been laid to rest in an honored grave within the city walls.

"I know it is a difficult thing to fathom, my lady," said Zechariah, speaking loudly for all the room to hear, "but in my opinion, it is the only way. We have heard nothing from Wulder Von Morix about the state of the League, and we cannot afford to wait until we do. We cannot be content to subsist. Stalwart hearts, strong swords, and good fortune won the Battle of Cervice. Avagad's demons will be back. If we simply sit in this city and wait for the next attack, we will become an island in a sea of demons while the world is overrun around us. Even if we can continue to hold the city, what have we won? Nothing but the privilege to die last!"

Leah shivered involuntarily. Innocen had said something eerily similar, days before. And now, as if Zechariah were reading her thoughts, he mentioned the murderous little man by name.

"The man called Ragny," said Zechariah, "who revealed his true identity as Innocen, infiltrated our organization on a hunt for Justin Holmes. Based on what Leah has told me about him, I surmise that he follows the tenets of an ancient order called the Cult of the Hyd. The Hyd were assassins who used aurym-powered strength and speed to feed off of human prey, the same as coblyns, believing it to fuel their spirit powers. He is just one example of the many dangers that will seek us out if we make ourselves stationary. Meanwhile, populations around the world are left to suffer."

Zechariah paused to look around the room.

"*Surviving* this onslaught should not be our objective," he said, shaking his steel hook for emphasis. "We have the responsibility to defeat it."

Leah's gaze wandered from Zechariah to the opposite side of the council chambers, where Gunnar sat next to Borris and Pool. His single eye was looking her direction, but as soon as she looked at him, it darted away, seeking the other side of the room. She had not yet had the opportunity to discuss with him the events concerning Innocen or the treachery that had cost Cimon Endrus and other good soldiers their lives. Both she and Lycon Belesys—who, she had learned, fortuitously landed on one of the lower balconies of the guardhouse during his fall instead of plummeting into the coblyn horde below—had barely escaped. She knew Gunnar blamed himself. But guilt may not have been the only thing bothering him. According to Innocen's own words, and supported by Lycon's account, Yordar Erix Nimbus had been killed in the same manner as Endrus and the others. The humble cook Gunnar had been traveling with was his brother's killer.

"With all due respect," said Marcus Worth. He did not stand; his leg had been badly broken by Innocen, and he was still on the mend. "You want us to uproot all these people *again*? To march them halfway across the world on a . . . a suicide mission?"

"Some might call it *all* the way across the world," said Zechariah.

Some of the advisors murmured to one another.

"It would be a journey almost the entire length of the Oikoumene to Erum," said Zechariah. "And you are right, lad. This is not a course of action to be taken lightly. It may mean the deaths of many of us. But only by attacking the enemy head-on and disrupting Avagad's hold on the world—maybe even catching him off guard and killing him—only then can we hope to gain an advantage. We cannot repel his invasions anymore. We must do the invading ourselves."

"Cut off the head and the body will follow," said Olorus. "It is not the first time we've relied on such a tactic."

"That is because it is a sound tactic," Zechariah replied. He brought his hook-hand down on the table in front of him like a judge banging a gavel, and it struck with a loud ping. "What have you all to say?"

Leah stood. All eyes turned to her, and she cleared her throat.

The sound of hurried footsteps interrupted her as a messenger suddenly rushed into the council chambers.

"This is a closed meeting," a man of the High Guard scolded.

"I apologize for the interruption!" the messenger said, gasping for air, but despite his apology, it was clear he had no intention of waiting for permission to speak. "A convoy has just arrived. From *Darvelle*! They request an audience with Lady Leah!"

"Perhaps they seek peace," spoke up Elder Thid of the Cru.

Olorus scoffed. "The last time Darvellians were admitted into this palace, they repayed our goodwill with a poisoned dagger."

"I'd be more concerned about flaming arrows," said Gunnar.

"How many are there?" asked Leah.

"No more than a dozen, my lady," said the messenger. "And they have brought a . . . gift."

CHAPTER 130

For only the second time since her return, Leah Anavion sat on the throne of Nolia. Soldiers of the combined forces of Cervice filled the room. Any Darvellians contemplating another assassination attempt would think twice about it now. But she did not think that would happen. Not this time.

Through the throne room entryway stepped the gaunt, jagged old frame of the former prime minister of Nolia, Illander Asher.

A pair of Darvellian guards shoved Asher forward. His hands were bound. He was still dressed in the vestments of power. Over his shoulders was draped an elegant, purple cape, and various emblems and golden tokens hung upon his chest.

He was marched to the front of the room. There, men of the High Guard held him at spear-point. His red-rimmed, old eyes locked on Leah, filled with baleful malevolence.

Despite her advantage over him, Leah's mouth was dry. She was less than a stone's throw away from the man responsible for the death of her entire family.

She hazarded a glance at Zechariah, standing beside her throne. He nodded to her reassuringly, and she took a deep breath. How she conducted herself in the face of this challenge would have a strong bearing on the opinions of the people assembled here—people she had been charged to lead.

Asher cleared his throat, dislodging a bit of something and swallowing it before proclaiming, "Lady Leah. The former princess of Nolia. The Oleander of the West. . . ." Asher sighed in an exaggerated sort of way. "I remember when you were just a baby, dear Leah. To think what crimes that sweet babe would mature to commit. How I mourn what could have been! Tragic, that such noble roots could grow to bear so bitter a fruit. It seems even the progeny of greatness is not without the occasional evil seed—"

"You killed my family," Leah said, cutting him off.

She let the words hang in the air a moment.

"You," she continued. "The prime minister of this nation and the king's most trusted advisor. You had the royal family murdered in their sleep. Then you blasphemed their memory by abandoning the lands our forefathers protected for nine generations. You forsook our allies in their time of need and crawled instead to the doorstep of an enemy, all while wearing a purloined crown on your liver-spotted head. You sabotaged this country on the orders of a foreign nation, and now even *they* see the folly of allying themselves with such a snake, and they bring you back to dispose of you where they found you. . . . After all these betrayals, a wise man would beg for mercy in the face of judgment." Leah drew her hand into a fist and pushed the volume of her voice to its limits. "Instead, you attempt to bring accusations against *me*!"

The words rang through the room long after the fact.

Asher blinked a few times. Even his practiced, political face could not hide the shock—shock, and maybe even a little begrudging admiration. It took him several seconds to find any words to respond.

"It was. . . ." he said. He cleared his throat again. "It was with the greatest of regret that I wore your father's crown. In the face of adversity, the people needed the confidence that only a king could give. The Nolian people are what really matter, Leah. Not titles, royal blood, or strength of arms."

Leah felt her nostrils flare. "As my father once told me, 'This is the tactic of the most adept of deceivers: to sow the seeds of their *un*-truths amid the fertile soil of that which *is* true.' Deceit, treachery, and misdirection. The tools of the politician. But you are not in any reelection campaign now."

Asher sneered at her, revealing rows of sharp, little teeth. "You mock politics, but they are what keep the power-mad nobility from turning government into dictatorship! Is that not what this is? Rule seized by military might alone? My eyes are not so old that I do not recognize your hired swords, Antony and Bard. Both are wanted by this nation for desertion and treason! It would not surprise me if they are the men who helped you murder your family. And who is this filthy, old beggar who stands so haughtily alongside our nation's throne? Is he the wizard who covered your tracks as you fled the country?"

Zechariah looked over his shoulder as if searching for the man Asher referred to.

"Zechariah is about as far from a beggar as you are from a king," said Leah. "As for General Antony and General Bard, they are men of honor. To that fact, many an individual within this room can attest. For while you were in Darvelle—doing what? Drinking fine wine and eating freshly picked fruit? While you satiated your appetites elsewhere, the country over which you claimed to rule was at war—a war in which Olorus, Hook, and every person in this room battled for their lives and their freedom."

Asher growled impatiently. He tried to take a step forward, but the two Darvellian guards held him in place. "Men and women of Nolia!" he screamed. "You are deceived by this traitor! We must take back the throne! Off with her head!"

"You are quick to hand out sentencing, Asher," Leah said calmly. "It would be a barbaric world, indeed, if the wanton orders of madmen like you held stock. Fortunately, our ancestors decided long ago that a court system was preferable to martial law. Your guilt or innocence will be determined by a jury, in a fair trial. For now, guards, please provide the former prime minister in a suitable holding place. One where he will not be tempted to leave the country when it is no longer to his liking."

"No!" Asher shouted as Nolian guards converged. Even with his resistance at its ugliest, it took little manpower to keep him under control. He was half dragged, half carried away.

Leah let out a long breath—a breath it felt like she had been holding for the better part of several months. Nothing would ever bring her family back, but maybe, now, they could rest a little easier.

"Darvellians," said Leah, turning her sights on the two guards before her. They shifted nervously. "Much blood has been spilled between our two countries. Too much, I had thought, for reconciliation." She smiled. "But this helps."

The Darvellian guards bowed low to Leah. As they respectfully exited the room, Hook tapped Leah on her shoulder. She turned to him, and he made several signs, trying to hide his hands from Olorus.

"Yes, I think you're right," said Leah. "It does seem like an appropriate time."

She turned to Olorus. There was a skeptical expression on his face.

"Appropriate time for what?" he asked.

Leah raised her voice to some guards at the back of the room waiting for her signal. "Bring her in!" she said.

"Bring who. . . ?" said Olorus.

From the outside hallway, a soldier stepped in. Leaning heavily on him for support was a short, old woman with white, wiry hair. Her frame was so bent that she had to turn her head sideways to look up the center aisle of the throne room. Even from here, Leah could see the joy on her face.

"Mother!" Olorus said, leaping down to run up the aisle.

Olorus reached old Mrs. Antony and embraced her in a gentle, careful hug. Her boney hands patted and rubbed his big, armored shoulders as they shook with sobs. Hook wore a satisfied smile.

In the midst of it all, Leah found herself thinking about Justin again. She wondered where he was, whether he was safe, and, most of all, when—if ever—she would see him again. She hoped so.

"Oh!" said Zechariah suddenly, stepping forward. "I had very nearly forgotten! Darvelle has sent you *another* token of goodwill. It would seem, by their sudden generosity, that your display of unification and leadership made quite an impression of them."

Zechariah held out a wooden box to Leah with his good hand. He pried open the lid with his hook, and Leah lost all breath. There sat a thick circle of gold, inlaid with jewels. The Nolian crown.

Zechariah took the crown from the box. The occupants of the throne room gave a collective gasp at the sight. Some called out with cheers.

Leah looked at Zechariah. He winked at her. She stared straight ahead, lost in the surrealism of the moment as he placed the crown atop her head.

General Olorus Antony stepped momentarily away from the embrace of his mother, pulled the shield off his back, and slammed it against the ground with a deafening clang. He lowered himself to one knee. Beside the throne, Hook repeated the stance. Gunnar kneeled, as well. As did Worth, Lycon, Adonica, Sif, Thid, and every other person in the room, expanding backward in a wave of shields and armor all lowering in submission. To her. The crown felt heavy on her head as she watched it happen.

"All hail, Leah Anavion!" bellowed the voice of Olorus Antony. "Queen of Nolia!"

"Hail!" the voices of Cervice exclaimed as one.

CHAPTER 131

Justin still remembered the Guardians' funerary rites from a time when he had witnessed them performed by Zechariah, in a stone tunnel at the base of the Shifting Mountains. Now, he witnessed them again—for the same man. It was the dead of night, and here, on the beach of a small island many miles from Esthean, the forty-three surviving members of the Ru'Onorath, including Cyaxares, Kallorn, Ezon, and Justin, paid tribute to their fallen brother.

The canoe sat on the edge of the beach. Ahlund's body had not been moved from it; he lay in the same position in which he had died. Around him in the canoe had been placed piles of fibrous palm fronds gathered from the island.

"He died in battle, a hero to his people," continued Cyaxares's eulogy. "And so, we offer provisions for his final journey."

She opened one of the few packs of supplies the Ru'Onorath refugees had managed to bring with them in their escape from Esthean.

Kallorn solemnly stepped forward. "Salt, to flavor the meat of his game," he said, scooping a handful from the sack in Cyaxares's hands. He waved his hand over the canoe to sprinkle it into the bed of the boat, over Ahlund's long body.

"And coin," Justin said as he stepped forward and tilted his hand, letting a few copper coins fall into the canoe. They landed on Ahlund's chest.

Justin took a last look at Ahlund's bearded face. Then he and Kallorn gripped the sides of the canoe. As Cyaxares struck a flint, producing a spark that ignited the palm fronds, Kallorn and Justin waded out into the shallows. By the time they were waist-deep, the fire was already raging enough that the heat was difficult to endure. Justin had to turn away to protect his face.

Finally, he and Kallorn gave the canoe a push. Sparks rose into the air as it floated out toward the open ocean.

Kallorn quietly watched it float away. Then he waded back in. Justin felt like he should say something meaningful before turning back to the beach, but he couldn't think of anything.

When he returned to shore, Kallorn and Cyaxares were waiting for him.

"Now what?" said Justin.

"We should try to seek out your allies," said Cyaxares. "We are vulnerable on our own like this."

Justin sighed, regretting that he'd even asked. Moving on, no matter what direction, seemed impossible right now. He turned back toward the ocean. The burning boat was drifting farther out. It looked like the flame of a single candle swaying on the vast ocean.

"I know you didn't have to give him a Ru'Onorath funeral since he was an outcast," said Justin. "So, thank you."

"We are all outcasts, now," Cyaxares said. "Ahlund lost his way for a time, but he was a better man than I gave him credit for. In the end, he sacrificed his life so the rest of us could escape. Only a true Guardian of the Oikoumene would do that."

Justin looked at Kallorn.

"Pardon my silence," Kallorn said with a stern face, watching the ocean. "But silence, to me, seems the most accurate remembrance of him."

In that silence, Justin stood with them and watched the flames of the canoe rise higher and higher, becoming a brilliant, flaming beacon on the waves—a truer testament to the life of Ahlund Sims than any hole in the ground ever would have been.

Justin felt Cyaxares touch his shoulder. She held out a folded piece of paper. It was the letter written in the hand of his father. Justin took it wordlessly and slipped it into his pocket, and Cyaxares left to join the rest of the group higher up the beach. Kallorn soon followed, but Justin stood a while longer by himself, watching the ball of flame on the water drift away until it became a dot.

Justin pressed his fingers to his head, then his shoulder, then his heart. Mind, body, spirit.

He lowered his hand and rested it on the hilt of Ahlund's broken sword at his belt. He fed a sliver of aurym into it. A ribbon of smoke hissed up from the blade.

Justin's odyssey continues in

SHADOWS OF THE FALLEN

Coming Soon

To find out what happens next, go to www.thefallenodyssey.com/anabasischapter for a preview of the next book.

Also available from Corey McCullough:

A KNIFE IN THE DARK: A SCIENCE FICTION NOIR THRILLER

Now available in ebook and paperback.

ABOUT THE AUTHOR

COREY MCCULLOUGH is an independent copy editor, proofreader, ghostwriter, and author. He lives in western Pennsylvania with his amazing wife Vanessa and their two beautiful daughters. His favorite pastimes are reading, writing, playing video games, spending time with his best friend (Vanessa), and, most of all, being a dad.

Instagram @cbenmcc
thefallenodyssey.com
facebook.com/mcculloughwrites
facebook.com/thefallenodyssey
mcculloughauthor@gmail.com
cbmcediting.com

CPSIA information can be obtained
at www.ICGtesting.com
Printed in the USA
BVHW072200150420
577708BV00001B/29